Critical Praise for *The Hanging* by Wendy Hornsby

"Hornsby's well-constructed eighth Maggie MacGowen mystery... offers a nuanced glimpse of campus life in the budget-crisis era, a plot with a nicely topical twist, and a cast of smart, appealing characters. Readers will cheer Maggie on as both new romance and fresh career opportunities beckon."

—*Publishers Weekly*

"...the plot moves smoothly ahead, with Maggie, of course, uncovering background information to help solve the murder as well as other possible crimes. The story develops slowly and surely, with excellent character development and smooth writing and a credible conclusion. Recommended."

—*Spinetingler Magazine*

"I think Hornsby is one of the best writers in the field, and this book has all her strengths: a great story, characters who engage and convince the reader, and the kind of language (and structure) that keep our eyes on the page.... A great setting, a terrific set of suspects, and the humanity of Hornsby's characters make this another winner in one of my favorite mystery series."

—Timothy Hallinan, author of the
Poke Rafferty & Junior Bender series

"VERDICT: Longtime series readers will be pleased by the eighth title in Hornsby's amateur sleuth series. The first-person narrative sets a familiar tone, plus side stories about Maggie's family and friends make for a comfortable read. Those who like academic settings and local politics will enjoy. Share with Sue Grafton and Hank Phillippi Ryan fans."

—*Library Journal*

D1557751

The Color of Light

Also by Wendy Hornsby

The Color of Light

A Maggie MacGowen Mystery

Wendy Hornsby

Perseverance Press / John Daniel & Company
Palo Alto / McKinleyville, California, 2014

Copyright © 2014 by Wendy Hornsby
All rights reserved
Printed in the United States of America

A Perseverance Press Book
Published by John Daniel & Company
A division of Daniel & Daniel, Publishers, Inc.
Post Office Box 2790
McKinleyville, California 95519
www.danielpublishing.com/perseverance

Distributed by SCB Distributors (800) 729-6423

Book design by Eric Larson, Studio E Books, Santa Barbara, www.studio-e-books.com

10 9 8 7 6 5 4 3 2 1

LIBRARY OF CONGRESS CATALOGING-IN-PUBLICATION DATA
Hornsby, Wendy.
 The color of light : a Maggie MacGowen mystery / by Wendy Hornsby.
   pages cm
 ISBN 978-1-56474-542-2 (pbk.)
 1. MacGowen, Maggie (Fictitious character)—Fiction. 2. Women motion picture producers and directors—Fiction. 3. Homecoming—Fiction. 4. Cold cases (Criminal investigation)—Fiction. 5. Police—California—Berkeley—Fiction. 6. Berkeley (Calif.)—Fiction. I. Title.
 PS3558.O689C65 2014
 813'.54—dc23
                    2013035789

Toujours, Paul

The Color of Light

Chapter 1

SIX GIRLS WALK DOWN the sidewalk away from the camera, seemingly unaware anyone is watching them. Foreshortened by the telephoto lens of the old Super 8 that captures them, weighted down by backpacks and school projects, they seem like spindly giants as they move through long morning shadows. They are ten and eleven years old, still coltish—leggy, hipless, breastless—apparently confident about their place in the small universe encompassed within this comfortable, leafy neighborhood.

A skinny girl wearing stovepipe blue jeans and red high-top sneakers, walking near the front of the pack, seems to be the primary target of the lens. The resolute set to her shoulders, head held high, suggests that she and her cohort are on a mission.

The camera's wide field of vision places the girls within the usual dance of morning along the narrow tree-lined street: a car backs out of a driveway, a gardener mows a lawn, a dog chases a squirrel, a deliveryman drives his route. Now and then branches obscure the shot as the cameraman pans to one side or the other with some apparent interest in stands of shrubbery or garden walls; potential hiding places? Clearly, it is the progress of the girls that draws him.

One by one, new arrivals enter the frame from either side and merge with the group, until there are twelve girls. Each newcomer greets the others with a hand slap or a conspiratorial nod of the head before falling into formation.

At the last driveway before the corner, a boy about the same age as the girls waits with his mother. The mother is quietly, unfashionably beautiful in a starched pastel blue shirtwaist dress. The boy is pretty like his mother, his straight dark hair slicked back from his forehead, roses in his round cheeks. Puppy fat makes him seem younger than the girls; his mother looks at him as if he is made of pure gold.

As the girls approach, the boy begins to strain against his mother's grip. The mother gives her boy a few cautionary words and receives a duty kiss in return. She releases him to join his friends. His polished black brogans make a sharp contrast to the intentionally scruffy, brightly colored sneakers worn by the girls.

The cameraman loses the children when they turn at the corner. By the time he catches up to them, they have formed a line across the road, shoulder to shoulder, facing down a group of boys who seem to have been lying in wait. There are half as many boys as girls, but the boys are bigger, older, railed out, already well into puberty, young toughs trying to look like bikers: blue jeans worn low on narrow hips, rolled cuffs, tight white T-shirts showing off budding biceps. The film has no sound track but the body language makes it clear that the toughs taunt the girls. But the girls, and their single boy, hold their ground.

The girl wearing red high-tops strides forward until she is nearly toe-to-toe with the hobnail boots of the opposition leader, a snaggle-toothed youth with a greasy blond pompadour. He cants his body forward and yells into her face while stabbing his middle finger toward the small boy who is shielded by the girls. Red high-tops shakes her head to whatever blond pompadour is saying. Frustrated, he pushes her hard enough that she drops one foot back to keep her balance. Instead of returning the shove, she crosses her arms and faces him directly, speaking in a voice so soft that he has to lean forward to hear her.

What she says seems, at first, to confuse him. But after he tries a verbal comeback or two, his face and his bravado suddenly collapse. Sobbing, he runs back through the line of his buddies and out of the frame.

I hit the Stop button and the image on the television screen faded to black.

"God, Maggie, you had balls." Detective Kevin Halloran of the Berkeley PD, my friend since childhood, sat forward in the big leather chair in my late father's den, where we were holed up in front of the television set, as we had when we were teenagers, too broke then for a real Saturday night movie date, or so he'd say. There was a wistful smile on his weathered face when he turned toward me. "Every kid in Berkeley knew you made Larry Nordquist cry. What did you say to the little punk?"

"Nothing I'm proud of," I said.

"Did you know that he's out on parole?"

"Gracie Nussbaum told me."

"If he comes back to Berkeley, you better watch yourself."

"That scuffle happened over thirty years ago, Kev," I said. "I'm not worried about Larry Nordquist."

"If you say so." Kevin lifted a shoulder, a dismissive shrug. "Gracie also tell you that Beto took over his dad's deli?"

"She did. I went in for a sandwich the other day," I said. "Beto gave me an extra pickle and comped my drink."

"That's our Beto," he said with fondness, as if Beto were still the chubby ten-year-old in the film, clinging to his mother's hand, and not the rotund forty-something he had become. "Beto would love to see that little movie, Mags, to see his mom. I forgot how damn gorgeous Mrs. Bartolini was. She was what? Chinese?"

"Vietnamese," I said, hearing the catch in my voice as I remembered what lay ahead for her the day the film was shot; what lay ahead for all of us.

"So?" Kevin dipped his head toward the television. "This is what you asked me to come over and see, you kids walking to school? You made it sound urgent."

"Beto told me you're looking into his mother's murder," I said.

He nodded. "I took it on as a favor to him."

"What have you found?"

"*Bupkis.*" He held up empty hands. "I started with *bupkis*, and that's exactly what I've come up with; nothing. After thirty years, whatever evidence there was—and there never was much—has disappeared, rotted, or died. Every lead petered out a long time ago. I'm only going through the motions because my friend Beto asked me to."

"So, you're not doing a serious, all-out investigation?"

"Of course I am." The question embarrassed him. "Department resources are tight, but I'm doing what I can with what damn little I have to go on."

His focus slid from me to the blank television screen and back again. "What's that have to do with—?" Before he finished the question he nailed me with a glare. "Hey, you're not thinking about doing one of your TV-show hatchet jobs on Beto's mom are you? Because I don't—"

"Dear God, no," I said, reaching for his arm.

"No 'Maggie MacGowen Investigates'?"

"I promise you, no."

"You promise, huh?" he said. He tried to look intimidating, but I saw a flash of the big tease he had always been hovering behind the effort. "You know you can't lie to me, Maggie MacGowen. We have a soul bond that's stronger than a blood oath."

Clueless, I asked, "We do?"

"You bet." He lifted the corner of his cheek to wink at me. "We got each other's cherries, Maggie. That's sacred."

"Since you put it that way," I said, trying not to laugh; he'd caught me off guard. "Cross my heart, no TV project on this one."

"Okay. Now that we have that settled, you want to tell me what I was supposed to see on that film besides scrapping kids in funny clothes and bad hair?"

"The film was shot on the same morning that Beto's mother was killed."

"On that very day? Thirty-some years ago? You can't know that. Hell, Mags, I barely remember breakfast this morning."

"Some things you don't forget."

He hesitated, thinking through what he knew and what he remembered before he shook his head. "After all this time, you can't possibly be sure."

"But I am." I leaned toward him. "The police came to school that day at lunch time. We all thought we were in trouble for fighting, but they were there to take Beto home to his dad before he heard about his mom from someone else."

"Even so, thirty years is a long time."

"There's something else."

I walked over to my dad's desk, took an envelope out of the top drawer and carried it across the room to him. He pulled out the single Polaroid photo inside, saw what it was, and blanched: In the faded photo, Beto's mother lies at the base of a granite outcropping at Indian Rock Park a few blocks from our homes, half-naked, long dark hair in a loose spill across her face. She looks more like a doll that has been dragged through mud and cast away by a willful child than like the quiet, reserved woman we had known in life.

"Jesus Christ, Maggie." He turned the photo face down on the table beside him. "Where the hell did you get this?"

"I was clearing out Dad's desk— you know Mom has given up the house. I found it locked in a strongbox with the film I just showed you."

"If you're thinking your dad took the picture, he didn't. It's one of a series taken at the murder scene by the original crime scene investigators," he said. "The rest of them are in the evidence box locked up in my office. The question is, how did your father get hold of this one?"

As an answer to his question, I took the yellowed envelope the photo had been in and pointed to the embossed return address, BENJAMIN G. NUSSBAUM, M.D., my father's closest friend.

"Doc Nussbaum," he said, nodding as he carefully placed the photo back inside the envelope. "He used to give the department a hand from time to time, sit in on autopsies when there was a gunshot wound involved so he could testify in court as our department expert. He was a M.A.S.H. surgeon during the Korean War so he knew a hell of a lot more about gunshot wounds than any of us ever could; we don't get a lot of experience with murder in Berkeley. He must have bagged the picture and given it to your dad. The question is, why?"

"That is the question, isn't it?" I said.

He aimed his chin toward the dark television screen. "Did your dad shoot that film?"

"As far as I know, he did."

"There's no record in the evidence log that he ever showed a film to the police."

"I'm sure that he didn't," I said. "Your people would have kept it."

"If you're right about what day that was, then you kids were just about the last people to see Mrs. B alive."

"That's why I thought you should see the film."

"Uh-huh." He sounded skeptical.

"Kevin, was Mrs. Bartolini raped?"

"Looks that way."

"Did they do a rape kit?"

"Sure, but it's long gone."

"You had the coroner do a search for it?"

"Hey, Maggie?" Voice low, words drawn out, sounding like my dad when he was about to deliver a scolding. "I know you play at being an investigator when you put together your TV shows. But just for a minute, why don't we pretend that I'm a real cop and I know what I'm doing?"

"I don't doubt your ability, Kevin," I said. "But this is new information to me. I'm shocked by it. Whenever I think about Mrs. B in death, I see her as she was in her coffin, looking as serene as a Christmas angel. Not like this." I tapped the back of the envelope. "This was brutal, angry. Help me out, here. What happened to her?"

He took in a deep breath and let it out slowly as if he felt put upon. "You saw; it was ugly. She was battered, maybe raped, shot in the chest, and dumped in a public place. That suggests that the perp meant to humiliate her or her family, or to upset the peace of the community."

"He succeeded in all the above," I said. "Who was he?"

"That's the question, isn't it? There was blood found on her teeth and lips that suggests she might have taken a chunk out of her attacker. A sample was collected."

"Is that lost, too?"

"Lost? No. Gone, yes," he said. "Thirty-something years ago, blood type was about all they could get from blood or semen. We didn't have DNA labs and cold case units back then. There wasn't enough of either found on her for typing, so the samples were disposed of during routine house cleaning when the coroner moved to a new facility. Okay?"

"Okay." I gave his knuckle a flick as I smiled up at him. "Just to be clear, I get paid fairly well to play at investigating."

"I didn't mean that as a shot."

"Sure you did."

He threw back his head and laughed. "God, I've missed you, Maggie."

He started to rise from his chair and I thought he was ready to leave. But he glanced at the dark television and a new thought seemed to occur to him.

"Why was your dad out there filming you that morning, anyway?" He looked over his shoulder at me. "Did you tell him there was going to be a rumble?"

"Hardly. Would you have told your parents that you were heading off for a showdown with a pack of middle-school bullies?"

"They'd have locked me inside the house," he said. "But your dad was there, he saw what was happening. Why didn't he try to stop it?"

"He taught me to fight my own battles," I said. "If things had gotten out of hand, he would have done something. But they didn't, did they?"

"Did you know he was there?"

"No."

"So, why was he?"

"Does it matter?"

"I can't know that until you tell me what you know. Everything you know."

I sighed, sat back down in my chair and rubbed my eyes. For a while—not long enough—I was married to a homicide detective. No one could ever successfully tell my Mike that there was something he just did not need to know. I had no reason to believe that my old friend Kevin, now Detective Halloran, was any less relentless than Mike had been. I also trusted that Kevin, like Mike, would be discreet about what he learned.

Kevin still watched me, waiting.

"It's a long story, Kevin."

He glanced at his watch. "I have time."

"Lordy." I did not want to go into all the sordid details, and sordid they were. I said, "The short version is, the woman who raised me, Mom, was not my birth mother."

"Everyone knows that now," he said. "It was all over the news last winter when your birth mother died. I DVR'd the interview you did on TV so I could watch it a couple of times. I record all your TV shows, Maggie. We all do."

"The woman used to lurk around me."

"Your bio-mom?"

"Isabelle," I said.

"Isabelle," he repeated. "Your dad withheld information from the police to protect Isabelle?"

"More likely he was trying to protect me and Mom from whatever Isabelle might do."

"And Doc Nussbaum helped him?"

I nodded. "He understood the stakes."

"So, you were adopted?"

"No," I said. "You know the story by now. Dad had an affair with a graduate student when he was in France working on a project. And, *voilà*, me."

"The student was Isabelle?"

"Yes."

"And your mom, meaning your father's wife, raised you?"

"What can I say? She's a saint."

Kevin *tsk*'d. "Your dad is the last person I would ever suspect of fooling around. The way he used to watch me, jeez, like he thought I was up to something."

"You *were* up to something," I said. "You were trying to get into his daughter's pants."

Kevin blushed at that. He looked over his shoulder and around the room where, nearly three years after his death, my father's presence still hovered. Leaning close to me, Kevin whispered, "Was your dad always out there, watching you? Us?"

I shuddered at that awful notion, thinking about some of the stupid stunts we pulled as kids. Fortunately, the statute of limitations had run out on even the worst of our transgressions.

"He couldn't possibly have been out there all the time," I said. "I think someone tipped him off whenever she was in the country so he could keep an eye on me."

"She? Your mother?"

"Isabelle," I said.

"He was afraid Isabelle would snatch you?"

"Among other things," I said. "When my dad took me away from her, my arm was in a cast. Dad had a restraining order against her."

"Did she ever try to kidnap you?"

"Not that I'm aware. But she did lurk," I said. "In the strongbox where I found the film I showed you, there were a dozen more film reels, and she is on every one of them."

"You are a big snoop, Maggie," he said, laughing. "You couldn't resist seeing what was on the old reels so you went out and had them converted to digital so you could see them, didn't you?"

"Occupational hazard I guess, just like you, Mr. Detective," I said, feeling no chagrin. "What would you have done?"

"Exactly what you did. If I could squeeze the processing fees out of the department budget." Kevin glanced toward the television. "Is *she* on that film?"

"She is."

"Show me."

I hesitated before restarting the disc where we left off, with Larry Nordquist running away down the street and his pals quickly dispersing.

My little group, triumphant, reassembled and continued on toward school. When we crossed the next intersection, a busy commercial street, Dad stopped following us and remained focused instead on the front of a neighborhood pharmacy. Behind the reflections of the street on the shop's front windows, people can be seen moving around inside the store. Someone—a silhouette—stands inside the door, looking out. After we passed by, the door opened and a slender woman—Isabelle—stepped outside. She watched us for a moment before she began to follow in our direction. Suddenly, she stopped and turned as if someone had called to her. Her face registered alarm at first, and then great pleasure when she must have seen that it was Dad who called out to her. Seeing her face light up chilled me; Dad did have that restraining order for good reason.

"That's her?" Kevin asked, moving forward for a closer look. "Your real mother?"

"The woman who gave birth to me, yes. But she wasn't my *real* mom."

"Can you zoom in on her?"

"Not very much." I paused the last frame and enlarged it until the image dissolved into a disorganized mass of pixels. "The film stock Dad used has low resolution. There isn't much that can be done with it."

"Did you ever meet her?"

"The only time I ever spoke with her was the night she died. But I didn't know who she was until later."

He cocked his head to study me. "Why weren't you going to show her to me?"

"Because she is not germane to the issue at hand." I hit Stop and watched Isabelle's scrambled image fade to black.

"*Germane?* Give me a break. I only went to San Jose State, not to Cal like you and your egghead friends."

"You chose to go to State because you thought you wouldn't have to work as hard."

He conceded the truth of that, a cocky grin on his face as he rose and crossed to the television. "I wanted to play football, but I didn't want to get hurt. Those guys at Cal are big."

He ejected the disc. "I need the original film reel, too."

"Thought you might." I went to the desk and took it from the drawer.

"Copies, too, please." He held out his hand.

"You have the only one."

"Yeah, sure."

"It's true," I said. "When the TeleCine technician at the San Francisco affiliate of my network made the digital conversion of the original Super 8 reels yesterday, he burned one disc each and downloaded the files to the Cloud."

"I have no idea what you just said."

"I can access the film from any computer, anywhere I can get Internet. But there is only one disc. So far."

"God, I feel like a dinosaur."

I was ready to say good-bye—I had work to do—but he began to walk a slow circuit around that very familiar room, probably for the last time, looking at pictures on the walls, books in the cases, various little mementoes my father kept around where he could see them. Reminders of a good life.

One beautiful spring afternoon, Dad sat down on a bench in the backyard for a little nap, and never woke up again. My mom stayed in their big old house in Berkeley, alone, until late this spring when I persuaded her to move closer to me and my college-age daughter, Casey, in Southern California. In early summer I had spent a few days with her in the house where she and my father had lived for half a century, the house where they raised my older sister and brother, and where they brought me when I was very young, helping her to decide what she wanted to take with her to her new apartment. The rest she left for me to deal with; the task was too huge for her, too fraught. So, there I was, spending a July week—maybe two—stirring up dust and occasional ghosts buried among the family's accumulated treasures and detritus as I cleared out the place for the next tenant, the university's housing office; the University of California, Berkeley, where my father taught, and my alma mater, was only a few blocks away.

Kevin lingered beside the leather sofa set in a niche among bookshelves. It was on that couch during the summer before my senior year in high school, on the night before Kevin left for college, that I surrendered to him that which Sister Dolores of Perpetual Sorrows, the morals and standards officer at the convent high school where my parents stashed me, referred to as my most precious jewel. Or as Kevin called it, my cherry.

Running a hand over the arm of the sofa, a wistful smile on his face, Kevin asked, "What are you going to do with the sofa?"

"I don't know yet."

"If you're going to dispose of it…"

"I can just see you dragging that home to your wife. How would you explain it?"

"Did I tell you we're not—"

I put up my hand to stop him. "I'm seeing someone, Kevin."

"Mrs. Nussbaum told me."

I laughed. "I don't know why anyone in this town bothers with the Internet when we have an information resource like Gracie Nussbaum."

"You gotta love Gracie." He flashed a smile that was so full of sweetness that I remembered why I had once found him so irresistible.

He picked up a small framed photo of the two of us in high school, flicked something off the glass and turned it to face me. "Your prom or mine?"

"Could have been either," I said, walking over for a closer look. "Since we went to different schools I wore the same dress to both."

"May I?" He had already slipped the picture into his pocket before I nodded assent.

I saw the grin that suddenly lit his face, but I didn't see his move coming. There was an arm around my shoulders and one under my legs and when I had re-established a relationship with gravity I was prone on the sofa with Kevin's substantial bulk atop me.

"Clever move, Kev," I said, pushing against his chest. "What's this about?"

There was the strangest look on his face, as if he were more surprised than I was about the position we were suddenly in. Ages ago, when we were dating, he thought that particular maneuver was just awfully funny. But he wasn't smiling as he gripped my side in his big hand and gently squeezed my rib cage as if he were checking a tomato for ripeness.

"Don't you dare tickle me," I said, batting his hand away. "I hated it when you tickled me."

"Yeah." His hand relaxed but he didn't remove it. He didn't smell the way I remembered, no Brut, no pepperoni—more like shampoo and scotch. "It's just... God, you used to be such a bag of bones."

"And now I'm fat?" I shifted sideways until I was out from under him, wedged on my side with my back against the back of the sofa. He relaxed, stretched out facing me.

"Jesus, no," he said. "It's just... You have more substance than you used to have. I wasn't expecting it."

"Funny thing, buddy," I said, giving him a nudge. "Last time you flipped me over your shoulder I was seventeen years old. A little girl. I'm all grown up now."

"That's the thing of it," he said, brow furrowed as he searched my face for something. Was he counting lines in my crow's-feet? "We were golden back then, weren't we, Maggie? Golden."

"You were a good boyfriend, Kevie." I combed my fingers through his mussed hair. It wasn't as thick as it once was, or as dark; the furrows made by my fingers exposed a lot of pink scalp and silver streaks. "Every Friday night, except during football season, you put on your letterman's jacket, borrowed a car and drove down to pick me up from school. You were handsome and smart and fun, and I was the envy of everyone in school."

"Everyone include the nuns?"

"Especially the nuns. You were a nice Catholic boy." I propped myself up on an elbow and looked down at him. "But that was then."

"Just for old times' sake, how about we get rid of all these clothes and have one more bare-assed roll around on this big sofa?"

"Might be interesting," I said, struggling to sit up; he gave me an assist. "But it's a real bad idea."

"Sometimes, though, don't you wish you could go back?"

"Not for a minute," I said, straightening my shirt. "I'm in a pretty good place right now, not perfect but pretty good. It took a lot of work to get here. I don't want to go back."

"What if you could, though, knowing what you know now?"

"Same answer." I swung my legs over his hips and pushed against him, trying to get to my feet. Instead of giving me a hand, he disentangled himself from underneath me and scooted around until he was sitting upright next to me. I stood and held out my hand to him. "I'd probably just make a whole new set of mistakes. Besides, when we were kids, if we knew half what we know now, we would have ended up in Neuropsychiatric. No thanks. To tell you the truth, some of the big secrets from back then, I wish they had just stayed secret."

He looked up from checking that the Beretta affixed to his belt was secure. "What secrets?"

"The truth about my parentage for one," I said. "And I could have lived the rest of my life without seeing that photo of Mrs. Bartolini."

"You could be right, but I look around at the way things are now and I wonder if the whole world has gone to shit. I mean, tell me honestly, what do we have to look forward to?"

"Kev?" I took his face between my palms. "Why don't you do what other guys our age do when they feel this way? Go buy yourself a Maserati."

He finally smiled. "On a cop's salary?"

"Then have a messy mid-life fling with a twenty-two-year-old blonde."

"Already tried that." His face colored. "Didn't work out so well."

"Could that be the reason you and the wife aren't...?"

"That's part of it."

I shook my head. "Kevin, Kevin, Kevin."

"This guy you're seeing," he said as he tucked in the front of his dress shirt and pulled his jacket straight. "It's serious?"

"It could be," I said. "Too soon to say. But I don't want to do anything that might muck it up."

"Let me know if it doesn't work out," he said, checking his watch. Suddenly, he was the cop again. "I have to get back to work."

"Me, too." I looked around the room at all the laden bookshelves that needed to be sorted and packed up. "You'll let me know what you find out about Beto's mom?"

He grew still, looking down at me with his cop face on. He was at least eight inches taller than me so I had to lean back to look up at him.

"I need to know, Maggie," he said, the heel of his hand resting on the butt of his gun. "Who did you invite over to see that film? Your friend or a cop?"

"I'm not sure."

"When Beto asked me to look into his mom's case again, I warned him that he might not like what I found out, especially if it implicates his dad in some way," he said, watching me closely. "Mag, what if my investigation turns up something that points to *your* father?"

"I'd like for you to tell me. As a friend."

"We'll see," he said. "We'll see."

Chapter 2

AFTER KEVIN LEFT, the house felt hollow, as a house does when all of its inhabitants have moved away. I didn't count myself among the missing because I hadn't lived there for a very long time. If I had left some essence or emanation anywhere, I thought it would be at my own house down south.

I went back to the task of cleaning out Dad's big old mahogany desk, the undertaking that had been interrupted the day before when I found the films locked away in a bottom drawer.

A man's desk is a very private zone. Who knows what you might find there, besides a random crime scene photo or films of the owner's former paramour, and various other things a man's widow might prefer not to learn about her late spouse? That's why Mom had left the job for me. And rightly so.

I found that Dad had kept a neat file of his correspondence with Isabelle, my natural mother, after she relinquished custody of me. These weren't love letters, far from it, at least on his part. But seeing them would have been a painful reminder to Mom of Dad's infidelity, though my very existence must have been daily proof enough that it had occurred.

Because it might be useful to me as Isabelle's estate wound its way through the arcane French probate system, I set the file in a box with other things I found in the desk that I wanted to keep: handmade cards from my brother and sister and me, an old address book, a few family photos, Dad's passport, an old wallet molded to the contour of his rear end by years of use. In the wallet I found an unfilled prescription for blood pressure medication, some expired credit cards, his faculty identification card and about fifty dollars in cash, which I stuffed into my own pocket.

Other than that, most of what I found was old pens, tangled paper clips, university stationery yellowing at the edges, and endless scraps of paper with indecipherable hand-scribbled notes and calculations; Dad, a physicist, doodled in mathematical formulae. I pulled out the top drawer, and as I dumped its odds and ends into a trash bag I could almost hear Dad's voice in my ear: *I think there's still some good use to be found in that red pen; One day when you need a paper clip, you won't have one.* I felt him so strongly that I actually turned my head to check behind me. Nothing there except dust motes floating in the sunlight streaming through the garden windows.

I was disappointed Dad wasn't there because I had so many questions to ask him. About Isabelle, certainly, but after seeing his little movie, it was the events of the day that Mrs. Bartolini—Tina—died that I needed to have explained frankly.

There are things that happen when we are children that sit restlessly on our shoulders for the rest of our lives and affect the way we venture about in the world. For me, the first of those events was the loss of my older brother—my half brother—during combat in Vietnam when I was very young. The second of course was the murder of Beto's mother a few years later. I began to understand at a tender age not only how fragile and precious life is, but also the randomness with which life can be stolen away.

Our parents, our teachers, Father John the parish priest—all the adults in our lives—sheltered us, as they saw fit, from the grim details about the hows and whats of Mrs. Bartolini's passing. Like the real scoop on the mechanics of sex, we were left with little more than rumors and our naive imaginations to figure out what happened to her.

The word *murder* alone conjures up vivid pictures in the mind of a ten-year-old, but when I was ten, a sheltered little shit, I was so ignorant of the ways of the world beyond the protective bubble of my neighborhood that I could not have comprehended what was done to

Mrs. Bartolini in the process of her dying even if someone had seen fit to tell me.

The squeaking of the back gate's hinges interrupted my ruminations. I went over to the windows to see who was there.

Toshio Sato, my parents' longtime yardman, pushed his cart of tools along the uneven brick walkway, stooping from time to time to snip faded roses from the flower border. For as long as I could remember, Mr. Sato had mown and edged half of the lawns on our street every second Monday, starting at the top of the hill and working his way down.

Mr. Sato stopped, took off his broad-brimmed straw hat and wiped inside the sweatband with a big white handkerchief. With his hat off, I could see that his thatch of black hair had become little more than feathery white wisps, but his back was still straight and his step was strong. For a man with his eightieth birthday in his rearview mirror, he looked very good.

Watching him, it occurred to me that he was only one of many grown-ups who routinely moved in and around our house and our neighborhood when I was a child, and to whom I generally paid scant attention. Other than Mr. Sato, there had been the dry cleaning deliveryman, Vera who cleaned our house twice a week and sometimes baby-sat me, Dad's students and colleagues, Mom's piano pupils, various friends and others. I wondered how many people also had access to the Bartolini house?

Taking the filled trash bag with me, I headed outside to speak with Mr. Sato. When I opened the back door, I startled him.

"Oh! It's you, Maggie." He patted his chest to show his heart was pounding.

"Sorry, Mr. Sato," I said, pausing on the porch steps. "Did I scare you?"

"Little bit, yeah." He pointed to his ears and shook his head. "Don't hear so good no more. Your mom, she lets the door slam so I know she's coming."

"I'll remember to do that," I said, walking down the steps so that he didn't need to crane his neck to talk to me. "How have you been?"

"Every day I find myself on this side of the grass and not under it, I think that's gonna be a pretty good day." He put his hat back on as he cocked his chin toward the flourishing vegetable patch growing in the sunny back end of the yard. He and Mom had planted it early in the spring before she went south to be near me during her knee replacement surgery and recovery. Before she decided to move down permanently. "Garden looks real good this summer. Too bad your mom's missing it."

"Thanks for keeping it up since she's been gone," I said. "Any ideas about what to do with all that zucchini?"

He laughed, shaking his head. "This time o' year, everybody's got too much zucchini. Gracie Nussbaum tried to give hers to the food bank, but they wanted some certificate from the Department of Ag about pesticides or something. Berkeley's one crazy place, eh? Even the poor people eat organic."

My eyes filled as I looked around the yard. Mr. Sato and Dad shared a love for roses and arguing politics; Mom grew herbs and vegetables. Roses and vegetables were planted in beds in the sunny south end of the yard. The shadier north end was a cool green lawn ringed by curved flower borders planted in the colors of the rainbow. And in the order of the colors of the rainbow: violet first, next indigo, then blue, a line of green, edged by yellow, then orange, and climbing the fence, vivid red bougainvillea. Dad, a physicist, planted the borders with the help of my older half sister and brother, Emily and Mark, fraternal twins, as a way of explaining to them the optical spectrum when they were taking their first physics classes. Later, Dad did the same exercise with me, this time planting flower borders on either side of the driveway in rainbow bands of color to explain the color spectrum of visible light to me. I still remember, though it has never come up in conversation since Dad's lessons in the garden, that what we perceive as green has a maximum sensitivity—color perception—at about 540 terahertz. If I was, or am a nerd, I came by it naturally.

As a family, we spent a lot of time in the yard. I was glad when Mom decided that the house was too much for her to keep up alone, and that she was now living near me. But we would both miss that garden.

"So," Mr. Sato said, face averted while I composed myself. "University gonna take over here, huh?"

"Yes," I said. "They're leasing the house for visiting faculty to use.

The housing officer is coming by this afternoon to look around. Do you want me to ask her to continue with your service?"

"Oh, hell no." He snorted, waving off the idea. "I retired ten, maybe twelve years ago. I'm living with my big-shot son and his family over in Menlo Park with all the other dot-com big shots. He's so rich he hired his own Japanese gardener. No, honey, I just been coming over here to hang out with your mom and look after my roses."

He took off his hat again and wiped the sweatband, a habit more than a necessity, I thought; it was a pleasantly warm day.

"Everything changes," he said, casting a glance around. "Was a time I took care of half the yards on this street. Now most o' the houses are full of strangers—you kids all grew up and went away—and some Mexican guy mows the lawns."

We both turned when we heard the squeal of the gate hinges. Standing side by side, we watched in silence as someone pushed it open enough to peer around. I don't know who was more surprised when a man's face appeared, he or us. The newcomer froze, staring, but Mr. Sato acted quickly, grabbed a long-handled garden fork out of his tool cart and aimed the business end of it at the man.

"How many times you gotta be told?" he said, advancing a few feet closer to the gate. "You quit coming in here, buddy."

"But I—"

The man took a half step further in, seemed confused or conflicted, or maybe he wanted to plead his case for being there. He looked weedy in frayed jeans, his brown hair pulled back from a receding hairline into an untidy ponytail. If I were homeless, I might find a yard with a nice garden full of food to be a good place to hang out, and I, too, might want to argue about being turned away.

When the man stayed his ground, not speaking, just staring, Mr. Sato pulled out his mobile phone. "You want me to call the cops again?"

"No, don't," he said, holding up his hands as he backed out the gate. "I'm going."

"Persistent bastard," Mr. Sato muttered as the gate latch snapped home. He put the fork away and rooted around in his cart for something. Search successful, he held up a hefty padlock for me to see. "I brought you this. Pest control."

I followed him to the gate and watched him attach the padlock. When it was secure, he handed me a pair of keys on a wire ring.

"Thank you." I put the keys into my pocket.

"Lock or no lock, watch out for that guy," he said. "I don't know what his deal is, but he seems bound and determined to hang out here. I've shooed him away a couple times. When I saw you come out the back door just now, I thought at first it was that asshole and he'd moved right in."

"You called the police on him?"

"Last week, I sure did," he said with righteous conviction. "I saw what kinds of mischief that knucklehead was capable of when he was just a punk kid. Who knows what he might do now?"

"You know him?"

The question surprised him. "You didn't recognize him?"

I shook my head.

"That's the kid you made cry that time. Remember?"

Impossible. "Larry Nordquist?"

"That's him," he said, thumping me on the back. "I pulled his dad's crabgrass out of half the lawns on Euclid. He didn't control his kid any better than he did his weeds."

"Mr. Sato, can I offer you a cup of coffee? I'd like you to take a look at something."

"I was hoping you'd ask. Your mom makes a good cup of coffee."

"She taught me how."

He followed me into the kitchen and helped me move some boxes off the table so there was room for us to sit. While he stirred cream and sugar into his coffee and chose a few cookies from the tin of shortbreads I offered him, I downloaded the film I had shown Kevin onto a laptop. When it came up, I paused it and turned the monitor toward him.

Mr. Sato took a pair of reading glasses out of his pocket and scooted his chair closer. "Whatcha got? One of your TV shows?"

"No. One of Dad's old movies."

"Hah!" He snorted again. "Your dad, crazy with that little camera, following you all ovah the place."

I was surprised: "You saw him?"

"Oh, sure. He had me watching for that girl. The French one. Me and the Nussbaums."

"Did you ever see her?" I asked,

"Oh, sure. Every time I see her, I go tell Al, he chases her away for a while."

"I didn't know."

He leaned forward, tapping my hand with a crooked finger as he grinned like a conspirator. "That was the idea, honey."

I took a breath; he took two more cookies and refilled his mug, perfectly comfortable in that kitchen.

"So, what'd you want me to see?" he asked.

I hit Play and the images began to move.

"Look at all you kids," he said, smiling. "Whole buncha little troublemakers, huh? Played hell with my flower borders, runnin' all over the place."

When the parade of girls passed a house where a gardener was mowing a lawn, I hit Pause again.

"Is that you, Mr. Sato?" I asked.

"Let's see, now." He adjusted his glasses on his nose and peered closely. Grinning, he said, "Looks like my truck; good truck, that one. Looks like my hat, too, so I'd say probably the handsome guy under the hat was me."

I fast-forwarded to the first frame that showed Tina Bartolini and Beto.

The sound he made when he saw them was something between a sigh and a groan. He said, "Poor little boy, lose his mother so young."

"Mr. Sato, Dad shot this movie on the same day Mrs. Bartolini died."

Eyes on the monitor screen, he sat back in his chair, nodding. No questions, no argument. No surprise.

"You took care of the Bartolinis' lawn, too, right?" I asked.

"For a while. But one of the guys I had working for me said something that the lady didn't care for. She was a very fine-looking lady, you know? Can't blame a man for noticing, but whatever he said he shouldn't of. I didn't blame Big Bart for hiring someone else. A cousin or something."

"Any hard feelings afterward?"

He shook his head. "I fired the guy, and that was it. Hired someone else, a better worker. Never a shortage of guys who need a regular paycheck."

I nodded toward the image frozen on the monitor. "Did you see Mrs. B that day, or speak to her?"

"I might have, you know, just coming and going. I don't remember; it was a long time ago."

"Did the police ever ask you about that day?"

Slowly he shook his head. "Not the police, no. They never asked me nothing."

The way he looked at me from the corner of his eye made me wait. I thought he was deciding whether he wanted to say something more. I topped off his mug, still waiting.

"Friends tell you something because they need your help," he said. "Ask you to keep it to yourself, you keep it to yourself long as it doesn't hurt somebody. You know, if your dad asked me to help him sneak that French girl into the house, I'd say, fuck yourself, Al, out of respect to Betsy. But he said, Tosh, help me keep that girl away from my baby, so that's what I did."

"Did the French girl have anything to do with what happened to Mrs. B?"

"No, no, no. 'Course not. But that's the thing, you know. Al asked me what I saw, and that was exactly nothing except maybe aphids on the Lopers' roses. If the cops asked me, I'd tell them the same, because it was the truth."

"No strangers lurking around, other than the French girl?"

"If I saw anyone, I woulda said. But I didn't."

"What did Dad ask you to keep to yourself about that day?"

"Just that he was out there with the camera," he said with a nod toward the computer. "We looked at the movie, but we didn't see anything the police would want to know about."

"Did Dad talk to your helper, too?"

He held up his hands, shrugged. "Dunno."

"What was his name?"

"Good question." He crossed his arms over his chest and gazed toward the ceiling as if the answer might be written there. After a moment, he laughed softly, tapping his forehead. "Almost… It'll come to me, maybe."

"Give me a call if it does."

"Yeah, okay. How come you're asking so many questions?"

"I don't know, Mr. Sato." I closed the computer and set it aside. "Curiosity?"

"Nosy." He grinned at me. "I see you on TV, you know. All the time nosing around about stuff. You was always like that, pestering about why, why, why before you could hardly talk."

"Dear God," I said, feeling heat rise on my face.

"I gotta go." He finished his last bite of cookie, washed it down with coffee, and picked up his hat. "My daughter-in-law has me picking up the kids from lacrosse camp. But first I gotta top the green beans."

"I'll give you a hand." I followed him out, grabbing a sun hat and a muslin shopping bag from the hook by the back door on the way. "Do you need something to take veggies home with you?"

"No. I brought a box," he said.

"I thought I'd pay Gracie a visit. Is there anything in our garden that she doesn't have in hers?"

"Gracie likes the herbs and tomatoes best," he said. "But she didn't plant a garden this year."

"Just zucchini?" I said.

"Not even. Zucchini planted itself, hitchhikers from last year."

In the middle of the garden, Mr. Sato had constructed half a dozen six-foot-tall tepee-shaped frames out of bamboo stakes for the green beans and peas to climb. The vines, heavy with crop, had grown to the top of the frames by June and were now putting out tendrils that waved in the air above. While Mr. Sato cut the stray tendrils, I snipped beans and peas and distributed them between my bag and his box. The young beans were so beautiful that I picked one, broke it in half and ate it; sweet and crisp and delicious.

"When you was little," he said, grinning at me, "you always ate those beans just like that. Sneaking 'em, like you was stealing 'em."

"They're so good." I popped a pea pod open and offered him the contents. With a thumbnail, he scraped the row of firm sweet peas into his mouth. "Better than candy."

"Is your little girl as crazy as you were?"

"My little girl isn't so little, Mr. Sato. She'll be a junior in college next year."

"She gonna come and help you out here?"

"No," I said. "She's spending the summer in Normandy with her

French cousins, getting to know them and learning how to make cheese."

"I forgot. Gracie told me something about that."

I knelt down to snip herbs. "How are your beautiful granddaughters?"

"Growing fast," he said, smiling proudly as he tied the herbs into bundles with garden twine.

"Are they dancing in the Obon Festival this weekend?"

"Oh, sure. To make the old grandpa happy, my son takes them to the Japanese Cultural Center for classes." He looked up at me. "You know, the kids got baptized Episcopalian by their mother. So, I ask my son, when you're in that big fancy church, which god does a good Buddhist boy like you pray to? You know what he says?"

"I can't imagine."

"He says, Pop, you were a married man. You know damn well it's the one my wife tells me to." He tapped his forehead and winked at me. "Smart boy, that one."

The garden was abundant. It didn't take long before my bag and his box were filled: young green beans and peas, three varieties of lettuce, peppers, cucumbers and squash, with fat red tomatoes safely nested on top with the herbs.

As I saw him out the gate, he said, "I still keep my greenhouse down south of San Jose. You come see me sometimes, okay? Bring your mom."

"I will," I said.

He aimed a finger at me. "You better."

I held the gate for him.

His parting words were "Lock up after me."

After I said good-bye to Mr. Sato, I called Gracie Nussbaum to see if she was home and wouldn't mind me dropping by. Like Mom, Gracie had a full calendar, so it was rare to find her at home during the day. But I was in luck, she was in and yes, she would love a visit.

I washed my hands, found a case for my laptop, gathered up the bag of herbs and vegetables, and set out for Gracie's house three streets over.

Gracie was waiting for me in the big wood-slat swing on her front porch. On a little iron table beside her there were a pitcher of lemonade and a plate of rugelach.

"What is all that you're carrying?" she asked as she rose to meet me.

"I was in the garden with Mr. Sato," I said, opening the bag to show her.

"Lovely." Gracie kissed my cheek. She let me carry the bag up the steps and said I should just set it beside the front door, she'd put it away later.

"Taking a break from house clearing?" she asked, handing me a glass of lemonade after I was settled on the swing.

"Yes, but I shouldn't," I said, steadying the swing so she could sit down beside me. "I haven't accomplished much today, one distraction after another."

"You know, dear, I always liked that Kevin Halloran." She passed me the plate of rugelach. "Ben did, too."

"Exactly what made you think of Kevin just now?"

"Didn't he drop by to see you?"

"Yes, but how did you know?"

"I ran into Karen Loper at Beto's deli. She told me she saw Kevin on your doorstep this morning. Didn't he marry one of the Riley girls?"

"He did. Lacy."

Gracie chuckled softly. "So, our boy has had his hands full, then."

"Seems he has," I said, biting into a raspberry-jam-filled rugelach and getting flaky crumbs all over my lap. "But Kevin can be a handful, too."

"I forget, do they have children?"

"Two. A boy in college and a daughter in high school."

"Hmm." She nodded, thinking that through. Gracie is a font of information about everyone in town, but she really is not a big gossip. There is never anything malicious in what she says. I think that Gracie is just sincerely interested in people and doesn't mind sharing benign information with others who might also be interested. People seem to be comfortable telling her the most amazing, sometimes excruciatingly personal things about themselves. Gracie sorts it, keeps confidences to herself but shares various comings and goings, births and deaths with mutual acquaintances.

"Gracie," I said. "Did you know that Beto asked Kevin to look into his mother's murder?"

"No." Her eyes grew wide and owlish behind her thick lenses. "Did he?"

"He did."

"Do you think that's wise?"

"Maybe not. But I understand why Beto would ask."

"I suppose." She seemed doubtful.

"Do you remember Larry Nordquist?" I asked.

She chuckled. "He's the boy you made cry."

"Is that all you remember about him?"

"I remember he had a very troubled home life." She leaned close as if to share a confidence. "Problem children sometimes are the products of problem parents, you know."

"Sounds reasonable."

"You ask, because?"

"The brouhaha that ended with Larry in tears began when he said something crude to Beto about his mom."

"I can't imagine anyone having anything crude to say about that lovely woman."

"At the time, I really didn't know what it meant. But Beto understood well enough to take a swing at Larry. God, Gracie, you should have seen it. Beto connected with a roundhouse punch right to the kisser. Then he ran like hell. Our Beto was little but, God, he was fast. Larry was mortified, so he challenged Beto to a real fight, Beto's gang against Larry's gang."

"Beto had a gang?" The notion seemed to amuse her.

"Sure. All of the fifth graders on our street."

"As I recall, Beto was the only boy your age on your street."

"Yep. It was a dozen girls and Beto against Larry and five or six middle-school bullies. In the end, it didn't amount to much. I took down Larry with a few cruel words and it was over."

"Sticks and stones," she said. "It began and ended with hurtful words."

"All day I've been bothered by what Larry said that started it all."

She put her hand on my knee and smiled sweetly. "So my darling Maggie has come over to ask her old Auntie Gracie a bouquet of questions about Larry Nordquist?"

"Not about Larry, but yes, lots of questions." I stuffed the end of the rugelach into my mouth, chewed fast and washed it down with lemonade.

"Gracie, I really know nothing about Mrs. B except that she was very sweet to all of us, very tolerant of the noise and chaos when we were around. But who was she?"

"How do you mean, dear?"

"For one thing, how did she end up with Big Bart Bartolini?" I said. "When we were kids, Mr. and Mrs. B were just Beto's parents. But when I think about it now, they were an odd couple. She was beautiful, refined, gracious, young. And Bart? None of the above. How did they ever get together?"

"Your mother is probably the best source for that information. She and Tina were quite close, you know," she said. "They worked together with Father John at your church, helping out Vietnamese refugees after the war over there ended."

"I'll talk to Mom later. But I wondered what you might know."

"Not very much, except that Tina and Bart met in Vietnam. He was a cook in the navy and her father was a food broker of some kind, and that's how they connected. For all of the differences between them, I can say that there was abundant love in the Bartolini household."

"Ah yes, love."

"You doubt it?"

"No," I said. "I saw it for myself. But when you said that, you reminded me what I said that made Larry cry."

"What did you say?"

"I told Larry that if he hurt Beto, no one would love Beto any less. But everyone would hate Larry more than they already did. I asked him if that's what he wanted."

"Oh, sweetie."

"I was ten, Gracie."

"Dear girl." She cupped my chin in her cool hand and turned my face toward her. "That poor boy went into a battle of the wits unarmed, didn't he?"

"I just didn't want to get socked by some pimply-faced boy, okay?"

"Okay." She began to rise. "Will you help me put away nature's bounty?"

She led the way, carrying the plate of pastries. I followed with the lemonade pitcher and the garden bag. In her kitchen as we rinsed the vegetables, conversation remained superficial while I tried to form the big question I had come to ask in a way that she might deign to answer.

"When is your cousin Susan arriving?" Gracie asked as I spun lettuce dry. "What's her last name now?"

"Haider," I said. "She'll be here sometime Sunday afternoon."

"I remember her from visits years ago. Nice girl. Pretty girl. Is she coming to help you with the house?"

"In a way. I asked her to look at some things from Mom's family while she's here, in case there are pieces she wants. She's been down in Livermore all week, taking a sommelier course at the Wente Vineyards."

"Studying wine?" Gracie frowned, skeptical. "I thought Susan had a very responsible job in Minneapolis."

"She does, something in marketing. But wine is a passion for both her and her husband. Bob took their daughter, Maddie, off trekking in the Rockies for a couple of weeks, so Susan flew out here for what she calls wine camp. She'll be with me on Sunday and then her book club friends will join her Monday for a wine-tasting tour."

"That does sound like fun. Maybe I'll tag along."

"I'll let her know you're interested."

"You'll have a houseful, Maggie. I understand your Jean-Paul is visiting this weekend, too."

What didn't she know about my life?

"We don't have any plans beyond Friday evening," I said. "He's coming up for an official event."

"The grand opening reception of the Matisse exhibit at the de Young Museum, isn't it?" she said. "Sounds very highbrow," she said, feigning haughty airs. "Sponsored by a French chocolatier."

I knew her source of information only too well. "How's Mom?"

"Fine, thanks. I just spoke with her this morning. She wants to talk to you about shipping her piano down."

"I thought we had that all arranged," I said. "She doesn't have room for it in her new apartment, so she's having it sent to my house."

Gracie wagged a finger. "I won't say another word. Might spoil her fun."

My mom had adjusted well to her new home, very well. But she sometimes felt lonely in the evenings. I called her every night at about the time she would be sitting down for dinner so that she would have company of a sort while she ate. Otherwise, she might just skip eating altogether. Seeing the gleam in Gracie's eyes I thought that Mom might just get an early call tonight.

The vegetables were put away in the crisper, herbs in small vases on the windowsill, tomatoes cushioned in a basket on the counter. Gracie dried her hands, leaned against the counter, and said, "Now, dear girl, what is the question you actually came over to ask me?"

I laughed: God bless Gracie. I pulled out a kitchen chair and sat.

"Gracie, on the morning that Mrs. Bartolini died, my dad was out following me around with his camera."

She nodded, matter-of-fact. "Isabelle's mother called to warn him to be on the lookout; Isabelle had flown across the pond again."

"Why did he film her?"

"He had a restraining order, you know. But she consistently violated it. He worried about what she might do; I think you were the only girl at your school with her very own stalker. Your Uncle Max told Al he should keep a record of every infraction in case she ever tried to claim custody. What he really wanted to do was get her barred from entering the country."

"There might be something on that film that would have been useful to the investigators, but I don't think Dad ever showed it to them."

"No, he didn't." She pulled out a chair beside mine and sat. "Maggie, dear, when Tina was murdered, we were all sent into a tailspin. Your dad forgot he'd even shot the film for I don't know how long. By the time he sent it to the developer and got it back again, the police had someone in custody. Al just put the film away. Why wouldn't he?"

"Someone was in custody? I never heard that. Who was it?"

"A young man. What was his name?" She scratched her head. "I'll think of it. Anyway, the man broke into an apartment in the south campus area, raped a woman student—brutal, what he did to her— and was caught when he came back to the building a second time. He looked like a good candidate for the murder."

"But?"

"The police couldn't tie him in any way to Tina's death so they had to drop that charge," she said.

"You know that my Ben worked with the police from time to time," she said. "Over cards one night at your house—it was some months later—he was telling your mom and dad and me about how frustrated the police were. They couldn't find any evidence that would tie the man in custody, or anyone else, to the murder. Somewhere during that discussion your dad remembered the film. He wondered if there might be something there."

"Why didn't he take it to the police?"

"You know the answer," she said sweetly.

"Because he didn't want the police to haul in Isabelle to ask what she might have seen."

"Exactly. But we took a very careful look at the film and we didn't see anything that we thought might be important to the police," she said. "We certainly didn't see that particular young man. We talked it over and decided Al should just hang on to the film for the time being."

"If something were there, would Dad have turned the film over?"

"Of course, dear. But as there wasn't…" She held up her palms and smiled; no harm, no foul.

The edges of that decision were a bit squishy, I thought. But I understood why they made it. At the time, my parents and the Nussbaums saw nothing untoward in the film of their neighborhood on an ordinary morning. But an outsider might. The passage of time makes all of us outsiders to the past. I thought that if Gracie saw the film again something might pop out that she had missed before.

I took my laptop case from the counter where I parked it when we came inside, pulled out the computer and held it up to Gracie.

"Want to go to the movies with me, Gracie?"

"What do you have, dear?"

"The film."

"Good lord, did you get the old projector working?"

"I couldn't find enough pieces of it," I said as I booted the film. "So I had the film digitized. Tell me what you see."

Gracie leaned toward the monitor, bobbing her head until she found the right lens of her trifocals to look through, and I hit Play.

"I don't recognize all you girls, but there's Tosh working on the Scotts' yard. And George Loper backing out of his driveway. The dry cleaner's van, hmm…" Her brow was furrowed when she looked up at me; I hit Pause. "I don't remember noticing before. What day of the week did Tosh do yards on your street?"

"Alternate Mondays," I said.

She nodded. "We had him the opposite Mondays. The dry cleaner only made home deliveries to our neighborhood on Thursdays."

"Interesting," I said. "Did they ever make special deliveries?"

"Never. If you needed something special you had to go over to their place yourself."

"Do you remember the deliveryman?"

She shook her head. "They came, they went. No one ever stayed long enough to know his route well. I think the pay was a pittance. Maybe it was a new driver and he was lost," she offered.

"But wouldn't he have been lost on Thursday instead of Monday?" I asked.

"You would think so, wouldn't you?" Suddenly her face brightened and she said, "Ennis Jones."

"He was the driver?"

"No, dear. That's the name of the man who was arrested, the rapist. Ennis Jones."

Chapter 3

WALKING AWAY FROM GRACIE'S, I dialed Kevin's mobile phone.

"Detective Halloran," he answered, though I knew my name came up on his caller I.D.

"You're busy," I said.

"Go ahead," was his cryptic response.

"Gracie Nussbaum picked out something interesting on the film I showed you," I said. "I thought you should know."

"What was it?" Someone in the room with him, a woman, wanted to know who he was talking to. He shushed her.

"It was the wrong day for the dry cleaner's van to be on our street."

"That's a tough one," he said. "But I'll check it out. Anything else?"

"Yes, but it can keep. Sounds like you're in a meeting."

"This is as good a time as any." The woman volubly disagreed. "Go ahead."

"Do you remember Toshio Sato?"

"The gardener?"

"Yes," I said. "He told me that he's caught Larry Nordquist hanging out in Mom's backyard a couple of times."

"Larry? At your mom's house?" Again he shushed the woman when she demanded to know whose mom. "What was he doing there?"

"Hanging out, apparently," I said. "Mr. Sato called the police last week. But Larry showed up again today."

"Were you there?"

44

"I was."

"What did he do?"

"Nothing, really. Mr. Sato shooed him away," I said. "You told me Larry was out on parole. What did the police do with the call?"

"I'll check it out and get back to you."

"Thanks," I said. "Sorry to interrupt."

It was a beautiful day, and it was nice to be outdoors. Instead of going straight home, I walked across the western end of campus and went into town. I had missed breakfast and lunch, unless you count one rugelach. I was hungry, there was nothing at home except garden vegetables to eat, and I wanted to see Beto. Not to tell him about the film—I wasn't ready for that yet—but just to spend a few minutes with my old friend.

Bartolini's Deli and Italian Market on Shattuck Avenue was busy, as always. Located half a block from the BART station, about equidistant between the Civic Center and the massive Cal campus, even at two o'clock in the afternoon there were seven people ahead of me when I pulled a number tab from the machine on top of the refrigerated deli cases.

Beto was hard at work behind the counter, serving customers and supervising three young clerks, sending orders to the kitchen, overseeing plates coming out of the kitchen, slicing and wrapping meats and cheeses as ordered, dishing up take-out containers of salads and casseroles and precooked entrees. He was so busy that I gave up on any notion of having any sort of chat with him. But I was still hungry.

When he noticed me he flashed me his big smile and called out, "Hey, Maggie."

"Hi, Beto." I gave him a little wave, took a bottle of cold water out of a drinks cooler, and found a table near some freestanding metal racks filled with imported pastas and delicacies and waited for my number to come up on the board.

While I was waiting, Kevin called. Without preliminaries, he said, "Patrol officers responded to Mr. Sato's call. Larry was picked up and brought in. He was released to his probation officer, but it was Father John who picked him up."

"Father John?" I said. "Our Father John? I thought he had gone off to Outer Upper Gadzookistan or somewhere."

"He's back in the parish," Kevin said, followed by "I have to go."

I thanked him, wondering about his abrupt tone. Something was up with him.

"Yo, is that my favorite TV lady?" Old Bart Bartolini, Beto's dad, came out from the kitchen when he spotted me. He kissed me on both cheeks. "Beto said you was in town." He lowered his chin. "Sorry to hear about your mother, honey. Betsy was one nice lady."

"Mom is fine," I said. "She moved down closer to me so you won't be seeing as much of her, but she's just fine."

He furrowed his brow, seemed confused; we'd had exactly the same conversation two days earlier.

"I thought you retired," I said, shifting the topic. "So why are you wearing that big apron?"

"Just helping out the boy," he said, sitting down heavily in the chair beside mine, grimacing as if his feet hurt. "You know, only till Beto gets the hang of running the place."

"Seems to me he's doing just fine." No need to remind him that Beto had worked in the store for most of his life.

Mr. Bartolini beamed as he looked over at his son. He could behave like an old curmudgeon with his employees and with overly demanding customers, but where Beto was concerned, there was nothing but sweetness and light.

"What a kid, uh?" He pulled a towel off his apron string, picked up my sweating water bottle and wiped the table under it. "Always a good worker, that one. I just wish his mom…"

His eyes filled, just as they had two days earlier, when he'd said exactly the same thing.

Mr. Bartolini was somewhere in his eighties. When he moved to Berkeley about forty years ago and opened his deli, he was a retired navy cook with a much-younger Vietnamese bride and a baby boy. If Beto was the apple of his eye, his wife, Tina, was the entire apple orchard. I could only imagine the pain her death inflicted on him. On both of them.

When I lost my husband, Mike, to cancer a little over a year ago, it felt as if the San Andreas fault had opened up and swallowed me whole. I would have given anything for a little more time with him. But Mike decided for himself when he'd had enough, and left this world on his own terms at a time of his own choosing. As much as I missed him, I accepted his decision. But someone else, a stranger maybe, had made that decision for Tina Bartolini. And that was not fair.

Mr. B took a deep breath and looked up at me from under his thicket of eyebrows.

"Everyone's sure gonna miss your mom," he said, patting my hand. "She was one of the finest ladies I ever knew. You know, when she first met my Tina, I thought there might be some, ya know, resentment, her being Vietnamese and your big brother dying over there."

"My parents would never associate Mrs. B with what happened to my brother."

"Yeah? Well some people did. Gave her a hard time."

"I'm sorry to hear that," I said.

"But not your mother. She helped Tina get registered in some English classes over at the JC. Then when the war over there went all to hell and refugees poured into this area, your mom hooked her up to the refugee assistance programs. You know, to help people coming in from Vietnam to get what they needed." He began to choke up again. "That was real important to my wife. Being able to help out like that."

During the entire conversation, Beto kept an eye on his father. When Mr. Bartolini reached a certain emotional state, Beto handed off the customer he was serving to one of his staff and joined us. He wrapped an arm around his father's shoulders and leaned down close.

"How you doing, Papa?"

"Good. Good." Mr. Bartolini wiped his eyes with the backs of his big hands and gave his son a game smile. "I was telling Maggie how sorry we were to hear she lost her mother."

Beto kissed his father on the forehead, gave me a watcha-gonna-do? look. I smiled. There was no point correcting Mr. Bartolini, again.

Mr. B turned to me. "You should try Beto's pastrami today. It's extra special."

"My pastrami is always extra special, Papa." Beto had been a sweet, round-cheeked little boy. He had become a sweet, round-all-over adult, very much like his dad, except with his mother's soft brown slanted eyes and none of Mr. B's curmudgeonly edges. "But you talked Maggie into having the pastrami day before yesterday. Today I have some really nice baked ziti with chicken, artichokes, some asparagus and good Greek olives. I think she'll like it."

"Sounds more like puttanesca than baked ziti," Mr. Bartolini said, winking at me. "But you're the boss, son. You're the boss."

"Maggie, I think your number is up," Beto said, pointing his chin toward the service area; my number was fifty-eight, the number on the call board was fifty-four. "Papa, stay put. Can I get you a coffee?"

Mr. Bartolini, who seemed fatigued, started to nod, but stopped himself. He turned and looked up at Beto, and as if scolding, he said, "I run this place for forty years. You think I don't know where to find the coffeepot?"

"Suit yourself."

As I rose to follow Beto, I patted Mr. Bartolini on the shoulder. "Take care."

"Try the pastrami," he said. "Today it's extra special."

Beto leaned his head close to mine as we walked toward the deli cases. "What do you think?"

"I think you're right, Beto," I said. "He's getting a little fuzzy around the sides. But he seems to be okay."

He nodded. "Some days are better than others, and today's not so good. If you asked him what happened this morning, he couldn't tell you. But ask about something ten, twenty, thirty years ago and he'll tell you every detail as if it happened yesterday."

"How old is he?"

"He'll be eighty-four in August." He glanced around, checked on his father, who hadn't moved from his seat. "For his age, he's doing all right. You know, I'd understand it if he wanted to go live in a happier time. But he seems to be stuck in a bad place. A very bad place."

"He misses your mom."

Beto gave my arm a squeeze, seemed to shrug off his mood as he went behind the counter where he had spent so much of his life, selling good food to hungry people. In one continuous flow, he grabbed a take-out container, asked one of his staff to serve his dad some coffee, and unpinned a card from the bulletin board next to a wall phone. He reached over the high counter and handed me the card.

"This is the number for the gal my wife told you about," he said. "She did a real good job on the estate sale for her cousin."

"Thank Zaida for me," I said, slipping the card into my pocket.

"How's it going over there?" he asked, referring to Mom's house.

"Making some progress," I said. "After my cousin and University Housing take a look around and tell me what they do or don't want, I'll be ready to call in someone to cart the rest off."

"It's a big job. Let me know if I can help." He had already piled enough ziti into the container for several meals before he added a last scoop and snapped on a lid. "But don't be in too big a hurry to finish over there; I'll miss you."

"I'll be around," I said.

"Hey, I heard Kevin knocked on your door." He looked up, gave me his version of a leer. "Thinking of rekindling the old flame?"

"Beto!" I feigned shock. "He's a married man."

"Tell *him* that." A sardonic laugh. As he filled a second container, unbidden, with grilled peppers and sausage, he said, "So, are you bringing your new guy to the party Saturday?"

"I should know better, but I'll ask him. What else can I bring?"

"Bring? To *my* house?" He pointed a big spoon toward his chest. "You gotta be kidding. Between my dad, my mother-in-law, Auntie Quynh and me we're having an Italian-Mexican-Vietnamese feast."

"Tums, then?"

He laughed. "Yeah. Bring some of those."

There was a local branch of the bank I use down the street from the deli. After I said good-bye to Beto and Bart, I shouldered my shopping bag, its contents much heavier and more expensive than I had anticipated when I dropped in to say hello, and walked over to use the ATM to get cash for the weekend. The bank had stationed a uniformed guard out front, probably to shoo away the street people who sometimes aggressively panhandled bank customers coming out with their pockets full of fresh money.

When I got closer, I recognized the guard, Chuck Riley, a retired Berkeley detective who lived down on the corner of my parents' street, across from the Bartolinis'. I knew him to be a blowhard, with a quiet, put-upon wife and two notoriously wild daughters, one of whom, Lacy, was married to my friend, Detective Kevin Halloran. Dad always said that Chuck must have been a pretty good money manager to afford a house in that neighborhood on a cop's salary, unless he or his wife, Marva, had inherited a fair amount, though that didn't seem likely. Marva canvassed the neighborhood regularly, selling everything from Amway to Tupperware; Mom avoided her. The Rileys still lived in the same house; maybe Chuck needed this post-retirement job to maintain it.

Like many old acquaintances I had run into that week, I noticed how much he had aged since I last saw him; they all probably said the same about me. Probably in his late sixties or early seventies, he was still thin enough to be described as lanky, but now a bit stooped. Age aside, he looked sufficiently intimidating in his crisply pressed uniform with a gun holstered on his Sam Browne belt to do his job. He gave me a fish-eyed going-over as I used my card to gain access to the ATM lobby.

"Hello, Mr. Riley," I said.

"It's been a while," he said, smiling when he recognized me. He touched the shiny bill of his cap in a sort of military salute. When the lobby door lock clicked, he pulled it open and held it for me.

While I waited for a man who had finished his business inside to fumble his cash into his wallet before leaving, I asked, "How are you?"

"Good enough," Chuck said, still holding the door. "How's your mother?"

"Mom's doing well. You know she moved?"

"George Loper mentioned that. You're in town closing up the house, I understand."

"I am." I shifted my shopping bag higher on my shoulder. "How's your family?"

"Hanging in." His smile became closer to a sneer when he said, "But I suppose Kevin already filled you in on the details, eh?"

There were ugly undertones in that question. What sort of nasty spin was Karen Loper putting on Kevin's visit to my house that morning as she made her rounds?

The answer to Chuck's question was, no. Kevin had said nothing about his wife's family at all, and never mentioned his wife, Lacy, by name.

Wallet satisfactorily stowed away, the man inside the ATM lobby finally came out. Without addressing Chuck's last remark, I said, "Nice to see you, Mr. Riley," and stepped past him. When I came back out a few minutes later, he had his back toward me, giving directions to a tourist holding a map.

I hiked the bag up on my shoulder again as I turned and walked away.

An afternoon breeze blew in off San Francisco Bay, full of salt and fish and a hint of petroleum fumes wafting up from the freeway. It was early for rush hour but traffic streaming out of the City was already so heavy that the line of cars seeping over the Bay Bridge and up the freeway looked like one continuous snake undulating along the shore as far as I could see in any direction. Grim going for those trapped in it.

Instead of cutting across the campus, as I normally would, I detoured for a look at my elementary school. On the way, I passed the pharmacy where Dad had spotted Isabelle watching for me. Bay Laundry and Dry Cleaners was two doors down. It would be pointless, I knew, to go in and ask whoever was there who might have been driving their delivery truck on a particular Monday morning over thirty years ago. But, nothing ventured, nothing gained, I thought, and not for the first time. Even though the chance of solving a thirty-year-old murder was remote, especially when there was scant surviving evidence, maybe the right question to the right person might dislodge an essential bit of information out of hibernation. Who knew?

I ask questions for a living, so I went in.

"Good afternoon." The young woman at the counter looked up from a chemistry textbook. "Picking up?"

"No," I said. After an awkward-feeling moment—what was my excuse for being there?—I pulled out one of my business cards with the network logo in the middle and asked if the owner was on the premises. The woman raised her eyebrows and looked from the card to me, and back again.

"Joe's out in the shop, but he's busy," she said. "Can I tell him what you need?"

I lied: "I have a few questions about running a family-owned business. If he could give me just a minute or two."

"I'll ask," she said in a way that gave me little hope. Probably for the best, I thought. Why waste his time?

A man I guessed to be in his fifties, wearing starched green work pants and matching shirt with the laundry's logo stitched over the pocket, came forward through the forest of plastic garment bags hanging from the overhead conveyor. He flicked my card as he studied me.

"I heard you were a local," he said. "My wife watches your stuff on TV."

I had to chuckle. "But you don't?"

He shook his head. "Too bleeding-hearts for me. No offense."

"None taken."

"Madison here said you have some questions."

"A few, yes," I said. "I know you're a busy man."

"That I am." He flipped up a section of the counter and gestured for me to come through. "But if I said no to you, the wife would shoot me. Come on back. We can talk while I work. This time of day I need to keep an eye on things."

I followed him into a huge room. It was a hive. At the far end, a bank of industrial-size washers and dryers sloshed and whirred while maybe a dozen people operated a variety of pressing and folding machines. Sorters wrapped and tagged the finished work and either hung it on the conveyor or placed it on shelves in what seemed like one seamless, efficient chain. A truck backed into a loading bay and three workers converged to unload bundles of soiled clothing, and then they loaded in clean.

Fascinated, I said, "This is a much bigger operation than I thought it was. Very impressive."

"You gotta keep growing or you get plowed under. We've taken over five storefronts since my dad retired." Joe weighed a stack of starched, maroon-colored dinner napkins on his hand, flipped the edges and took two off the top before he sealed the stack in plastic and stuck a routing label on it. "You wouldn't know how big the plant is unless you went down the alley."

"How many employees?"

"Here at the laundry, we have eighteen. Another four at the dry cleaning plant up in Richmond." He leaned in close to offer a confidence, though he still had to shout over the noise of the machines. "Up there, they aren't as anal about the cleaning chemicals as they are here in town. But in case that's what you're nosing around about, this ain't no sweatshop. We run a green business, we pay better than minimum, make our Social Security contributions on time and offer health coverage to full-time workers. And we don't discriminate against nobody. Hell, take a look around and you can see I got a god-damn mini-U.N. working for me.

"Everything is run strictly by the letter of the labor codes. Here in the People's Republic of Berserkeley, if I break some law of political correctness, whatever it is at the moment, a squadron of hatchet-faced do-gooders will land on me like a bomb and organize a boycott. Which I can't afford. Is that what you want to know?"

"Interesting," I said, laughing. "But I'm more interested in your delivery schedule."

He scowled. "There a problem? My drivers are bonded."

"No problem," I said, watching the truck driver scan his load before signing off on a computer-generated manifest.

"My drivers are good guys. They draw a good wage and they stay with me for a long time."

Feeling hopeful, I asked, "How long?"

He wrapped another stack of napkins. "Fred's been with me about a dozen years, Satch eight or nine. Jaime, my dispatcher back there, drives backup if someone calls in sick. He was the first man I hired when Dad retired twenty years ago. I don't mean to knock my dad, may he rest in peace, but he had a big turnover of drivers. I say it makes better sense to take good care of your key people so they stick around."

I was disappointed; none of them had been on the job long enough to help me out. I asked, "Do you change their delivery routes regularly?"

"Nope. The schedule is the same as it's been since forever." He tapped a city map on the wall behind him that was divided into a dozen numbered zones. "Mondays and Fridays are commercial pick-up and delivery, restaurants, mostly. Tuesdays, Wednesdays, and Thursdays are home delivery. If someone needs something off-schedule, they have to come in for it."

I pointed to my neighborhood, Zone Nine on his map. "Would there be any reason for one of your trucks to be here on a Monday morning?"

"On a Monday?" He scowled, shook his head, counted and wrapped another stack of napkins. "Never. On Mondays, besides half

the restaurants in town, we pick up from the party rentals and cater-
ers—after the weekend events, you know—so we have to scramble. If
one of my trucks took a detour into Nine on a Monday, I'd be getting
calls about late deliveries."

"Did you change the schedule after your dad retired?"

"Nope. Give him credit for that. He only had the one truck, and
now we have three because we have more customers. But the schedule worked then, and it works now."

I took out my laptop, loaded Dad's movie, fast-forwarded to the
shot of Bay Laundry's truck backing out of a driveway, and froze the
frame. I turned the screen so he could see. He paused in his work to
take a look.

"Where'd you get that?" he asked, chuckling. "That's Dad's old
van. If it's still around, it belongs in a museum."

"This is an old film," I said. "What does it tell you?"

"That's upper Zone Nine," he said with a little shrug. "So that was
taken on a Thursday between eight and ten."

"It was shot on a Monday around eight A.M."

He shook his head. "Not possible."

"Can you think of any reason why the truck would be there on a
Monday?"

Again he shook his head. "Like I said, we keep a tight schedule."

The second of his delivery trucks backed into the loading bay and
the off-loading, reloading scramble began anew. I saw the driver slip
into the men's room.

"What happens if one of your trucks breaks down?" I asked.

"We take good care of the rolling stock so that doesn't happen very
often. But when one does go down or goes in for regular servicing,
we bring in the truck from the dry cleaning shop. They do a pick-up
here in the morning and a delivery in the afternoon, so in the case of
a breakdown, we just hang on to it for the day."

"Is that truck the same as the other two?"

"It's an Econoline, yeah. But it's unmarked. The Richmond plant
is in a crappy area, so we try to keep a low profile up there."

I took another look around before I offered Joe my hand. "Thank
you for your time."

"Sure thing." He pulled my card out of his breast pocket. "Mind
putting your John Hancock on here? For the wife, you know."

"A pleasure." I don't at all understand the appeal of autographs, especially the signature of someone like me, who has, at most, minor celebrity. But I scrawled my name on the face of the card and handed it back. "Say hello to her for me."

As he walked me back toward the front, I asked Joe where he was on the date Mrs. Bartolini died. The question seemed to puzzle him, but after a moment to think back, he said, "I was in the navy, stationed in Japan."

I thanked Joe again, said good-bye, and started off again toward home. On the street where we had faced down Larry Nordquist and his gang all those years ago, I stopped and looked around.

Funny how two disparate events, the "rumble" and Mrs. B, became inextricably entwined in my memory. For me, the link was more than a coincidence of time. It was also the words that Larry yelled at me that day as we stood toe-to-toe in the middle of the street; his words still seemed to hang in the air at that place. "Gook kid and his gook whore mother. Saigon slut."

I remembered the way Larry's spittle felt on my cheek when he spat out those words. Ugly, frightening words, so foreign within the protective bubble of my existence then. Ugly still.

With a shudder, I continued toward home. When I reached my own street, I turned and took a last look at that place; no one was there.

Beto, his wife, their children, his father and his mother-in-law all lived together in the corner house where Beto grew up. It appeared to be a happy arrangement for all, one that was perfectly natural to Beto's Mexican-born wife, Zaida. As the domestic *jefe*, Zaida had overseen an extensive home remodel that added a second story, so that now the house looked very different from the original, right down to the front yard where a lawn and rose garden had been replaced with a native-plant xeriscape.

Just about the only parts of the house that had been left untouched were the bedroom Mr. B had shared with his wife and a niche in the front entry that held a small golden Buddha. Every morning, fresh flowers, food and burning incense were carefully placed in the niche to honor the lost wife and mother, and the ancestors she left behind in Vietnam.

A car horn startled me as I stood looking at the Bartolinis' yard. I turned and saw Beto's Aunt Quynh behind the wheel of a huge SUV. She waved as she pulled in off the street. I walked up the drive and waited for her to park.

Quynh was Mrs. B's older sister, a smaller, less pretty version of Tina. After the Americans pulled out of Vietnam, because Quynh had family in the U.S., the Hanoi-based government sent her to a re-education center, where she was sentenced to work in the rice paddies somewhere outside Saigon until, by some mysterious means, she managed to escape. From a Red Cross camp in Hong Kong, she was able to contact Bart. It was only then, maybe a year after the fact, that she learned that her sister was dead.

I remember the excitement when Bart brought Quynh home from the airport shortly after she made contact. She lived in her sister's house, taking care of Beto, until he was ready for college. We all loved her. It was clear, though, that for Beto, Quynh was his aunt, and never a replacement for his mother.

"Quynh," I said. "How nice to see you."

Grinning, she placed her palms together and bowed, the traditional Vietnamese greeting. "What is this 'Quynh' you say? You don't call your auntie 'Auntie' no more?"

"Auntie." I bowed to her, though I wanted to throw my arms around her. She opened the SUV's back hatch and handed me a five-gallon plastic bucket full of live lobsters without preamble.

"You can take two?" she asked, holding up a second.

"Sure." I reached for the handle. "Are these for the party Saturday?"

She nodded. "You want to take one home, make a nice dinner?"

"Thanks," I said, turning a bit to show her the shopping bag dangling from my shoulder. "But I stopped by the deli and Beto gave me enough food to hold me for a while."

She grinned, stacking three long, foil-wrapped roasting pans together. "That Beto, he takes care of his friends. He tells me you have a new boyfriend."

"When a man is fifty, do you still call him a boyfriend?" I walked beside her into the house.

She shrugged her narrow shoulders. "What else you gonna call him?"

"I call him Jean-Paul."

"You better bring him Saturday so Auntie can get a look at him."

I smiled, and did not tell her that Jean-Paul and I had made no plans past Friday night. I looked around the immaculate kitchen for a place to set the buckets; the lobsters scrabbled their banded claws against the sides, looked up at me with sad, beady eyes.

"Auntie, you're here!" Zaida, Beto's wife, came in from the backyard. "And Maggie!"

First she took the pans from Quynh, leaning in to kiss her cheek.

"Anything else to bring in?"

"Whole car full," Quynh said.

Zaida opened the back door and called out, "Boys, need some help, please."

Carlos, the younger of Beto's sons, came in and took both buckets of lobsters from me as his mother gave instructions to the trio of teenagers trailing after him to finish unloading Quynh's car.

"Carlos," she called after her son. "Put those bugs in the garage refrigerator. They'll go to sleep until Grandpa is ready for them."

"Looks like you have your hands full," I said to Zaida as she closed the back door after her son.

"Everything's under control." She wrapped her arms around me and smooched my cheek. She was lovely in a way that Gracie would call zaftig, deliciously curvy. "How's it going over at the house, Maggie?"

I held up my hands. "It's going. Thanks for the estate sale referral, but I think we'll just donate stuff and be done with it."

"Anything I can do to help." She squeezed my arm. "Just whistle. I'll send the boys over to work and bring a bottle of wine for you and me."

The boys were back with the bags, pans, and cartons from Quynh's car.

"I might take you up on the offer," I said as Zaida gave instructions to her adolescent help about where everything should be put. "And right now I think I can help you best by getting out of your way."

"Bye, sweetie," she said, looking up from the refrigerator. "Can't wait to meet the new guy."

Quynh walked me out, but first we stopped in front of the memorial niche in the entry, at one time a telephone alcove, and placed a ripe plum and a pink rice cake next to the golden Buddha presiding there. She gave me a joss stick to light, lit one herself, and placed them in a brass holder. Again she put her palms together and bowed, this time to the spirit of her deceased sister. We shared a quiet moment, each left to her own thoughts.

At the door, when I said good-bye to her, she hugged me, as she used to.

Feeling a bit nostalgic about the old neighborhood, so full of memories, I made my way up the hill to Mom's house. Just as I was unlocking the front door, my mobile phone buzzed in my pocket. The I.D. screen said Jean-Paul Bernard, the boyfriend, new guy, the fella. I checked my watch as I answered the call; the woman from the university housing office was due to arrive in only a few minutes. I sat down on the front steps to talk with Jean-Paul while I waited for her.

I wanted to invite him to come home with me after the Friday night reception in San Francisco, but felt oddly shy about doing so. I liked him very much, enjoyed being with him enormously. But, so far, we had proceeded into our relationship with caution, first because we were both fairly recently widowed, and second because, as the appointed French consul general to Los Angeles, he served at the will or the whim of his country's current administration and could be recalled to France at any time. My home base was LA, and probably always would be.

Cautious or not, when I opened the phone and heard his voice, I flushed all warm and girly.

"I arrive in San Francisco early tomorrow," he said after the usual *I'm fine–you're fine* was taken care of. "But there are official duties that will occupy me for most of the day. The reception opens at eight so we need to be there by seven-thirty to meet the French museum contingent and check on arrangements. I have commandeered the San Francisco consul's car and driver. What time should I come for you?"

"Don't even try to pick me up," I said. "Evening traffic out of San Francisco is impossible. I'll hop on BART and meet you."

There was a little back and forth, but when I explained how long it would take for him to make the round trip from the City to Berkeley and back again during rush hour, he reluctantly agreed. We decided I would meet him at about 6:45 at the San Francisco consulate on

Kearney Street, near Union Square, giving me time and a place to freshen up before the event.

"Exactly what is the dress code?" I asked. He had only extended the invitation the previous afternoon during a brief conversation that was soon interrupted on his end by a work-related issue.

"Dress code?" he asked.

"Where on the scale between street sweeper and Marie Antoinette should I aim my attire?"

"Ah. I didn't tell you? So sorry. What an idiot I am." I heard papers rustle, then a muttered *merde* before he came back on the line. "The worst, I'm afraid. Black tie. Is that a problem?"

"No," I lied. Who packs formal evening gear to go clear out the family manse? There was enough time, however, for me to come up with something; the Bay Area is hardly a shopper's wasteland.

"*Chérie*," he said before I had found my opening to invite him for the weekend. "How is the house clearing progressing?"

"Slowly," I said. "I didn't realize how much there was to do."

"I have no reason to be back in Los Angeles until Monday morning."

"If that's an offer, I accept," I said. Bless his heart.

"The weekend dress code is what you call grubbies?"

"Yes. And bring something to wear to a backyard Hungry Ghosts celebration Saturday afternoon."

"I am afraid to ask what that is," he said.

"It's an Italian neighbor's version of the Vietnamese version of the end of Hungry Ghosts Month. As I understand it, the gates of the underworld have been open all month and the spirits of our ancestors have been wandering among us. If you've taken care all year to honor your ancestors and they lived good lives and died well, they won't cause mischief to you. But if they've been neglected or they lived or died badly, then they are doomed to wander as lost and hungry spirits. They slip through looking for food and maybe a living person to trade places with. You have to make a special effort to bribe the hungry ghosts so that they go back into the underworld for another year. And that's what we'll do Saturday."

"Ghosts?" he said, sounding bemused.

"You don't believe in ghosts?"

"I believe they reside in the imaginations of the living."

"*C'est ça*," I said, borrowing the expression from him.

"What does one wear to a Hungry Ghosts celebration?"

"Anything comfortable as long as it isn't black. Think backyard barbecue."

He laughed. "*Bon*. I'll bring chocolates."

A Prius pulled up to the curb in front of the house and a woman in her early forties got out. From the looks of her, slacks and a tailored shirt, and her accoutrements, a clipboard and a camera, I assumed she was the staffer from the housing office. She paused on the sidewalk to take a few pictures of the front of the house. I rose and started down the walk to meet her.

"I need to say good-bye," I told Jean-Paul. "I have a visitor."

"*À demain*," he said.

"Until tomorrow."

Chapter 4

IT SEEMED TO ME that the woman from University Housing, Evelynne M. Sanchez according to the card she gave me, had a bit of an attitude, as if she were put upon by the chore of this visit. I did not understand why she would be. It seemed to me, and to the people Mom had spoken with at the housing office, that Mom was doing the university a favor by leasing the house for their use.

The cost of housing in the San Francisco Bay Area is wickedly high, a problem whenever the university wants to recruit talented researchers and faculty. In recognition of that problem, and as a sort of memoriam to Dad who always put up visiting colleagues, the rent Mom was asking covered property taxes, insurance, a reserve account to cover repairs and maintenance, and little else. The bite was far below the going market rate for a house its size in the area. I did not expect Ms Sanchez to bow down in gratitude, but I thought a certain level of professional politesse was called for.

"How much of this furniture will remain?" she asked, running her hand over the surface of a very old table with a marquetry-work top that Dad had found left on a curb by a student who was moving out of an apartment.

"The house will be fully furnished," I said. "But exactly which pieces will be here and which won't I can't say until Monday. A family member is coming to decide on things she might want."

"The pianos?" Ms Sanchez asked.

"Mom is keeping the baby grand, but the upright in the sun porch is staying if you want it."

As she opened kitchen cupboards stocked with crockery and cutlery and pots and pans she said, "You know to expect wear and tear. If any of this—" Ms Sanchez turned over a dinner plate and checked the trade mark on the bottom before putting it back on the shelf. "Things do get broken."

"Mom expects that families will live here," I said, stowing Beto's food containers into the refrigerator. "And that they will make themselves comfortable for the duration of their stay. She isn't leaving anything that is particularly valuable or irreplaceable."

I walked her upstairs and showed her the bedrooms and the bathrooms.

"As far as I know, the house is in good repair," I said as we toured. "Mom put on a new roof late last winter and repainted all the rooms upstairs. The water heater is only a couple of years old and the gravity heater in the basement has always been more than adequate. The house is within the university's Wi-Fi umbrella, so residents will be able to connect online using their Cal accounts."

"Is there a full basement?" she asked.

"No," I said. "The gravity heater is in a big cement-lined hole under the house. There's an access hatch in the dining room."

I saved the master bedroom for last because it was a mess. Mom had left her wardrobe rejects in a heap on the bed for me to bag and deliver to the women's shelter thrift store. Stacks of books on the floor were waiting to be boxed and taken to the library's used book store.

A muslin garment bag hanging on the closet door caught my eye. Mom had debated whether to take the dress inside with her, or to leave it. In the end, she decided that she could no longer bring herself to wear something that plunged in the back. She could also not bring herself to throw that particular dress onto the heap with the others. For decades, the dress had been her favorite to wear out on special evenings. It was a genuine couturier designed and crafted floor-length gown, made originally for some San Francisco society maven; her initials were embroidered into a side seam. Mom bought it at an Opera Guild rummage sale, but even at rummage sale prices it had been a splurge for her.

While Ms Sanchez was looking through the en suite bathroom, I took the dress out of the bag and gave it a careful going-over, thinking that I might have something to wear to Jean-Paul's reception after all.

The dress was as timelessly elegant as I remembered: long sleeves, a ballerina neckline, the lines kept from being severe by an almost daring plunge in back and the graceful way the skirt swirled around the legs. The fabric, a tissue-thin black silk and wool knit, had some benevolent give. Cut on the bias, the dress was narrow through the midriff and then gradually flared; a wonderful dress to dance in. I hadn't asked Jean-Paul if there would be dancing.

The dress did show some signs of age, but who doesn't after forty? The cuff end of the right sleeve was a bit frayed, but I could turn that under with a couple of stitches. If the lighting at the reception was subdued, as it should be at a party, who would notice a couple of tiny moth holes here and there? If the dress fit, and didn't fall apart on me, it would be better than just fine.

"I remember that dress."

I wheeled around, startled. I hadn't heard Ms Sanchez come back into the room. "You do?"

"Your mother wore it to a couple of concerts," she said. "My mom said it came from Paris."

"Originally, I think it did," I said, looking at her more closely; why did she seem so cranky? And who was she to recognize the dress? "Mom bought it at a rummage sale."

With her knuckles on her hips, she challenged me: "You have no idea who I am, do you?"

This was not the first time someone had asked me that particular question. Because I work in television, I meet a lot of people. Frequently those meetings consist of little more than a handshake and a comment about the weather or something just as impersonal and noncommittal. But sometime later they might see me on the living room TV and the nature of that glancing acquaintance changes in their minds. Generally, when I encounter them a second time and nothing familiar registers, I apologize for my memory lapse and ask for help. But because we were in my home town and I had once known a goodly number of its inhabitants, I gave Ms Evelynne M. Sanchez another looking-over before saying anything.

Through the open window, I heard someone shake the back gate hard enough to make Mr. Sato's padlock knock against the wood. The racket jarred me, but it was also a welcome interruption. I folded the black dress over my arm and went to the window to look down into the yard.

"What is it?" Ms Sanchez asked, standing close behind me.

I couldn't see who was out there, but I had my suspicions. Through the open window I called down, "Hello there."

Whoever it was stopped shaking the gate. There was a pause. Then I heard running feet.

"Who is it?" Craning to look over my shoulder, Evelynne M. Sanchez pressed against me. A bit too familiar, I thought. And that's when enlightenment came: Evie Miller. She sat behind me in fifth grade and was on the same swim team in middle school. What I remembered most about her was that she was forever leaning forward in her chair to see what I was doing or to talk to me, demanding attention.

"I don't know, Evie," I said, turning back around and edging away from her. "Maybe just some kids. With luck it's someone who wants to steal zucchini. If it is, I hope they come back."

"So you do remember me." She sounded sarcastic, though she smiled. "Took you a while."

"It's been a long time," I said. "Middle-school graduation, maybe?"

"We doubled to the prom," she said, scolding. "Junior year."

"So we did." Did we? All I could remember about the other couple in the backseat of Kevin's dad's car the night of his prom—I went to a different high school than he and Evie—was a lot of fluffy pink satin, frothy blond hair and the sounds of some serious groping going on back there. Was that Evie and her date? Guess so.

I showed her around the yard and she filled me in on her life so far: married a boy she met in college, had one daughter, now in college like my own. Her husband got caught fooling around with someone else I was supposed to know but could not place, so here she was, single again and on the prowl.

"Know any available guys?" she asked. "I married cute. Now I want rich. You must know plenty of rich guys in Hollywood. Age doesn't matter."

"I'll keep my eyes open," I said as I walked her back through the house.

"You always had the cute boyfriends," she said.

"Only one boyfriend, ever," I said. "Kevin."

"Have you seen Kevin recently?" she asked, snooping, I thought.

"I have," I said because there was no point equivocating about it, not after Karen Loper had made her rounds. The old home town was a tough place to keep secrets.

"You know about him and Lacy."

"We didn't talk about Lacy."

"She's really jealous of you."

"She has no reason to be."

"Oh, Maggie," she scoffed. "Think about it. Even Larry Nordquist had a crush on you."

"Bullshit." And it was. As a kid, I was a scrawny nerd.

"Remember the day you made Larry cry?" she said, grinning. "God, I thought I would plotz when he took off running."

Was she there? I studied her face, trying to picture her among the dozen girls walking to school that day. It took a moment, but I could place her in the film, a profusion of brightly colored ribbons in her curly hair.

"That was a long time ago," I said.

"For you maybe." Looking up at the house, she repeated, "For you."

"Good to see you, Evie."

She stood inside her open car door, chin on fists resting on the car's rooftop.

"Maggie?"

"Yes."

"Our childhood wasn't always like a dance in an opera, was it?"

"No, it wasn't."

"I mean, Beto's mom, bullies—well, Larry—boys who always want-ed…" She looked down the street toward the house where her family had lived. "But we made it, didn't we?"

"So far," I said, repeating one of Mike's expressions. "So far."

Chapter 5

THE REST OF THE AFTERNOON, I sorted and boxed books. By the time the shelves in Dad's study were empty, the sun was low in the sky, my nose itched from dust and my arms ached from lifting and stacking heavy boxes. I left a hefty sampling of books on the shelves for the tenants because it seemed to me that a house isn't furnished unless there are good books. The rest were sorted into three waist-high zones, one each for the public library sale, the University Library Special Collections, and books I wanted to keep.

The day was still warm, and there was an hour or so of daylight left, so I poured myself a glass of wine, piled some of Beto's cold ziti into a bowl, and went out to the backyard to eat in the fresh air. I took a seat at the long plank table under the grape arbor where my family always ate summer meals, and called my mom. I was feeling a bit adrift in the swamp of my childhood and wanted to hear her reassuring voice.

"What progress?" she asked.

"Some." I told her about the visit with Evie Miller Sanchez.

"Should I remember her?" Mom asked.

"The Millers lived two doors down from the Jakobsens."

"Oh, sure. They moved away years ago."

"Anyway, after Susan has chosen what she wants and I've carted off the things I'm taking home, Evie will come back for another look."

"Thank you for taking care of it all, dear; I was having nightmares."

"It's manageable," I said. "The interesting part has been seeing the old crowd again. After college, I'd come home to see you and Dad, but I never made a point of looking up anyone except Beto."

"You never stayed around long enough," she said. "Maybe if you'd gone to high school with the others, you'd be more interested."

"Somehow I doubt it," I said. "Kevin Halloran dropped by."

I heard Mom chuckle. "I knew where this conversation was headed before you called, Margot. I spoke with Gracie just after you left her place. She told me that Beto wants Kevin to look into his mother's murder, and that you have some questions for me about Trinh."

"Trinh?"

"Tina Bartolini," she said. "She anglicized her name. I got used to calling her by her own name when we were working with the refugees."

"Gracie seems to think you were her closest friend, Mom. But I don't remember that."

"I don't know that I was her closest friend, but we did spend quite a lot of time together."

"Working with refugees?"

"That, and before," she said. "Your dad and I met the Bartolinis at church when they first moved in; you kids were just toddlers. Bart told your dad that Trinh felt out of place, very lonely, didn't speak the language. I helped her enroll in English classes at the community college and invited her to bring Beto to the parish playgroup with us. She met the other mothers, Beto met the other kids. We went to Father John's scripture study together."

"I thought Mrs. B was Buddhist."

"Culturally, privately she was," Mom said. "But nominally she was Catholic. For very practical reasons, when Vietnam was under French rule Trinh's grandfather, who was a highly placed bureaucrat, had the family baptized. He sent his daughters to be educated by French nuns just as his grandfather had sent his sons to study with Mandarin scholars. The survivors adapt, don't they?"

"I remember Father John giving a blessing at the Bartolinis' Hungry Ghosts celebration every summer. And I also remember him standing back when the hungry ghosts were offered bribes to stay away."

Mom laughed. "A man has his limits."

"You're missing the hungry ghosts this weekend," I said.

"Probably for the best," she said. "Bart seems to think I've already passed over into the next realm. God only knows what the man might do if I showed up in the flesh. Honey, you'll have to burn offerings on my behalf this time."

"For any ghost in particular?" I asked.

I heard what sounded like a stifled sob and wished I could unsay that careless remark. Of course, I thought, there was someone in particular she wanted remembered: my dad.

"Sorry, Mom. A dumb thing to say."

"No. It wasn't."

She took a deep breath and what she told me next was not at all what I expected.

"Margot, people assume that Trinh became dependent on me because I reached out to her. But the opposite was true. I needed her help more than she ever needed mine."

I never thought about Mom needing help from anyone. She always seemed so competent in everything she undertook. So in charge. Curious, I asked, "What did you need her help with?"

"Where to begin?" She took a moment to decide that before she began to tell me. I leaned back, looked across the yard that had given her and Dad so much happiness, and listened.

"You know, dear, that your father and I were deeply opposed when your brother, Mark, enlisted in the army with the intention of serving in Vietnam." I was very young, but I would never forget the night Mark dropped that bombshell on our peacenik parents. "When Mark was killed over there, I was so angry and so bereft that your father began to worry about my sanity. I was ready to go to Washington to take out that huddle of sanctimonious old bastards who perpetrated the damn war."

"I remember, Mom," I said. "But you worked your way through it, you came back to us."

"Thanks in no small part to Trinh," she said. "My son died in a place I knew nothing about, among strangers. We received a flag-draped coffin with about twenty pounds of scorched flesh and bone sealed in a plastic bag with a new uniform, neatly folded, inside. But most of my boy was still in a jungle, unburied, unidentified. If I could have, I would have gone over there and found him and brought him home.

"Father John took me by the hand and walked me down to Trinh's house. He asked her to describe Mark's resting place for me, to tell me all about the people who were around him. And she did; she was wonderful. She told me about her own family and what the war had done to them. It was helpful, but it wasn't until later, when the war collapsed that I was able to put my grief in perspective and get on with life."

"Why?"

"The floodtide of people who came in," she said. "Do you remember?"

"You brought a family home with you. I remember sharing my clothes."

"Most of the families in the parish took in a refugee family that summer," she said with a laugh. "That was Father John's doing: 'Say three Hail Marys, take in a family and sin no more.'"

"Sounds like Father John," I said.

"Yes. But what Trinh did was far more important," she said. "She took me with her to the refugee camp in the Presidio—a huge tent city. There were so few services, and so many people who came over here with nothing. We were able to help, to really help. It was the best therapy in the world for me. I couldn't do anything for Mark, but I had something to offer people who got snagged in the same fuckup."

"Language, Mom."

She laughed.

I said, "Mr. B told me that some people took out their anger about Vietnam on his wife."

"Some people are idiots," she said. "Even among the refugees Trinh helped there were people who resented her for the comforts of her life, or for who her father was or was not. Some people need enemies."

"Did she have enemies?"

"Trinh? I wouldn't think so. But she may have inherited a few. You know, dear, the sins of the fathers…"

"Ouch," I said.

"Which reminds me." She went through a list of instructions for disposing of Dad's research notes. She finished with a non sequitur: "Did you know that Father John is back in the parish again?"

"I heard."

"He'll probably say a blessing at the Bartolinis' party Saturday. Just to be on the safe side, will you ask him to say a rosary for your brother?"

"Sure." I started to say she could ask him herself. Instead, I asked, "Mom, what happened between you and Father John?"

"The right to choose."

That was explanation enough.

"Gracie said something about your piano."

"Yes." She suddenly sounded enthusiastic. "I want to ship it to Ricardo's studio instead of your house."

"Sure." Ricardo, my former roommate's father-in-law, was a retired high school music teacher. When his son and daughter-in-law, Roger and Kate, built their home in a canyon near my own home, they also built two casitas—little houses—one for Roger's parents and another for his grown children from his first marriage. Out of self-defense, Kate and Roger had added a sound-proofed music studio at the back of their property for Ricardo, whose music indeed made a joyful noise. I asked Mom, "What's up?"

"I told you how much fun I had teaching Ricardo's piano students when he and Linda were out of town."

"You did," I said. "Are you planning to take on students of your own?"

"Just a few, yes," she said. "Ricardo offered me the use of his studio; we'll work out a schedule. But beyond that, dear, Kate and Roger made me an offer that I did not refuse."

"Should I be worried?"

"No, not all. In fact, the opposite," she said. "Margot, Kate and Roger offered me the second casita."

"For piano lessons?"

"No, dear, to live in."

"Good God," I said. "Gracie will think you've been sucked into a cult."

"If I have, it's a lovely one," she said, laughing. "And now, dear, you won't have to worry about me being alone. I know that the reason you have resisted starting your film project about Isabelle's family is that you did not want to leave me alone while you were off shooting in Normandy."

"The reason I haven't started the film is that the network has not approved funding."

"Then call your Uncle Max and have him light a fire under those network people as he always does. And go to Normandy. I know it's what you want to do."

"I'll work on it." If only it were that easy.

When Mom had her mind made up, it was pointless trying to argue with her. The truth was, though my producer had approved the Normandy project, the network goons had not. And maybe would not. Even my Uncle Max, who was both my lawyer and my agent, had not been able to budge them this time. The issue, I was beginning to understand, was not the project, but me.

When we said good-bye, I gathered my dishes and headed back inside, thinking, tomorrow is another day.

I washed my glass and bowl and went upstairs to try on Mom's black dress. It draped, it twirled, it fit quite well; the knit fabric was accommodating. Mom, who is taller than I am, had to wear flats with the dress. With heels, the length would be just fine for me. I had a dress to wear Friday night.

Mom owned a small collection of family jewelry that she left behind for my cousin Susan and me to divide. Other than the ruby earrings that Mom still wore—the matching necklace had gone to someone else a generation earlier—there was nothing of significant monetary value in the lot. Because I had no genetic or legal relationship to Mom or her family, I had qualms about keeping for myself anything that had come from her side of the family, even though Mom had scolded me to get over my reluctance.

From Isabelle, my late bio-mom, I had already inherited some very nice and very old pieces of jewelry that I appreciated for their beauty, but that had no significance to me; I never knew Isabelle. On the other hand, there were several things that I remembered Mom wearing on special occasions, and that made them precious to me. But sweet, warm memories did not change my opinion about rightful ownership.

The best piece rested inside a flat red leather box; a late nineteenth-century brooch shaped like a dragonfly. It was big, nearly three inches from wingtip to wingtip, but it weighed almost nothing. The body and wings were little more than open platinum filigree studded with bright gemstones: garnet, opal, tourmaline, zircon, peridot. I knew it was the signature on the back that made it valuable, and not the

materials it was made from. And for me, all of its value was in its asso-
ciation with Mom. When she wore the rummage-sale black dress, she
wore the brooch pinned high on her shoulder, as if the dragonfly had
just landed there and was about to take off again. To a kid—me—it
was magic.

I decided that the dress and the brooch would have at least one
more outing together. I carried the red leather box and the dress into
my old bedroom thinking that I could easily shop for shoes in Berkeley in the morning.

When I had put the dress away, I returned to Mom's room and
began bagging clothes and boxing books. It only took a short time
before her bed and the floor next to it were clear. Packing is the easy
part; the hard part is shifting the stuff from place to place. Six trips
down the stairs and into the garage later, the clothes and books were
packed into the bed of Mike's pickup truck, ready to be delivered in
the morning.

Tired after a long day, I poured myself another glass of wine and
curled up in one of the big leather chairs in Dad's study—I was keeping the chairs—to watch *Casablanca* for the umpteenth time. Just as
Ilsa was telling Sam to play it for her, "for old times' sake," there was
a great banging on the front door. I set my wine aside and went to the
entry hall to see what the racket was.

Through the glass panels on the front door, under the porch light,
I could see a woman, red in the face, seemingly the worse for drink,
pounding hard enough to rattle the windows. I don't know if she
could see me in the darkened foyer as clearly as I could see her,
but she obviously saw some movement. She screamed, "Maggie, you
bitch! Kevin, come out here!"

That's when I knew who she was.

I pulled out my phone, found Kevin's number, and hit Dial.

When he answered, I said, "Your wife is on my front porch."

"What's she doing?"

"Banging on the door, calling for you. Where are you?"

"On my way over. Sorry."

"Should I open the door?"

"Definitely not." He coughed. "Maggie, do me a favor and go back
inside. Don't watch."

"If you say so." But I was concerned that Lacy might hurt herself, so I slipped into the shadows and watched her from a side window. After a few minutes she wore herself out and slumped down onto the porch with her back against the door, and wept.

Kevin arrived shortly after that in his unmarked police car, argued with her for a moment before he took her by the upper arms, set her on her feet, and marched her down the front steps and strapped her into the front passenger seat of his car. Before he got in on his side, he looked back at the house, searching for something he apparently did not find.

I stood there in the dark, feeling like an intruder into a very private world as the taillights of Kevin's car faded into the night. I now knew who had been in the room with Kevin when I spoke with him on the phone that afternoon.

Chapter 6

OUT OF HABIT, whenever I visited my parents, I slept in my old bedroom, though there was nothing left of me, or of mine, in that room. Long ago, my single bed was replaced by a double, the walls were painted and new curtains were hung. It was only when the lights were out and I lay there in the dark that I felt I was back in a familiar place.

Light from the street, interrupted by the leaves on the trees in the backyard, made the same blue-gray lace on the ceiling, framed by the skewed, angular shadows of the windowpanes, as always. I fell asleep listening to the usual lullaby of night sounds: a neighbor's dog, the occasional car or a back door closing, the creaks and groans of the old house settling, wind through the branches of the sycamore below my open window.

Sometime, deep in the night, I jolted awake, aware that something in the rhythms of the night had been disturbed. I sat up in bed and listened, heard nothing, but got up anyway, feeling uneasy. Ever since my daughter was tiny, I have always slept with the bedroom door ajar so that I can hear the house. I can't sleep otherwise, especially when I am alone. Barefoot, I tiptoed to the door and peered out into the hall. The hall was lit only by street light coming in from the window at the far end, but I could see that no one was there.

Dad, for his own peace of mind, had placed a mirror in the stairwell positioned so that he could see the downstairs hall all the way to the entry and the window in the front door without going down the stairs. I crept along the side of the hall, avoiding the squeakier center, until I could see into the mirror. There was still no sound, but I could see a disturbance in the pattern of shadows coming from the door to Dad's den; someone was in there. When I heard what sounded like a drawer being slowly opened I slipped into the nearest bedroom, my brother Mark's, and dialed 911. In a whisper, I gave the dispatcher my address and told her that someone was inside the house. She told me to stay on the line and to stay upstairs, out of sight. I told her I would stay out of sight, but I needed to hang up so that the intruder wouldn't hear the phone or see brightness from its screen. She was protesting when I turned off the phone and dropped it into my pajama pocket.

I waited to see if I had already alerted the intruder before I went back out into the hall where I could see into the mirror again. Shadows shifted along the floor outside Dad's office as someone moved about inside. Suddenly, a narrow shaft of bright light flew out through the gap between the doorjamb and the door's hinged edge, showing me, roughly, where in the room the burglar was; near the desk.

After a while, the intruder either grew more bold or more desperate to find whatever he was looking for—there was nothing of value to be found, other than some of Dad's books—and made the occasional noise moving things around. Maybe he made enough noise that he didn't hear the police pull up outside.

I called 911 again, filled in the dispatcher who answered, and told her where the intruder was and that the front door was locked. I asked her to tell the officers that I was coming down to open the door for them. She told me to wait, but already the noise from the radios on the shoulders of the two patrolmen who walked up onto the porch had alerted the person in the den. I heard him unlatch and open a window.

I flipped on the stair lights, and holding up my hands so the police looking in through the windows could see they were empty, ran down the stairs and unlocked the door.

"He was in the den," I told the officers, pointing the way. "He may have gone out the window."

There was a sudden cacophony of neighborhood dogs behind our house, the growing ruckus a good hint about the direction the intruder had taken. I was told very firmly to stay put by one officer while the other radioed for backup as he rushed into the den. Lights came on inside. And I stayed put.

Porch lights went on next door at the Lopers', too. I muttered, "Shit," and turned on ours as well, as two more black-and-whites pulled up to the curb, light bars flashing.

Before anyone got around to talking to me, there was a circling chopper overhead, lighting up the neighborhood with its big night-for-day spotlights. After explaining what all the boxes were about, and after agreeing not to touch anything, I was asked to look around the den to see if anything was missing.

Several of Dad's desk drawers had been left hanging open.

"I emptied the desk earlier today," I said. "There was nothing to find except maybe a stray paperclip."

Mystified about what anyone would want in that room, I pointed to the stack of boxed books the university had selected. "Some of those books have value for a few connoisseurs, but they weren't touched. The computer is a good one, but it's a few years old. And it's still here. The TV, ditto. I have no idea what anyone would want in here. Unless it was someone who was just shopping and got interrupted before he could look elsewhere."

"You didn't see anyone?"

I shook my head. "I saw his—or her—shadows, and saw that he had a flashlight, and I heard him. But, no, I didn't come down the stairs and introduce myself."

"Were the doors and windows locked?"

"The doors all were," I said. "I thought all the windows were, but I can't swear to it."

The questioning officer, Bo Peng, just nodded as he looked around.

Right away, I thought of Larry. But Kevin knew already that he had been coming into the yard, so I decided that it was best to answer Officer Peng's questions without volunteering anything, and trust that Kevin would know what to say about Larry.

The search moved outside very quickly, following the intruder's escape route across the backyard and probably over the fence, then, according to the first barking dogs, down the flood control ditch behind our house, headed toward the bottom of the hill. Once the police arrived, it seemed that every dog in the neighborhood had joined the chorus.

Officers searched the entire house and yard, making sure the intruder wasn't there. When they were certain he was gone, and hadn't left a friend behind, Officer Peng checked all the doors and windows again, wished me good night and left.

For the rest of the night, sleep eluded me except for short naps full of bad dreams. I was hyper-aware of every sound, until about five when the neighbors began to stir. Comforted by the gentle racket of garage doors, the paperboy, and the heels of early dog walkers along the sidewalk, I fell into a deep sleep that lasted only until the trash trucks came up the street about two hours later.

First thing that Friday morning, I went for a run to clear my head. The day was still young, but already heat was building in the East Bay, drawing ocean air over San Francisco like a cold, gray shroud. Berkeley, in the north, was clear and it was still cool enough for an uphill sprint. I ran across the bottom of Grizzly Peak and over the few blocks to Indian Rock Park, where Mrs. Bartolini's body was found.

Indian Rock Park is a volcanic outcropping of stark gray granite that juts up out of the middle of a green hillside neighborhood; it is barely one block square. We used to play there as kids. Great for hide-and-seek and climbing, and sometimes just for hanging out. I knew from the Polaroid I found in Dad's desk that Mrs. Bartolini had been dumped near one of the park entrances. At that place, there are a park sign, a bike rack and a drinking fountain. A set of steps hewn into the granite rises from that point to give rock climbers access to the tallest of the volcanic towers. Though Mrs. B lay only a few yards from the street, she had been placed in a sort of bowl formed by large boulders so she would not have been visible to passersby.

During weekends, the park is packed with rock climbers and kids and family picnics. But on a school day, it would have been deserted except for the occasional dog walker, or soul looking for a place for quiet contemplation, or kid ditching school. There are no rest rooms and there are vigilant neighbors close by, so the park is not attractive as a haven for homeless people.

We had continued to play among the rocks after Mrs. Bartolini died, though never alone. I don't remember anyone being afraid as much as titillated when we saw some blood on the dirt where her body had been. There wasn't very much blood and it disappeared soon after, probably washed downhill during the next rainstorm. With great ceremony, we built a small stone cairn as a memorial at the place where the blood had been, and for a while remembered to lay flowers on it. At some point, the cairn was dismantled by some boys playing caveman war, and no one rebuilt it. I won't say that we forgot her, because we didn't. But I think we began to forget to remember her link to the place.

I took a drink from the nearby fountain and walked over to the site, scuffed the dirt with my toe, expecting what? A magic clue? Nothing turned up except some buried cat droppings.

The steps cut in the granite took me up to an overlook. From the top, I could not see the base of the rock where our cairn had been, but I could look down into the yards of several of the houses below. People in those yards, though they could see the taller towers and might have seen people coming and going on the street, would not have been able to see Mrs. Bartolini.

On my way down, I saw a cross chiseled with care and precision in the granite directly above her resting place. Someone had made an effort. Someone remembered.

A fresh breeze came up off the Bay. Chilled, I started for home. When I turned onto the top of our street, I saw Chuck Riley in full security guard uniform with his shoes shined and his service Beretta fastened on his belt, walking down the hill in front of me, going toward his house. Out for a little morning stroll, a visit to a neighbor's house before work, passing out Mary Kay catalogues for his wife, in full regalia? Why not, I thought. Once a cop, always a cop.

A car came down the hill behind me. The driver—I don't know who it was—called out, "Morning, Maggie" as it passed me. Chuck heard, turned, and headed back up the street toward me.

"Out for a run, huh?" he called out. "Nice morning for it."

"Very nice," I said, slowing to a walk. "You on your way to work?"

"Pretty soon." Chuck reached the end of our front walkway before I did and waited for me. "What was all that excitement up here last night?"

"I had a break-in," I said, still breathing hard.

"I'll be damned. They take anything?"

"Other than my peace of mind, no, not that I've found," I said, sopping up my face on my sleeve. "But there isn't much left in the house that's worth taking."

"Did you see who it was?"

"No. Just shadows. I don't know how he got in, but it looks like he went out over the back fence."

"That would take some doing, wouldn't it?" he said, grinning broadly. "Probably some punk kid, out looking for anything he could find. He was probably more scared of you than you were of him."

"Small comfort," I said.

"One way to get your peace of mind back is to install a good floor safe," he said. "I can connect you to a reliable dealer, probably get you a nice discount."

"I'll think about it," I said, but wouldn't. The Rileys, as I remembered them both, always seemed to have something to sell or a discount they could arrange for you.

"I need to get going," he said. "But if you have any more trouble, don't hesitate to give me a call, Maggie. I'm just down the way and I can be here in a hurry. The neighbors have always known they can call on me any time of the day or night if they need a little help." As emphasis, he patted the service revolver on his belt.

"Thanks," I said. "I'll keep that in mind."

"And give that floor safe some serious thought." With a wave, he turned and walked back toward his home.

After a quick shower, I fired up Mike's pickup and started making deliveries, grateful for a reason not to be alone in the house. Books went to the library, clothes to the thrift store. And two big boxes piled high with fresh garden vegetables went to a soup kitchen in the basement of an old church in downtown Oakland.

Juggling the heavy produce boxes, one on each arm, I managed to get down the back stairs and into the large community room without either falling or dropping anything; my arms were sore from lifting and carrying the day before.

As I set the boxes on the first table I came to, I heard a familiar voice call out.

"Hey, McGurk." Father John, once my parents' parish priest,

leaned through the service window from the kitchen. He had a white paper cap on his head and an apron over the jeans and polo shirt he wore that day instead of his usual white cassock, looking fairly convincingly like kitchen help. "How long since your last confession?"

"I don't know, Padre," I said. "What year is this?"

"I thought so." He grinned at me as I rubbed a kink out of my arm. He looked fine, a little pale, thinner, certainly older. I hadn't seen him since my sister's funeral six years earlier. "What'd you bring me?"

"Green beans, zucchini, yellow squash, carrots, potatoes and tomatoes," I said. "Parsley, sage, rosemary and thyme."

"Bring it in, let's have a look."

I carted the boxes into the kitchen and set them down next to the big stainless steel sinks. Looking around the empty kitchen, I asked, "You all alone?"

He glanced heavenward, grinning. "I am never alone, child. But Cook is AWOL this morning, so yes, no one is here except me." He handed me a paper cap like his and an apron to put on. "He's a good cook, when he can find it in his heart to show up. Give me a hand, will you? We feed lunch to two hundred at noon and the soup isn't even started."

"You can't feed that many people all by yourself," I said.

"The church ladies will be here later to set up the service line and do the salad and bread. But they won't have soup to serve unless we get busy."

He unloaded the boxes into the sink and looked at what he had to work with. "I was hoping you'd hidden a couple of fat chickens in here. Getting enough protein into the meal is always a problem. But this is nice, very nice."

There were four giant soup pots on the restaurant-size stove. He poured gallons of chicken broth into the pots and started it simmering while we washed and chopped vegetables and herbs. Everything was dumped into the pots, along with about ten pounds of brown rice and a tub of leftover spaghetti.

"Do you do this every day?" I asked him.

"People eat every day," he said, fitting lids onto the pots. "Hey, McGonagle, I have a good idea. Why don't you do one of your programs about homeless people, break some hearts, loosen some wallets?"

"Already did that one, years ago," I said. "You should work on your skills dividing loaves and fishes instead."

"Every day I ask for God's help with that particular sleight-of-hand," he said with a chuckle. "And today he sent me you."

"If there's a miracle in this story, it's Mr. Sato's green thumb." I untied my apron and hung it back on the hook he had taken it from and gave him my cap.

He asked about Mom and my daughter, Casey, and I filled him in.

"And how are you?" I asked, watching him closely as he decided how to answer. He leaned back against a counter, arms crossed over his chest, looking down.

"Floor needs a good mopping," he said instead of answering the question.

"Kevin Halloran told me you were back in the parish," I said. "I wanted to say hello, so I called the church and asked about your schedule. I was told you'd be here."

He turned his face up to me, grimacing. "What blabbermouth did you talk to?"

"Lorna Priddy," I said. "She told me you're in remission."

"My missing cook calls it recess," he said. "When I was diagnosed, the diocese offered to assign me a rocking chair at the old priests' home to wait until Our Father calls me home."

"I can't imagine you accepting that deal."

"Me either. So I asked if there was a rack available in the rectory at St. Mary's that I could use until the recess bell rings. Cancer be damned, there's still some use in me."

"Your soup's starting to smell good."

He asked me to stay and help serve lunch, but I had too much to do. I did, however, agree to stay and keep him company until the church ladies arrived. There was something fragile about him that had never been there before; I sensed that he very much did not want to be alone, any more than I did.

I knew he wouldn't tell me anything about his relationship with Larry Nordquist if I asked him directly—that penitent–confessor bar. But I thought he might talk to me about the work he and Mrs. Bartolini had done with Vietnamese refugees. It seemed to me that at the end of a failed war there would be people from all sides who, as Mom suggested, still needed enemies, and he might have some ideas about who they were. But I could not bring myself to launch into that topic just then. He seemed so happy, so relaxed that I did not want to upset his peace.

Instead, we talked about nothing and everything as we stirred the soup and argued over seasonings. He was curious about my current film project, a two-hour special scheduled for fall Sweeps Week. He had met the subject of the film, a murdered former congressman, and found him to be sympathetic to issues relating to poverty.

I told him, "I'm calling the film *There Was a Crooked Man.*"

He began to recite the poem, "'There was a crooked man and he walked a crooked mile / He found a crooked sixpence upon a crooked stile…' Was your congressman a crooked man?"

"You'll just have to wait till September when the film airs," I said. "Then you can decide for yourself."

"I liked the man," he said with a little lift to his shoulders. "Maybe I don't want to learn something that might change my opinion of him. I think I'll just read a book the night of the broadcast."

"That's up to you," I said, knowing from experience that there was a lesson in the offing.

"Maggie, I'm not your only old friend who's back in town."

"Oh? Who?"

"Larry Nordquist. Do you remember him?"

"I saw him yesterday," I said, wondering where Father John was headed, but happy that he had brought up the subject.

"Was he okay?" he asked.

I shrugged. "He came and went. Seems he's been hanging around in Mom's backyard."

"Who'd you hear that from?"

"Toshio Sato," I said. "Mr. Sato was with me yesterday when Larry came into the yard."

"Ah." He didn't look happy with that answer.

"Father John, Larry is on parole for murder—"

"Manslaughter," he corrected. "Involuntary manslaughter. He got into a bar brawl and the other guy lost."

"Okay. The thing is, he's out on parole. When the police picked him up last week, it was you who came to fetch him, not his parole officer."

"His parole officer called me because I'm Larry's employer," he said. "Larry is my missing cook."

I chuckled. "I shoulda known."

"I thought maybe you did when you popped in here out of the blue this morning," he said. "Thought maybe you wanted to talk to him."

"You read me like a book, Padre."

"Comes with the job, child," he said.

"And?"

He raised a shoulder, a small self-deprecating gesture. "And yesterday, when I told Larry that you were staying at your folks' place he got very agitated. It was all I could do to get him to finish making the spaghetti before he shot out of here. When he didn't show up today, well, I was a bit concerned that maybe the demons he struggles with got the better of him. Or you did."

"Should I be watching my back?"

"Not on his account," he said. "When he's sober, he's a peaceful man."

"Small comfort," I said. "Father John, someone broke into the house last night."

"You think it was Larry?"

"I didn't see who it was, and I don't think anything was taken," I said. "Why does Larry hang out around at Mom's?"

"Maybe he figured you'd show up sooner or later." He hunkered down to put his eyes on a level with mine. "He's worried about it, but he wants to talk to you, Maggie."

"Whoever came into the house last night was definitely not looking for conversation," I said. "If Larry has something he wants to say to me, he could have said so when he came into the yard."

"One of the things they don't teach 'em in the slam is social graces. He's very resourceful—he's had to be to survive this long. When he's ready to talk to you, he'll figure a way. I can't believe there's any harm in him where you're concerned. Talk to him, child, you might just learn something that would change your opinion of him."

"I knew you were working a lesson into that conversation."

"Occupational hazard."

We heard a clatter of feet and overlapping conversations coming down the stairs: The church ladies had arrived.

"My cue to leave," I said.

"Bye, McGuff." He folded me into an embrace. "See you at Bartolinis' party tomorrow?"

I remembered to ask him to say a rosary for Mark while the hungry ghosts were being consigned back to hell. He promised that he would, but he would do so in the church.

On the drive back to Berkeley, I tried to calculate how many times over the last few days I had been called *honey, dear,* or in Father John's case, *child.* Just two weeks earlier, the senior network producer who was my boss had suggested that it might be time for me to have a little tuck taken under my chin and maybe a little nip in my eyelids. In the TV world where I worked, I was an old lady, over forty. Among my mom's friends I was still a kid. The reality was both and neither, I thought.

There was a good shoe store in Berkeley on Shattuck, catty-corner from Beto's deli. I found a big enough space to park Mike's pickup truck in a public lot off College, suffered through a few comments about the environmental irresponsibility of driving such a big vehicle—people in Berkeley feel quite comfortable about sharing their opinions—and walked over to Shattuck.

I was in luck. The perfect pair of shoes—high-heeled silver sandals—was displayed in the front window of the store. At least, they were perfect until I tried them on. I could hardly walk in them, much less dance. I settled instead for practical, medium-heeled black slingbacks. The dress was long. Who'd see the shoes? Besides, I might actually be able to wear the black shoes again.

The next errand on the list was getting in some basic supplies for house guests: eggs, milk, juice, bread. As I left the shoe store, I noticed that the ragged man—face shrouded by the hood of his stretched-out sweatshirt—who had been curled up on the bench in front of Beto's deli when I arrived was now upright, pacing back and forth.

Since the Summer of Love in the 1960s, Berkeley has been a magnet for street people. Old hippies, hippie wannabes, tokers and tweakers, musicians and purveyors of tie-dye garb and handmade bongs, professional panhandlers and various other folks who have slipped away from the bonds of the nine-to-five world, hang out in the city's parks and set up stalls along the streets. Generally, they are a harmless and colorful element of local daily life; a street festival every day.

The man pacing around Beto's store, however, did not seem harmless to me. He seemed agitated, as if on the verge of something. I dialed Beto's mobile phone to give him a heads-up.

"It's okay, Maggie," Beto said. "Why don't you cross the street and talk to him?"

"Who is he?"

"It's Larry Nordquist. He's been out there since yesterday afternoon. Someone told him you've been coming by, so he's out there waiting for you to show up."

I'd only had a quick glimpse of him the day before, a face peeking around the garden gate. With his head covered, I did not recognize him. I was still staring at the pacer—Larry—when he caught my reflection in the deli window. I took a breath, steeled myself, and began to cross the street. He stopped dead, watched me for a beat or two. And then he took off running.

Beto stood in the open deli door, watching.

"What was that about?" I asked as I walked inside with him.

"Larry is making amends to people he thinks he's harmed," he said, taking his place behind the refrigerated cases. "At any rate, he's trying to."

It was just past eleven o'clock and the store was still fairly quiet, the lull between the breakfast and lunch-time storms.

"Which one of the Twelve Steps is making amends?" I asked.

"I don't know." Beto picked up two plates, piled salad greens on them and topped both with hefty scoops of curried chicken salad. "At least he's working on his problems. When he came in yesterday to make amends with me, he told me he needed to make amends with you, too."

"Guess he changed his mind."

"He said with you it would be harder."

Beto handed the plates across to me. While he gathered forks, napkins and hard rolls, I carried the plates to a table.

"I'm not sure he was sober when I talked to him," he said, taking the seat opposite mine. "I don't know if it was alcohol or something else, but he was on the verge of freaking out the whole time."

"Was he apologizing about that fight when we were kids?"

His mouth was full so he answered by toggling his head back and forth, meaning yes and no. He reached around and pulled two bottles of bubbly water out of a drinks cooler.

"What did he say?"

Beto winced. "It wasn't so much the fight, as the day it went down. Do you remember?"

"Who could forget, Beto?"

"Well apparently that's what's been on Larry's mind. No statute of limitations on guilt, huh?"

"What does he think connects the two?"

"He told me that after the fight he was still plotting what he was going to do to us next when he heard about Mom. He was afraid we'd think he was the one, you know, who did that to her. So he took off for a while."

"I never thought Larry had anything to do with it," I said. "Did you?"

He flushed bright red. "When Dad told me Mom died, I thought I was being punished for fighting. Major bad karma."

"Ah, Beto." I covered his hand with mine.

He patted my hand and smiled gamely. "What? Don't you like your lunch?"

"Almost as special as your pastrami."

He laughed. "Then eat it."

After a few quiet bites, he said, "I got lots of counseling, Maggie. Your mom referred us to a child psychologist who wanted me to reason my way through my feelings. How do you reason your way through something like that? Father John told me that I needed to believe that Mom was happy in heaven, sitting next to God. That just pissed me off, because if she was sitting around anywhere being happy, I thought she should be with me and Dad in our house."

"Perfect kid logic."

"You know who really helped the most?"

"Who?"

"The Buddhist priest Mom got to know in the refugee camp," he said. "He told me that Mom's spirit was really angry because of the way she died. That made total sense to me, because, like I said, I was pretty pissed off, too. Then he told me I could comfort her by making fresh offerings to her every day. He told me she was always close by. That was the answer I liked the best, and that's the one I picked."

"Makes sense," I said. "I asked Father John to say a rosary for my brother, Mark. But this year I think I'll burn some offerings for him, too."

"Cover all the bases, Maggie." He laid his fork across his empty plate and leaned back in his chair, content, smiling. One of his staffers came and took the plates away.

"You know," he said, "Mom started that Hungry Ghosts celebration in our backyard because when the refugees first got here after the war, none of the local Buddhist temples followed the Vietnamese lunar calendar. Think of all those ancestors left behind in Vietnam, all those people who died in the war and never had a proper burial. All those unhappy hungry ghosts who could come through and cause mischief if they weren't taken care of. The problem was, the Gates of Hell open and close a whole month earlier in Vietnam than they do in China and Japan. Way too late to deal with pissed-off ancestors."

"There are Vietnamese temples around now," I said. "But you still have the celebration in your backyard."

"Of course we do. That's where Mom is."

The store was getting busy.

"I'll be sure to say hello to her tomorrow," I said, rising. "Thank you for lunch."

He put his arm through mine and walked me to the door. "Talk to him, Maggie."

"That's up to him."

As I walked back toward the lot where I parked Mike's truck I glanced at a shop window and spotted Larry following me from across the street, staying several yards behind me. It was creepy. He had to know where I was going, so why dog my steps if he wanted to talk to me? I stopped and turned to face him. But he ducked into an open doorway and I wasn't about to chase him down. Instead, I got back into the truck and headed for the closest supermarket for some staples.

No one was behind me when I pulled into Mom's garage and closed the door. I thought immediately about the person who had aggressively pushed on the locked back gate when Evie Sanchez was with me, and then the break-in. Both times, whoever it was had run away. Larry both times? Possibly. Father John said he was resourceful. Stymied by the locked gate and possibly the thorny bougainvillea on the trellis beside it, maybe he had found another entry point. But why? If he, or anyone, wanted to talk to me, he could knock on the front door.

Before going upstairs to make beds for weekend guests, I made a circuit of the downstairs, taking care that every door and window was securely locked. When I left the house to meet Jean-Paul, I double-bolted the front door. Striding to the downtown BART station, my bag of evening clothes slung over my shoulder, I saw no one lurking, but I was still wary. I regretted turning down Jean-Paul's offer to pick me up in a car.

Funny, I thought, during all those years that Isabelle stalked me I remained completely oblivious to her and any peril she might have presented. So why, when no one was there, was I feeling as spooked as I was? It wasn't Larry; I didn't think he intended harm, even if it was he who broke into the house. Maybe it was all the talk about hungry ghosts. Or was it that I had been sleeping in my old bedroom for the last several days knowing that I had yet to pack away the monsters that lived under the bed? In any case, for the weekend, Jean-Paul and I would be using the room across the hall.

When I came around the curve in the street and caught the first glimpse of Beto's driveway, I knew what at least one source of my discomfort was. I had seen that damn picture of Mrs. Bartolini's battered corpse.

On an ordinary Monday morning, in a peaceful neighborhood, a monster had slipped through our veneer of safety and created mayhem. Was he still among us? Had he been inside my house the night before?

Chapter 7

JEAN-PAUL WAS ON THE SIDEWALK in front of the French consulate, watching for me. He came to meet me, smiling his shy, upside-down smile, holding his arms wide for me to walk into. I put my arms around him and offered my face for *les bises*, the kiss on either cheek, plus the third for close friends and lovers that is the standard French greeting.

He was dressed for the evening in a beautifully tailored silk tux, minus the jacket.

"You're gorgeous," I said. And he was.

"I've missed you." He kept his arm around my waist as he led me inside to the guest apartment where I was to change; I clung to him. Looking down into my face he asked, "All is well?"

"All is well. You're here."

While I dressed, he lounged across the guest bed, looking as gracefully elegant as a panther, talking to me as I transformed myself from bedraggled commuter to evening butterfly. Or dragonfly, as it were.

Mom had sewn a piece of felt into the shoulder seam of the black dress as an anchor for the dragonfly brooch so that it wouldn't pull the delicate fabric. Jean-Paul watched me engineer the placement of the brooch, as I had watched Mom do the same.

"Beautiful," he said.

"The brooch?" I said.

"No, *chérie*, the woman who wears it."

I stretched out beside him, curling myself into the contours of his body. "I've missed you."

"I am afraid," he said, kissing the side of my neck, "that if we don't get up from here right now, we will not get up at all. And, sorry to say, we will be greatly missed."

We weren't in a hurry about it, but we did get up, and we left. A driver named Rafael, who doubled as a security guard for the San Francisco consul general, ferried us to the de Young Museum of Fine Arts in Golden Gate Park. At the door we were greeted by the museum people, the staff from the Georges Pompidou Center in Paris that had accompanied several of the Matisse works, and the chocolatier who was underwriting the event as a way to announce the opening of his first American shop, a confectionary in the Ferry Building on the Embarcadero; commerce and culture wed.

Before the invited guests arrived, we were given a brief tour of the reception preparations and the exhibit. The museum's main concourse had been transformed to represent a street in Montparnasse, with faux sidewalk cafés and shops, and a street musician playing an accordion. The terrace at the far end of the concourse, where dinner would be served, had become a Parisian garden bistro, lit by candle light. As we walked through the special exhibits gallery on the lower level, I turned to Jean-Paul and asked, "Where is your San Francisco counterpart?"

"Monsieur le consul general of San Francisco?"

"Oui."

He lifted one shoulder, pretending to be studying a painting. "We did le swap. He is in Los Angeles tonight at the opening of a French film."

"Le swap, huh?" I said, putting my palm against his cheek and turning his face toward me. "When did this come about?"

He made a moue, trying to hide a smile. "It took two days to negotiate with my colleague, but the deal was sealed day before yesterday, just before I called you. I thought an evening out would be a nice break for you. All I had to do was persuade my colleague that he would enjoy spending an evening with some film stars more than he would an evening with Monsieur Matisse."

"Et voilà," I said.

"Yep." He kissed me quickly.

M. Matisse's opening drew an interesting collection of local luminaries, both political and social. I ran into an old friend from my days working at KQED, the PBS outlet in San Francisco. We had a good catch-up conversation while Jean-Paul took care of some official duties. He made a charming short speech in two languages, thanking various dignitaries for their support, and hanging medals around the necks of some of the people responsible for mounting the exhibit in furtherance of Franco-American friendship. Or something.

As he escorted me in to dinner, he put his head close to mine and said, "There is a bit of a stir among the Centre Pompidou staff about your dress."

"What? This old rag?"

"Exactly." There was a mischievous glint in his eyes. "I was asked— accused might be a better word—of having the dress lent to you for the evening out of the couturier's archival collection."

"And you told them?"

"That I know nothing about such things, which is the truth." We found our seats and he held my chair for me. "But, if you don't mind, what is the provenance of *la belle robe?*"

"I found it in Mom's closet yesterday after I spoke with you. I hadn't brought evening attire with me."

"Of course," he said, taking his seat beside me. "She perhaps acquired it at the couturier's shop during a trip abroad?"

"Hardly," I said. I looked over and saw the staffers with their heads together, watching us. I smiled. "She bought it at a rummage sale."

"What is that?"

"Like a *brocante*." A French flea market.

He laughed, his gaze following mine to the little clutch of curious women. "Let's tell them nothing."

Afterward, as we rode together in the backseat of the Town Car, headed across the Bay Bridge toward Berkeley and the work that awaited me there, I felt a bit like Cinderella after the ball. Except that Prince Charming was riding in the coach with me.

Jean-Paul was quiet, looking out his window at the play of lights on the water below us. The Bay Lights installation was still up, twenty-five thousand LED lights illuminating the length and height of the west span of the Bay Bridge. It was dazzling, but I'd had a very bad night before and a very long day, and the car was very plush, so I was struggling to keep from nodding off. When Jean-Paul took a deep breath and cleared his throat, I came to a bit, wondering if perhaps I was about to find out why he had gone to all the trouble to arrange le swap. He broke the silence with a question.

"Has your network come across with funding for your film in Normandy?"

"Not yet," I said. "My producer wants it, but the network hasn't, or won't, approve a budget."

"What is the hold-up?"

"I think it's me," I said, patting the flesh under my chin. "Jean-Paul, I am old for television."

He folded my hand into his. "In Europe, a woman your age would just be coming into her own."

"Maybe," I said, "if her own wasn't a career in front of a camera."

He tipped his head slightly to one side, acknowledging that what I said could be correct. He asked, "Perhaps the issue is the cost of making a film abroad?"

"Not if I can shoot the film I want," I said. "The heart of the project will be conversations with my grandmother at the farm in Normandy during harvest, and then at her Paris home late in the fall. To keep the point of view at an intimate level the only crew I need is a cameraman."

"Guido?" he said.

"Yes. Guido and I can do this one alone, the way we did field reports when we were still covering news stories together. Because we will stay with Grand-mère and we don't need a big crew, the production costs will be minimal. But if we don't get funding soon, we'll miss the harvest this year. Grand-mère is ninety-three. Next year may be too late."

"If the network does not come through, would you go ahead with the film if an alternate source of funding could be found?"

"If I could come up with both funding and a distributor I would certainly give it some serious thought," I said.

"May I make inquiries?"

I tried to read his expression as freeway lights danced across his face. "Why do I think that line is the opening gambit for something?"

He laughed when I defined gambit; though his English seemed flawless, occasionally a word or its use would stump him.

"All right, yes," he said. "I am caught."

"So?"

"I have some contacts," he said. "Perhaps, if you approve, I could make some calls."

"Of course. Thank you." Something was up. I could hear it in his voice. "What am I missing?"

"Maggie, you know I am nothing except a businessman who accepted a political appointment to serve as consul general." When I acknowledged that I did, he said, "On the other hand, the consul general here in San Francisco is a career diplomat. His appointment to San Francisco is a stepping stone for him. But for me? Well, I am an interloper. What do you say, a temp?"

"Yes," I said. "You've told me."

"If I were at all political, and I am not, I would have been recalled a long time ago so that a true diplomat could take over. But, the new administration has been kept very busy, crisis after crisis. As there has been no emergency to handle in my assigned region, and I have managed not to disgrace my country and have actually been of some small service, I have been left in place." He turned and gave me a pointed look. "I have been here far longer than I expected to be."

"Have you been recalled to France, Jean-Paul?" I asked, dreading the answer.

"Not yet," he said. "But I understand that it will happen."

"When?"

He wrapped an arm around me and pulled me close. "After the summer holidays, perhaps. When the government goes back to work."

"How do you feel about that?"

He raised his shoulders, frowned. "My son received his exam results."

"Yes?"

"Dom qualified to enter the preparation course for admission to the *grandes écoles*," he said.

"Congratulations," I said. This was big news, indeed. Very few

French students pass the *baccalauréat* exams at the level necessary to qualify for the nation's premier public universities. The bombshell here was that, having qualified to prepare for the *grandes écoles*, seventeen-year-old Dominic would not be finishing high school in Los Angeles. And I doubted his father was ready to send him back to France, alone. "When do his classes begin?"

"In September."

"Ma'am?" The driver, Rafael, interrupted the dark pall that settled over the car after Jean-Paul's announcement. "Were you expecting someone?"

I looked up as we slowly came to a stop at the curb in front of Mom's house. A man sat on the top step, holding a baseball bat across his knees.

"It's the next-door neighbor," I said. "Something must have happened."

Rafael opened Jean-Paul's door first, and then stood close beside me after he handed me out of the car and walked me up to Jean-Paul.

"Mr. Loper?" I called, staying near the car as George Loper rose and started down the steps toward us. "Is there a problem?"

"That damn hoodlum." He smacked the side of his leg with his bat. "I told him that if I saw him hanging around here anymore, I wasn't going to call the cops again. Next time I'll take care of him myself."

"Are you talking about Larry Nordquist?" I asked.

"Damn right," he said.

I saw some movement behind the big hydrangea next to the front porch. So did Rafael. Before he could move or say anything, I gripped his elbow. When he looked down at me I mouthed, *No.* He got the message and he stayed where he was.

Loper, sounding like the patronizing jerk I remembered him to be, said, "I don't want the guy skulking around, not with you alone in the house."

"I'm not alone now," I said. I introduced Jean-Paul to him.

"Well, well." Finally, Loper smiled as he offered his free hand—the one without the bat—to Jean-Paul. "The boyfriend we've heard so much about. My wife would love to meet you, Mr. Bernard. She's a regular Francophile. Can I offer you a drink? A little nightcap?"

"Thank you," Jean-Paul said. "Perhaps another time. I'm afraid that it is quite late."

"Rain check, then," Loper said, releasing Jean-Paul's hand.

I wished him good night and thanked him for his concern. As he turned to leave, he winked at Jean-Paul while aiming a finger at me.

"Take good care of our girl, now," he said. "Trouble seems to follow her around."

Jean-Paul said, "Good night." He sounded genteel; he meant *Go away*.

We watched Loper until he reached his own front walk.

Rafael asked, "What do you want done?"

I knew he was referring to the person hunkered behind the hydrangea. I said, "Would you please help us with the things in the trunk?"

The three of us huddled over the open trunk. I explained to them who Larry was and that I wanted to speak with him. "Please don't let him get away. He'll probably try to run."

Rafael laid out a strategy. Jean-Paul gathered our bags and Rafael collected the two towers of green silk-covered candy boxes that the chocolatier had given Jean-Paul to hand out as promotional gifts. With Jean-Paul on the porch beside me and Rafael waiting at the bottom of the steps, I unlocked the front door.

As soon as I opened the door, the two men sprang into action. Jean-Paul dropped the bags and dove right, toward the hydrangea, flushing out Larry. Larry, rising from a crouch, was off balance, easy pickings for Rafael, who grabbed the smaller man, pinned his arms behind him and marched him into the house.

"Hello, Larry," I said, as he was quick-walked across the threshold past me.

"Yo, Maggie," he said, giving up his resistance to Rafael. "Long time no see."

"Do come in."

Rafael sat him down in a chair in the living room as Jean-Paul moved into position blocking the most obvious escape route, with Rafael standing as backup near the locked front door. Larry seemed agitated, sweating profusely, as he noted where Jean-Paul was. I wondered, as Beto had, if he was on something.

I said, "Can I offer you a cup of tea, a glass of juice?"

"I could use a shot of something a hell of a lot stronger than tea." Larry pushed off his hood and shook out his ponytail.

"Sorry," I said. "That's all I can offer."

"Yeah." He settled into his seat and looked around the room. "It's nice here. Really nice. Comfortable, you know. Not all formal like I expected. Some places, jeez, they're so done up you're afraid to touch anything. Know what I mean?"

"You've never been inside the house before?" I asked, thinking about the person in the house the night before who moved about as quietly as a shadow, as if he were familiar with the layout.

"Oh, yeah, sure," he said, his tone bitter, defensive. He picked up a coaster from the table beside him, glanced at it and tossed it back down. "Like maybe you invited me to your birthday parties with all your prissy little friends? That never happened."

I heard self-pity in his tone and found it worrisome. I said, "I heard you wanted to talk to me."

"Yeah, well." He flicked his chin toward Jean-Paul, a question in the gesture. "It's kind of personal."

"Larry, this is my friend Jean-Paul Bernard. Jean-Paul, meet Larry Nordquist." They exchanged perfunctory nods. "Larry, Jean-Paul is staying, and so is Rafael."

He swiveled in his seat to find out where Rafael was.

"Why don't we just get it over with?" I sat on the sofa, facing him across the coffee table. "Before someone like Mr. Sato or Mr. Loper knocks your block off for sneaking around."

He dropped his head, chagrined. But he remained quiet.

"Sir," Jean-Paul said. When Larry looked up, he said, "It is quite late. Miss MacGowen has had a very long day. If you have something to say..."

Larry nodded, but seemed unable to begin. I tried to nudge him along.

"Beto told me you want to make amends to people you feel you have harmed," I said. "You and I had a couple of run-ins when we were kids, but I don't feel you harmed me."

Again he glanced at Jean-Paul. "Did she ever tell you she beat the crap out of me?"

"I never laid a hand on you," I said.

"But you still won, didn't you?"

"I'm sorry I hurt your feelings that day," I said. "Is that what you want to talk about? That fight? What you said that day?"

"No." He swiped the arm of his sweatshirt across his glistening face, took a deep breath, and squared his shoulders.

"Maggie," he said. "I did wrong you. And I'm sorry if what I did hurt you or put you in danger."

"If it's not the fight, then what are you talking about?"

"I saw you on TV," he said. "When that woman died."

"You mean Isabelle Martin?"

"Freaked me out," he said, nodding. "I mean, I knew her. When I saw her picture on TV and they said she was your mother I about lost it, you know? Because I knew her."

"What do you mean, you knew her?"

"It's kind of hard to explain." He scratched his neck, looked behind him, hoping maybe for some help to appear.

"Do your best."

"The woman who died? Miss Martin?" he said. "Way back then, she got me to report about what you were doing all the time. She gave me stamps and paper, and I wrote stuff to her. Sometimes she called me on the phone and asked about you."

"You spied on me for her?"

"She paid me." He shrugged, a sheepish grin on his face. "I didn't look in your windows, or anything. I just told her about school, like the time you played some kind of bird in the school play."

"I was an owl," I said. "Fourth grade."

I glanced up and caught Jean-Paul smiling. Rafael must have thought that the situation was under control. Quietly, he slipped outside to collect the bags and chocolates we had left behind. But when he came back, I heard the snick of both deadbolts shooting home. So did Larry: He watched Rafael the way that prisoners watch their keepers, always knowing where they are, always wary, afraid that they'll be called out.

"What you did was—" I searched for the right word.

"Bizarre," Jean-Paul supplied.

"Definitely, bizarre," I said. "But I never knew about it. And nothing happened to me because of what you did."

"Doesn't matter," he said. "I still needed to tell you."

"Thank you for your honesty, Larry," I said. "I'm sure it was difficult for you to come forward."

"*Pffh.*" Uttered with an eye roll as if coming clean were no big deal.

I said, "A couple of people think you might have been sleeping in the backyard here."

"That's bullshit," he said with a smirk. "Why would I do that? You think I'm homeless?"

"I don't know what to think," I said.

"The thing is, I come by now and then to water the garden," he said. "That old Jap gardener only shows up maybe once a week. If it was left to him, the whole yard woulda dried up and died a long time ago."

"How in the world did that come about?"

He pointed at his chest. "You mean, me watering the place?"

"Yes."

"Oh, yeah, well, see." His face colored. "I was always curious, you know? I mean about what it was like back there. I used to hear your family out in the yard all the time, and I always wondered what it was like on your side of the fence. So when I heard no one was home here, I just came in to take a peek."

"You could hear us?" I asked. "I don't remember that we were especially noisy. Where were you that you could hear us?"

"That's the thing of it," he said. "I kind of made myself comfortable in the bushes where I was tonight and sort of listened."

"To my family?" Creepy, I thought. But he didn't seem to think it was especially strange. "Because Isabelle Martin paid you to?"

"Not exactly," he said. "But that's how it got started. One day, you guys were eating dinner outside, the way you did. I was just hanging out in the bushes, minding my own business, when she showed up. Scared the shit out of her when she stepped on me."

Feeling absolutely nonplussed, I looked over at Jean-Paul. He seemed thoroughly puzzled, but fascinated as well.

"Why?" I asked Larry.

"You all seemed so normal," he said. "I only wanted to know what that was like. You know, being normal."

"And Isabelle gave you an excuse to keep spying on us," I said.

"Not an excuse, exactly," he said. "When she caught me, she promised that she would tell on me unless I wrote to her about you. She scared the shit out of me, too."

"Dear God."

"Yeah. But what I told you already, that's only part of it." He looked around, his glance shifting from Rafael to Jean-Paul. "I know you, Maggie. Or I used to. We could talk about it, you and me. But I don't know these guys."

"They're my friends."

"I don't give a flying fuck who they are; I don't know them." He brushed his hand across his balding pate where he once had a pompadour and finally I recognized the old Larry. The punk. The lost boy. The bully. He checked again on Rafael and began to rise from his chair. "If you want to hear what I have to tell you, lose the friends."

Mr. Sato was right, I am nosy as hell. I wanted to know the rest of what he had to say, but I didn't want to be alone with him, not when he was so agitated. Clearly, Larry wanted to be the one calling the shots. There was a chance, I thought, that if I could keep him talking he would change his mind and open up.

I asked, "How long did you spy on me?"

"Couple o' years." He stayed on the edge of his seat, poised to go. "Until that day—"

"Until the fight?"

"That day, anyway."

"Beto's mom died that day," I said, watching his face. When he nodded, I asked, "Is that what you want to talk about?"

"Something like that." He stood abruptly. "When you're free to talk—just you—let me know."

"You know where to find me," I said.

"Yeah." He pulled the hood of his sweatshirt back up over his head and started toward the door. Rafael stepped aside; the man was not a prisoner.

"Do you need a ride anywhere?" I asked, hoping to find out where he was staying at least; Father John did not know.

"Who, me?" He had a sardonic grin. "You offering me a ride in that hearse you drove up in?"

That wasn't my offer to make. I turned to Jean-Paul.

"Certainly," Jean-Paul told him. "Just tell Rafael where you wish to go."

"S'okay," Larry said. "I have wheels."

We followed him to the door.

"Larry," I said as I threw the bolts. "Next time you see me, don't rabbit."

"Yeah, sorry about that." He paused in the open door to zip up his sweatshirt. "The thing is, I've caught you on TV a couple times, but I haven't seen you in person since way back. So the other day when I saw you in the yard, you know without all that TV makeup crap on, saw just *you*, I freaked. I mean, I really lost it."

"Why?"

"Because you look so damn much like that Miss Martin. And I know she's dead."

He stepped outside. With his head hunched low, he checked for enemies, and quickly walked away into the night.

Chapter 8

"Looks to me like a string of substance abuse–related offenses." Sergeant Richard Longshore, an old friend who works in the Homicide Bureau of the L.A. County Sheriffs, read to me from Larry Nordquist's rap sheet. I called him first thing Saturday morning, while Jean-Paul was in the shower, and asked him to find out who I was dealing with before I tried to shake the rest of the story out of Larry.

"Petty theft, shoplifting from a liquor store, public nuisance—urinating. He did some weekends in custody for drunk-and-disorderly; looks like he's a scrapper when he has a bag on. There are some possession and possession-for-sale charges that got him county jail time, but he always bounced out early because of overcrowding. We have DUI, DUI, DUI, driving on a suspended license while under the influence. Solicitation, public intoxication."

"Solicitation?" I said.

"Earned a buck or two on his knees to buy drugs," Rich said. "He's a problem child, Maggie, but it was all petty crap until he went down for aggravated burglary. Because he took a firearm to that party he drew three years at Soledad and his first strike. The firearm enhancement put him in the bigs, so when he was charged with manslaughter—couple of drunks got into a fight and one died—he drew a full five years as guest of the state, and strike two."

"Maybe going away for a while was good for him," I said. "Gave him a chance to dry out, got him into a twelve-step program."

"Don't hold your breath," he said. "And take care. If he draws one more strike, he goes down for a long, long time. Guys in his position can get pretty desperate if they have something they need to cover up. And it sounds like maybe your boy does."

"Did you find anything about Ennis Jones, the man who was once accused of the Bartolini murder?"

"Pretty much what you thought I would," he said. "He pulled fifteen-to-life on two counts of rape, one of lying-in-wait. Served five before he was sent to a sex aversion program at Atascadero. Died six months later in an altercation with another prisoner, also a convicted sex offender. End of his story."

Jean-Paul came out of the bathroom with a towel around his waist and began dressing in work clothes: old jeans and a T-shirt.

"Thanks, Rich," I said.

"Maggie?" Rich said. "Don't try talking to the Nordquist guy alone, all right?"

"He said that what he has to say is for my ears only."

"Too damn bad," Rich said. "Unless you want your family to be doing some sad singing and slow walking, you don't go in with the guy alone. Got it?"

"Yessir," I said, laughing. "Thank you. You've been a big help."

He offered his usual sign-off, "Watch six," meaning I should guard my rear.

"What did Rich have to say?" Jean-Paul asked as he tied his sneakers.

"Essentially what you said."

"Smart man, our Sergeant Longshore." He rose to his feet. "So, what is the plan of attack?"

"Le garage," I said. "And a trip to the dump."

His eyes lit up. "In the pickup?"

I handed him the keys, which he pocketed. He loved Mike's big truck and was happy for any opportunity to drive it. For all of his polish, he was still just a boy drawn to planes, trains and automobiles, the bigger the better.

Opening the garage door was like putting out an OPEN HOUSE sign in the front yard. As Jean-Paul and I tackled fifty years' worth of accumulated stuff packed into, onto, and around every shelf, cupboard and workbench, the lookie-loos, the curious, and the concerned from one end of the street to the other felt free to drop by to offer advice and comments, or just to chat. My mother would have served coffee.

There were a couple of invited helpers added to the mix. My former San Francisco housemate, Lyle, and his husband, Roy, arrived carrying a giant box of recyclable trash bags. Lyle, who had always been our resident handyman, started on Dad's workbench, culling useless and duplicate tools to make one good set. We were leaving those tools that the tenants might need, from wrenches to plungers. The rest were up for grabs.

My parents were products of the Great Depression. They were loath to throw away anything that might conceivably have some use left in it, especially if it was connected to an electrical cord or an on/off switch. There was, for example, a drawer full of dead batteries that someone, caught up in magical thinking, must have thought could be brought back to life somehow. The batteries were just part of a vast, sometimes oozing, collection of electronic junk. All of it was put into bags and deposited into the bed of the pickup for delivery to a toxic and electronic-waste station.

Roy, an information technology specialist, went to work on anything computer-related. He removed the hard drives from the dead and outdated computers stacked in a back corner, and consigned the carcasses to the truck. When his corner was cleared, Roy went inside to back up and then wipe Dad's files from the computer in the den. Roy had built the system shortly before Dad died and thought very highly of its capabilities. We decided that it would stay in the house because visiting faculty might find it useful, if for no other reason than that it was connected to a very good laser printer; visiting faculty might not travel with printers.

Jean-Paul went into the cupboards and began pulling down boxes of Christmas ornaments, camping and sports gear, and various semi-rejects that someone thought were too precious to toss but not precious enough to store inside the house. He received lots of opinions from the peanut gallery on the driveway: you could sell that on eBay, you should have a garage sale, the high school might want the well-used and thoroughly outdated sports equipment, and the library would love twenty years' worth of *National Geographics*. Who wouldn't?

When a Dumpster arrived—a refuse box in Bay Area–speak—for nontoxic discards, the deliverymen received a great deal of advice about placement on the driveway: Leave room for the pickup to come and go, don't block the garage door, stay out of the flower borders. Like the rest of the actual working crew, the deliverymen paid scant attention to the kibbitzers and placed the Dumpster where it would be convenient for them to pick up again.

The noise of the Dumpster delivery attracted Mr. and Mrs. Loper from next door.

"How long will that thing be there?" George wanted to know. From his tone and expression it was clear that he did not think the big, ugly metal trash box enhanced his neighborhood.

"They'll pick it up Monday," I said, tossing in a pair of very dusty old sleeping bags. "And replace it with an empty. I hope to be finished with all of this by the middle of next week."

George followed me into the garage, talking to my back as we walked. "I've been keeping my eye out for Nordquist this A.M. He always seems to pop up first thing in the morning, so I began to think he might be sleeping in your backyard. Last night I was out there when you drove up, hoping to catch him before he tucked himself in for the night."

"What were you planning to do with the baseball bat?" I asked.

"Just a little inducement to stay away, if you know what I mean," he said. "A twelve-bore would put a stop to him."

"You don't own a twelve-bore," his wife, Karen, admonished; she had followed us in. "Or any other firearm, for that matter. I won't allow those things in my house." She winked at me as she tipped her head toward her husband. "Who knows what a hothead might do if there were a lethal weapon handy at the wrong moment?"

George paid no attention to her. He went over to "help" Lyle with Dad's tools.

"So good to see you, Maggie," Karen Loper said. She had aged a great deal since I saw her last. Living with George Loper would age anyone in a hurry, but it wasn't only wrinkles and gray hair that had changed her. She held her left hand protectively and her left foot lagged a bit when she walked; a stroke?

"Sorry I haven't dropped by sooner to say hello," she said, standing to the side while I unloaded the family's collection of outdated

textbooks from shelves. Boxes and dusty boxes of them. "But you've
had so much to do and I didn't want to get in your way. I was talking
to Sunny last night—"

"And how is Sunny?" I asked. Her daughter had once been one of
my best friends.

"Oh, she's fine. I worried when her youngest went off to college
last fall. That empty nest nearly killed me, you know. But not Sunny.
Since she made partner at the law firm she's been too busy to notice
how empty her house is."

"Good for her," I said. "Say hello for me."

"I shall," she said. "Was that Evie Miller I saw over here the other
day?"

"It was. She's working with University Housing."

"Too bad about her and Tom."

"Maggie?" Jean-Paul stood in front of one of the floor-to-ceiling
cupboards that lined the back wall and clearly wanted some guid-
ance about what to do with its contents. I was happy he interrupted
before Karen got further into her tale of someone else's woe. While
Gracie Nussbaum passed along information, Karen was a notorious
and sometimes malicious gossip. I very much did not want to hear
about Evie and Tom, whoever he was.

"Excuse me," I said to her.

"Of course." She patted my shoulder. "I'll get out of your way."

She wandered out to talk to another neighbor on the driveway, and
I went to see what Jean-Paul had found.

Inside the cupboard, among other things, there were two large plastic laundry baskets filled with little developer's boxes full of old family
slides and movies. I groaned.

"I will leave them to you," Jean-Paul said, smiling as he moved on
to old paint cans, paintbrushes, and household chemicals that needed to go to the toxic waste dump.

I pulled the laundry baskets down, knelt on the floor beside them
and started looking at the notations on the film boxes. There were
photos and movies of family trips and school plays, Christmas pag-
eants and birthdays, and roses—many roses—and they needed to be
at least looked through. But later. The baskets would have to come
home with me to be sorted on some lonely rainy night.

As I shifted the baskets to the corner of the garage designated for things I was keeping, I noticed a handwritten notation on the end of a slide box: GARDEN–CHRYSLERS, and a date. Dad was proud of his Chrysler Imperial roses, to be sure, but what interested me was the film developer's date stamp. I began pawing through the basket, looking for more boxes dated around the time that Mrs. Bartolini died.

"What the hell is wrong with you people?" George Loper shouted, waving what looked like a small jeweler's box perilously close to Lyle's face. Lyle stood looking back at him in stunned silence.

I jumped to my feet and saw that Jean-Paul was already rushing toward the tool bench where George was fulminating at poor Lyle.

"Dammit," George spat. "A young man gives his life in service to his country, and this is how you people honor him?"

"George!" Karen snapped, coming back into the garage. As she tried to make haste to intercept her husband, her limp became more pronounced.

I put myself between George and Lyle, who stood mute, ashen. "What's the problem here?"

"This." He opened the little box and pushed it close to my face. I took it from him so I could see what had upset him so.

My brother Mark's Purple Heart. It was given to my parents, along with some other medals and a tightly folded flag, during Mark's funeral.

"Where did you find this?" I asked George.

"In a drawer with a bunch of—" He sputtered, trying to get the next word out. "Crap."

"I can't imagine why you were going through my father's drawers," I said quietly, closing the box. "Or why you are so concerned about what he kept in them."

He had more to say, but I didn't want to hear it. Looking into his eyes, watching his red and angry face, wondering if he would explode like a character in a cartoon, I said, "We can manage from here, Mr. Loper. Thanks for dropping by."

Karen was at his elbow. "Honestly, George."

He spun on his heel and stormed out.

"He's a veteran," Karen said, attempting to apologize for him, or to explain something about him, but gave it up with a shake of her head and walked out behind him. The other neighbors in the drive, perhaps sharing chagrin for being snoopy, drifted away.

"Sorry, Lyle," I said. I heard my voice break. I knew he was upset, even though he said he wasn't. But he went inside to check on Roy's progress just the same. Jean-Paul took me in his arms and I buried my face against his shoulder, taking a minute to catch my breath. Like my mom, I wear grief for my big brother close to the surface, and George had no business scratching at it.

"Some work crew." I knew the voice; my Uncle Max had arrived. "Everyone standing around snogging when there's work to be done."

I looked up over Jean-Paul's shoulder. Uncle Max stood there with his arms akimbo and a grin on his face, a welcome sight. I asked, "Where did you come from?"

"I'm told I was born in Duluth," he said, ever the smart-ass. "But I was too young to remember. So, what was all that fuss and feathers I walked in on?"

"Snoopy neighbor. Not to worry."

"Says you." He tapped Jean-Paul's shoulder as if he were cutting in on a dance floor. "You have a monopoly on the lady's hugs now, Bernard?"

"A lovely thought," Jean-Paul said, releasing me.

Uncle Max enveloped me in a bear hug and smooched my cheek. Holding me at arm's length, he said, "I got an interesting call early this morning. Very, very early."

"Did you?" I said, pulling free.

"From Paris. Canal Plus wanted to talk deal. Something about backing your Normandy film project." He gave Jean-Paul a pointed glance. "Anyone here know anything about that?"

I turned to Jean-Paul. "Does anyone?"

He responded with a shrug and a moue with a guilty grin behind it. "Perhaps someone spoke with an acquaintance."

"I thought so," Max said, mimicking Jean-Paul's shrug. "They made a decent offer. Problem is, there's this network that thinks the project is already theirs."

"But?" I said and waited.

"But the network needs to shit or get off the pot," Max said. "There are two sides to the contract, you and them, and you both have performance obligations. You have done your part. Now it's their turn. If the guys with the checkbook don't come across with funding by early next week, they are in breach and you are free to take the project elsewhere."

"That is good, yes?" Jean-Paul said.

"Maybe good for you, Kemosabe," Max said, pointedly. "But, Maggie, only you can decide what's best for you. I promise that if you walk away with this project, no matter how badly the network is behaving, they will sever your relationship. Permanently. Are you ready for that?"

"I need to talk with Guido before I do anything," I said. Guido Patrini had been my film production partner for a long time. The decision absolutely was not mine alone to make.

"Guido told me he can get himself up here tomorrow," Max said. "You two can talk it over."

That bit of news didn't quite please Jean-Paul. I suspected he was hoping that we would have more time alone together, to talk. I took his hand and gave it a squeeze.

Max looked around at the apparent chaos we had made of the garage, stuff piled out of cupboards and in the process of being separated into various zones by category: keep, donate, dump. It looked more chaotic than it was; I could actually see the end.

"Max," I said. "There's work to do. Go up and change your clothes. Jean-Paul and I are in your room. We'll put Guido in my room and Susan in Mom's room. So why don't you take Mark's room?"

"Where do you want me to begin?" he asked.

"Legal and financial records," I said. "There's a stack of labeled boxes in Dad's den. I was going to take them home to go through, but you can save me the portage."

"Where's the shredder?" he asked.

"In the den, next to the records."

Jean-Paul and I worked alone together in the garage for the next couple of hours, sorting, dumping. And talking. It was a dusty chore, but there was something oddly romantic about doing it together. I appreciated that he stuck with me without ever grumbling or suggesting a break, kept a sense of humor about it all. By the time we had emptied the cupboards along the back wall and dispatched their contents, this is what I knew: The two of us also had some very serious decisions to make, together.

Lyle came out of the house carrying a big box filled with house-hold chemicals. As he deposited the box in the truck, he announced, "Lunch is ready."

"I wondered what you were up to," I said. I closed the garage door and we followed him inside.

"You can thank Roy." Looking over his shoulder at us, Lyle said, "Wash those hands."

"Bossy as ever," I said, laughing.

Years ago, when I was a fledgling divorcée and Casey was in elementary school, we lived in a wonderful old house in the Pacific Heights neighborhood of San Francisco; I was still working for PBS. Lyle was our across-the-alley neighbor, someone we waved to when we took out the trash or backed out the car, or ran into each other in the market. When an earthquake reduced his house to rubble and left ours habitable, though damaged, we took him in. For a month, we thought. But contractors and repairmen were hard to come by for a long time after the quake, so he just continued on with us, one month after another, until there was no pretense any longer that one day he would go home, even when the quake repairs were long finished. The three of us lived together like a family until he met Roy and I met Mike, and Casey and I moved down to LA. We still considered Lyle to be family.

"What's for eats?" I asked when, freshly scrubbed, Jean-Paul and I joined the others in the kitchen.

"Homegrown tomato–basil bisque and grilled cheese sandwiches," Roy said proudly. "First thing, before I got to work on anything else, I went right out and picked the Romas from the garden to get them stewing. There are so many tomatoes out there that we could open a stand out front."

"Or you could pick them all and take them home so Lyle can make his famous marinara sauce," I said. "There should be enough to last you all winter."

Lyle's face collapsed. I thought he was going to cry.

"Now what?" I said, spoon poised above my bowl.

"You're leaving me again, aren't you?"

"Where'd you get that idea?"

"The dopey look on your face."

"For heaven's sake." I reached around for a box of tissues and handed it to him. "Get a grip."

"Lyle," Jean-Paul said, catching his eye. "Have you ever visited France? You will love it."

I thought it was time to shift to a new topic. I turned to Uncle Max and asked, "Why would Dad keep Mark's Purple Heart in his workbench?"

Max considered the question for a moment before he offered, "He loved to putter in the garage and your mom never went out there. Maybe he wanted to put it somewhere Betsy wouldn't happen upon it and get upset. Or, maybe he wanted to keep it where he could take it out and look at it from time to time privately. You know, keep it close."

"'Al's out in the garage making sawdust,' Betsy always said." Lyle was smiling again.

"So she did." I ate my soup, thinking about Mom moving into the noisy, happy sphere of the Tejeda family. A good move, I thought as I returned Lyle's smile. A very good move.

Jean-Paul cleared his throat. I looked over at him, expecting him to say something, but after glancing from me to Max, he didn't.

"Yes?" I said.

He considered for a moment before he retrieved the medal box from the counter where he set it when we came inside for lunch.

"I was curious," he said, unpinning the medal from the velvet lining it was attached to. "I had never seen a Purple Heart before."

He laid the medal on my palm, and holding my hand in his, he turned the medal over and showed me the back. Below FOR NATIONAL MERIT the recipient's name was engraved.

"Max," I said, handing it to him. "This isn't Mark's Purple Heart. It's Dad's."

"I'll be damned," he said, running a finger over the letters. "I forgot he earned one."

"Korea," I explained to the others. "Dad took shrapnel in his shoulder, his leg and his butt."

"Because of Korea, my brother Al didn't want Mark to go to Vietnam," Max said. "He thought he had gone to war so that his son wouldn't have to."

Max pinned the medal back into its box. He took a last look before he closed the lid. Holding the box against his chest, he appealed to me: "May I?"

"Of course," I said. He slipped the medal into his shirt pocket and finished his soup.

After lunch, Jean-Paul and I left the others bent to their tasks and drove off with the load for the waste station—the toxic dump—in Martinez. I brought along the three boxes of slides I had found that Dad shot around the time that Mrs. B died. As Jean-Paul drove, I took them out one at a time and held them up to the light through the windshield.

"What are you looking for?" he asked.

"Whatever I can find." I dropped yet another picture of a perfect rose back into its box and took out another. Roses, roses, me, Mom, me again, me holding a rose. I was nearly to the end of the last box, dated the month after Mrs. Bartolini was murdered, thinking that there was nothing to see. At least, nothing useful. I pulled out the last two frames and held them up side by side.

"What did you say?" Jean-Paul asked.

"Did I say something?" I shrugged: had I? "Eureka, maybe?"

"No. I think it was, 'When is a rose not a rose?'"

"The answer is, When it's a man." I handed him the last slide from the box. The previous frame showed Mr. Sato holding a deep red Chrysler rose by the stem in one hand and the neck of a beer bottle in the other. There was a man standing beside him, but Dad, interested in the rose, had cut him off so that all I could see was a hand with short, brown, calloused fingers wrapped around a beer bottle. The next frame, the last frame, was a risk shot taken after the thirty-sixth picture on a thirty-six-picture roll. There was only half a frame of film left before the beginning of the black trailer that wound the film on the spool. But that half frame was enough. Dad had captured the face of the man standing next to Mr. Sato. He wore a gardener's wide straw hat and a wide smile. And I had never seen him before.

"Do you like flowers?" I asked Jean-Paul.

"Of course." He gave the slide a quick look before handing it back. "Why?"

"After we dump our load, I thought maybe we could go see some flowers."

"Is there time before the Hungry Ghosts party?"

"The party goes on all day and most of the night, so we can show up at any time," I said. "The ghosts will still be there when we get there. They always are."

Chapter 9

I HEARD JEAN-PAUL'S SUDDEN INTAKE of breath when we turned onto the access road to Mr. Sato's greenhouse. In front of us, spread across flat fields almost as far as the eye could see, an ocean of flowers in full bloom, their colors more vivid than film could ever capture. The perfume in the air was nearly overwhelming.

At one time, this area south of San Jose was covered by flower nurseries. But over the years, piece by piece, the land had been sold to developers who replaced the nurseries with stucco housing tracts and boxy gray industrial parks and shopping centers. But nestled among warehouses and cinderblock fences, an oasis of commercial nurseries had managed to survive.

Mr. Sato, perched on a canvas director's chair in the shade of his greenhouse, was surveying what remained of his once-vast patch of roses through binoculars. When he heard the crunch of gravel under our truck tires, he turned the binoculars on us. Slowly, he got to his feet and directed Jean-Paul where to park.

"Hey Maggie, you come to see my roses?"

"They're amazing," I said, shaking his hand. "But we came to see you."

Introductions made, he offered us shade, chairs, and beer, in that order. We gladly accepted all three; it was at least twenty degrees hotter south of San Jose than it was in Berkeley.

After some preliminary chitchat, I took out the two slides that had parts of the man I did not recognize and asked Mr. Sato to look at them.

"Sure, sure," he said, slipping his reading glasses back into his pocket and handing the slides back to me. "That's Duc."

"Duck?"

He spelled the name for me. "Vietnamese guy. Duc Khanh."

"Did he work with you?"

"Yep." He rocked forward. "Worked for me a couple years. Best helper I ever had. I was real sorry when he quit."

"I think this picture was taken around the time that Mrs. Bartolini died."

He reached for the slides again and held them both up to the light, the effort to remember apparent in his frown. After a moment, he nodded.

"Yep, I think you're right," he said. "The other day you asked me about my helper back then but I couldn't quite pin it down, you know? But now I see this—" He flicked the corner of a slide frame. "That's the good thumping my rusty old brain needed. Yeah, Duc was working with me then."

He took another look at the slides. "Chryslers, you know, after they flower in the summer they have a short bloom again in the fall. That year, though, this rose just kept going till Christmas. Not a few pissy little late roses, but big, beautiful ones. So red they were almost black on the ends. And the perfume. Jeez, knock you out. Soon as that one went dormant, me and Duc pruned it and took cuttings."

I had to smile. My dad would sequence events by the way his roses performed during a particular year, or the stages of their bloom when something happened. Like Dad, Mr. Sato would remember the roses that year more clearly than he would lurking strangers.

"Did Dad ever talk to Duc about that day?"

He shook his head, unsure. "But now I remember why I fired the guy who worked for me before Duc."

I asked, "Why?"

"Let me run it down, see if I can put it all together." He scratched his chin, thinking. "The kid I had working for me for a long while— Fernando something, good worker, too—got picked up by Immigration and sent back to Mexico. I was in a jam, lotsa work to do. Your mom turned me on to a list of refugees needing jobs. That's where I found a guy named Van. He was a good enough worker when he put his mind to it, but he kinda thought he was above mowing lawns, you know? Always calling in sick. I had to take on Duc part time to fill in; found him on the same list. Like I said, Duc was the best helper I ever had, learned real quick. So when Van said something that bothered Mrs. Bartolini, I told him to take a hike and I hired Duc full time."

"Do you remember what Van said to her?"

"No. But I got the idea it had something to do with the old country. Her father, maybe."

"Do you have any idea where Van or Duc are now? I'd really like to talk to them."

He grinned at me. "You're still my nosy girl, Maggie."

"Can't help it," I said.

He turned to Jean-Paul. "Better watch yourself, boy. Don't ever try to sneak one past our Maggie."

"Wouldn't dare," he said, laughing out loud.

"Van? I don't know what happened to him. But you wanna talk to Duc?" Mr. Sato raised an arm and pointed to the south. "There's Duc."

I followed the trajectory of his arm, but all I saw was the commercial nursery on the far side of his greenhouse.

"Where?" I asked.

"Next door. I used to have six acres here," he said, pulling out his telephone. "Now all I got's this greenhouse. Duc bought me out a long time ago."

He hit speed dial on his phone, had a quick conversation, and put it away. "He's there now. Go on over. Said he'd like to meet you."

The office of Khanh Wholesale Nursery was a freshly painted red barn, perhaps left over from the area's rural past. Except for the koi pond moat around a Zen garden with a Buddha in a pagoda in the middle, it could have been a barn anywhere in America. In front of the Buddha there was an ancestor offering of fresh fruit and a giant bouquet of pristine white roses.

We walked inside, happy for the air-conditioning. I recognized Duc from the slide as he walked across the reception area to greet us. He was older, of course, but his smile was unchanged. He was a small man, weathered to a nut brown by years of working outdoors, wearing crisply pressed chinos and a green polo shirt, with work boots on his feet. The skin on the hand he offered me was as hard as the handle of a hoe, but there was a gentility about Duc's speech and carriage that suggested a formal upbringing.

"So, you're Al's girl," he said by way of greeting. "How's your mother?"

After assurances that Mom was just fine and introductions were made all around, he said, "I want to show you something."

He led us out through the back into the open nursery fields. There were plants of all sorts, but more than half the land we saw was covered with roses arranged in tiers by color and variety, some in the ground and some in pots. Maybe a dozen workers were on duty pruning, harvesting, moving irrigation drip lines, and pulling weeds that dared to intrude through the well-manicured soil. It was an impressive, bustling operation.

"My friend Tosh says you have some questions," he said as we walked through ranks of white roses. The sun beat down on our bare heads; heat came up through the soles of our shoes. Duc and Jean-Paul seemed unaffected; I wished for a hat.

"I've seen your program, of course," Duc said. "Your father and Tosh wouldn't forgive me if I hadn't. Are you working on something for television?"

"Not for television, no." I looked to Jean-Paul, hoping that a plausible excuse for asking the man questions that were truly none of my business would occur to me. I sighed: where to begin? How much to impose? In the end, I said, "To tell you the truth, it's personal."

He cocked his head, looked at me expectantly, and waited for more.

"It's about Tina Bartolini — Trinh," I said.

"Ah, Nguyen Trinh, yes." He dropped his eyes for a moment, a private smile on his face. When he looked up, he said, "A very long time ago, your father asked me what I saw in the neighborhood on a particular day. Is that what you want to know from me?"

"Yes, if you don't mind."

"I'll tell you what I told Al: I saw nothing out of place. No strangers, no wandering ninjas, no black-hooded gangsters. Just grass and flower borders and mulch."

I smiled, a bit chagrined for having asked. "Thank you."

"But that isn't the only question to ask, is it?"

"No."

"Maybe I can help: Did I know Trinh?" he said. "I did. Our families came from the same village. It was Trinh who introduced me to your mother, and it was your mother who enrolled me in the refugee employment program where I connected with Tosh. Later, when I wanted to start my own nursery, Tosh took me to your father, who helped me get a small business loan. And here we are."

"Interesting," I said. "I never knew exactly what it was that my mother did at the refugee center."

"One *mitzvah* after another," he said with a slight bow. "And so?"

"I heard Trinh's father was a food broker in Vietnam," I said.

"That's one way to describe what he did," Duc said. "Once again, one thing led to another. During the war against Japan, he made sure that supplies from the western Allies got to the resistance troops, chiefly the Viet Minh, who were fighting Japan. After the war, the French colonial government came back. They took over the Allied supply network, except now they were using it to fight the Viet Minh who were then fighting against the French for independence. No matter which side Trinh's father chose, he would create enemies. I don't know anything about his ideology, but he chose the side that offered the greatest economic security for his family."

"The French," I said. "And after them, the Americans."

He nodded.

"A man named Van worked for Tosh before you," I said. "Did you know him?"

"Thai Van, yes. Not very well, but yes."

"It was because of something Van said or did to Trinh that Mr. Sato fired him," I said. "Do you know what that was about?"

We had reached the division between pink and yellow roses. When Duc stopped and took small clippers from his pocket to snip off a perfect yellow rose, I wondered if I had asked one question too many, or ventured into a sensitive territory. But after Duc ran the stem through a thorn stripper, he handed the rose to me with a little bow and a sad little smile.

"I don't know what happened between Van and Trinh," he said. "I can't believe that she would have been happy to see him so near her family, even if he said nothing to her."

"Why?" I smelled the rose and passed it to Jean-Paul. I asked Duc, "Was Van dangerous to her?"

"Dangerous?" Duc said as we walked on. "I can't say. Van was a bitter man, like his father. But dangerous?"

"Who was his father?" I asked.

"Thai Hung, a nationalist leader," he said. "During the world war, Hung was an organizer in the resistance against Japan. After the Japanese defeat, he led a faction that opposed not only France but also Ho Chi Minh and his Viet Minh. Thai Hung believed Ho was trying to replace one form of European oppression, the French, with another, namely Ho's Moscow-bred Marxism. To his way of thinking, Trinh's father, at one time or another, was complicit with all of the oppressors of the people of Vietnam. That is, he was an enemy."

"Did Van agree with him?"

He held up his hands; who knew? "Like his father, Thai Van was a committed nationalist who lost his country but would not give up his cause. Last I heard, he was part of a group that thinks it is the legitimate government of the Republic of Vietnam, in exile. They're down south in Orange County somewhere. Little Saigon, probably."

Duc leaned closer, as if to share a confidence. "There is an American expression: You can take the boy out of the country but you can't take the country out of the boy, yes?"

"Yes," I said.

"I know in context the reference is to rural Americans when they go to the city," he said. "But it could as easily refer to the inability of a man like Van to adapt to a new environment. When he saw how Trinh lived, he said that her willingness to become, if you will, an American, living with an American, the mother of an American, was a betrayal of her ancestors."

"We have another expression," I said. "The sins of the fathers are visited upon the sons."

He thought about that. After a moment, he said, "Flowers I understand. People, not very much."

Jean-Paul, still holding the perfect yellow rose, looked around at Duc's flourishing little empire. He asked, "Were you a gardener in the old country?"

"No." Duc chuckled softly. "But when I came here, there were no openings in my chosen field. Gardener's helper was the best job I could find on the refugee center's help-wanted list."

"What was your field?" I asked.

"In Vietnam, I was a flyer," Duc said, stooping to pull a weed. "VNAF—Vietnam Air Force."

"What did you fly?" Jean-Paul asked with apparent interest.

"F-5s for the most part," Duc said. "Light fighters."

"Of course, American aircraft," Jean-Paul said. "My father, when he was stationed at Nha Trang, trained VNAF pilots on the old F8F Bearcat. Single-engine, piston driven, but a good work horse. A bomber."

I turned to him. "Your father was in Vietnam?"

"*Bien sûr.*"

"When?" I asked. The man was full of surprises.

"At about the same time your father was fighting communists in Korea, my father was fighting communists in Vietnam." He slipped his hand through the crook of my arm. "He was there until maybe a year after Dien Bien Phu. I think he came home in 1955. The French left soon after, and then the Americans arrived."

In French, Duc said, "Before my time."

"And mine," Jean-Paul said. "Do you still fly?"

Duc shook his head. "In 1975, I left Saigon in a commandeered fighter jet with my wife and children buckled into the co-pilot's seat. When I landed on the *Midway*, I hung up my pilot's wings. Thanks just the same, but I now prefer growing flowers to dropping bombs."

Duc stopped in the middle of an area planted with magnificent deep red roses and spread his hands.

"Here we are, Maggie. Your father's progeny."

"Chryslers," I said.

"This is where it all began for me," he said. "Your father gave me cuttings from this rose, Tosh leased me a corner of his land and coached me, and little by little I went into business for myself. I acquired a field here, a field there, a bit at a time, and now I plant about forty acres."

Jean-Paul said, "In France, we have an expression: *Petit à petit, l'oiseau fait son nid.*"

"Meaning?" I asked, as Duc laughed.

Duc answered, "Rome wasn't built in a day."

He walked us back to the office and offered refreshments. As warm and thirsty as we were, we needed to get home.

"Thank you for showing us around," I said. "What you have accomplished is very impressive."

"Yes," Duc acknowledged as he walked us out to the truck. "But possible only because I had help. Now, if there is any way I can be helpful to you, I would be honored."

"Can you help me find Thai Van?"

"Maybe," he said. "I'll make some calls and get back to you."

Two of his gardeners were waiting for us beside the truck. Each held a bucket full of long-stemmed roses, one white, one red.

"You told me you're going to the Bartolinis' *Vu Lan* celebration," Duc said. "Please take the white roses to Trinh's son, in memory of his mother. The reds are for you, in honor of your lovely mother. White for the deceased, red for the living."

I glanced at the giant bouquet of white roses in the ancestor shrine in front of the office, then at Duc.

He nodded; yes, his mother had passed into the next realm.

During the drive home, Jean-Paul was thoughtful. I handed him a bottle of cold water from the cooler bag Lyle had sent with us. He drank half of it in a long gulp.

"Tired?" I asked.

"A little, sure. It's very warm."

I checked the dash clock. "I think there's time for a short nap when we get home."

He gave a curt nod as he negotiated his way around a road boulder in the high occupancy lane who was cleaving strictly to the speed limit, backing up freeway traffic behind him. I leaned my head against the seat, sipped my water and tried not to doze off.

We were passing downtown Oakland when the first shot pinged the truck somewhere on my side.

"Get down!" Jean-Paul snapped, pushing me down with one hand as he skillfully slipped the truck between two cars in the next lane. Hunkered below the window, I scanned the mirrors I could see, looking for the shooter as a racket of car horns and squealing tires roared around us. Jean-Paul changed lanes again, dodging, weaving, looking for a clearing to gain some speed, to get away. I saw a silver car, no more than a flash of late afternoon glare in the side mirror, as a second shot plowed through the tops of the white roses in back and exploded the rear window, filling the cab with a confetti of rose petals and glittering shards of glass.

Chapter 10

"JESUS CHRIST," UNCLE MAX HUFFED as he ran his hand over the bullet hole in the truck's right side panel. "I can't let you out of my sight, can I?"

"Stuff happens," I said.

"To you, it does."

He was shaken. Jean-Paul and I'd had a couple of hours to get over the worst of the effects of the attack, but we were still edgy, scared. Somehow, needing to reassure my uncle that we were all right helped to settle me down. I gave him a hug and kissed his cheek, passed him a barely used tissue I found in my pocket to dab his eyes. He pulled in a couple of deep breaths and took another look at the bullet hole before he wandered over to listen in on the account of the incident that Jean-Paul was giving to a Highway Patrolman.

We didn't need Max to play lawyer, but he couldn't help himself. I had only asked my dear uncle to come and fetch us home from the Highway Patrol impound lot in Oakland, but I realized that maybe it was a good idea that a lawyer was there. The Oakland police had come by earlier, taken a look at the truck and our identification. When they saw Jean-Paul's diplomatic credentials there was a moment of alarm until he assured them that he was certain there were no international implications. The patrolmen were only too happy to declare that we were innocents caught in local gang crossfire, have us sign their brief written report, and to leave. The Highway Patrol was being far more

thorough; the shooting had shut down their freeway in both directions for over an hour, so there were questions that must be posed.

I was taking our belongings out of the truck and transferring them
to Max's car, waiting for a tow truck to show up to take the truck for
repairs, when a Berkeley PD black-and-white pulled into the lot and
Kevin climbed out.

"Thanks for calling," he said, giving my back a pat as he looked at
the truck's broken back window. "What happened?"

I told him what I had seen, which wasn't much.

"It's downtown Oakland," he said with a dismissive shrug.

"That's what Oakland PD said."

"So who's this Thai Van guy you said I should check out?"

I gave him the short version of the story of Thai Van and Mrs. Bartolini, and Duc Khanh and Toshio Sato.

"And while you're checking on people," I said, "you might want to
have a little chat with our old friend Larry Nordquist. Late last night
we found him lying in wait for us when we got home. He suggested
he knew something about the day Mrs. B died, but he said he would
only tell me about it if we were alone."

"I saw the report on the break-in at your place," Kevin scolded.
"Why didn't you call me last night?"

"And have you on my doorstep two nights in a row? The neighbors
are already talking."

He narrowed his eyes at me. "Who?"

"George and Karen Loper."

"Fucking busybodies."

Max, who had noticed Kevin when he pulled in, decided that it
was time to amble over to see who this newcomer was.

"Uncle Max," I said, "you remember Kevin Halloran."

Max raised his eyebrows, studying Kevin as he offered his hand.
Recognition suddenly dawned.

"Jesus, Mary and Joseph, if it isn't little Kevin," Max said, holding
Kevin's big hand in both of his; Kevin towered over Max. Seeing the
grin on my uncle's face, I dreaded what was coming next. "Or, as my
brother Al called you, that damn bundle of hormones."

Poor Kevin turned several shades of crimson; I probably did, too. I
nudged Max. "That's Detective Halloran, to you, buddy."

"Nice to see you again, sir," Kevin said, his voice changing register a couple of times, the way it would when he was fifteen, about the age he was when first confronted with my doting uncle.

"So, Detective Halloran," Max said, finally releasing Kevin's hand. "What brings you all the way from Berkeley?"

Kevin canted his head toward me. "Nancy Drew here called me. After someone took a couple of shots at her, she finally decided it was time to let me know where she's been poking her nose."

"It's a nice nose, though, isn't it?" Max said, grabbing me around the shoulders and pulling me close so he could pick glass shards out of my hair. "She paid a lot for it."

"No comment," Kevin said, grinning, his normal color returning. He asked me to walk him through my version of the shooting. With Max listening attentively, I told him the sequence of events as we walked a circuit around the truck. Kevin took pictures of the bullet hole in the right side panel before he climbed up into the truck bed for a closer look into the cab through the gaping window. As he plucked a fragment of broken glass from the frame, he asked, "Truck registered to the boyfriend?"

"No," I said. "It's mine."

He snapped his head around, checked to see if I was kidding him.

"It's my truck, Kevin," I said. "Sometimes itty-bitty girls have big trucks, too."

"I didn't say anything," he demurred.

"You didn't have to. If it helps, the truck belonged to my late husband."

That he could accept. "Where are you having it towed?"

"The insurance agent recommended the body shop at the Ford dealership on MLK, Jr. in Berkeley."

"They do good work."

The tow truck, a big flatbed, arrived to haul the pickup for repairs. Kevin exchanged cards with the driver and with the Highway Patrol investigator, oversaw the process of securing my pickup. As the driver signed paperwork proffered by the investigator, Kevin dialed a number he read off the card the driver had given him. After some automated switchboard folderol, he was put through to the service manager, to whom he gave sharp instructions for the truck to be locked in a secure area of the body shop over the weekend, and not to be touched until he arrived Monday morning.

"What was that about?" I asked when he put his phone away.

"The slug didn't pierce the truckbed liner, so it's probably still lodged inside the side panel," he said. "Looks like the second slug is embedded in the dash. I want to be on hand when the panel comes off, see if I can find it. Ditto for the dash."

I cringed. I had hoped the repairs would entail no more than replacing the window and slapping a patch on the side panel so that I could get the truck back right away; I needed it. But now it sounded like a rental truck was in the offing. And a big bill.

Max, damn him, introduced Kevin to Jean-Paul as my first big flame. That bit of slang did not need explanation. Jean-Paul offered his hand and a few gracious words while the two men, though they stayed in place, circled each other visually, like bantam cocks in the henhouse. I slipped my hand through Jean-Paul's arm, leaned my head against his shoulder and asked, "Can we go home now?"

"Yes." He covered my hand with his. "If there are further questions, the authorities will call us."

"I'm sure they will." I felt something scratchy under my collar, gave my shirt a good shake and half-a-dozen more bits of glass fell to the pavement. Jean-Paul had a row of tiny cuts across the side of his face that showed the trajectory of the window's explosion. He had turned his head to check on me just as the second shot went through the back window and been hit by fragments of glass as they flew past; thank God he was wearing sunglasses.

We left Kevin speaking with the Highway Patrol investigator when we climbed into Uncle Max's rented red Cadillac, and drove out.

I sat in the backseat and listened to the two men discuss the incident.

"I believe it was a Toyota, maybe a Honda," Jean-Paul told Max. "Silver-gray. Perhaps a Camry or an Accord. Several years old. Because of the angle of the sun, I could not see the driver, but my impression is he was alone."

"Tall, short, dark, fair?" Max asked.

Jean-Paul shook his head. "*Qui sait?* I concentrated on getting out of his way, not seeing who he was."

Max looked over his shoulder at me. "Maggie?"

I also shook my head. "I ducked. All I saw was something silver bobbing and weaving through traffic, trying to stay with us."

Jean-Paul reached between the seats and took my hand. "I keep thinking about what that neighbor said this morning, about wishing he had a twelve-bore. So help me, this afternoon, I never wished for anything more than I did a great big gun to stop that lunatic."

"Good thing we didn't have one," I said. "Who knows who you would have taken out."

Max caught my eye in his rearview mirror. "Maggot, where is your dad's Colt?"

"His what?"

"Gun."

"Dad never owned a gun," I said.

"Actually, honey, he did."

I shrugged. "Ask Mom."

"He certainly never told Betsy about it," Max said. "She wouldn't have a gun in the house."

That I knew. I needed just a few minutes with Dad; he'd left me with so many unanswered questions.

"But he went ahead and bought one," I said. "Why?"

"Isabelle," he said, as if that explained everything.

"Just how crazy was she?"

"From day to day?" Max said. "Hard to say. But whenever she showed up here it was because she was off her meds and in a manic stage. Impossible to predict what she might do. Your dad caught her inside the house one night, in your bedroom, watching you sleep."

"So he bought a gun?"

"He didn't buy it," Max said. "The neighbor acquired it somehow and gave it to him."

"Which neighbor, George Loper or Jake Jakobsen?"

"It wouldn't be Jake, now, would it?"

"No," I said. "Jake is far too sane. But George Loper..."

"Your dad had asked the neighbors to keep an eye out for Isabelle, told them she was a former student who'd gone off the rails, which was only ten degrees off true," Max said. "Loper came over one day and handed your dad a new, unregistered, unfired Colt Commander.

Told Al that if he wanted to try it out, he should go way out into the desert and make sure he was never seen so that if he ever needed to use the damn thing he could ditch it afterward and there would be no way to trace it back to him."

"Except George knew," I said.

Jean-Paul had listened with rapt attention. He asked, "This George, is he in law enforcement or perhaps the military?"

"He's a rocket scientist," I said. "Rumor is, he's brilliant."

He laughed. "*Bien sûr*. The mad scientist next door."

"You laugh," I said. "But if he gave Dad an unregistered gun, you know he has one himself."

Chapter 11

A PAPER EFFIGY OF A LARGE HOUSE, and then a car and a bundle of hell money—gifts for ancestors—caught fire and burned in a flash, sending smoke and fine ash fluttering among the dozens of red Chinese lanterns strung like bright laundry above the Bartolinis' backyard.

"Beautiful," Jean-Paul said, looking up at the lanterns.

It was nearly sundown by the time Jean-Paul and I arrived to honor the hungry ghosts. We brought the dozen or so white roses that had survived the events of the afternoon, now arranged in a vase, and several green silk-covered boxes of decadent French chocolates, some for the living, some for the dead. A red table and chairs were set in a place of honor for the ghosts who had come to eat among the hundred or so neighbors and friends who filled the yard. We placed a box of chocolates among the offerings heaped atop the red table, and then, like the other invited guests, gave the area a wide berth so that the ghosts could feast undisturbed.

There was a soft presence beside me. "Is that you, Maggie?"

Pa, a Buddhist monk Mom befriended during her work with refugee services, seemed to have floated out of the backyard throng; his long-sleeved white robes all but covered his feet. He put his palms together prayerfully and bowed when I introduced him to Jean-Paul. Jean-Paul acknowledged the greeting with a slight bow of his own, diplomatically not offering his hand.

"I was looking for your mother," Pa said to me as he tucked his hands into his sleeves. With quiet yet profound concern, he asked, "You brought white flowers?"

"The flowers are for Mrs. Bartolini," I said. In his circumspect way, he was asking if Mom had died. "Mom couldn't be here this year."

"Your mother is well?"

"Very well." I told him about Mom's move south and his expression brightened. "I'll tell her you asked about her."

With another bow, he excused himself and floated off again.

As we ventured toward the buffet tables, I looked for Beto or his dad in the crowd. Among a noisy clutch near a beer keg, I spotted Kevin's wife, Lacy, and her younger sister, Dorrie, both of them listing a bit, as if the lawn underfoot was a storm-tossed sea. Kevin was nowhere to be found.

Lacy's name had suited her perfectly when we were kids. She was quick and bright then, a tiny, wiry, athletic little daredevil who plied her dimples to charm our way out of messes she generally got us into in the first place. Dorrie was as close to being Lacy's opposite as a sibling could be. Stolid, cranky, slow-moving and annoying. A tattletale. As a grown woman, though she had become quite striking, she did not seem any happier.

Dorrie saw me, whispered something to Lacy, threw back her shoulders, and headed in my direction with an alarming air of purpose. I gripped Jean-Paul's arm and readied myself. Before I could warn him to be prepared to hear whatever was on Dorrie's mind, Beto pushed through the mob from behind us bearing a raffia-wrapped bottle of chianti and a stack of plastic cups. Dorrie backed away.

"What kept you? I was about to send out a search party to go find you guys," Beto said. When I introduced him to Jean-Paul, he offered a cup from his stack in lieu of a handshake. As he filled both our cups, he nodded toward the bouquet. "Are those for Mom?"

"Yes," I said. "They're from an old friend of hers."

"Who's that?"

"A man named Khanh Duc," I said. "Remember him?"

Beto frowned, thinking. He said, "Maybe. Let me get my kid to take over refill patrol, and we'll take the flowers inside to Mom."

He summoned his teenaged son, Bartolomeo Bartolini III, by calling out across the masses, "Yo, Trips."

"Yo, Pop." Trips, a lanky, handsome six-footer, more Bart than Beto,
squeezed through the crowd. He draped an arm across his father's
shoulders, leaning on him; he towered over Beto. "What's up?"

Greetings and introductions taken care of, Beto handed his son the
cups and the bottle and took the flowers from me. "I'm going inside
with Maggie and Jean-Paul for a minute. I need you to keep an eye on
Lacy. If she gets out of hand before Uncle Kevin shows up, I'm going
to ask you to drive her and her sister home, okay, son?"

Trips took a quick glance in the direction of Lacy and Dorrie, and
nodded. Raising the wine bottle, he asked his father, "Can I have
some of this?"

"Of course, my angel." Beto patted his son's smooth cheek. "In
three years, when you're legal."

As Beto led us inside to place the roses in the shrine to his mother
I said, "Uncle Kevin? Since when?"

"Kevin is Trips's godfather."

"I didn't know," I said.

"Guess you wouldn't," he said. "Where were you eighteen years
ago?"

I shrugged, "Dallas, I think. I worked at a local TV station there
until Casey was three."

He grinned. "Well, you missed a good party."

"My loss."

Beto placed the vase in the entry niche shrine next to the golden
Buddha, making space among the offerings to his mother that were
already there: a plate of fresh fruit, a circlet of pearls, burning incense, pictures of her grandchildren, and a rosary. After a moment of
silence, Beto reached behind the Buddha, took out a prayer card and
a St. Mark's medal and handed them to me.

"Father John left these for you," he said. "He offered rosaries for
Mom and Mark at mass this morning."

"Is he here?"

"Been and gone. He came over early, said a blessing, ate some food
and took off. He tires out pretty fast now."

I suddenly felt like crying. Too much day, adrenaline let-down, too many shadows from the past rattling around. Jean-Paul noticed, wrapped an arm around me and kissed my forehead. I took a deep breath, composed myself and smiled at him. He was still carrying chocolates.

"These are for you," Jean-Paul said, handing the remaining silk-covered boxes to Beto.

"Holy cow," Beto said when he saw the label. "Wow. I've only heard about this stuff. Primo. I saw they're opening a shop in the City."

"Yes, next week," Jean-Paul said. "I'll see that you get an invitation to the opening, if you wish."

"I'd love to go, yes, thank you," he said. With an elbow he nudged me. "Looks like Ghirardelli has some competition in San Francisco now."

"I think they'll survive," I said.

Bart shuffled in, walking like his feet hurt. Without his usual verve, he said, "There's my girl. How are ya, Maggie?"

I kissed Bart's proffered cheek and introduced him to Jean-Paul. He noticed the roses and asked, "Did your dad bring those over? I didn't see him come in."

I exchanged glances with Beto, who said, "He's on his way, Papa."

"Good, good," Bart said. "Every year he brings white roses for my Tina."

"Papa," Beto said, "this time, an old friend of Mom's sent the flowers."

"Yeah?" His head seemed heavy. "Who's that?"

Beto turned to me. "What was the name?"

"Khanh Duc," I said, looking for a flicker of recognition from Bart. "He used to spend a lot of time with Dad in the yard. Maybe you met him?"

But Bart didn't seem to hear. His eyes were glassy, his skin an alarming shade of gray. Probably exhausted by party preparations, I thought, and the noisy mass of people underfoot. Beto took him by the elbow and turned him toward the living room.

"Let's go sit down, Papa. Take a load off." Bart did not protest. Over his shoulder, Beto said to us, "Go eat, for God's sake. Papa's been cooking for two days. So have Zaida and her mom and Auntie Quynh."

Bart, his back to us as he shuffled out, raised a hand and waved. "Try my ravioli aragosta. But hurry up before it's all gone."

Jean-Paul and I stood for a moment in the quiet of the entry hall, sipping the very good chianti. Looking at me over the top of his plastic glass, he said, "Your father is expected?"

"The spirits of the dead are here, remember?"

"However..."

"Bart's having some memory issues," I said. "He seems to think Mom is dead. And Dad isn't."

"I see, yes. A man of a certain age, *n'est-ce pas?*"

"*Oui.*" I took his arm. "Let's eat. The food will be an Italian–Mexican–Vietnamese fusion, and the head chef recommends the lobster pasta."

The partiers outside seemed to have grown noisier during the short time we were in the house with Beto; the Bartolinis were as generous with drink as they were with food. I heard Lacy's high-pitched laugh above the din as we headed toward the buffet tables.

The side gate opened and Kevin blasted through like a sudden squall. He nodded curt greetings to various people but kept moving on a straight trajectory toward his wife. When he reached Lacy, he took her by the upper arms, nearly lifting her off her feet. I heard him say, "What were you thinking?" as he fast-walked her toward the gate with Dorrie following in their wake. When he passed us, there was the merest hesitation when he noticed me. I thought he wanted to say something, but he just shook his head and kept going.

A general tittering followed their exit, but it soon died away. Apparently, that scene, or some version of it, had played a few times before.

Gracie Nussbaum sidled up next to me. All she said about the drama was "Oh, my." And that just about summed it up.

Jean-Paul and I filled plates at the long buffet table and ate standing up, talking to old friends and neighbors. Jean-Paul, always charming and self-effacing, seemed to be having a good time. Certainly he was more relaxed, I thought, than he had been at the more formal museum party the night before. He went back to the table for seconds of Beto's mother-in-law's little carne asada tacos and the ravioli aragosta tossed in garlic and olive oil. Then he mediated the ongoing but good-natured little competition between Beto's wife, Zaida, and

his Aunt Quynh over the former's ceviche and the latter's Vietnam-
ese-style shrimp rolls. Jean-Paul engaged the cooks in a conversation
about the ingredients while he sampled both dishes. Both women
preened for him. Charm the man had, as well as a good appetite and,
apparently, an iron stomach.

Trips came by offering wine refills. "Uncle Kevin asked me to tell
you he'll catch up with you later."

"Too bad he couldn't stay," I said.

"Lacy needed to go home," Trips said, doing a pretty good imita-
tion of a drunk slurring his words. I tried not to laugh. He leaned in
and said, "If you ever want to talk to Lacy, you need to catch her pretty
early in the day. Otherwise—" He waved the bottle, and walked off
to serve other guests.

Just as Jean-Paul headed toward the dessert table, I heard someone
call my name. When I turned to see who it was, I nearly bowled over
Lacy's sister, Dorrie.

"Dorrie!" I grabbed her by the shoulder to steady her. "So sorry."

"So, you remember my name?" She seemed surprised.

"Of course I do. I thought you left with your sister."

She laughed, but there was nothing happy in the sound. "Kevin
extracted Lacy. I wasn't about to get into a car with the two of them,
not when you're in town and she's had a few."

"When I'm in town? What's that have to do—"

She held up her hand to forestall the question. "Maggie, you don't
know what it's like for her. All through high school, she had the biggest crush on Kevin, but he was with you and wouldn't even look
at her. Now, every time one of your shows comes on TV, it just stirs
up all those old feelings again because everyone in town, including
Kevin, watches you. Then for a couple of days afterward, that's all
anybody talks about. Whether they agree with what you said on the
show or not, it's all Maggie, Maggie, Maggie everywhere Lacy goes,
especially if she's with Kevin. For a woman like Lacy, the attention
you get around here is painful."

"What do you mean, a woman like Lacy?" I asked.

"Well, hell, think about it," Dorrie said, as if I missed the obvious.
"Lacy always thought she should be both the soprano and the con-
ductor in her own opera, if you know what I mean. But she peaked

in high school. Head cheerleader, then has-been. And look at what you've accomplished."

"Jesus, Dorrie, there are eight or nine Nobelists in Berkeley. For Lacy to compare herself to me, a face on TV, that's just—"

"Normal," she said firmly. "It's bad enough for her when Kevin sees you on the tube, but when she heard that you're in town and he's hanging out at your house, well, she just can't handle it."

"Hardly hanging out," I said. "He came over once, on police business."

"That isn't the way Lacy heard it."

"Heard it from whom?"

"That damn Mrs. Loper. I think she gets off on stirring things up between people."

I nodded; it was true.

Jean-Paul edged his way back to me, trying to keep slippery homemade flan from sliding off his slick plastic plate. He offered me his spoon. "Try this."

I did; it was wonderful. "Jean-Paul, this is an old friend, Dorrie Riley."

"Dorrie Riley Ross," she said, glowing a bit as she offered her hand to Jean-Paul. Dorrie wasn't unattractive, and I have to admit that when Jean-Paul turned his attention toward her, just being polite, I slipped a few inches closer to him, making it clear that he was not available. And did not admire myself for doing so.

I said, "Please reassure Lacy that she has no reason to concern herself with me."

"But she does, you know," Dorrie said, giving my hand a quick squeeze. "She does."

Dorrie moved off into the crowd. I saw her speak to Beto before she slipped out the side gate.

There were dark circles under Jean-Paul's eyes. I said, "Had enough fun for one day?"

"Enough for several." He patted his flat belly. "And more than enough to eat."

It was time to say our good-byes. We found Beto tidying the buffet table.

"Thank you," I said, walking into his hug.

"So happy you came," he said. He offered his hand to Jean-Paul. "Hope you can join us again next year."

When I asked where we could find his father, he said, "He knocked himself out getting things ready; you saw how he was. Sometimes when he's tired, he gets, I don't know, combative. So, I put him to bed to keep him from getting into trouble."

"Tell him we had a wonderful time."

Beto was grinning when he asked, "Did your dad have a good time, too?"

"I'm sure he did," I said.

We left by the side gate.

"So?" Jean-Paul wrapped an arm around my shoulders and pulled me close as we walked down the driveway past the garage. "See any ghosts tonight?"

"Many." My eyes trailed to the vase of white roses dumped atop a very full trash barrel. "Many."

Chapter 12

"I CAN THINK OF only two places in this house where Dad might hide a gun," I said. "One is his desk, but I have already emptied it. The other is his workbench in the garage."

Jean-Paul threw his head back and laughed, something I had rarely seen him do. I looked over at him as I slipped off my jeans. "Sir?"

"My dear." He pulled me against him and laid us back on the bed. "I am doing my very best impression of the romantic Frenchman, but, alas, apparently to no effect."

I rolled on top and straddled him. "You're doing a fabulous job of it, Monsieur. Top drawer. A-number-one. *Le dernier cri.*"

"But?"

"Your target, *moi*, is just too damn scattered at the moment to focus fully on the program."

"*Et donc?*"

"So, give me ten minutes for a quick look, and I promise that when I return I will give all my attention in mind as well as body to your fine efforts."

"A look in the garage?"

"A quick one." I kissed him.

His wheels were turning, thinking. After a moment, he lifted me off him and said, "*D'accord.*"

I pulled my jeans back on, found my flip-flops, and hurried down the stairs through the quiet house and out through the butler's pantry to the garage. Roy and Lyle had taken Uncle Max with them to Yoshi's, a jazz club in San Francisco. Max's note said he would stay overnight and take BART back in the morning. He'd left us the keys to his rented car in case we needed wheels in the meantime.

Lyle had finished sorting through most of the drawers and bins in and around Dad's workbench before George Loper flamed out and progress halted. I rummaged through the remaining jumble, finding nothing more interesting than a book about constructing martin houses, a project Dad apparently never got around to, possibly because mosquitoes are not a big problem in Berkeley. I tossed the book into a trash bag and kept searching. Surely Dad wouldn't hide a firearm where anyone might happen upon it. So, then, where? Unless he had disposed of it.

I had a wrench in one hand and a rubber mallet in the other, standing beside the workbench, looking around for inspiration, when the door to the side yard opened.

"Larry?" I raised the wrench as a reflex when he came through the door.

"Whoa." Larry held up both hands. "Don't throw that thing at me, okay?"

"What the hell are you doing here?"

"I saw you." He gestured toward the window in the side door. "And I saw you were alone, so I thought, No time like the present."

"That door was locked; I checked it."

"Yeah, well." Sheepishly, he held up a key. "I know where your dad hid it."

"Have you been coming in here all along?"

"Shit, yeah," he said, sounding almost angry. "I told you that."

"No, you did not."

"I told you I was looking after the garden, didn't I?" he said, as if speaking to an idiot as he aimed a thumb toward the rack of garden tools. "How the hell did you think I could do that without, oh, I don't know, maybe a rake and a hoe?"

I put down the wrench and held out my hand for the key, which he gave me. The key was old, rusty where it attached to a small metal ring, but shiny, recently oiled where it fit into the lock.

"How long have you known about the key?" I asked.

He shrugged. "Just about always, I guess."

For a long time, the same key could open all three of the small garage doors: one to the side yard, one to the backyard, and one into the house; my parents used the garage more as a workshop and garden shed than as a place to park cars. Somewhere along the way, when I was nine or ten, Dad had installed a new lock and a deadbolt on the door into the house. Max told me that Isabelle had been found in my room one night, watching me sleep. Any parent would have changed the lock after that.

"Did you tell Isabelle Martin where to find the key?"

"Mighta," he tossed off as if giving her access to the house—to me—were of no consequence.

"You went into the house, too, didn't you?"

"Just one time," he said. "I thought there was no one home, but then I heard someone running the vacuum cleaner and I got the hell out."

"No," I said. "More recently, like night before last."

"What are you talking about?"

"Someone broke into the house Thursday night."

"Oh sure." He slapped the end of the workbench that separated us. "Anything happens, just blame old Larry, the town delinquent."

"I'm sorry," I said. "But you said you were in the house."

"Yeah," he said, very matter-of-fact about it, like wasn't everybody walking into the house? "But that was a whole long time ago. And it was just that one time. I mean, I tried to, but the next time the key didn't work."

I nodded; it had been before Dad changed the lock. I asked him, "What were you looking for?"

A shoulder rose and fell. "Like I said, just to see what the house was like."

"Why us?"

"That's the thing I wanted to tell you about." He looked around, moved a step closer to speak in a soft, confiding voice. "I sorta looked in a lot of houses."

"Just to see what they were like?" I asked.

"Yeah. And what people were doing," he said. "I saw a lot of things."

"Private things," I said, suddenly feeling cold.

He nodded, his old cockiness coming back. "What I said to Beto that day, it was the truth. I saw it for myself."

"You called his mother a Saigon whore."

He smirked, head bobbing up and down to affirm that I had hit on the answer. "She was. A great big whore."

The door into the house opened quietly and Jean-Paul, barefoot, came down the two steps into the garage; he held a gun in his hand. To distract Larry from turning around and seeing him, and possibly running off again, I made a lot of noise pulling Dad's stool out from under the workbench. I sat so that, to talk to me, his back was completely to the door where Jean-Paul stood.

"That's a disgusting thing to say, Larry."

"Okay, but what I saw her and the guy doing was pretty damn disgusting, too," he said. "Old Bart would be at the store and Beto was at school and this guy would come over and, jeez, like you said, disgusting."

"But not so disgusting that you turned away."

"Boys will be boys," he said, flashing his snaggletoothed grin.

"Shouldn't you have been in school?"

"The thing is, I used to ditch a lot. Then they'd suspend me for ditching." He sneered: "Assholes."

"Who was the man?" I asked.

A phone rang inside the house, making Larry turn toward the sound. He spotted Jean-Paul.

"Maggie, *ça va?*" Jean-Paul asked without venturing further into the garage.

"We're okay," I said.

Larry turned back and wagged a scolding finger at me. "I said, just you."

"Hey, Larry, you broke into my house late at night," I snapped. "What did you expect? That Jean-Paul wouldn't come out and check on me?"

He seemed to think that was reasonable, and did not question that Jean-Paul had brought a gun with him.

"Who was the man?" I asked again.

He shrugged. "We were never introduced, if you know what I mean."

"But you saw him. Can you describe him?"

His gaze slid toward Jean-Paul. "Maybe I don't remember. It was a long time ago."

"Is there something that might help you remember?"

"Could be. I'll think about it and get back to you."

He headed toward the door. But he stopped with his hand around the doorknob and looked over his shoulder at me. "Do you remember what you said to me on that day?"

"I do. And I'm sorry that what I said hurt you so much."

"The thing is," he said, turning his face away from me. "What you said, it was true, too. I was pissed off at Beto, hell, I was pissed off at all of you guys and your perfect lives. I thought that if I told him what his mom really was, it would put the stupid little prick in his place." He fell silent for a moment, sighed, before he said, "But you were right. Bringing him down wouldn't make people like me."

With that, he turned and left, shutting the door behind him.

After he was gone, I opened a drawer in the workbench where I had seen a package of steel hasp locks and a pair of padlocks. I handed them to Jean-Paul, took out the can of screws and the electric screwdriver, and together we installed the locks on the inside of both the garage doors to the backyard and to the side yard, the door Larry said he had been using the key to open. With that same key, Isabelle had been able to access my bedroom, until Dad put a deadbolt on the door into the house.

"I'll call a locksmith in the morning," I said.

"Probably wise."

He picked up the gun he had been carrying when he came out to the garage.

"Where'd you find that?" I asked.

"I'll show you."

We went into Dad's den and over to his desk. The desk I so carefully emptied.

"After you went downstairs, I began to think," Jean-Paul said as he pulled out the bottom drawer, the same drawer where I had found the strongbox with the movies and the crime scene photo of Mrs. B. "Where would a man hide a gun so that his wife and child, and certainly the cleaning woman, would not happen upon it, even if they looked for it? Perhaps the underside of a drawer?"

He put his hand against the inside of the drawer and turned it over to show me the bottom. The wood was too pristine to have had something affixed there for a couple of decades.

"So, where did you find the gun?" I asked.

"*Voilà.*" He removed his hand and a wood panel fell out. Dad had made a false bottom, creating a fitted compartment for the gun and a box of ammo and a cleaning kit, and a top to hide them.

"I'll be damned," I said, imagining Dad at his garage workbench, carefully crafting a safe place for his contraband firearm. "I'm not surprised. If Dad could hide a mistress and their daughter from his wife for a couple of years, he would certainly figure out how to hide an itty-bitty gun."

Jean-Paul picked up the Colt automatic and weighed it on his palm. "Not so small, my dear. This weapon was standard military issue at one time, excellent stopping power."

"Max said it was unregistered. Do you think it's traceable?"

He gave me a little French shrug and a moue while he considered. "Probably traceable from the manufacturer to first point of sale. But from there?" He turned the Colt over and looked at the serial number. "I'll make some calls, yes?"

"Be careful with that thing," I said. "Is it loaded?"

"It was, yes, but no longer." He opened the top desk drawer and showed me the gun's magazine and a box of .45 ACP shells. "The ammunition is very old, certainly unstable. Perhaps you might ask your Detective Halloran to have it taken away for disposal."

I had qualms about doing that. "If I tell Kevin about the ammo, he'll ask about the gun it belongs to. I may want to keep the Colt if it's unregistered and untraceable. You never know when that might be handy to have."

He reloaded the gun. "My dear, should I be afraid?"

"Not you," I said. "It might be your sweet *tuchis* I'll need to save."

Chapter 13

"BUT IT WAS A LOVELY IDEA," I said, peeling a red rose petal off Jean-Paul's cheek. "Incredibly romantic."

"In theory, yes. There was such a large bucket of red roses, and what to do with them all, yes?" He got up to scoop crushed petals off the sheets and drop them into the trashcan he had brought in from the en suite bathroom. "But in application, a bit sticky."

"I think I'll dream about seaweed," I said.

He laughed as he slid back between the sheets and wrapped me in his arms. "I shall leave rose petal–strewing to the movies in the future."

"Maybe so," I said, picking yet another petal off his bottom. "But it was still a lovely idea."

He yawned, reached across me and turned off the bedside light.

The house was quiet, all doors securely bolted, windows locked, the loaded Colt in a drawer next to the bed. I nestled down against Jean-Paul and hoped for sleep, but I still buzzed with the events of the day. Every time I began to drift off, an image, a fragment of conversation, the sound of gunfire and shattered glass would seep through and set my mind racing again. I felt restless. If I had been alone and at my own home, I would have gone for a run in the canyon below my house. But that wasn't something I would do in the middle of the night in a dark Berkeley neighborhood. I tried to lie still to let Jean-

Paul sleep. I thought he had dropped off when he kissed the top of my head and spoke into the dark.

"Did your father speak about what he did in Korea?"

"No," I said. "Dad might say he hadn't been so cold since Korea, or that if he wanted to camp out he'd rejoin the army—he'd say a hotel without room service was as close to camping as he ever wanted to get again. And I knew about his wounds; couldn't miss the scars when he wore shorts or swim trunks. But he didn't talk about what happened over there, and I knew not to ask because it made him sad."

"*Oui*," he said. "Same with my father. He talked about the airplanes he flew in Indochina, but not much else. One time, he took me to an air show and told me about flying the Bearcats. Papa had far more to say about what the Germans did to his family during the world war than about what the French did in Indochina when he was there ten years later."

I smiled at that. My recently discovered French grandmother, Élodie Martin, had much to say not only about what the Germans did in Normandy, but also about what she and the women in her village did to the Germans: a bloody tale she told with relish, and one I was hoping to capture on film.

"What happened to your family during the German occupation?" I asked.

"My father was just a boy at school in Paris when the Germans conscripted him and forced him to work in a munitions factory in Belgium. His father died in a prisoner of war camp," he said, an edge of sadness in his voice.

"Papa was a reasonable man, an intellectual," he continued. "But for the rest of his life he refused to buy anything made in Germany or to invest in any company that held German interests. I cannot tell you the scolding I got when I bought a Mercedes. He would always say, 'Scratch a German, find a Nazi.' And there was nothing anyone could say or do that would make him change his mind."

"Wars do not necessarily end when the armistice is signed, do they?"

"No." He stroked my back. "It is not only war we are talking about, is it, *chérie*?"

"No?"

"The police are investigating the death of your friend's mother, yes?"

"Kevin Halloran is."

"And he is competent?"

"He seems to be."

"And yet, when you found a lead on a line of inquiry, you did not inform him immediately, but went yourself, first."

"You mean Duc?"

"Yes, Duc, and this Larry who keeps popping up late at night." After a pause, he said, "Do you believe what Larry told you?"

"About Mrs. Bartolini? Sorry to say, but I do."

"Maggie, my dear, I hear your questions and they all seem to come back to your father. Are you afraid he was involved in some illicit way with the woman or with her death?"

I started to deny it, a protective reflex. Instead, I said, "I think he knew something that worried him enough that he made inquiries. But he never went to the police."

"Because he was protecting someone?"

"Probably."

"Perhaps he found what he was looking for," he said.

"He would have gone to the police if he had."

"Unless it was too dangerous," he said, raising my hand to his lips. "And perhaps it still is. Maggie, I have to leave tomorrow." He lifted his head up enough to see the bedside clock; it was already Sunday. "Today, actually. Please come with me. Lyle and Roy will finish the work here."

It was an attractive idea. I thought about it, but told him, "I can't leave until Tuesday at the earliest. My cousin is coming this afternoon and staying overnight. We have some decisions to make before I can finish up here. There are haulers to arrange, a cleaning crew to boss around, truck repairs to see about, and—"

"Yes, yes, but you should not be here alone."

"I'll hardly be alone," I said. "Max will be back, Guido is coming up to talk about what we're going to do about the Normandy film, and Susan will be here in the afternoon. Her entire book club will show up Monday."

He was quiet for a moment.

"I love that you are concerned, but I'll be fine," I said.

"Everyone leaves again on Monday," he said. "Yes?"

"They do."

He yawned. "I have business to tend to in Los Angeles, but I'll be back Monday evening."

I did not protest. Instead, I snuggled down against him, and fell asleep.

FIRST THING in the morning, we went for a run up Grizzly Peak Road. I had been bending, stooping, and lifting for nearly a week and cherished my early morning runs to stretch my legs, breathe fresh air, and clear my mind. Jean-Paul ran easily next to me, though I knew he was the better runner and could have sprinted ahead or run circles around me. I had hoped to show him the view from the peak of San Francisco rising like Camelot out of the Bay. But the City was shrouded by its summer cloak of gray fog, as usual, and we couldn't even see the top of the Transamerica Building. Jean-Paul seemed more interested in the towering redwoods on the Cal campus below us than on the postcard-quality view of the towers of the Golden Gate Bridge rising up out of the gloom.

Altogether, it was a good run. By the time we returned home, my head felt decluttered, as it generally does after a good run or a hard swim. A few bits and pieces of what happened in my neighborhood thirty-some years ago were beginning to come together.

Back at the house, after showers, we made breakfast and took it outside to eat at the big table under the grape arbor. On Sunday mornings, both of us had transcontinental phone calls to make. My college-junior daughter, Casey, was spending the summer on her grandmother's farm estate in Normandy with about half a dozen cousins who were more or less the same age. Jean-Paul's son, Dominic, was staying in Paris with his aunt, now gearing up for a two-year preparatory course before he entered one of the *grandes écoles*. It was already late afternoon in France when we pushed our breakfast dishes aside and took out our phones.

"Mom, great, I was waiting for you to call," Casey said with unusual enthusiasm for this Sunday ritual. "When are you flying over?"

"Does my darling daughter miss me?" I asked.

"What? Oh, yeah. Sure, of course. But when are you coming?"

"One way or another, in a couple of weeks. What's up?"

"Are you bringing a whole film crew or just Guido?"

"Probably just Guido," I said. "Why?"

"We had this great idea—"

"We?"

"David and Dom and I."

I turned to look at Jean-Paul, who had the strangest expression on his face. I knew he was speaking with his son, Dominic. Catching Jean-Paul's eye, I asked Casey, "Dom Bernard?"

Jean-Paul heard me and was nodding when Casey affirmed, "Yes. You know his grandmother is Grand-mère's friend. She brought him to see the farm."

"Let me guess, his grandmother and your great-grandmother are plotting something," I said.

"They're matchmaking," she said, very matter-of-fact. "As always. Grand-mère hopes that you two will get married and move to France so you can come over every Sunday for dinner."

From the look on his face, Jean-Paul was hearing something similar from his son. He smiled and lifted a palm in a whatcha-gonna-do? gesture.

"Anyway, Mom?"

"Yes, dear."

"We had this great idea to film promo spots to raise awareness about the amazing local farm products. You know, globally."

"Sounds like fun," I said. "Where will you broadcast your spots?"

"We need to talk to Jean-Paul about that. Dom says that's his area of expertise."

"We'll talk more about it when I get there."

"We've drafted a shooting script. I'll email it to you so you can punch it up."

"Casey, I didn't know you were interested in filmmaking."

"You kidding?" she said with some heat. "No way. I've seen what you have to put up with. Nope, not my gig. But I am really getting into cheese making. Who knew, huh? The chemistry of it is fascinating."

She told me that she and some of the cousins were leaving in the morning on a road trip into the Dordogne to do some kayaking and hiking. I refrained from offering a string of maternal warnings and wished her godspeed. She promised they would be back, intact, before I arrived.

Jean-Paul was in the midst of a business-related call when I said good-bye to Casey. I called Mom next.

"The piano mover is scheduled for first thing tomorrow," she told me. "Can you be there when they arrive?"

"I'll wait for them."

Mom gave me the mover's number in case there was an issue. She updated me on her plans to move into the Tejedas' casita, and seemed very upbeat about the prospect. After I filled her in on progress with the house, I said, "I ran into an old friend of yours yesterday, a man named Khanh Duc."

"Oh, dear. Duc. I was just thinking about him. Funny how that happens, isn't it? I hadn't thought about him for years, and then out of the blue you mention him."

"I don't remember him," I said. "But he apparently spent a lot of time with Dad."

"I suppose. They had roses in common."

"Were you thinking about him because I brought up Mrs. Bartolini the other day?"

I heard her let out a deep breath before she said, "Yes."

"Is there a story there?"

"If there is, it isn't my story to tell," Mom said.

"Duc told me he and Mrs. B were from the same village in Vietnam."

"Maggie, you're digging."

"I am," I said. "Shamelessly. I heard something last night that cast what happened to her in a whole new light. Was there something between her and Duc?"

"I couldn't say," Mom said. "I only know they lost touch after their families were evacuated to Saigon."

"Until she ran into him at the refugee camp at the Presidio?"

"Yes."

"Did something develop after that?"

"Can we just say that they were old friends, and leave it at that?"

"I'm not sure," I said. "There was another man from their village that I think you knew."

"Van Thai?" she asked. "Yes. A very angry man."

"Do you have any idea where he is now?"

"None at all. Van worked for Tosh for a while. When Tosh fired him, he moved out of the area. I doubt I ever heard his name again until today."

The conversation was making Mom very uncomfortable. She knew something. But if Mom didn't want to talk about it, she wouldn't, so there was no point pursuing the issue. Didn't matter; her reluctance to answer had been answer enough. I changed the subject to Susan's expected arrival and news about various neighbors.

After we said good-bye, I called Kevin. His phone went straight to voice mail, so I left a message: "I want to see Mrs. B's murder book. And we need to talk. Very soon."

I hit speed dial and connected with my assistant, Fergie. I gave her the little I knew about Thai Van and his father, Thai Hung, and asked her to go into the network's news archives to see what she could find. And, if possible, find out where Van was now. As long as we were still connected to the network, I might as well use their resources.

A call from Uncle Max beeped the line. I ended the call to Fergie and said hello to Max.

"I'm on my way to SFO to pick up Guido," Max told me. "Do you want me to rent you a van or a pickup while I'm at the airport?"

"Please," I said. "I hope I'll only need it until Tuesday."

I looked at my watch as I calculated Max's travel time. If Guido's plane was on time and traffic on Bayshore wasn't too god-awful, they would be here in a couple of hours. I said good-bye to Max, turned off my phone and put it in my pocket.

Jean-Paul had wandered over to the garden. When I joined him, he was wiping bloom dust off a perfect tomato.

"What can be done?" he said, taking a bite out of the tomato. The juice ran halfway down his arm. He shook it off. "My mother is plotting with your grandmother."

"It's kind of cute," I said, wiping his chin with the tail of my shirt. "Very teenagery. Or is it dynastic? We aren't cousins to some degree, are we?"

"Not that I am aware. And certainly there is no great fortune at stake."

"Well, let them have their fun," I said.

"All is well with your mother?" he asked. "I didn't hear the usual laughter when you were speaking with her."

"She doesn't want me asking her questions about Trinh Bartolini."

"But she should know that only makes you more curious."

I laughed. "You'd think she would by now."

He touched my cheek. "I overheard you asking Fergie to locate Thai Van. There are some resources I can call on, if you want."

"Would you?"

"I should know better, but I will, as soon as I am back in Los Angeles."

"What time is your plane this afternoon?" I asked.

"Too soon." He looked at his watch. "Rafael is coming for me in the consul's car."

"Is there anything you want to see or do before you go?"

He smiled. "I can think of a couple of ways to pass the time that might be quite interesting, but instead, I want you to make good use of me for the little time remaining so that we can lock the door and leave here by Tuesday afternoon."

"Well then." I handed him a stack of sticky-note pads. "Pink is for the furniture I'm taking. Yellow is for Robnett family pieces my cousin needs to look at. Thrift store items are green and need to go to the garage for pick-up, and blue is staying here. Dad's books also need to go out to the garage."

We spent the rest of the morning affixing sticky notes and hauling stuff to the garage where it would be accessible for the trucks from the thrift store and the university library to haul away. Fortunately, the kitchen was finished. Roy and Lyle had sorted the kitchen cupboards when we were at the dump on Saturday, leaving full complements of dishes, pots, pans and utensils the tenants might need neatly stowed in the cupboards. The rest was carefully packed and labeled and ready to go. There was a nearly complete set of very old Wedgwood china for Susan, my parents' wedding china for Casey one day, and a few things that I wanted to keep. Lyle and Roy had taken with them a set of brightly colored vintage Fiestaware they had always admired. The rest we carried out to the garage for the thrift store truck that was due Monday morning.

The locksmith showed up while we were moving things into the garage. He reminded me about Sunday rates and I told him to install good bolts on all the doors, and to check all the windows on the ground floor to make sure their locks were good. And then we left him to his work.

When Max and Guido arrived, Jean-Paul and I took a break for lunch.

There was a frisson in the air between Jean-Paul and Guido, most of it emanating off Guido. We were longtime co-workers, good friends and nothing more. Except for one night when we were in Central America trying to file a news report about an attempted coup while we were under fire and had only a bottle of mescal for sustenance. Whatever happened that night—both of us blamed our lack of precise memory on the mescal—was never mentioned afterward. But Guido, of the Sicilian Patrini clan, just couldn't help being a bit possessive, and despite his efforts not to be, paternal.

I admit to feeling some relief when the front doorbell rang and interrupted their overly polite conversation. Though it was early, when I opened the door I expected to see Rafael standing on the welcome mat. Instead, it was Father John, wearing his white cassock and looking quite angelic.

"Come in," I said. "This is an unexpected pleasure. We're just sitting down to lunch. Will you join us?"

"I rarely say no to a meal." He followed me through the house to the backyard, commenting on the jumble the place was in at the moment. "Was there an earthquake I missed?"

"Looks like it," I said. "What brings you?"

"I need a favor," he said. "Beto was going to take all the food that the hungry ghosts and hungry friends didn't eat at the party last night and deliver it to the soup kitchen. I'm counting on it for lunch tomorrow. But he called me a bit ago to say that he had to take Bart to the hospital in the middle of the night and is still with him."

"What happened to Bart?" I asked.

"I don't know," Father John said. "But it looks like he'll be okay. I told Beto I would go by and see him later. But in the meantime, Larry, my fine cook and backup delivery boy, is nowhere to be found, again. Beto suggested I borrow your truck to pick up the leftovers and get them to the church basement."

"Sure. My truck's in the shop but we have a van," I said. "Do you need help loading the food?"

"I'd appreciate that," he said. "And there's one other little thing."

"Why am I suddenly quaking in my boots?"

He grinned. "I don't drive anymore."

After lunch, Uncle Max, doing a bit of matchmaking himself, volunteered his and Guido's services to Father John so that Jean-Paul and I could have our last few minutes alone. Before they left in the van Guido rented at the airport at Max's behest, we picked everything out of the garden that was ripe and sent it along.

The silence that followed the three of them out the door felt loaded, as if a bomb were about to drop inside the house.

"It was an interesting weekend, yes?" Jean-Paul slipped his hand into mine and walked me into the living room. Looking weary, and still holding my hand, he dropped into an easy chair.

"Interesting, yes," I said, perched on the arm of his chair. "It isn't every weekend that I dance in a couturier gown one day and get shot at the next. Or make love on a bed of rose petals."

"Ah, the damn rose petals." His cheeks colored from chagrin. "I was afraid I would bore you."

"You, bore me? Dear God, Jean-Paul, you may be the least boring man I know. I was afraid that the chaos of this weekend would frighten you away."

"I don't frighten easily." He canted his head to one side and quietly studied me for a moment, pensive.

"Maggie, you know that my wife, Marian, and I were very happy, as I know you and Mike were. I have missed her so terribly these last two years. Between us, everything was so—" He searched for the right words. "Peanut butter and jelly. I don't know how else to say it. Comfortable, I suppose. Sometimes, you remind me of her."

Last thing I wanted to hear: You remind me of my dead wife. Perhaps reading my reaction, though I tried not to show anything, he smiled in a self-deprecatory way, acknowledging a flub, and I relaxed.

"About the rose petals," he said, pulling me across his lap. He swept some loose hair from my cheek and tucked it behind my ear. "I was trying so very hard to be a dazzling French lover; it is expected of my countrymen, is it not?"

"You do your nation proud, Jean-Paul."

"*Tu es très gentille.*" With his palm against my cheek, he looked deep into my eyes. "You reminded me this afternoon that a small, spontaneous gesture can touch one's heart more profoundly than the most elaborate *grand geste.*"

"Did I?"

"Without any hesitation, you wiped my face with your shirt and then carried on as if it were the most ordinary thing in the world for you to do."

"It was. There was tomato juice on your chin."

"It was a gesture between intimates," he said. "Something I have missed very much."

"Yes." I put my hand over his, happy, comfortable, yet wary: Where were we headed?

"What I tried to say and got all muddled up earlier was that Marian always took whatever was thrown at her in stride—no fuss. It is a quality I cherish in you as well."

"Oh, I can make a dandy fuss," I said.

"No doubt. But when I stupidly did not tell you that evening attire was required for the reception Friday, you never complained, and on short notice found a solution that turned heads. Maggie, if you had shown up Friday wearing this stained shirt..." He tugged my shirttail. "You would have turned heads."

"I'm sure I would have." I laughed, wrapping my arms around his neck. "I can hear them now, 'Who's the babe with the imprint of the consul general's face on her shirt?'"

"Exactly." He kissed the top of my head. "Natural, like peanut butter and jelly."

Rafael arrived before that conversation could walk us further into the woods than we were ready to go.

Jean-Paul went upstairs and quickly changed into slacks and a dress shirt for the flight to Los Angeles. Because he would only be gone for a day, he took nothing with him except a book he found in Dad's den.

George Loper must have heard the Town Car pull up because he was on his front porch, standing watch, when I walked out with Jean-Paul.

Jean-Paul eyed him warily over my shoulder. "How long until Max and Guido are back?"

"Any time now."

When he made no move to get into the car, probably thinking of some way he could stay, I said, "Go. And hurry back."

I watched the Town Car disappear around the corner before I turned to go inside. George Loper was still on his porch. When I went in, I turned both of the new bolts on the door, hearing a very satisfying pair of clunks when they shot home.

I took advantage of the few available moments before the next wave of people arrived to gather myself. I found a bottle of good pinot noir in the stash Mom left behind for me, uncorked it, poured a glass, and to avoid the racket of the locksmith's drill, carried it out to the back-yard. It was early maybe to indulge in wine, especially when there was so much work to do, but it was summer and the afternoon was warm and sweet-smelling. I took a few minutes to do absolutely nothing except savor the day and sip my wine and walk around the garden. I felt buried beneath stuff, old family stuff, and not all of it was of a physical nature. It could just wait a little longer, I decided. I took out my phone and called Beto.

"How's your dad?" I asked.

"He'll be okay," Beto said. "Looks like he woke up in the night all confused, didn't know where he was. He went walking around in the dark and took a pretty good tumble. The docs are keeping him overnight again to check him out. They're talking about doing a brain scan tomorrow."

"He got overtired getting ready for the party."

"Probably," Beto said. "You saw how he was. He had a little fit dur-ing the party and I sent him to bed. I probably should have asked Doc Saracen to put down his beer and his egg roll and come inside to take a look at him right then. Twenty-twenty hindsight, huh?"

"I'll hope for the best."

"Hey, did Father John get in touch with you?"

"He did. My uncle is helping him."

"Our old friend Larry was supposed to do the delivery, but he flaked out."

"You weren't bothered that Larry was coming to your house to pick up the leftovers?"

"Why should I be?" he said. "That was then, this is now, if you know what I mean. We deliver bread from the deli to Father John's kitchen every morning. I've always had one of my guys make the run so I wouldn't risk bumping into Larry. But after talking to him, I know that was just stupid on my part. The man atoned; time for all of us to move on."

"Dear God, Beto," I said. "You sound like a grown-up."

"I'm just parroting Father John."

"And you sound tired," I said. "But it was a great party."

"Must have been," he said. "Dad wasn't the only casualty of the evening."

"Who else?"

"Lacy," he said. "Kevin put her in rehab last night."

"I'll light a candle."

"If only it were that easy. Hey, girly, I gotta go. I'll call if anything comes up."

"Please do."

Next, I texted Kevin: "Call me. Now."

* * *

Max and Guido were back and it was time to talk film business. Under the grape arbor, we went over our options for the Normandy project. Max had left several messages for Lana Howard, our executive producer at the network, but she hadn't responded to them—not a good sign. He was fairly confident that the network would eventually release funds to us, but the issue was when. Whatever they did, it was clear that our position with the network was increasingly fragile. We had alternatives. We could wait out the network. We could take the project to the French television production company and hope that a long-term relationship with them would develop. Or, as Guido preferred, we could strike out on our own and try to scare up independent funding and distribution. All three prospects had both potential benefits and unknown perils.

In the middle of the conversation, my phone buzzed. I looked at the I.D. screen. "Lana," I said, flipped on the speaker function and set the phone in the middle of the table.

"Lana," I said, speaking loudly. "This is the Lord's day. Why are you at work?"

"Are you underwater or something?" Lana snapped. "You sound weird."

"You're on speakerphone," I said. "I'm here with Max and Guido."

"With Max and Guido? I was hoping you and I could have a little private talk. Where the hell are you?"

"We're in Berkeley," I said. "Where the hell are you?"

"I'm in the middle of Malibu Canyon, sitting in my car in front of your house. That cowboy neighbor of yours wouldn't tell me a god-damn thing about where to find you."

"You could have called before heading up there."

"That's exactly what the bastard said." She was in full rant mode; I knew it only too well. We had worked together for a long time, and it had never been easy. Not, as Jean-Paul would say, a peanut butter and jelly relationship. "Your damn uncle—and I know you can hear this, Max—gave me some cockamamie story about you and Guido taking your production to someone else. After all these years, I can't believe you'd kick me to the curb like this."

"Lana, no one has kicked anyone, yet," Max said. "But you know how important this project is to Maggie and Guido, and how narrow the time window is. That makes me think that this foot-dragging over the budget is your own sweet way of kissing us off."

Guido chimed in, "That's how I read it."

"You read it wrong," she said. "This foot-dragging is more probably the head shed's way of kissing *me* off."

Max didn't need much time to consider that before he shook his head.

"You walk out on me," she said, "and I'm toast with the network."

"Television is a young man's business, Lana," Guido offered, wink-ing at me as he said it. He had more gray than black in his sideburns and a wrinkle or two; he was exactly my age. "A tough game."

"Yeah?" Lana countered. "Well I'm neither young nor a man, Guido. As long as you can shoulder your cameras you'll be okay in the business. And you, Maggie, my little sister, with a nip and a tuck and some good highlights you can last another ten, fifteen years in front of those damn cameras. I don't have your advantage of makeup and lighting when I go into meetings with the children who run the network now."

"By saying that, you aren't helping your case, my dear," Max said. "It's time for you to test whether you have enough mojo left at the network to take care of Maggie and Guido. Tell your money goons that they have until noon Tuesday to release funding, or we walk with the project. And, maybe just for the exercise, we sue them for breach of contract."

He snapped the phone off without uttering a sweet word of goodbye. Grinning, he said, "Bullshit. Pure manipulative bullshit."

Guido wasn't so sure. "If they dump Lana, will they keep us?"

"No one is dumping Lana," Max said. "She has too many of those goons by the *cojones* for them to release her."

"I liked the little sister gambit," I said. "Last Christmas she canceled our series without shedding any tears over it, and brought us back three months later without any fanfare or apology. If that's family, Guido my love, maybe we should run away from home."

"Is that a decision?" he asked, looking hopeful. "You know what I want to do."

"Lana was right about one thing," I said, feeling every one of my years. "You have better job prospects than I do if we fall on our faces. I propose this: We give Lana until Tuesday noon to move the network to fulfill their end of the contract. But if the money isn't in our account by the stroke of twelve, then Max should accept the French offer for the project. After that, we'll see where we are. Whichever way it goes, I have a feeling that after this one, we'll be on our own again the way we were when we started out."

"Suits me," Guido said. "But is that a good or a bad thing for you?"

"Hell if I know," I said. "Max?"

"Nothing we can do until Tuesday." He fiddled with his snazzy watch. "I've started the countdown. Lana has exactly forty-six hours, eleven minutes to move her people. In the meantime, you two need to book your flight to Paris and pack your bags. I'll drive you to the airport, myself. One way or another, you will commence filming in Normandy by the first of August."

There was a little more give and take, but that's where we left it.

Roy and Lyle had worn out Max with the clubbing the night before, so he went upstairs to take a nap. Guido and I sat down to talk about old business. There were still some continuity issues with the *Crooked Man* film we had been working on since late spring. The air date wasn't until fall Sweeps Week, but we had put in long hours to get it finished early so that we could leave for France as soon as the financing arrived.

We were happy with the film overall, but it still needed a final tweak for us to be completely satisfied with it. We made notes about what needed to be done, and then Guido headed off to San Francisco to use an editing bay at the studio of the network's local affiliate. He planned to work late and bunk overnight with Lyle and Roy. If all went well, by Monday afternoon he might have a finished version to show me.

I saw him off, turned my phone back on and checked for a message from Kevin: nothing. I texted him, "Call."

As soon as I sent the text, the phone buzzed. Not Kevin, though, but my cousin Susan. Would I mind if she arrived just a bit later than planned? She had met some interesting people during her week at wine camp—her sommelier course—and wanted to join them for a last glass of wine before everyone took off. I told her she should have fun. There were no specific plans for dinner, except that we would dine out and Uncle Max would pick up the check.

The locksmith finished his work, showed me what he had done, and handed me a bill that made my eyes roll back in my head. I dug my checkbook out of my bag, and paid him. He handed me a receipt and a fistful of nicely labeled keys to add to the growing collection. I pulled a bowl out of a kitchen cupboard and dumped them all into it.

Fergie, my assistant, hadn't checked in to tell me what she had found about Thai Van, so I called her.

"Do you know how many Thai Vans and Van Thais there are?" she asked. "I looked into the Vietnamese nationalist groups in Little Saigon, and didn't find your guy. A lot of people anglicize their names, so he could be calling himself Tommy Van or Vincent Thai, or Epaminondas, for all I know. But I did find his father, Thai Hung. That is, I found his obituary. The son is named in the obit, but that's it."

I thanked her for her efforts and asked her to keep at it. And then I went back to work.

I was making my third trip to the garage with kitchen boxes when the service manager at the Ford dealership called with a bit of good news. Though their body shop was closed on Sunday, the police had just released the hold on my pickup, a surprise because Kevin had told me that the ballistics techs couldn't get to it until Monday. As soon as I came in and signed the repair estimate, the service manager would order parts so they could get to work on the truck first thing in the morning. I needed my truck back. I told him I would be right down.

I texted Kevin again, asking him to call ASAP this time and adding three exclamation points. Then I wrote a note telling Max where I was headed, took his car keys and drove his rented Caddy to the dealership on MLK, Jr.

"Looks like you got caught in the shootout at the OK Corral yesterday." Bill—that's what his shirt said—at the service desk slid a sheaf of papers across the counter toward me. "You were the second vehicle we got in yesterday afternoon with gunfire damage. Everyone in your truck get through it okay?"

"Fortunately," I said as I read over the estimate. I cringed: new side panel, new dashboard, new disc player, rear window, and on, and on. Insurance would cover all but the deductible, but from the list of work to be done, I wouldn't get the truck back as soon as I hoped. I signed the bottom and slid the paperwork back. "Everyone okay in the other car?"

"No injuries," Bill said. "Side-view mirror was blown off, there are a couple of divots in the door frame. Shots must have gone straight through that car and into yours."

"Small silver car?" I asked.

"A Ford Focus." He looked up from separating my copy of the estimate from the original. "Did you see it get hit?"

"Everything happened pretty fast," I said. "Who was driving?"

"I'm sorry," he said, smiling as he handed me my copy. "We don't give out personal customer information. You never know who might be suing who, right?"

"Just curious," I said. "When do you think I can have my truck back?"

He looked at the calendar on the wall behind him as he counted on his fingers. "Friday, maybe, if all the parts come in. More likely not until next Monday or Tuesday."

"Peachy," I said, dismayed. With luck and hard work, I would be at home, sleeping in my own bed by this Tuesday night. I needed the truck to haul things I was taking with me. Now it looked like I would have to rent something bigger than the van Guido drove from the airport, or hire a hauler. The next problem was getting my truck picked up and stored until I could get back up and fetch it. I could ask yet another favor of Lyle and Roy, but I was loath to. That big truck would be a pain to handle on the narrow streets of their San Francisco neighborhood. Maybe I could impose on Beto to pick it up and keep it for a little while.

As I folded the paperwork I saw the signature of the policeman who released the car. I asked, "When was Detective Halloran in?"

"He left just before I called you."

Bill wrote my name in big red letters across the top of my work order and dumped it into a rack on the wall behind the desk. As he did, I saw the name atop the work order filed just ahead of mine.

I thanked Bill, and left.

Kevin was waiting for me outside in the parking lot. He opened the passenger door of his unmarked city car and said, "Get in."

"What happened to *please?*" I said as I passed him on my way into the car. He just shook his head. He looked like hell, unshaven, edgy, but in his situation, who wouldn't? Beto told me Kevin had just signed his wife into rehab. When was the last time he'd had a full night's sleep?

While he fumbled for his seat belt, he asked, "What's the bite for your repairs?"

I pulled out my copy of the estimate and handed it to him. The amount on the bottom after the dollar sign made him blanch.

"Have you filed a repair claim with your insurance company yet?" he asked.

"It's taken care of," I said.

Slowly, he turned toward me. "Is that a yes?"

"I called my agent yesterday. She got the incident report from the Highway Patrol and gave approval to the dealership to make the repairs. Other than waiting for the repairs to be done and paying the deductible, I'm finished."

All the blood drained from his face. He started to say something, but his eyes filled and he looked away.

"Take your time," I said, pulling a tissue from the box in the console and handing it to him.

He blew his nose and drew a couple of shaky breaths, started the car and drove out of the lot. At the first red light, he reached behind his seat, grabbed a blue three-ring binder and handed it to me.

"This what you want?" he asked.

I looked at the binder's spine, saw the name TRINH "TINA" NGUYEN BARTOLINI, the date of her death and her case number. When I texted Kevin earlier and asked for the investigation log—the murder book—I now held in my hands, I had expected a big argument, and for legal reasons there probably should have been one. But with no whining, bribery or cajolery, he had brought me the original old-style, paper-and-ink murder book that was assembled by the detectives who originally worked Mrs. B's case over thirty years ago. The paper was yellowing and smelled of dust and maybe some mildew. I could see finger marks and penciled notations, and foxing on the edges of pages thumbed by detectives one year after the next ever since. No digital file could ever have the authenticity this hard-copy record bore.

"Where are we going?" I asked.

"The crime scene," he said. "Indian Rock Park. Okay with you?"

"Fine with me," I said, scanning the log of evidence collected by the coroner: gunshot residue, blood type, fingernail scrapings, hair, pubic hair, sexual assault kit, bullet(s), clothing. The coroner's narrative report and a diagram followed.

Even though the Deputy Medical Examiner's choice of words, meant to be objective—just the facts—revealed no emotion, I found it difficult to remain detached. I kept seeing Mrs. B as I had known her in life and as I saw her in her coffin, dressed in white, as serene as a Botticelli angel. I had witnessed autopsies where case-hardened medical examiners wept, but still wrote their reports with bland objectivity. Nowhere did the report on my lap mention that Mrs. Bartolini was a beautiful young mother when she died, or that her death affected an entire community. Had Alameda County Deputy Medical Examiner R. Suzuki known how special my friend's mother was? Was she handled with dignity? Or was she merely the next victim in the assembly line of victims to be dealt with?

The medical examiner's report said the cause of death was a through-and-through gunshot wound to the chest. The victim had a large contusion and abrasions on her right hip, contusions on the right shoulder, contusions and abrasions on the right temple area. The

injuries were consistent with a fall onto a hard, flat surface. Carpet
fibers found in the hip abrasions suggested she was unclothed when
they occurred. Though there was evidence of recent sex, and semen
was collected, there were no vaginal or anal contusions, abrasions, or
tearing. No tissue was found under her fingernails. The blood inside
her mouth could have been her own.

Kevin stayed on MLK, Jr. to Hopkins. I didn't look up until he took
the hairpin loop to connect with Indian Rock Avenue so fast I had to
grab onto the hand rest to stay upright. I said, "Careful, Officer, you'll
get a ticket."

Finally, a trace of smile crossed his face, but it wasn't much. Something was up with him, and I had a very bad feeling I knew what it
was.

Kevin pulled over near a park entrance, got out and waited for me.
I brought the murder book along, opened to the plastic sleeves that
held the Polaroids taken of Mrs. Bartolini lying among the boulders
nearby.

According to the first homicide investigation report, Mrs. B's body
was discovered by a mailman who stopped on his route during his
lunch break to fill his water bottle at the fountain near the park sign.
But because there are no rest rooms in the park, before he filled his
bottle he went between some boulders to relieve himself, and that's
when he saw her.

Feeling a little queasy to be standing on the spot where she was
found while looking at photos of her body, I turned to look down
across the Bay, saw that the sun had already dropped into the fog bank
obscuring the Golden Gate. It was late in the day, already cooling off.
The rocks around us would radiate accumulated heat for hours after
the sun disappeared. Mrs. Bartolini had been found before noon on
a cool but sunny fall day. She was lying in the shade, but the rocks
around her would have been warm.

I looked back and forth between the Polaroids and the place.

"Kevin, what time did we head off for school in the morning?"

"Around eight, I guess."

"Mrs. B died some time between then and just before noon, right?"

"Yep."

"When she saw Beto off that morning, she was wearing a powder blue shirtwaist dress and low-heeled black pumps." I held the coroner's evidence log for him to see. "According to this, when she was found she was wearing a white blouse and nothing else."

"Okay."

"It isn't a blouse." I pointed at the button placket visible in the Polaroid close-up of her chest area, a bloody mass speckled with black gunpowder burns. "It's a man's shirt."

As he looked at the photo, he fingered the placket at the neck of his polo shirt, checking which side the buttons were on. He said, "I'll be damned."

"According to the medical examiner, Mrs. B was naked on the bottom when she fell or was pushed. At some point, and in some order, she had intercourse, put on a man's shirt, and was shot in the chest."

"That's what it says."

"Where is the shirt now?" I asked.

"In a sealed evidence bag locked up in my office."

"Is there a laundry mark? Maybe remnants of fluids from more than one person?"

He glanced askance at me. "How much do the TV people pay you to snoop, Sherlock?"

"I'm doing okay."

"I'll send the shirt to the crime analyst and ask him to check it out." With the back of his hand, he wiped away sweat running down the side of his face. "See anything else?"

"Lots of blood on the shirt, but there wasn't very much blood found here in the park," I said. "She was murdered elsewhere and dumped. It wouldn't take a very strong person to carry her because she barely weighed a hundred pounds."

"That we know, but no crime scene was ever determined," he said. "You think you know what happened?"

"I have some ideas," I said. "How long can I keep the book?"

"You can't keep something you never saw," he said. "It's an open murder case and that's a confidential police document. Besides, I don't ever, ever want Beto to get a look at what's in there. I keep the book."

I looked around for a boulder in the shade to sit on. "Then give me a minute with it, okay?"

"Take your time." He started up the steps that were cut into the face of a granite tower. "Whistle when you're finished."

I opened the book and began reading the investigation reports. Mrs. Bartolini's body was identified by Patrol Officer Ray Gutierrez, who knew her because he frequented the Bartolini Deli and because he and the victim attended the same church. The police captain who responded to the scene dispatched Officer Gutierrez to collect Father John and to go with him to inform Bart of his wife's death. Bart took the news as expected, hard, and was driven home from his place of work by Officer Gutierrez. Father John stayed with Bart while Officer Gutierrez went to the school to pick up Beto. Father John was worried enough about Bart's state of mind that he summoned the family physician, Dr. Benjamin Nussbaum, who administered a sedative. Any questioning of Mr. Bartolini was postponed until, in police-report-speak, "such a time that he was not under the influence of sedation."

The first conversation between Bart and the police happened three days after the murder. Bart went by the police station to retrieve his wife's wedding ring so that she could be buried with it, and stayed to answer some questions posed by Detective Charles Riley. According to the interview summary, he was at the deli all that morning. His lovely wife had no enemies. Period. I could hear what my late husband, Mike, would have to say about the softball questions Chuck Riley lobbed at Bart, who should have been his first suspect. But Mike worked detectives in great big, occasionally murderous Los Angeles, and not in relatively peaceful little Berkeley. Kevin had already told me that his department didn't get much experience working homicides. Everyone in town knew Mr. B, and knew that he doted on his beautiful young wife. But still...

What happened to Beto? I flipped through the pages but found nothing except that when the police left the Bartolini house that evening, Beto, Father John, Doc Nussbaum, and Dr. Brian Halloran, the head counselor at the high school—Kevin's father—were "inside the residence."

"Hey." Kevin's shadow fell across the book. I looked up and spotted him leaning over a ledge about fifteen feet above me. "Did you know there's a cross chiseled on the rocks up here?"

"I saw it the other day," I said. "But I don't remember seeing it before."

"Me either." He started down the steps. "Last time I was up here I think I was with you. We wouldn't have seen it though, because it was dark when we came up to watch submarine races."

"*Uncle* Kevin," I said, ignoring the remark. "When did you and Beto become such great friends?"

"It started then." He indicated the book on my lap as he walked toward me. "Old Bart was a basket case after Mrs. B died."

"I remember. The report says your dad was at their house that afternoon."

"Father John asked Dad to go over and talk to Beto, to make sure he had what he needed. They decided that because Dad was a school counselor and Mom was a nurse, they'd be able to look after Beto until Bart could pull himself together, so Dad brought him home. He stayed with us off and on for maybe a year, until Aunt Quynh got out of Vietnam and contacted Bart. There were a lot of crazy rumors going around. Dad wanted me to make sure the kids at school weren't…"

He searched for a word. I said, "Kids?"

"I was going to say little shits." His color was better than it had been when he picked me up.

"That's when you started walking to school with us." My shade had disappeared so I got up and moved into the shadows cast by the rocks.

He followed me. "Yeah. I'd walk him over to your street and meet you guys, make sure you didn't stop to rumble with any more bullies on the way to school."

"I keep seeing Father John's hand in our lives," I said, leaning my back against the rough, warm stone. "He's the keeper of everyone's deepest, darkest secrets. I wonder how he can sleep at night."

"Maybe he doesn't." Kevin fell quiet, his focus on something far, far away. "Maybe that's why he's sick."

"You're not going to say Father John is dying for our sins, are you?"

"No." The corner of his mouth came up in a semblance of a wry smile. "Dying from the weight of them, maybe."

"Kev?" I put my hand on his arm and waited until he looked down at me. "You ready to tell me why you decided to show me the murder book?"

There was a fresh breeze coming in off the Bay, and we were in the shade, but he broke out into a sweat again and seemed to have difficulty breathing. I was afraid he would pass out. I put my hand against his cheek and made him meet my eyes.

I said, "Beto told me you signed Lacy into rehab last night."

He shook his head. Choked with emotion, he managed to say, "I committed her on a seventy-two-hour psych hold. Danger to herself and to others."

"Namely, a danger to me?"

"You had it figured out, didn't you?" he said.

"After overhearing what you said to her last night when you manhandled her out of the Bartolinis' backyard, I started to wonder," I said. "But it wasn't until I saw your name on the work order for repairs to a certain shot-up silver car that I actually knew."

"That crazy bitch," he said, dropping his head into his hands for a moment before he straightened up and faced me. "Yesterday afternoon, I went over to the dealership to make sure your truck was locked in a secure area until the ballistics techs could go over it. And there was Lacy's car, already parked at the body shop. She shot off her own side mirror, for chrissake."

"The good news is, Lacy is a lousy shot and no one got hurt."

He let out a long, labored breath. "My career is over."

"Oh, sweetie, lots of cops have crazy wives." I patted his shoulder. "If they all got fired when their wives spun out of control, there would be no one left to write tickets. You'll get through this, Kevin. Just tell me you haven't done anything really stupid yet, like filing a false report or making anything disappear?"

"I've thought about it."

"Does Lacy have a psych history?" I asked.

"Oh, yeah."

"Then get her a good lawyer and let it all play out, Kev," I said. "It's up to the Oakland PD to file charges, and so far they don't seem inclined to get overly involved. Your insurance company will probably pay mine off and then cancel your coverage, but that's the worst they'll do."

"I'll have to file a report with my department," he said.

"Do what you need to do," I said. "I won't press charges, Kevin. You didn't need to try to bribe me with the murder book, but I'm glad you did."

He let out a long breath, one he may have been holding for the last day. "Know a good lawyer?"

"Uncle Max will," I said. "He's at the house now. Take me back to my car and then you go right over and talk to him."

"Are the Lopers on patrol?"

"Of course they are, but surely you haven't forgotten the secret way into my backyard?"

He laughed, a big, full-chested *ha-ha-ha* that verged on sobs. Without warning, he pulled me against him and held me in a tight bear hug.

"God, Mag, I've missed you."

"Just don't flip me, Kev," I said, my face pressed against the front of his sweaty polo. "And don't tickle me. Okay?"

"Okay." He set me on my feet and released me. "Not this time."

As he drove us back down the hill, I turned toward him. "Yesterday, no one knew where Jean-Paul and I were going, not even us. So, how the hell did Lacy track us down?"

"She followed you," he said.

"All day? Impossible. I would have seen her."

"How many silver cars do you think were out there on the freeway yesterday? Would you notice one little piece-of-shit Focus?"

"Maybe not. So, has Lacy been lying in wait for me?"

"She didn't have to," he said. "You know where her folks live, right?"

I nodded. "Across from Beto."

"The other night, when I picked her up from your house, I took her to her parents' house because I didn't want my daughter to see her like that. She had it in her head that I was hanging out with you. When she saw your truck go by on Saturday with a man driving, she assumed it was me. So she grabbed her dad's gun from a drawer in the front hall table and lit out after you."

"And stuck with us all afternoon?"

He nodded. "All afternoon, probably dogging you, waiting to get a good shot. This isn't exactly pickup country so your truck wasn't hard to follow."

"It wasn't me she was shooting at, though, was it? It was you."

"What can I say?"

"Hell hath no fury?" I said.

"Crazy jealous bitch?"

"Hey, Kev?"

"Mmm?"

"The other night, when Lacy was pounding on my front door because she thought you were inside with me, what if the door had been unlocked and she had been able to come in, and if she'd had her dad's gun with her then, what would she have done?"

"Probably woulda shot you through the heart."

Chapter 14

"OH MY GOD, MAGGIE." With delicate hands, my cousin Susan took the dragonfly brooch out of its red leather box and held it up to the light. The gems sent streamers of bright color across the room. "I had no idea this still existed. There's a portrait of our great-grandmother on the wall at home. In it she's wearing this brooch. Dad told me it was a very special anniversary gift. I can't believe I'm holding it."

"It's beautiful, isn't it?" I said, feeling just a pang of regret seeing the brooch for probably the last time. "Mom always wore it on special occasions. I hope you enjoy it as much as she did."

"Me?" Susan seemed taken aback. "Thank you for showing it to me, but it's your mother's."

"Mom says it's time for the next generation to wear it."

"But it should pass to you and Casey, not me."

I shook my head. The brooch had passed from mother to daughter in Mom's family for three generations. But I was not part of Mom's bloodline. As much as I cherished my memories of evenings when Mom dressed up, and last thing and with some ceremony, pinned the brooch to her dress, I felt that the jewel could not rightfully come to me. I was, however, keeping the black dress I wore on Friday night, and that was memory enough.

I said, "The brooch should go to you and your daughter, Maddie."

"What does your mom say about that?"

"I told her what I think, and she left the decision to me."

"Oh my." Susan held the brooch against her shoulder and looked at it in the mirror over Mom's dressing table before she put it back in its box. "I'll have to think about that."

Standing beside her, I looked at Susan's reflection in the mirror. She was still as pretty as I remembered her, blue-eyed, with dark blond hair, and tall like the women in Mom's family. Indeed, she closely resembled Mom and my deceased older sister, Emily. Growing up, people often said I was Daddy's girl, though I had no clue until last fall how literally true that was. My sister and brother and I all had Dad's long nose, and looked enough like each other that if it ever occurred to me that I hadn't inherited Mom's height or her hair, it also never occurred to me that I might not be biologically connected to her. That revelation struck me the very first time I met Isabelle's mother, Élodie Martin, and saw how closely I resemble her.

"Susan," I said, "the brooch is a Robnett family heirloom. It needs to remain within your family."

She met my eyes in the mirror. "Maggie, I would be lying if I said that I wasn't absolutely shocked when I found out that Aunt Betsy isn't your birth mother."

"You and me both," I said, laughing a bit, surprised by her frankness. The topic was awkward for me, but I had brought it up.

"No one in the family ever said one word to me about it," she said. "You know why?"

"Too scandalous for words?" I asked.

"No, not that at all," she said, turning to face me. "Truthfully, I think everyone just put it out of their minds, a non-issue, if you will. You were a fully enfranchised member of the family, and how that came about, well, so what?

"Last fall, when Aunt Betsy called Dad and warned him that you had found out about your relationship to the Martin woman—"

"Isabelle."

"Isabelle," she repeated. "And because you are who you are, the whole story would be on TV. Dad summoned us for a family meeting so that he could tell us about you and her before it went public. He said that there are some secrets that are just too big to be kept forever. They always knew that the truth would come out someday. He said they had only hoped it wouldn't happen before you were old enough to understand."

I laughed. "I'm not sure I'll ever understand, and I'm even less sure that I want to. Maybe some secrets should just stay secrets."

"Maybe so." She put an arm around me and bent her head close to mine. "Maggie, to my parents—to me—you are family. Period."

We went downstairs to drag Uncle Max out to dinner. He and Kevin had been holed up together in Dad's den for a couple of hours, supposedly talking through Kevin's legal issues, though I thought they had wandered far afield by now and it was time to extricate Max.

On the stairs, Susan leaned toward me and spoke in a very soft voice. "The man with Max looks so familiar. I know I've seen him before. Who is he?"

"I'm sorry I didn't take care of introductions earlier, but the poor guy's in a bit of a legal pickle at the moment and I didn't want to interrupt them," I said. "You have seen him before, though. That's Kevin, my high school boyfriend."

"Kevin? Oh my God," she said, a little giggly. "Remember that Christmas my family flew out? I think we were maybe juniors in high school."

"I remember," I said. "You were having a blizzard. When Mom told your dad that it was eighty degrees out here, your family was on the first available flight out of Cleveland."

"Your parents made you drag me along everywhere you went."

"They didn't make me, Susan. I wanted to. We had fun, didn't we?"

"Poor Kevin, though. He was so cute."

"He still has his moments."

Max looked up when we appeared at the den door. "Ladies?"

"Ladies are hungry," I said.

Kevin lumbered to his feet. "Sorry to hold you up."

We went through proper introductions. Kevin did his best to be gracious, but I could see the effort it took.

"Anyone else need a drink?" Max asked. Sometime during the afternoon, he had decanted a bottle of red wine that he wanted Susan, a newly certificated sommelier, to try. He poured wine into wide-bowled goblets and I handed them around.

As I gave a glass to Kevin, in the interest of moving us all closer to the front door, I asked, "Join us for dinner?"

"Thanks, but I can't." He held up the wineglass. "This hits the spot, but I need to get home. I'd rather tell the kids myself about what's going on than have them hear it on the street. Or worse, on Facebook."

"Chin up, my boy." Max clinked his glass against Kevin's. "I'll make those calls and get back to you tomorrow."

Susan was looking closely at the marquetry table next to Dad's reading chair. The table had a blue sticky, meaning it was staying.

"This is pretty," she said.

"It's something Dad dragged home." And it was.

Berkeley has a transient population of students. Many of them furnish their residences with cast-offs they find in family attics, garages, and barns. Who knows what treasures might lie buried under their piles of textbooks, laundry, bongs, hookahs, and dirty dishes for the length of their tenure at the university? When they break up housekeeping and move on to the next thing, students frequently dump their furniture on the curb, making it available for anyone to pick up before the trashmen haul it away.

My dad and Dr. Nussbaum now and then would carry home pieces of furniture that caught their eye. That's how Dad acquired his big early-twentieth-century desk and the round marquetry table that he put beside his reading chair. Not a skimpy end table, it was big enough and sturdy enough to accommodate a lamp, a decanter of scotch and a tray of glasses, a telephone, and maybe three stacks of books at a time. It was tall enough that everything on top was within Dad's reach.

Now the table held only a lamp, a telephone, the wine decanter, and a yellow legal pad covered with Max's precisely made notes from his conversation with Kevin.

Susan nodded with appreciation when I told her how Dad had acquired it.

"He had a good eye; it looks like an exceptional piece," she said. "Two of my friends who are coming tomorrow, Ann and Angie, are antiques dealers. They're more interested in jewelry, but they'll be able to give you a rough idea what its history is. You might change your mind about leaving it."

While we were talking about furniture, Max saw Kevin out. When he came back into the den he poured himself more of the wine. Holding it up to the light, he said, "What do you think about that wine, Susan?"

"It's lovely," she said. She twirled her glass and put her nose into the bowl. "Full-bodied, earthy, a hint of anise, I think." She took a sip and seemed to chew it before she swallowed. "There's a nice mineral cleanness. I get hints of pepper and black cherry with a bit of chocolate in the finish. What is it?"

"It's a Central Coast blend. The label calls it 'Red Table Wine' and I like it," he said. "Heavy on zinfandel, I think."

"The instructor in our course had good things to say about the Central Coast red wines," she said. "He told us he thinks that Napa Valley has become a sort of Disneyland for wine drinkers, overcrowded and overpriced. The real innovation is happening at small wineries down south."

Max and I agreed that Napa Valley is overcrowded with tourists, especially during the summer. We both preferred the Central Coast wine region, in no small part because it is easier for us to get there from LA. I told her about a favorite oceanfront boutique hotel in San Simeon, a short and beautiful drive over the Santa Lucias to some of the wineries her instructor recommended. Before we left for dinner, she had placed a conference call to the friends who were joining her in the morning, and received permission to cancel their hotel reservations in Calistoga and find new accommodations in San Simeon. That mission was accomplished with two more phone calls, and they were set to explore the wine country further south.

"I have never heard of five women reaching consensus that easily," Max said as he ushered us out the front door.

"We're from Minneapolis, remember," she said, patting his shoulder as she passed him. "They were sold at 'oceanfront.'"

We walked down to a small Indian restaurant across the street from the drugstore where Dad had captured Isabelle on film. All through the meal, I kept looking out the window at the door she had stepped out of, almost expecting her to be there, waiting for us when we left the restaurant.

Jean-Paul said that ghosts live only in the imaginations of the living. That doesn't mean they aren't real.

"Worn out, Maggie?" Max asked when he noticed that I had dropped out of the conversation.

"A bit, yes." I folded my napkin under the edge of my plate. "It hit me today that once we hand the house keys over to the university, I won't have a connection to this place anymore."

"You still have friends here," he said.

I thought about that for a moment before I said, "What I have here is a history. All in the past."

He caught the waiter's eye and signaled for the check. "Susan, it's time to take our girl home and tuck her in."

As we turned up our front walkway, George Loper came out onto his porch.

"How long is that damn Dumpster going to sit there?" he wanted to know.

"It's scheduled for pick-up tomorrow," I said.

"Okay then. If it's out there any longer, it's going to start smelling."

"Good night, Mr. Loper," I said, pulling out the house keys. There should have been nothing in the Dumpster that smelled worse than old rubber balls or well-worn tennis shoes, but I had to admit that, as I passed it, I caught a whiff of something that had acquired a certain gamey tang. Maybe a neighbor had contributed some household garbage to the mix inside.

Later, with Max snoring in the room next door to mine and Susan safely tucked in bed in the room at the end of the hall, I slept the sleep of the dead.

MONDAY MORNING, five trucks were scheduled to come and haul things to various destinations. The first of them arrived early, before we had finished our first cups of coffee. Uncle Max declared that he would be most helpful if he stayed out of the way. He took his telephone and his yellow legal pad to the backyard to make phone calls on Kevin's behalf and I went out front to make sure that whoever was backing into the driveway did not go off the side into Dad's beautiful flower borders.

A staffer and a student assistant from the university library came to pick up the books the science librarian had selected from Dad's collection. They loaded the boxes quickly and were hardly out of the driveway before the truck from the thrift store arrived. The pile of donations in the garage seemed huge, but the crew worked efficiently and had it loaded in a surprisingly short time; I could again see most of the garage floor. As the driver handed me a receipt for Mom's tax records, I asked him to please come again on Tuesday for what I hoped would be one last load.

With space in the garage now cleared away, after I swept the floor I would be able to bring out the things I was taking home so that the house cleaning crew scheduled for Tuesday could do their work unimpeded by extraneous clutter. We were still waiting for the piano movers to pick up Mom's baby grand and the haulers who would ship Susan's pieces to her home in Minneapolis. The refuse company promised to pick up the Dumpster and replace it with an empty as soon as a truck was available; as the day grew warmer, the gaminess coming from the Dumpster grew more pungent.

Susan had looked closely at everything marked with a yellow sticky note, deciding what to keep and what to leave. She knew right away that an armoire in an upstairs bedroom and the long mahogany sideboard in the dining room that had come from the family farm in Ohio, furniture that was oversized for most contemporary houses, belonged in the nearly century-old house in South Minneapolis she and her husband Bob had restored. There were other pieces that she found interesting or were very old, but thought might not be worth the cost and hassle of shipping. With a felt marker, she put question marks on their sticky notes.

I am not much of a decorator. My cousin is. She helped me shove aside the furniture I was taking home with me so that we could see what would be left for the tenants. There were a few pieces with blue sticky notes, designating that they were staying, that she thought I might want to think about keeping, Dad's chair-side table among them. She put question marks on those notes as well.

Father John called when I was in the kitchen getting us each a fresh cup of coffee.

"McGumption," he said, "My stalwart cook, Larry, is still MIA. I could use some help with lunch today. Sorry for the short notice, and I know you have things to do, but I was hoping you might be able to give me a hand."

"I would, Padre," I said. "But there is just too much going on here this morning for me to leave. Why don't you call Kevin Halloran? Tell him I said he should help you. It'll do him good."

"Fine idea," he said. "Fine idea." He did not, and would never, say a word about why he thought so, but I knew. Kevin could certainly have used some of Father John's wise counsel, or just a good listener, as long as the price to pay wasn't a string of Hail Marys and Our Fathers; Kevin had fallen away from the church long before I had.

With her friends due in from the Oakland Airport at any time, Susan and I retreated to the dining room. She helped me move a stack of boxes someone had set on top of the access hatch to the gravity heater under the house so that the inspector coming Tuesday could get at it. Then we sat on the floor in front of the sideboard she was taking and sorted out its contents. She was interested in the old linens. There were tablecloths, napkins, runners, and doilies variously embellished with crocheted edges, Madeira work, embroidery, ladder-stitched hems, hand-painted or silk-screened flowers and bucolic scenes. Some had come down through Mom's family, some from Dad's, and some my parents had acquired during their fifty-eight years together. Neither Susan nor I had any idea what came from where, and it didn't really matter. As we went through them, taking turns making selections, we got caught up on family and each other.

"I always loved Max," she said, setting aside hand-crocheted antimacassars I didn't remember ever seeing before—too fussy for Mom's taste, and mine. "But he's awfully young to be your uncle. Is there a story?"

"A short one," I said. "When Dad was in college, his mother died. A year or two later, my grandfather married again, a younger woman, and they had Max. When Max was about ten, his parents died in an accident on an icy road. And Max came to live at our house."

"You and I weren't around yet, were we?"

"No. Mark and Emily were just toddlers, I think, and they were fourteen years older than me. Max was like their big brother, but he always made them call him Uncle. Me, too, when I finally showed up."

Susan folded a linen tablecloth and matching napkins into a box. "I was sorry Bob and I couldn't come out for Emily's funeral. I was abroad somewhere, working on a project."

"Your mom and dad came," I said. "It was good to see them. But to tell you the truth, my parents were so numb that I doubt they noticed who was there and who wasn't. They were burying their second child, and it's just not supposed to happen that way for parents."

"No it isn't."

Odd though, that before I thought about Mom and Dad at Emily's funeral, an image of Bart Bartolini at his wife's service flashed behind my eyes.

My sister lay locked in a coma for several years before she decided to die. I think that all of us who loved her suffered through the worst shockwaves of grief at the beginning, when she was shot, so that by the time of her funeral, though we were all sad because the inevitable had at last occurred, there was more than a little relief that her ordeal, and ours, was at last over.

It had been very different when Mark died in Vietnam. For weeks, maybe months, after the news of his death came, my parents moved through space and time as if they were deaf and blind tourists from another place floating among us in their own fragile bubble. They didn't always hear me when I spoke to them, they answered questions I never asked. From moment to moment they forgot where they were and what they had been doing. Dinner burned on the stove. And Max slept on the floor in my room until the worst was over.

That somnolent, semi-coherent state they were in is the way I remember Bart after his wife died. It would have been as pointless for the police to interview him then as it would have been to ask Mom to recite the Gettysburg Address after Mark died.

"Maggie?" Susan rubbed my hand. "I'm sorry. Talking about Emily made you sad."

"No." I sat up straight and took a deep breath. "I'm just very ready to be finished here."

The four book club friends arrived in a flurry of excited conversation. All those female voices brought Max inside.

It took a few minutes to sort Ann from Angie and Jean from Maureen:

"The baby in the seat behind me cried through the entire flight."

"I love this house. It reminds me of my grandmother's."

"Is that a Stickley chair?"

"It was so humid when we left home, and it is so lovely here. What a relief."

Max, ever the charmer, was in his element. "We have the advantage of that great big offshore air-conditioner," he said, responding to the comment about the weather. "What you need in Minnesota is an ocean."

They laughed, and he loved hearing it. They were all, like Susan, smart, attractive career women. They had met many years earlier, when they worked in the marketing department of the company that made sticky notes, and stayed friends. Two of them, Jean and Maureen, still worked there, though the other three had moved on. As a group, they felt right at home when they saw all the furniture festooned with little pastel paper squares.

"I'm tempted to call my boss and offer him a new marketing angle for the product," Maureen said when Susan explained my labeling system. "If he goes for it, Maggie, you'll get a finder's fee."

"I wouldn't turn it down," I said. She was kidding, I wasn't.

Ann and Angie, who dealt in antiques, declared Dad's chair-side table to be too valuable to leave behind. Who knew what abuse the tenants might heap upon it? I had already decided to take it with me, but hadn't pulled off its blue note. I was taking the chair and its mate, and it had occurred to me when Susan brought my attention to it that the table belonged with them; I would somehow make space for the three pieces in my home workroom.

There was a discussion about a rocking chair in the sun porch that Mom said her great-grandfather had made. The experts agreed that the rocker was very old, quite plain, worth little, and absolutely charming. It was labeled for transport to Minneapolis.

During the upstairs foray, the dragonfly brooch caused some excitement and a lively debate about its age and market value. I heard the front doorbell, gave the brooch a last fond glance, and went down to see who was there.

Gracie Nussbaum greeted me by pinching her nostrils together. "What is in that Dumpster, dear? Something you found in the back of the freezer?"

"It does smell ripe," I said, ushering her inside. "The refuse people promised they would pick it up today."

She pressed her cheek against mine. "How's it coming over here?"

"We're almost to the end, Gracie," I said. "We're just waiting for the trucks to come and haul away Susan's things and Mom's piano. I know, I think, what's going home with me. When all that's cleared away, we're ready for the cleaning crew and then University Housing's walk-through."

"What a relief it will be for you to have it done." She turned toward the stairs when she heard the women's laughter. "Is Susan upstairs?"

"She is."

"If you'll excuse me, dear, I'll just go up and say hello." On her way up the stairs, she glanced back at me. "You should call your mother."

I heard a truck out front and opened the door to see who it was. I called up the stairs to Susan. Her hauler had arrived.

Despite the advice offered by five women executives, the hauling crew made short work of strapping protective quilted pads around Susan's pieces and loading them all onto a pallet that was set on the truck's hydraulic back gate. When everything was arranged on the pallet, the load was tightly cocooned inside heavy plastic wrap. Susan signed the bill of lading, and watched to make sure that her pallet was correctly and securely labeled. Before they closed the truck's big door, she slipped the crew chief some cash and offered an admonition about her expectations for a safe delivery.

After a few near misses with the Dumpster and the flower borders, the truck was on its way down the street. There was a collective sigh and a moment of silence.

"Mission accomplished," Jean offered with a grin.

"Thank you for everything, cousin." Susan wrapped an arm around me. "We'll collect our bags and get out of your hair now."

"Stay for lunch?" I asked.

"Thanks, but we really should get on the road," Maureen said. She turned to Gracie. "Where do you live?"

"Just a couple of blocks over," Gracie said. "My bag is all packed and ready to go."

I laughed. "Have you signed on as tour guide, Gracie?"

"No dear, I'm just a hitchhiker. Your mother is driving up to San Simeon this afternoon to meet us. She wanted to visit with Susan. The change in plans made that much easier for her. And she didn't need to talk very hard to persuade me to come along."

"Oh" was all I could think to say. Mom didn't need to clear her plans with me, but I admit that I felt quite left out of the loop. I was tired. A few days on the coast would have been a welcome break. Not today, though. But soon, very soon. I managed what I hoped was a smile. "Have fun."

Gracie took my arm as we all walked back into the house. "Your mother would have called, dear. But you know how you dig, Maggie. She simply does not want you to delve further into Tina Bartolini's private life. And it is private, you know. After all these years, can we let her memory rest in peace?"

"You sounded like Mom just then, Gracie."

"I tried my best to." She wagged her finger at me. "Why do you dig so, Maggie, dear?"

"I've given that some thought, Gracie. I think it's because I always knew that people were keeping secrets from me. And on some level, I knew the secrets were about me."

"Did you?"

"I'd have to be deaf and blind not to."

Apparently that was a good enough answer for her. She smiled up into my face and patted my cheek. "Promise me two things, dear?"

"Maybe."

"Promise me you will call your mother right away. And promise me that this time you won't grill her about events she feels are best left buried."

As I watched Susan go upstairs for her bag, I thought about something she had said earlier. Some secrets are too big to be kept forever. I thought it was also possible that some secrets were too big to be revealed.

"Maggie?" Gracie gave my arm a squeeze to get my attention.

"Maybe," I said.

Max carried Susan's bag to the six-person van they had rented for the trip. A "mommy van" Angie called it.

"I wish I could be of more help to you," Susan said, taking my arm as we walked toward the van. "This is such a big job. But I think I can be most useful now by just getting out of your way."

"You've helped more than you know," I said. "I enjoyed the little time we've had. Now, go have a wonderful time."

"You will try to join us by the end of the week?"

"I'll do my best," I said.

Max handed her into the van. After we waved good-bye, Max, with a heavy sigh, said, "God, would I love to be in that van."

"Call Susan. They'll turn around and come back for you." I told him Mom and Gracie were joining the party and he might as well.

"Nope." He draped an arm over my shoulders and pulled me against him. "I promised Jean-Paul I won't let you out of my sight until he gets back tonight."

"He'll be here soon enough. If you want to go, then go."

He shook his head. "Even if he hadn't asked, I'd be staying. You and Casey are all the family I have left, kiddo. Nothing happens to you on my watch. Besides, we have work to do."

I pulled away enough to look up at him. "You're not going to start sleeping on my bedroom floor again, are you?"

The question took him aback. "You remember that?"

"I do," I said. "Something Susan said this morning reminded me. Why did you do that?"

"I don't know, exactly," he said with a little shrug, releasing me. We walked back inside, away from the smelly Dumpster. "It was probably more for my sake than yours. After Mark died, I didn't want you to wake up in the night feeling sad and alone. I wanted to be there if you needed me."

"Uncle Max, Susan asked me why you're so much younger than Dad. It occurred to me that when you lost your parents, you were about the same age my friend Beto was when his mother died."

He thought for a moment before he nodded. "Pretty close, yeah."

"I don't know very much about what happened to your parents."

He knuckled my head. "You weren't around yet, squirt."

"Max, after they died, did you sometimes wake up feeling sad and alone?"

"That was some conversation you and Susan had," he said, trying to pull off a scowl but failing. "But, yes, sometimes I did. I thought I had plenty to be sad about. You know, strange room, new town, new school, Mom and Dad gone, living with my big brother. But Al and Betsy just folded me into their household like I was one of their own. Mark and Emily were little pains in the ass and I fell in love with them. It all felt very normal very soon."

"I suppose I should thank you for softening the ground around here so that when Dad got me away from Isabelle and brought me home, Mom didn't toss me out on my ear."

"Yep, you were exactly what Betsy needed all right, one more little pain in the ass to bring up."

The piano mover came. The three-man crew locked Mom's beautiful instrument onto a triangular steel-frame dolly, wheeled it out the front door and lowered it off the porch on a portable hydraulic lift. I asked the crew boss, a giant of a man named Hong, if I could pay him to also shift some furniture out to the garage for me.

"Sure," he said when I showed him what I needed moved. "That's nice stuff. You just going to leave it out in the garage?"

"Eventually it's going to my house."

"Where's that?"

I told him, up in Malibu Canyon, not far from where he was taking the piano.

"When I take the piano down, I won't have a full load," he said. "I can haul your stuff at the same time for you. We have a concert hall job for the next couple of days so we won't head south until Friday. If that's okay with you."

I told him that was just fine, and it certainly was. One less thing for me to contend with. We negotiated a price, shook hands, and I went out to sweep the garage floor while Hong's crew loaded Dad's chairs, the pretty marquetry table, a few other pieces of furniture and about two dozen boxes of random stuff, much of it to be sorted later, when I had time.

Before Hong got into his truck, he scooped a collection of fast-food wrappers out of the truck's cab and took them to the Dumpster.

"Pee-yoo," he declared after lifting the Dumpster lid enough to drop in his trash. "Haven't smelled anything that rank since some guy ran over the neighbor's dog and dumped it in my trashcan. Like to never got the stink outta the can."

"It does smell," I said, looking up from sweeping. "The Dumpster is supposed to go away today."

Still carrying the broom, I went out front and directed Hong's wheels away from the flower borders as he pulled out onto the street. After I waved the movers good-bye, I went over to the Dumpster and lifted the lid to see what was causing the horrible stench. Had someone dumped in some domestic roadkill? A Fluffy or a Rover who strayed into the street at the wrong moment? Whatever was in there did smell dead.

The stench hit me like a hot, viscous wave. I turned my head to fill my lungs, then holding my breath, with the end of the broom handle I started pushing aside refuse to see if I could find the source. Under a pile of old kitchen gadgets, Dad's outdated professional journals, and various junk cleaned out of bathroom cupboards, there was an opened-up sleeping bag that I did not recognize. I reached in and lifted a corner of the bag.

I don't know how I got there, but next thing I knew, I was on my butt, on the driveway, back against the Dumpster, vision blurred, ears ringing, bowels threatening to let go. Anoxia, maybe? I tried to stand but seemed to have left my legs somewhere else.

Max was beside me somehow.

"Jesus Christ." He slammed down the Dumpster lid before he grabbed me under the arms and half dragged, half carried me across the driveway to the patch of front lawn. I saw Karen Loper hobbling down her front steps and summoned enough presence of mind to raise an arm, point at her and croak, "Go away," loud enough for her to hear. Reluctantly, she went.

I lay back on the cool grass and tried to breathe.

"I heard you scream," Max said. "What the hell happened?"

"Call 911."

"Maggie, honey." Worry clouding his face, he looked me all over, checked the back of my head for blood, felt my limbs. I reached into his pocket and took out his phone. I was connected to the 911 dispatcher before he finished his examination.

"What is your emergency?" the dispatcher asked.

"It isn't exactly an emergency," I said. "Not anymore. But could you please ask the police to get over here, right now?"

"What is your emergency, ma'am?"

"A man is dead."

Chapter 15

I HANDED THE PHONE TO MAX and tried to sit up. That horrible smell coated the inside of my mouth and nose and seemed to prevent new air from getting into my lungs. I lay back down, looked up at the clouds, and tried to breathe.

From somewhere in the distance, I heard Max talking to the emergency dispatcher on his phone. Next I heard the squeal of the Dumpster lid rising, heard him utter, "Holy Jesus, Mary and Joseph," and then the lid slammed back down. Sirens approached almost immediately. And the refuse haulers arrived to pick up the Dumpster.

The sirens stopped and there was some shouting before the refuse haulers went away again. I just pulled up my knees, spread out my arms on the grass and looked up at the sky. Was I supposed to have intuited when George Loper said the Dumpster stank and I heard that Larry Nordquist was MIA that the missing church cook, childhood bully, and adult felon was taking his eternal nap among my family's castoffs in that big green iron box on the driveway? It seemed that he wanted to be brought inside our family circle, but, man, had he chosen the wrong way to do it.

I felt tired. Psychically, physically tired. Too many people coming and going, too many people hovering. Too many family relics to deal with. Too much good-bye. I knew that Mom was right when she said that some bodies need to be left as they are, where they are. Except that Larry, after sweltering in that box in my front yard for a while, did need to be removed. Soon,

Dark blue–uniformed Berkeley cops came pouring out of black-and-white cars and Max went to meet them. More arrived on bicycles, others ran up the steep street. They all converged around Larry Nordquist's less than auspicious catafalque. I intended to stay as far away from the activity as I could.

I don't know how long I lay there, quietly working things through. Sooner or later one of those badge-wearing people was bound to come over and yank me back into the here and now, so I savored my moments of solitude.

Kevin lay down on the grass next to me and rested his head on his hands. "Looking for the Big Dipper?"

"Too early for that," I said, watching the shapes I conjured out of the few sparse stratocumulus clouds above me morph into new shapes, change again.

"You want me to call Father John?" he asked.

"Not for me," I said. "And it's a little late for Larry. Besides, Father John is busy making soup. I thought you might be helping him."

"He called," Kevin said. "But unlike some people, on Monday mornings I have to go to work. My daughter went over with a couple of her friends to help out. I thought she could use a little time with the padre."

"She okay?"

He bobbed his head, maybe yes, maybe no. "Any idea how Larry ended up where he is? And when?"

"Maybe," I said. "Can we talk about it later?"

"Take your time."

I sat up, stayed still for a moment until my head adjusted to the new altitude. The driveway looked like a police convention.

"I hope at least one of your guys stayed behind at the cop house to turn out the lights and lock the door." I looked over at Kevin. "When was the last time you had a murder in Berkeley?"

"It happens, even here," he said. "You think Larry was murdered?"

"Did you get a look at him?"

He nodded.

"Then you know."

Probably because nothing else was happening in Berkeley on that beautiful Monday in summer, a fire department paramedic truck pulled up. With nowhere else to park, it stopped in the middle of the street. Two excruciatingly young men got out. One ran toward the Dumpster, the other ran to me. As I sat on the lawn next to Kevin, the medic took my vitals, shone a flashlight into my eyes and asked me what day it was.

"Monday," I said. Uncle Max came over when he saw the ministering paramedic. "I don't remember having lunch, so it must not be noon yet."

"Everything check out?" Max asked as the paramedic rolled up his blood pressure cuff.

"A little shocky, but she's okay."

"Then excuse us, please." Max took me by the hand and helped me to my feet. "Anyone who wants a word with my niece will just have to wait."

Max walked me inside through the front door, giving the Dumpster a wide berth. In the kitchen, he reheated the leftover tomato bisque that Roy had made two days earlier. I retched when I saw the color of the soup he set in front of me. I pushed the bowl away, folded my arms on the table and rested my head on them. I kept seeing the seeping red canyon cleaved between Larry's staring, pale gray eyes.

Max knelt beside my chair and put a hand on my back.

I turned my face enough to see him. "Did I do this, Max? Did I set something in motion?"

"That's two questions," he said. "Different answers. First question: You give yourself too much credit, Maggie. What happened to that poor guy isn't your doing. Second question: Maybe you did start something."

I fell into his arms and wept. He tolerated the snuffling only so long before he reached for the tissue box on the counter and handed it to me. I sat back, blew my nose and took a few deep breaths.

"You know what Mike would say, don't you?" he said.

"Mike said a lot of things." I pulled out a fresh wad of tissues and blew some more.

"Your Mike would say, you make your bed, you lie in it," he said. "Larry Nordquist is lying in the bed he made for himself."

"That's a bit harsh," I said. "Whatever he did, the poor bastard didn't deserve what he got."

"Maybe not." He struggled to his feet and cleared the soup off the table. "Is there anything you need to tell me about this Nordquist fellow before the police start asking you questions?"

I shrugged. "Like what?"

"When was the last time you saw him?"

"Saturday night after we got home from the Bartolini party," I said. "It was late, after ten anyway. I went out to the garage to look for Dad's gun."

"Did you find it?"

"Jean-Paul did," I said. "Dad built a false bottom into one of his desk drawers and hid it there."

"Mm-hmm." He nodded. "That's something Al would do." A sudden thought seemed to hit him with a jolt. "You didn't happen to fire the gun?"

"No, no. I never touched it. Don't worry, Larry left here, intact, under his own steam," I said. "He got in on his own, too. He knew where Dad kept a garage key hidden and he just walked right in."

"What did he want?"

"He's in a twelve-step program, though I think he's fallen off the wagon. He's been going around making amends with people for any wrongs he thinks he did them. But I think he wanted me to say that I had done him wrong, too," I said. "When we were kids, we had a fight because he was trash-talking Mrs. B. And I won. He wanted me to know that what he said was true."

"Trash-talking Tina Bartolini?" He tossed away that notion as ridiculous. "What negative thing could he possibly say about Tina?"

"It turns out Larry was a bit of a Peeping Tom," I said. "He told me he saw her with a lover."

That gave him pause. He thought over the possibility, shaking his head, trying to reject it. Finally, he said, "Never. Not her."

I pointed at my chest. "Remember how I got here?" I said. "My dad, the salt of the earth, pillar of the community…"

"Point taken." But still skeptical, he asked, "Did Larry tell you who this supposed lover was?"

"He wouldn't say. But he did confess that he showed Isabelle where to find the key to the garage."

That bit of information cleared up a mystery for him: how Isabelle had gotten into the house at night to creep into my room. He said, "The little prick."

"*De mortuis nil nisi bonum,*" I admonished.

"Honey, I'm a lawyer. If I never spoke ill of the dead I wouldn't do much business," he said. "Where's the gun now?"

I pointed up. "Loaded, in a drawer next to my bed."

"I'll take care of it," he said.

There was a knock on the connecting door to the dining room. Before we had a chance to answer, Kevin pushed through. "How's everyone in here doing?"

"We're still mostly vertical," I said.

"Ready to answer some questions?"

Max sat down beside me and took my hand. I knew that if Kevin asked me anything that Max, my attorney, thought I shouldn't answer, he would squeeze that hand as a signal to stay quiet.

Before he sat down, Kevin took a glass from the cupboard, filled it from the tap and drained it in a few gulps. He refilled the glass before he sat down across the table from us. "It's that smell, you know. You just can't get rid of it. Have any lemons?"

"Look in the fridge," I said.

"What's going on out there now?" Max asked as Kevin opened the refrigerator and began his search.

"Our crime scene investigator has taken over. The department is working crowd control; it's getting to be quite a circus." He found a lemon in the crisper, took it to the sink and cut it in half. "Most of the neighborhood is out there, trying to get a look. Wouldn't be surprised if someone started selling ice cream and balloons. I saw a media satellite truck down the street. I advise you to stay put until they're all gone."

I asked, "Shouldn't you be out there, Detective, detecting?"

"Not much we can do until the scientific team finishes." Kevin squeezed one half of the lemon into a glass of water and rubbed the other half under his nose. He sat down opposite us, with the glass in front of him, and took out a notebook and a pen. "But we can get some of the bread-and-butter questions out of the way while we're waiting."

He clicked his pen and looked at me. "You ready?"

"Fire away."

In answer to his questions, I told him about Larry's visits on both Friday and Saturday nights. I hesitated before telling him what Larry said about Mrs. B, but somehow, whether true or not, that nugget seemed important, and so I did.

Kevin clicked his pen a couple of times, apparently concentrating on something he had written before he looked up at me.

"Why didn't you tell me that yesterday?" he said. "We spent all that time up at Indian Rock, and you never mentioned Larry or what he said."

"Yesterday it was gossip," I said. "Today it could be something else."

Like a good detective, he put some effort into keeping his expression neutral. He reacted with some interest, however, when I told him about finding George Loper on my front porch Friday night, lying in wait for Larry, who was hiding behind the hydrangea. I told him that Larry had been coming into the yard all summer to look after Mom's garden. Both Mr. Sato and George Loper had shooed him away; Mr. Sato had called the police, as Kevin well knew because I'd asked him to look into it.

Thinking about Loper's baseball bat and the gash I saw on Larry's forehead, I asked, "What was the cause of death?"

"Too early to say." He changed the subject to time frames: when did I last see Larry, when had we last deposited refuse into the Dumpster? What had we last deposited into the Dumpster? The Dumpster was out front and accessible to anyone; had I seen anyone other than people in my household use it? The answers were: Larry was last seen around eleven o'clock Saturday; the big clean-up happened Saturday, but on Sunday we were still tossing out bags and boxes of junk gathered the day before. I hadn't seen anyone other than our household use the Dumpster, but I wasn't keeping watch over it. The last deposit I knew about was Hong's fast food wrappers a little over an hour ago.

"The Dumpster started smelling bad on Sunday night," I said. "George Loper made sure we noticed."

"What happens now?" Max asked.

Kevin shrugged. "Nothing happens until the medical examiner clears the scene. My chief may call in a special homicide squad from the county sheriff to advise our department, but that decision will depend on what the M.E. has to say."

A uniformed officer pushed through the swinging door. "Halloran?"

"What is it, Peng?"

"Guy outside wants to see you." The officer, Bo Peng, handed Kevin a business card. "He seems pretty upset, and he's damned insistent."

Kevin handed me the card and waited for me to make a decision, yes or no.

I passed the card to Max and rose from the table. "It's Beto. I'll go get him."

Kevin put up a hand. "Better if you stay put—it's a zoo out there. Peng will bring Beto in."

Beto entered the kitchen in a rush, face red, tears streaming down his cheeks. Kevin held out a chair for him and got him a glass of water from the tap.

"Is it your dad?" I asked.

"What?" Beto seemed confused by the question at first, but then he waved it away. "No. God, I mean, it doesn't look good, but he's hanging on. Jesus, Maggie. Zaida called me at the store and told me that there were cops all over your place and that the coroner's van showed up. I thought—"

He looked from me to Max, and back at Kevin, his lower lip quivering.

"We're okay, Beto." I passed him the tissue box. Kevin put his big hand on Beto's shoulder to calm him.

Beto mopped his face, blew his nose, and managed to gulp in a couple of deep breaths. After a big exhale, he said, "Sorry. Flash of déjà vu, I guess. Panic response. Last time I saw that many cop cars in one place was—" He couldn't get the words out.

Kevin said, "Your mom?"

Beto nodded as he reached for more tissues. With red-rimmed eyes, he looked at me. "What the hell happened here?"

I said, "It's Larry Nordquist."

"He's dead?"

"Very," Max said.

"Holy Mary, mother of God." Beto crossed himself. "But I just saw him."

"When?" Kevin asked.

Beto finally managed a sort of smile. "Is that an official question, Officer, sir?"

"Damn straight, bro. When did you last see Larry?"

"Saturday afternoon," Beto said. "He drove Father John to our party and waited out front. I went out and asked him to come in, but he said he wasn't in a party mood."

"What time did Father John leave?"

"You're kidding, right?" Beto turned enough in his chair to give Kevin a snarky look. "You know how many people came and went Saturday? Well I don't. And I sure as hell didn't play time keeper. All I can say is that Father John wasn't feeling very well so he didn't stay long; he prayed, ate, and ran."

"He left before Jean-Paul and I arrived," I said. "Don't ask me the time, but the sun was still up."

Kevin asked Max next: "Where were you Saturday night?"

"After I got Maggie and Jean-Paul home from that shoot-'em-up in Oakland Saturday afternoon, I took BART into San Francisco. Stayed over with friends and came back yesterday."

"How well did you know Larry Nordquist?"

Max just shrugged. "Never met the guy. Only time I ever saw him was this morning, in the Dumpster."

"Any more questions, Mr. Cop?" Beto asked, good humor returning.

"Yes, one." Kevin flipped to a clean notebook page and clicked open his pen and faced Beto. "You said you were at the deli when Zaida called you."

"I was," Beto said. "Elbow deep in sliced pastrami."

"And you didn't bring us lunch?"

"Fuck you, bro." Beto, grinning now, snatched up Kevin's notebook and tossed it at his chest. "I don't cater this sort of shindig. But I tell you what, Kev. Let your guys know that today only, if they come into the store and mention your name, I'll give them ten percent off their meal."

"Such a deal," Kevin said, turning to me. "Junior here normally gives the boys a thirty percent discount and free drinks."

"Are you two finished?" I asked. When they looked my way, I asked Beto, "How's your dad?"

"The ultimate diagnosis is, he's old and worn out. Doc thinks he had a transient ischemic attack, probably not his first. Could have an aneurysm. His chances for a major stroke before Christmas are excellent. While they have him, they're evaluating him for Alzheimer's and other dementia," Beto said. "But at the moment, except for some spaciness and cuts and bruises he got when he fell, he feels pretty good and he likes the nurses, even if he can't remember their names."

"We should all hope to go the way Maggie's dad did," Kevin said. "He sat down to take a nap and just never woke up."

"Halloran?" Max furrowed his brow. "What's the possibility this Nordquist idiot climbed into the Dumpster for a snooze and got hit in the head by something that was thrown in on top of him?"

Kevin held up his hands. "Not my question to answer."

That scenario didn't seem likely to me. I turned to Max. "I didn't see anything piled atop the sleeping bag that covered Larry that could have cleaved his head so cleanly and so deeply. Not through the padding of the sleeping bag. For what it's worth, I know that sleeping bag did not come out of our house."

Max covered my hand with his. "You okay?"

I shrugged; yes and no.

"Kevin," I said to get his attention. "Father John has been looking after Larry. Has anyone contacted him?"

"Dunno." He pulled out his phone and hit speed dial, asked that question of whoever answered, explained briefly who Father John was and his relationship to Larry, and volunteered to notify the padre. He said, "But, sir," a few times and got no further with whatever he wanted to interject into the conversation. He seemed deflated when he put the phone away.

He met my eyes. "The chief hasn't sent anyone to inform Father John. There will be more questions for you later, but they can wait. Do you want to go with me to talk to John?"

"I want to go, yes," I said, checking the time on the wall clock; Father John should still be serving soup. "But not with you. You said the media are already here. Under the circumstances, the two of us shouldn't be seen in public together."

When he started to protest, I said, "There are TVs in the psych unit, Detective."

Kevin suddenly seemed to fold down into some deep, dark place. Beto leaned in close to him. "Kev?"

After a long sigh, Kevin said, "The chief took me off the case. He says I'm too close to it."

"Hard to argue that one," Beto said. "What's that about the psych unit?"

Kevin ignored Beto's question. "Chief said I have enough on my plate right now to take on a new case. The bastard."

He glared at me and Max. "I did what you guys told me I should do. I told the chief everything."

"I didn't say it would be easy, did I?" Max said.

Kevin hung his head. "Damn, if she even sees me coming out of this house."

"Who?" Beto's focus bobbed from person to person, like a spectator at a three-man tennis match. "What psych unit? Do you mean Lacy? But she's in rehab, right?"

"I'll tell you about it later," Kevin said.

"Okay. But what about Father John?" Beto said. "Someone, a friend, needs to tell him. "

I turned to Max. "Will you go with me?"

"Be honored," he said. "Okay with you, Halloran?"

Kevin nodded. "Probably better if he hears it from you. But he's still down in Oakland. How are you going to get there? The street out front's totally blocked. If we start moving cars out of the way so you can get that red Caddy out, you're going to have every asshole holding a camera jamming it in your face. I don't think you want that."

I turned to Beto. "If the street's blocked, how'd you get here?"

"In the store delivery van," he said. "But I had to park a couple of blocks away and hike up the hill."

"You, walk?" Kevin patted Beto's round front. "At least something good happened out of this mess."

"Beto," I said. "Do you remember the secret way into my back-yard?"

"Yeah." If he was feeling a bit out of the loop before, he was thoroughly mystified now.

"Do you think you could still get out that way?"

He glanced down at the roundness Kevin had patted. "Got a ladder?"

Kevin rose and tugged on Beto to get him up. "I'll give you a boost."

"Where are we going?"

"We're going to get your van. Maggie and Max can take it down to Oakland. On the way, they'll drop us off at the store where you're going to make me a great big pastrami sandwich and I'm going to tell you all my troubles."

On his way toward the back door, Kevin pulled out his phone and told someone we were leaving.

I glanced at Max's shoes to make sure his had rubber soles, saw that they did, and asked, "You ready?"

"Lead on, McDuff."

We went out to the back corner of the yard, behind Mom's vegetable garden. One summer while my family was away on vacation, with Beto's help, Kevin, an amorous youth, had sawn through the back crossbeams of a two-foot-wide section of the redwood fence that surrounded the yard, and installed crude hinges. A hard push at the right place would open a piece of the fence wide enough for the boys to sneak through. That was the easy part.

To get to the back side of the fence, the boys first had to navigate their way up a narrow, concrete-lined rainwater run-off channel that ran between the backyards on my side of the street and the backyards behind ours, cross a weir where a second run-off channel intersected, and crawl through a culvert. The prize at the end of the obstacle course, if the boys were successful, was a little unchaperoned outdoor summer evening hanky-panky with their girlfriends; Beto was dating Sunny Loper from next door at the time, a situation her parents did not approve of.

And so, many years and quite a few pounds later, the four of us were going to run that course.

With surprisingly little effort, Kevin managed to pull the panel open on its rusty hinges.

Max looked through the opening and down into the run-off channel beyond with more than a little skepticism. He turned to me.

"Now I know why my brother was so worried about that boy."

I had to smile, remembering how earnest Kevin had been on his mission to lose his virginity.

"You know what Mike would say?" I asked. "Love is a hurting thing."

"That may not be all that hurts by the time this is over." Max followed Kevin through the opening, paused and grinned back at me. "Always an adventure with you, kid. Always an adventure."

Chapter 16

THE PASSAGEWAY OUTSIDE the Oakland church basement door was packed with shopping carts, every one of them heaped with someone's worldly goods: bedding, clothes, green trash bags full of cans and bottles redeemable for cash. A marmalade cat groomed herself in the sun atop the pile in one cart while a tired old mutt slept in the shade under another. A rich, human effluence filled the air as we made our way through the jumble.

The church ladies were just finishing with lunch service in the big fellowship hall. A few stragglers among their customers lingered over coffee, some in conversational groups, others off by themselves except for maybe the voices in their heads. A ragged man with a long, tangled beard played *Rhapsody in Blue* on the old upright piano at the far end of the room. The piano needed tuning, but he played with such expression, such beautiful phrasing that Max and I paused to listen before we went in search of Father John.

"He said he needed to sit down for a minute," a woman clearing a table told us. "You might go up and check in the sanctuary. He enjoys the solitude there after the worst of the noise down here is over for the day."

We found the sanctuary easily enough, but not Father John. The vast chamber was lit only by sunlight streaming through the stained glass windows on the east side of the chancel, very pretty, but not very useful. It took a moment for our eyes to adjust, but when they did we still saw no John; I had expected to find him on his knees before the chancel rail. I was about to suggest that we look elsewhere when I heard a little snore. We walked down the center aisle looking into the pews on either side until we found him, stretched out, his apron wadded under his head for a pillow. I sat down next to his feet and gave the toe of his sneaker a shake.

He awoke with a snort, seemed disoriented for a moment after he opened his eyes wide. Still lying on his back, he said, "Tell me I didn't die in my sleep and here's an angel come to take me away."

Max laughed. "No such luck, Padre."

John raised his head to look around me for the source of that voice. When he saw it was Max, he sat up and swung his feet to the floor.

"Well if it isn't that old sinner, Max Duchamps." He offered his hand to my uncle. "Good to see you, friend."

"Been a while," Max said. He nodded toward the altar. "You do realize this is a Presbyterian church, John."

Father John, smiling, shrugged, good-naturedly dismissive. "Last I heard, the Presbyterians were Christians in good standing. They also made their commercial-grade kitchen available to feed the hungry, so who am I to quibble?"

"Are you all right?" I asked him.

"Oh, sure." He rubbed his cheeks. "The chemo knocks me out sometimes. I have found that a house of worship on Monday mornings is just about the quietest place in town to catch a few Zs.

"So?" He turned an accusatory eye on me. "You told me you were too busy to help with lunch, but here you are. What brings you, child?"

I felt tongue-tied. I had delivered the sort of bad news I had come to give him before, but it does not get easier. Ever. I managed to say, "It's about Larry Nordquist."

"Not good news, I fear, about my AWOL cook."

"Father John." I put my arm around his shoulder. "Larry's body was found this morning. He probably passed away sometime Saturday night."

"Ah." A shaft of blue light crossed his face as he looked up, crossed himself. A set of rosary beads appeared out of his pocket, wrapped around his hand. After a moment, as if speaking to no one in particular, he said, "I knew when I didn't see him for a while that something had happened to him, but I didn't expect that. No, not that. Not that."

We sat in the sepulchral quiet of the sanctuary for a bit before Father John let out a long breath.

"An accident?" he asked.

"It doesn't look that way," I said. "And not by his own hand."

"Thank you for telling me."

Max asked, "Do you know how to get in touch with his family?"

"I do." After another contemplative breath or two, he rose to his feet. "Can you give me a lift back to the rectory? There are calls to make."

For the trip back to Berkeley, I conceded the passenger seat of Beto's delivery van to Father John and climbed into the back. I upended a plastic milk crate, folded a shop rug to use as a cushion, and made a seat of sorts in the pass-through space between the two front seats. It was a familiar enough arrangement. From time to time, on weekends when I was in high school, if Bart needed servers for an event he was catering, Beto would press a few of his friends into service and we would ride to the event in the back of the van with the food. Bart worked us hard but he paid us well; I remembered it being fun.

The service pans and trays that had been used to deliver Hungry Ghosts party leftovers to the soup kitchen, now empty and carefully washed, were stowed on a shelf near the back door, ready for return to Beto's deli. The pans and trays rattled around a bit, but overall, the short trip wasn't unduly uncomfortable or unpleasant.

Max broke the silence that had settled over the cab. "John, how do you handle the weight of all the secrets you have to keep?"

Father John thought for a moment. "The confidences of the confessional don't belong to me. I pass messages on to the boss upstairs and counsel the sinner to repent. And to fix his mess."

"Can you really do that, just hand it off?"

Father John shook his head. "Not always. Sometimes what I hear makes my heart feel heavy. Hell, sometimes what I hear curls my toes. Why do you ask, counselor? Is something weighing on you?"

"At any given moment? You bet," Max said with a sardonic little chortle. "Lordy, the crap I hear from my clients. But my job isn't fixing them or saving their immortal souls. All I have to do is represent their issues before the law. Sometimes, though, it's damn hard to sit by and do nothing when I'm told something that could really help someone out, but I can't say a damn word."

Father John reached across the space between their seats and clamped a hand on Max's shoulder. Smiling, he said, "Have you tried going to confession, my son, to unburden your soul?"

Max laughed. "I gave that up a long time ago, Padre."

"If I put a couple of easy chairs and a bottle of good scotch in the confessional, counselor, would you give it a try?"

"I might." Max reached back and tapped my knee. "What are your plans tonight?"

"Jean-Paul is flying in," I said. "So you're relieved of duty."

"So, John," Max said. "You up for a steak dinner?"

"I know just the place," Father John said. "Pick me up at seven."

We dropped off Father John at the rectory and headed down Shattuck. As soon as we pulled the van into its parking space in the alley behind the deli, Beto started making lunch for Max and me. Kevin was already gone, and the lunch-hour crowd was beginning to thin. Max and I found a table near the front windows and sat down.

"How was it riding in back, Maggie?" Beto asked as he set pastrami on rye in front of us. He uncorked a frosted bottle of prosecco and poured it into three tall flutes; it had been that kind of a day.

"It was nostalgic," I said, clinking my glass to his as he pulled out the chair next to Max. "Like the old days, when we went on jobs with your dad. Do you still do catering?"

"Oh, sure. More, actually. We cater a lot of lunch and breakfast meetings at Cal and Rotary, that sort of thing. When Dad still had the place alone, because those gigs always come at slam time here in the store, all he could ever do was drop off food platters and run back to work the counter. By the time I came aboard, he was already slowing down, so catering pretty much stayed status quo. But once our kids were in school, Zaida took over that end of the business, and she's done a fantastic job, really grown it. She brought in Auntie Quynh to make desserts and help serve. If it's a really big event, she hires her friends to do the serving, just like in the old days when Dad hired us on weekends. Now they have all the business they can handle." Beto grinned. "I'm so proud of her."

"That's just great," Max said. "Really great."

"It is," I said. I remembered that his mom used to work in the store during the lunch-hour rush. She'd see Beto off to school, and then she'd walk over; Mrs. B never drove a car.

"Any new word on your dad?" I asked Beto.

He shook his head.

"I'll go over and see him this afternoon sometime."

"He'd like that," he said. "Look, if you're going to the hospital, could you do me a big favor? Dad asked for a couple of things, but Zaida and Auntie are busy getting ready for a dinner gig and I can't get away until closing. If you'd go by the house and get a bag for him, it would be a big help. Auntie will be at the house frosting cakes until four."

"I'm happy to help," I said.

My phone buzzed; it was Kevin, so I stayed where I was and took the call.

He asked, "You get Father John squared away?"

"We did. He's going to call Larry's family."

"I'll tell the chief."

"You're really off the case, then?"

"Yeah." There was a pause. "Hey, Maggie, the D.A. is filing charges against Lacy for the shooting. Arraignment is scheduled for Wednesday."

"That's rough," I said. "Max is here. Do you need him?"

"No, but thanks. He put me on to a good local guy. On the advice of Max, we've started the process of getting Lacy formally committed to a long-term program. Her seventy-two-hour hold runs out tomorrow. We want her to be inside when the papers are served."

"Makes sense," I said.

"You'll be called to make a statement."

"I don't have much to tell, Kev. I didn't see who shot at us."

"They might ask you about some other things, too."

"We'll worry about that if it happens."

"Yeah. Hey, maybe I should have a word with Max."

"Hold on." I handed the phone to Max and he walked outside with it.

Beto picked up his empty plate and stood. "Let's hope they can keep Lacy in the hospital long enough this time to do her some good."

With that, he walked away to tend to customers.

I finished my sandwich, visited the ladies' room, and came back to find Max waiting for me.

"The cops are sending a car to drive us back to the house," Max said.

"Where's Larry?" I asked.

"He's at the morgue. The crime analyst took the Dumpster somewhere they can comb through everything in it, so the police are finished at the house."

"Bless their hearts," I said, fighting to keep the pastrami down as I envisioned the forensic technicians going through everything in that putrescent iron box. I hoped they had good face masks and gloves.

A police cruiser pulled up outside and we said our good-byes to Beto. When we drove up to the front of the house, I looked at the mess left behind by police, gawkers, and media folks with dismay. The flower borders I had been so careful to protect from truck wheels all morning had been churned underfoot. I said a silent apology to my dad, and called Tosh Sato for advice. Right off, Mr. Sato asked about the Chrysler roses that formed the outer red band of Dad's rainbows of flowers.

"Ground to confetti," I said.

When he finished swearing, he gave me instructions for gathering the remains and putting them in water; maybe he could salvage cuttings. He'd be over in the morning with some new plants. We could not restore the borders to their former glory, but we could make them presentable.

While Max headed inside the house to make sure all was secure, I pulled on Dad's heavy leather rose-trimming gauntlets and did as instructed, gathered the broken, thorny remains of the roses and set them in buckets with water. I thought of my dad, digging in the dirt, his mind light-years away as he worked through some thorny physics conundrum or another, searching for patterns, always searching for patterns.

I got out the big shop broom and began sweeping up the plant mess. No longer lined up in tidy color tiers, their petals were all in a jumble, the way bands of visible light might look if they were disassembled by a shattered prism.

It occurred to me that no one except my family would understand the significance of Dad's planting pattern. Sure, they made a pretty rainbow, but why they made a rainbow had meaning only for us, the targets of Dad's lessons about the optical spectrum. Any sort of plant would do to replace them, because the house's tenants would likely not care about the terahertz waves in the color blue. Or red, or yellow, or…

"Dammit, Dad," I muttered. Still carrying the broom, I ran through the garage and stood in the middle of the backyard, looking at the intact rainbow flower borders, the rose beds, the climbing vines on trellises, the vegetables, and I swore again.

I called out, "Max!"

He came out the back door with a phone to his ear. As he walked toward me, he held up a finger for me to wait while he finished his call.

"I'm afraid to ask," he said, pocketing his phone. "But what now?"

"Tell me what you see?"

He shrugged, surveyed the yard. "Grass, flowers, green beans and tomatoes."

"I should have asked, what don't you see?"

Looking around again, he said, "I need a hint."

"White," I said. "You don't see white."

I pointed to the closest flower border, raging with midsummer color, and said, "R, O, Y, G, B, I, V."

He threw back his head and laughed. "Okay, I get it. Red, orange, yellow, green, blue, indigo, violet—the colors of the visible spectrum. And no, of course you don't *see* white. White has no hue, it is the sunlight itself."

"Dad put you through the color drill, too, did he?"

"Yep, first year physics in high school. You can't have thought I'd be spared the Al Duchamps lesson on optics can you? Who do you think he practiced that stuff on before he subjected you to it? Me, his baby brother, that's who. Did he make you read Newton, too?"

"Of course he did. I left Dad's copy of *Opticks* on a shelf in the den for the edification of the tenants and their children."

"Fat chance anyone will pick it up." He looked around, puzzled. "What brought that up?"

"Dad didn't plant white roses, or white anything else."

"I see that."

"But every year he took white roses to the Bartolinis' Hungry Ghosts party as an offering to Mrs. B's spirit."

"A good Catholic boy like your father taking offerings to a ghost?"

"Aha!" I whapped him on the back a little harder than I intended to and rubbed the place to make any sting go away. "The flowers came from someone else. But Bart always thought they were from Mom and Dad. This year Beto and I told Bart that Khanh Duc sent the flowers. And they got tossed out."

"By Bart?"

"I don't know," I said. "Jean-Paul and I saw the bouquet, still in its vase, on the trashcan when we left the party. It was around that time that, according to Beto, Bart had a meltdown and got sent to bed. Later in the night he had a sort of mini-stroke."

"Where are you going with this?"

"I have no clue."

"Don't tell me that." Max wrapped his hand around my upper arm the way he had when I was little and was intent on launching into some stupid daredevil stunt that Max was equally intent on stopping. "You have something in mind, and no matter what it is, I know and you know that I'll get dragged into it."

"That would be up to you, though, wouldn't it?"

"Yes, my beloved. Yes. So, what's up?"

I looked into his bright blue eyes, Dad's eyes. "Max, what I know is, you all—you, Mom, Dad, Gracie, Dr. Ben, Mr. Sato, Father John, and I don't know who else—have a great capacity for keeping secrets."

"Are we talking about Isabelle now?"

"In part," I said. "My friend Beto's mother was murdered in a terrible way. A very terrible way. Dad and Ben, I believe, knew something. Mom is protecting someone or something. And Gracie, I think, is protecting Mom. Larry may have died because he owned some part of that secret. And you? You told Father John that you are weighted down by all the crap you have to keep to yourself."

"I said that?"

"All but," I said. "Help me, Max. What do you know?"

He shook his head. "When Tina died, I was practicing law in Los Angeles. I was out of that loop entirely."

"Entirely?" I said, very skeptical.

He thought for a moment. "Mostly. I knew Tina, of course. Your mom had me volunteer for a couple of Legal Aid shifts at the refugee camp in the Presidio and Tina was my translator. I don't remember seeing much of her after that."

"Did you do any legal work for Mrs. B?"

"Yeah, some," he said. "I don't remember all of it, but the big issue was her sister, Quynh. A lot of people were worried about relatives that stayed behind in Vietnam, lots of rumors that the relatives were being punished because of them. I helped them go through the International Red Cross—la Croix-Rouge—and the Swiss Embassy to get information. She needed help finding Quynh."

"And you found Quynh?"

"I didn't," he said. "We traced her to a re-education camp up near Hue, but then she disappeared. There was a kind of information underground among the refugee community that could sometimes get news out of Vietnam, or into Vietnam. But Tina didn't trust them. She said they were spies for the communists, so we kept searching through official channels, but she died before Quynh was located."

"How did Quynh get out?"

He held up his empty palms. "One day she called Bart from a refugee camp in Hong Kong. I have no idea how she got there."

I said, "I think it's time to go see Bart at the hospital."

"Just to pay your respects, I hope. He's a sick man."

"Of course, just to pay my respects. Beto asked me to stop by the house and get some things Bart wants."

"Later though, okay?" He looked at his watch. "Look, sweetheart, Maggie, I need you to focus on more pressing business right now. Lana has dodged my calls all day. So has the head of her division. I checked your network account and no funds have been released to you."

"What are the odds the network will come through by tomorrow?"

"They get longer every minute that passes without word," he said. "I went ahead and scheduled a phone conference with the folks at Canal Plus for five minutes past noon, our time, tomorrow. And I'm working on a backup, in case they both fall through."

"Good idea."

He furrowed his brow. "Where's your phone?"

I pulled it out of my pocket and showed him the dark screen. "Out of juice. I forgot to put it on the charger."

"Go give Guido a call," he said. "He's been trying to reach you. He asked me to tell you that he made the revisions on *The Crooked Man* you two talked about. He put what he hopes is the last draft of the film in the Cloud for you to look at. In his opinion, it's finished. I think it's best that you go take a look at it now, as in right now. Guido's headed for the airport. If you think the film's ready to go, I want that project submitted and signed off by end of business tonight so that, come noon tomorrow, there's one less thing the network can jerk you around about if they still haven't released funding for Normandy."

"Good thinking." I handed him the broom. "I'm on it."

As I went inside, I heard Max sweeping the driveway. Bless his heart.

I called Guido as I waited for our film to download from the Cloud file where he had stowed it. He was at the San Francisco airport waiting to go through security. Before he had to drop his phone into a plastic bin with his shoes and go through the scanner, he explained the changes he had made. While I waited for him to get re-assembled and call back, I fast-forwarded to the segments we thought needed some tweaking, saw what he had done, admired his technical skill for maybe the thousandth time, and relaxed. Before Guido boarded his short flight to Burbank, we agreed that the project was finished, and it was good. Very good, indeed.

When he was buckled into his seat, he made a last call before he had to turn off his phone for takeoff.

"What if Lana balks, and won't sign off?" Guido asked.

"Smile enigmatically and tell her that's exactly what we hoped she'd do," I said. "Drop a hint that the other folks we're talking to would love to have *The Crooked Man*, too. She'll call Uncle Max and he'll explain how many different ways he's going to sue her."

"So, we're really going to Normandy," he said, sounding very happy indeed. "If you can stay out of the line of fire long enough."

Max had some pressing business to deal with, so I took his Cadillac and went to see Bart without him. But first I stopped by the house, as I promised Beto I would, for some things Bart wanted.

Auntie Quynh answered the door wearing a baker's cap and apron, holding a pastry bag in a plastic-gloved hand.

"Oh, good, you're here," she said, leading me toward the kitchen. The counters were covered with trays of exquisite bite-sized pastries. "I'm just finishing up; Zaida will be here soon to get me. Big party tonight, you know, down in the Marina. Carlos and Trips are with Bart now, but we need them to come home and get ready to work tonight. We didn't know how we were going to get Bart's bag to him until you said you'd take it."

She leaned toward me. "You know how Bart gets grumpy when things don't go his way."

"I do." Eyeing the pastries on the counter, I said, "A couple of those would cheer him up."

She handed me two little pink boxes tied with red string. "Top one is for Bart, bottom one is for you." She pointed a finger at me and tried to look stern, but didn't quite pull it off. "For after dinner."

"Thank you," I said. "What else do I need to take to Bart?"

"Come with me." She pulled off her cap and gloves and untied her apron.

As we headed toward the back of the house, I asked, "Do you still have your bakery?"

"Oh, no," she said. "Auntie got old and retired. No, I just do this for Zaida a couple times a week. Otherwise, I'd just sit in a chair and rust."

She led me into Bart's bedroom, the sanctum sanctorum of the house, left untouched since the day Mrs. B died.

Quynh stooped quickly to get a pair of fleece-lined slippers from under the edge of the bed. Holding them, she slid open the closet doors, found a canvas overnight bag and put the slippers inside.

"Honey, there's a checkered robe in the other end of the closet," she said. "Will you get it for me?"

I slid the doors the other way and found the cotton robe on a hook at the end. That half of the closet was still full of Mrs. B's clothes, neatly hung on hangers. After all those years, couldn't Bart bring himself to remove them? Or was he just used to them being there?

Quynh carefully folded the robe I handed her and put it into the bag on top of the slippers. As I watched her, I said, "Auntie, does it bother you to talk about Vietnam?"

"Not so much." She walked across the room and opened the top drawer of the dresser. "What do you want to know?"

"I remember when you came here, how sick you were at first," I said. "I know you were in a re-education camp in Vietnam, but I never heard how you got out."

"Just like Indiana Jones," she said, taking a few pairs of white cotton socks out of the drawer. "When the communists took over Saigon, they sent me to work in the rice paddies because I was a capitalist—I owned a little market—and I had to learn how to be a hardworking proletariat. I stayed in that place maybe three years. Then one night, a man came into the hut where I slept and gave me a shot of something to keep me asleep, and then he took me away, up into the mountains."

"He kidnapped you?" I said.

"He and his friends kidnapped a lot of people," she said, packing the socks into the bag. "In that place he took me to, everybody had families living outside Vietnam. At first, I thought that we were put there for special punishment, but the others told me we were being held for ransom. Only, when their relatives followed instructions to deposit money in a certain bank account, the kidnappers asked for more. And more."

"You must have been scared to death," I said.

"At first, yes." She packed reading glasses and a book from the nightstand before she went into the en suite bathroom for a toothbrush and other toiletries. She talked as she collected. "But there was food, I didn't have to work in the rice paddies anymore, and no one beat me. Every now and then, someone did get out, so I just waited for my sister Trinh and Bart to do what they could. I knew Trinh would figure out a way."

Bag packed, she zipped it closed and handed it to me.

"So what happened?" I asked, walking back to the kitchen with her.

"I told you, Indiana Jones," she said. She put Bart's little box of pastries inside the bag and handed me mine. "One day, a man I knew from our family's village came with some money, American money, and said he wanted me to go with him. When the kidnappers said it wasn't enough money, my rescuer whistled for some friends who ran in carrying M-16s."

She smiled. "I guess it was enough guns."

"They got you out?"

She nodded. "I rode on the back of a scooter to the sea. A boat came for me, and took me to a refugee camp in Hong Kong."

"And that's where you were when you called Bart," I said. "And found out about your sister."

"Yes," she said.

"That's quite a story, Auntie," I said. "It has both a happy and a sad ending. My mom and my uncle told me how hard your sister tried to get you out. I'm sorry she wasn't around when it finally happened."

"Yes, but it was Trinh who got me out," Quynh said, very matter-of-fact.

"How so?"

"The man who rescued me," she said, "he was always in love with Trinh. But our fathers were enemies so they were not allowed to see each other. It was for memory of her that he did what he did."

"What was his name?"

I thought I knew the answer when I asked the question, but I was very wrong.

She said, "Thai Van."

Chapter 17

BETO'S SONS, CARLOS AND TRIPS, were in chairs on either side of their grandfather's bed, stockinged feet up on the bed, playing video games or texting or watching movies or whatever teenagers do on their cell phones. Bart was snoring like a hibernating bear. Both boys put their feet down guiltily and stood when I came in.

I whispered, "How is he?"

Trips, who was closest to me, came over and whispered back, "After all the tests he had today, he's out for the count. If the nurses would leave him alone, he'd sleep through the night."

"Auntie said to tell you to go home, shower, and get to the Marina," I said.

He checked his watch. "What time is Dad getting here?"

"As soon as he closes the store," I said. "I'll wait for him."

"Thanks," Trips said, pulling on his shoes. "Grandpa gets a little crazy when he wakes up alone in a strange place."

After they left, I unpacked Bart's bag, put his book and glasses where he could reach them and the pastry box where he could see it. The slippers went on the floor beside the bed, and the robe I draped over the back of one of the chairs next to the bed. Socks and toiletries went into a night table drawer, and the bag went into the small wardrobe.

The room was dimly lit and quiet. The only sounds were people out in the hall and the steady beeping of the heart monitor. I sat down in the chair with the robe over the back and took out my phone.

Jean-Paul had left a message earlier in the day, before I recharged the phone, telling me his flight plans. I checked my watch. If his plane left on time, he should be in the air at the moment. And because there wasn't a second message telling me there was a delay, he most likely was in the air. He also told me that Rafael was picking him up at the airport. I left a text message asking him to have Rafael drop him at the hospital if his plane landed on schedule. I waited a few minutes for a response. When there wasn't one, I knew his phone was turned off, so I texted Kevin. I told him where I was and asked if he could come right over; we needed to talk.

A nurse bustled in to take Bart's vital signs. When she put the digital thermometer in his ear, he stirred, opened his eyes and looked around. Seeming confused, he looked from the nurse, who was wrapping a blood pressure cuff around his arm, to me, and then around the room. His eyes lit on the things on the night table, and then on the robe behind me.

"Is my wife still here?" he asked, his voice a low rasp.

I exchanged glances with the nurse.

"Your wife just stepped out for a minute," the nurse said, taking off the pressure cuff. "She wants you to go back to sleep."

"Okay," he said, and closed his eyes again.

I followed the nurse out to the corridor. "How's he doing?" I asked.

"Are you family?"

"Friend," I said.

She smiled. "He's stable, but he's still pretty confused. And he can get volatile. Whatever he says, just go along with it to keep him quiet."

"Okay." I glanced back into the room; Bart was snoring again.

After checking for messages, I turned the phone to silent ring, sat back down in the chair beside Bart's bed and watched the heart monitor—it was hypnotic. I don't know how long I sat there, probably half an hour, before Kevin came into the room. He made sure Bart was sleeping before he gestured for me to follow him out into the corridor. We left the door open so we could see Bart, but we stood on the far side of the wide passageway so he couldn't hear us if he wakened.

"Why am I here?" Kevin asked, nervous, looking down the corridor toward the nurses' station.

"Because no one will question you coming to see Bart at the hospital," I said.

"Fair enough," he said. "What's on your mind?"

"I need to know whether you're seriously looking into Mrs. B's case, or you're just saying you are to humor Beto."

His eyes flashed with anger. "Did Beto put you up to this?"

"No," I said. "Why do you think he would?"

"He asked me the same damn question."

"What did you tell him?"

He glanced toward Bart. "I told him that of course I'm performing a serious investigation."

"Is that the truth, though?"

"Yes, it is," he said. "But I wish it weren't. Honest to God, Maggie, the further I get into the case, the more I have to ask, what good is it going to do anyone to drag all that up again? You told me yourself that you could have gone your whole life without knowing the truth about your parentage or seeing that crime scene shot of Mrs. B. Now you tell me that Mrs. B was sleeping with some guy. Beto worships his mother. Does he need to know that? Does Bart?"

He braced a hand on the wall next to my head and put his face close to mine. "And Bart, jeez, look at Bart. I'm at the point in this that I need to ask him the hardball questions no one asked the first time around or I'm stuck. But who is that going to help, Maggie?"

"I think the real question is, who benefits most if you bury the investigation?"

Still standing uncomfortably close to me, he said, "I'm sure you have an opinion about that."

"A few," I said. "Has Chuck Riley asked you to walk away?"

"My father-in-law? No." He moved back half a step. "Why would he?"

"He was the original detective assigned to the case," I said. "He's the cop who neglected to ask Bart those hardball questions, among other things, when he should have. I didn't see a record in the murder book that Chuck ever roused himself to look into Bart's bedroom, sent carpet samples to the crime analyst, looked for blood or bullet hits. Why do you think that was?"

"Chalk it up to inexperience."

"Bullshit," I said, leaning in toward him, forcing him back a bit, and looked right up into his face. "Your department is small, but they've always been damn good at what they do."

"Well, thanks for the vote of confidence, I guess."

"Have you talked about the case with your father-in-law?"

"Why wouldn't I?" he said. "You said it yourself, this was his case in the beginning."

"I guess that's the part I keep going back to," I said. "You told me you took Lacy over to her parents after her meltdown at my house the other night because you didn't want your kids to see her in that state again."

"Yeah."

"Did you explain to Chuck when you took Lacy to him why I had asked you to come to the house earlier that day?"

He lifted a shoulder, dismissing the issue as inconsequential. "No reason not to."

"Tell me, what experienced cop, tasked with watching over his highly agitated, pathologically jealous, not very sober daughter would leave a loaded gun where she could easily get her hands on it?"

"You can't think Chuck put Lacy up to taking shots at you," he said.

"At you, you mean. I don't think she was gunning for me on the freeway, and neither do you—you said so. Who planted the idea with her that you were at my house on Saturday?"

"Oh for cryin' out loud." He turned away from me and pressed his back against the wall, arms folded defensively across his chest.

"You can still pass the case to someone else if you don't have the stomach for it," I said. "Conflict of interest alone should have kept you from taking it on at all."

After he fumed to himself for a few moments, he looked down at me. "You got anything more you want to throw at me?"

"I wouldn't put it like that," I said. "Have you done anything with the shirt Mrs. B was wearing when she was shot?"

"I gave it to our crime analyst," he said. "To our department's licensed, certified, professional analyst, in case you're wondering. And so far, he's told me that the shirt has DNA from more than two people on it, but the DNA profiles won't be ready for a while. And, FYI, the shirt's a size fourteen and a half."

"I doubt Bart has worn a fourteen and a half since his first communion," I said. "If then."

"You want me to say the shirt belonged to this guy, this lover, you say Mrs. B was fooling around with?"

"I don't want you to say anything you can't substantiate, Kev. But think about this: When I saw Mrs. B the morning she died, she was wearing a blue shirtwaist dress. She looked like she was ready to go to work at the deli."

'You told me that before," he said.

"I saw that blue dress hanging in Bart's bedroom closet this afternoon."

He said, "I..." and got no further. We stood there, side by side for a moment, watching Bart sleep.

The elevator doors down the corridor opened and a dietary tech came out pushing a tall cart full of dinner trays, making a great racket of it. Bart stirred. He began kicking off his blankets as if he were trapped by them, waving his arms against unseen foes. I rushed to him, afraid he would pull out his IV line. The blips on the heart monitor spiked crazily. I caught his hands and held them.

"Bart, it's okay," I said. "Look at me. Bart."

With effort, he focused his eyes on me and stopped thrashing about, but he still seemed confused, frightened. He saw Kevin standing at the end of the bed and dropped his head back on his pillows and lay quiet, seemed dazed. After a minute, he looked at me and said, "How are ya?" And then he paused, as if he couldn't dredge up my name.

"I'm fine," I said, watching the heart monitor settle back into normal rhythms. "And how are you?"

He raised the arm with the IV and managed a smile. "Guess you should ask the doc that."

The dietary tech came in with Bart's dinner tray.

"Good evening, Mr. Bartolini," he said, awfully damned cheerful, setting the tray on a wheeled table and moving it into position over the bed so that Bart could eat sitting up. "We have something really yummy for you tonight."

"A nice veal scaloppini with marinara sauce and a side of fettuccini aioli?" Bart said, scooting further up on his pillow as he searched for the controls to raise the head of his bed.

"Close," the tech said, lifting the cover off Bart's tray. "How about vegetable soup, mashed carrots and a ground turkey patty?"

Bart took a look at the food and pushed the table aside. He glanced at the robe on the back of the chair and said, "My wife was here a minute ago, I was just talking to her. Where'd she get to?"

Kevin paled. I said, "She'll be right back, Bart."

The tech caught my eye on the way out, gave a little shrug. "I'll leave the tray; he might get hungry."

"Go ahead and take it," Bart said. "Tina will bring me in something nice for dinner."

As a distraction, I opened the drawer in the bedside table and pointed. "You asked for some things from home, Bart. They're here."

He looked over, smiled. "My Tina takes good care of me."

There was a tap on the door and I turned. Jean-Paul came in carrying a muslin shopping bag from a local market. We exchanged *les bises* and he shook Kevin's hand before I introduced him to Bart as if it were the first time; Bart seemed to have lost complete track of Saturday night.

After a few minutes of stilted conversation, Kevin asked, "Who's spelling you here, Maggie?"

"Beto, after he closes the store."

Kevin checked his watch. "He'll be here pretty soon, then. Why don't you two go on ahead? I need to talk to Beto."

When I said, "Thanks, we will," Jean-Paul seemed relieved.

I went over to the bed and kissed Bart's cheek. "We'll see you later."

"Thanks for coming by." He still hadn't called me by name. "I was real sorry to hear about your mom. Real sorry. She was always so good to Tina."

Kevin walked us to the elevator and pushed the down button. In a sardonic tone, he asked, "You think Bart can handle those hardball questions now, Maggie?"

I shook my head. "We both know it's too late."

The elevator came and we said good-bye to Kevin as we stepped inside. He turned to go back to Bart.

Happy to be alone with Jean-Paul, I asked him, "What's in the shopping bag?"

"Dinner," he said, pushing the button for the lobby. "I was hoping you might agree to a quiet evening in."

"That would be so nice."

"I have some interesting news for you," he said as the doors began to close. "Something we should discuss."

A hand shot into the opening and triggered the door to open again. We both looked up, surprised by the suddenness of the move, curious. I was also disappointed that there would be another passenger.

It was Kevin, but he didn't get in. Staying in the corridor, he held his hand against the door's sensor to keep it from closing.

"Sorry I got a little frosty there, Maggie," he said. "I don't want you to go away thinking that I'm not taking what you said seriously, because I am. It's just that this whole thing has been…"

He dropped his head, searched for the right words. When he looked up again and met my eyes he said, "It's been hard. Real hard."

"I understand that," I said. "And it isn't over yet. But you'll get through it."

"Says you." He removed his hand and let the door close.

Alone, I wrapped my arms around Jean-Paul, pressed my lips to his, and held him in that clutch until the doors began to open again in the lobby. Jean-Paul was thoroughly cooperative, as he always was; a quality I appreciated.

"Lovely," he said, offering me his arm. "I missed you, too. What's new?"

"How much time do you have?" I slipped my hand through the crook in his elbow.

"All the time in the world." He covered my hand with his. "All the time in the world."

We ran into Beto as he came out of the parking garage carrying a big bag from the deli.

"That better be veal scaloppini," I said.

He laughed. "Is that what Papa's asking for now? This morning it was a meatball sandwich. He'll have to make do with wedding soup and lasagne."

"He seems to think your mom has been to see him," I said as warning.

Beto's smile was rueful. "He's been talking to her for a while now. I have a feeling that she's coming to get him soon."

"What do the doctors say?" I asked.

"He has a leaky aneurysm in his brain. It's a race between a blood clot and a blowout."

"Oh, Beto." I reached for his hand.

"It's okay," he said, squeezing my hand and working up a game smile. "I think Papa's ready to go with Mom. I think he's been ready for a long time."

Chapter 18

I WAS STEPPING INTO THE SHOWER, eager to wash away the grime of the day before we began making dinner, when Jean-Paul walked into the bathroom holding the red leather jewel box I had sent home with Susan. I was mystified; I thought I would never see the box again.

"Where did you find that?" I asked him.

"On my pillow," he said. "I was curious."

"Is it empty?"

"No." He opened the box and showed me the brooch inside. "I remember that when you took off the dragonfly after the reception on Friday you said it was to go to your cousin. I know you are very fond of the brooch but you were quite clear that it should be Susan's. And here it is. What changed your mind?"

"I didn't change my mind," I said. "I gave it to Susan last night."

"Then she has made it a gift to you," he said, closing the box again. "A very fond and generous gift, yes?"

"*C'est un beau geste,*" I said.

"*Bien sûr.*" He patted my naked bottom, smiled, and walked back out of the room.

When I went downstairs, shiny and clean again, I found Jean-Paul in the kitchen washing lettuces he had picked out of the garden. He handed me the dripping colander of greens. "Ever since you told me your uncle was going out for steak tonight, I have been thinking about steak. Big, red, bloody steaks. The grill is started, potatoes are baking in the oven, and the salad I leave in your hands."

"You've been busy," I said, taking a redwood salad bowl out of the cupboard. "Anything else I can do to help?"

He paused from peppering the meat. "Open some wine?"

"I can manage that." I uncorked a bottle of cabernet and poured two glasses. He clinked his glass against mine, took a sip, and nodded his approval.

During the drive home from the hospital, I had given him, in broad strokes, a summary of the events of the last day and a half. I had almost convinced him that he shouldn't beat himself up for going home Sunday afternoon and leaving me to find Larry alone. Whether he had been there or not, the outcome would have been the same. When I reminded him that Larry probably was put into the Dumpster not long after he walked out of our garage on Saturday night, very likely at about the same time that Jean-Paul and I were enjoying each other on rose petal–festooned sheets, he conceded that what happened to the man was nothing we could have either foreseen or prevented.

"The important thing," I said, tearing radicchio into the bowl, "is that except for some last odds and ends, we're finished here. The cleaning crew comes in the morning. When they leave, we hand the keys over to University Housing, and we're gone."

"Finished?" The question sounded loaded. "All finished here?"

I looked around the kitchen as I took out plates and silverware and stacked them on the tray that he had already loaded with various condiments. There were no boxes stacked anywhere, and no more cupboards to sort or empty. I said, "Yes, finished."

"I wasn't referring to the house."

"Ah." I sighed, feeling weighted. "That other thing."

"The murder of your friend's mother."

"I think Beto and I are the only people who want to know what happened to her," I said. "Everyone who knows something is stonewalling me in the same way I was stonewalled about Isabelle."

"Then one day Isabelle walked up and introduced herself to you."

"I doubt that whoever shot Trinh Bartolini is going to walk up and say hello."

"Maybe next summer at the Hungry Ghosts celebration she'll speak to you herself."

"Enough about that, Jean-Paul," I said. "You told me you had some news."

"Three things, yes," he said, cocking his head, watching me. "How do you say it? What do you want first, the good news or the bad news?"

"How bad is the bad and how good is the good?"

"That depends, I think."

"Let's get the bad news over with, then. Should we drink a lot of wine first?"

"We should keep clear heads." He took both of my hands in his and looked into my eyes. "*Chérie*, I made a call or two and I found Thai Van for you, but he will be no help."

"I should know by now that when you say you'll make some calls, the earth will move."

"I don't know about moving the earth," he said with a little laugh. "But making the right call can sometimes open a door. It is the business I am in, yes?"

"I'm not exactly sure what your business is. Or was, before you were appointed consul general," I said. "But, what did you find out about Thai Van?"

"Maggie, he died a very long time ago."

I mulled that over before I asked. "In Vietnam?"

"You knew?" he said, brows furrowed.

"No," I said. "But I began to suspect it. Earlier today, I was talking with Beto's Aunt Quynh—you met her."

"Shrimp spring rolls?"

"Yes. And tonight's dessert," I said, moving her pink pastry box toward him. "Anyway, Quynh told me that she was kidnapped from a re-education camp in Vietnam and held in the mountains for ransom. One day Thai Van came in like Indiana Jones, she said, with men armed with M-16s, and rescued her. He fell off everyone's radar at about that same time. It would have been difficult, probably dangerous, for him to go to Vietnam then, and very difficult for him to get back into the U.S. I wondered if he just stayed there."

"When was that?" he asked.

I gave him a rough idea of the time frame and he nodded.

"Thai Van died in a firefight around then."

"How did you find that out?" I asked.

"If I told you my sources," he said, smiling his upside-down French smile, "I'd have to kill you."

"I'll take that risk."

"I made a call to a friend, who called a friend," he said with a little shrug, picked up a long barbecue fork and headed for the back door. I grabbed the wineglasses and followed him out.

"You're CIA," I said, handing him his glass. "I've always suspected it."

"It would be DGSE in France," he said, as he prodded flaming coals in the barbecue. "*Direction générale de la sécurité extérieure.* But no. Please don't be disappointed, but it's simply a matter of having connections."

"Maybe so, but they're pretty hefty connections."

"You know I attended one of the *grandes écoles.*" That little self-deprecating shrug again. "Most of the upper echelon of the French civil service attended the same university. A very small club, if you will. It was because of connections with certain people I became friends with in school that, after Marian died and I moped around like a wounded duck, they arranged for my appointment as consul general to Los Angeles. I don't know whether my friends were hoping a change of scenery would cheer me up, or they just got tired of seeing my sad face."

"I think I like your friends," I said.

"I hope that you will," he said, setting the fork aside. "The coals won't be ready for the meat for another half hour."

I asked, "How does your contact know about Thai Van?"

"You know that Vietnam was once part of French Indochina," he said. "Our troops came out a very long time ago, 1955 to be exact. But like any messy divorce, there were property entanglements to resolve and long relationships that were not severed. Remnants of our intelligence apparatus remain in place to this day."

He took my hand and walked with me over to the garden, where the last of the day's sun lingered. While I snipped basil for the salad, he told me that Thai Van's father, Thai Hung, had been a leader in an organization of Vietnamese refugees down south in the Orange

County community now called Little Saigon that raised money, re-cruited support and trained men to launch an invasion of Vietnam and overthrow the People's Republic. A Bay of Pigs sort of endeavor, as it were. The FBI planted informants in the organization to keep close watch on the father and the son and their cohort.

"There were reports that Thai Van split with his father," Jean-Paul told me. "The regime in Vietnam had its own spies in the U.S., so they knew what Thai Hung was up to. Word got back to Van that his relatives were being punished for his father's activities. For their sake, Van begged his father to step away, but he refused."

"Did you learn anything about what happened to Quynh?"

"No, not specifically her. Probably she was sent for re-education because of her family's position before the takeover," he said. "But the kidnapping for ransom was a different matter. There were those in po-sitions of authority in the regime who used intelligence gathered by the state for their own criminal enterprise, kidnapping and extortion being one of several. Desperate acts in desperate times, yes?"

"Don't be too generous," I said. "Extortion is a vicious game any way you play it."

"*Bien sûr.*"

"Quynh also told me that the ransom money was deposited into an account here. Is there anyone you could call to find out about that?"

A little shrug while he considered. "I can try. And that brings us to topic next."

"Is this good news or bad?"

"Again, that depends on what you make of it," he said. "You wanted to know if your father's Colt is traceable, so I asked a friend to trace it. He learned that your gun was part of a large order placed with the manufacturer by the United States Army and it was then shipped to the National Armory in San Francisco. From there, it was allotted to a National Guard unit where, as far as I can ascertain, it remains."

"Except that it doesn't," I said. "It's in a drawer upstairs."

"A mystery, yes?"

"But there's someone we can ask." I put my hand through his arm. "How long until your coals are ready?"

"Maybe twenty minutes."

"Shall we call on the neighbors?"

"Dear George? Certainly. Shall I go upstairs first and collect some fire power?" He was smiling so I laughed, but I wasn't at all sure if he was serious or not about getting the gun out of the drawer.

As we walked next door, I asked, "You said you had three pieces of news. The last one, good or bad?"

"Depends."

"Of course it does," I said, laughing. "So?"

"A question for you first: How long will you be in Normandy?"

"Through the fall, at least." We reached the Lopers' front porch and started up the steps. "I'll probably make at least three more trips later so that we can capture all four seasons at the farm."

"Would you consider staying for the entire year?"

"I think you'd better tell me your news now."

"It's official." Jean-Paul rang the Lopers' doorbell. "I have been recalled to France."

I hoped no one would be home: recalled to France? We had a lot to talk about. But we heard voices and some scuffling and then George opened the door. He seemed surprised to see us but he quickly gathered himself and plastered on his men's-club welcoming smile.

"Come in, come in, neighbors." He offered his hand to Jean-Paul. "Karen and I saw you drive up, sir, and we were hoping you'd take us up on that rain check for a drink." As he led us into the living room, he called out, "Karen, we have visitors."

The preliminaries were somewhat painful, lots of smiling, some stilted small talk. While George went off to the kitchen to make martinis, Karen caught us up on her family news and the news of several other families, some of whom I did not recognize, but I smiled and mm-hmm'd as if I did, clutching ever harder to Jean-Paul's arm. In return, I gave Karen as little information about my family as I could without sounding rude. Yes, those were piano movers at the house this morning. Mom had her piano shipped to her new place so she can give lessons again. I did not mention that Mom's new place was going to be the Tejedas' casita. Casey is just fine, enjoying college, and yes, she's still as tall as my sister, Emily. I am fine, and I understand that my programs can be uncomfortably thought-provoking. Thank you for your condolences for my husband's untimely passing, and no I don't mind that you didn't send a card at the time. I changed the subject when her inquiries veered toward Jean-Paul.

The topic Karen was dying to get into was the policemen's circus at our house that morning. She told us we could not talk about any of *that* until George came back with drinks or he would never forgive her. But Karen, being Karen, couldn't keep herself from nipping around the edges of it, like the kid who loosens the tape on his Christmas presents beforehand so he doesn't waste time when the Go signal sounds on Christmas morning.

"We have heard all sorts of stories from the neighbors," she said. "But of course, it's all just rumor and gossip, you know. Very unreliable. The police aren't saying anything until they've notified the next of kin. You can understand that we're curious. I mean, a dead man, right under our noses."

She didn't offer that last as a joke.

George came back carrying a tray with crystal martini glasses, a frosty silver cocktail shaker, olives on toothpicks, and a bowl of salted nuts. As he poured the drinks, he wasted no time getting right into the topic du jour.

"Maggie, who was it the police dragged out of the Dumpster over at your place this morning?" he asked, extending a glass toward me. "A vagrant?"

"It was Larry Nordquist," I said, watching his reaction closely. He froze in place, stooped over, glass halfway to my hand. I reached up and took it from him, but he still needed a moment for that nugget to sink in before he could unfreeze and stand upright again. Either he was a magnificent actor or he was genuinely surprised. I thought that the latter was more likely.

"I'll be damned," he said finally, remembering what he had been doing and getting back to his hosting duties. "I will be damned. Karen, did you hear that? It's the guy, that juvenile delinquent, who's been such a pest all summer. What happened to him? Overdose maybe? He crawl up in there to shoot up and never wake up again?"

"Coroner hasn't released the cause of death," I said.

"Of course, by the time he was found, we could smell him," George said baldly. "I told you the other night that Dumpster would start to smell, didn't I? But I never once thought a decomposing human would be the source."

"George." Karen shuddered. "Don't talk like that."

Ignoring her, he raised his glass. "Here's to the poor bugger. Guess he won't be hanging around anymore."

"Honestly," Karen said. She rolled her eyes at him before she sipped her drink. "You do make a fine martini, George. But please, the language."

After a healthy quaff, she leaned forward in her chair and stretched a hand toward me. "It was very considerate of you to come over and tell us, Maggie. If you hadn't, we wouldn't have slept a wink tonight, worrying about some lunatic out there on the loose. It makes me think about that other time—when was that, George? No one got any sleep then, either."

"Do you mean when Mrs. Bartolini died?" I asked.

"Oh." The question surprised her. "Of course that was a terrible, terrible thing. But, no, I was thinking about that poor woman who was shot in her own home right in front of her children. Was that about a year before the Bartolini woman died? Anyway, a man, a Black Panther or something, just pushed his way into her house and shot her, left her for dead. It happened only a few blocks over. Your mother knew her; what was her name?"

"Do you mean Fay Stender?" I asked, appalled anew by this callous woman. Fay Stender was a brilliant attorney, a Berkeley native who stayed in town to raise her own children. During the wild and crazy 1970s, Stender became involved with the radical prison reform movement, defending underground superstars like Soledad Brother George Jackson. It was Stender who got Jackson's prison letters published, making him a media star for a moment. The man who broke into her home and shot her was a con named Edward Brooks who may have been put up to it by the Black Guerilla Family, a deadly California prison gang, to avenge her abandonment of Jackson. She would not provide him with a gun in prison, and they parted ways.

Fay Stender did not die the night she was shot. A year to the day after, in terrible pain, she took her own life.

"Was that her name, George?" Karen asked her husband. "Fay Stender?"

"Yes," he said, sounding sanctimonious. "She was a local, you know. Came from a good family. I knew her father. Salt of the earth."

He stopped short of saying that Stender was "one of us," as perhaps Trinh Bartolini had not been. I remembered well that the Lopers did not want their daughter Sunny to date Beto, though she loved him crazily. But I never knew what their objections were. Until that moment.

Karen was still going on about how they were afraid men like that gangster would burst in and murder them all in their beds when I turned my attention to George.

I asked George, "Were you really afraid?"

"Well, of course we were."

"Afraid enough that you armed yourself?"

The question took him aback. He gave his wife a guilty glance, suggesting she did not know that he had a gun. Before she could chime in with the inevitable barrage of questions, I asked, "Is that when you gave my dad an unregistered handgun?"

He looked at me over the rim of his empty cocktail glass. "How the hell do you know that? We promised to keep that to ourselves."

"A gun?" Karen half rose from her chair. "George, you gave Al a gun? Where did you ever get a gun?"

"You had one, too," I said.

"You never told me," Karen harped. "Why didn't you tell me?"

"There were kids in the house," he snapped. "I acquired a gun and I put it where no one would run across it, but where I could get at it if I needed to. Maggie, your dad told me his was well hidden, too."

"It was," I said. "Mr. Loper, is that what you were looking for in Dad's workbench Saturday when you found his Purple Heart?"

"*His*, who?" he asked.

"You found Dad's Purple Heart," I said. "Not my brother's."

He picked up the cocktail shaker for something to busy his hands while that sunk in.

"I'm sorry, Maggie," he said, sounding rueful. "I overreacted when I saw that medal just piled in with the screwdrivers and drill bits. It's just, I'm a veteran, too, you understand. I earned a Purple Heart of my own and I know what that means. But hell, if your dad wanted to keep his medal out with his tools who am I to say anything about it?"

"Were you looking for Dad's gun?"

He averted his face from me when he nodded. "I was afraid it would get into the wrong hands after you turned the house over. Some kid of a visiting professor could run across it. You know how curious kids are, into everything."

Jean-Paul set his glass on the coffee table, on top of an Avon catalogue that had Marva Riley's contact information stamped on the front in red. He asked, "Mr. Loper, may I ask where you got the guns?"

George looked at Karen, who hadn't yet caught up with the idea that there had been a handgun in her house, under her nose, for over thirty years, and she never knew about it. Karen liked knowing things.

"Second Thursday of the month, we always got together with the Rileys from down the street for bridge. It was serious bridge, but after a few rubbers we'd take a break. The guys would always go out to the backyard for a cigar and a stiff drink and leave the wives to talk about kids or whatever girls talk about.

"One Thursday, not long after the Stender shooting—we were at the Rileys' that time—Chuck brought out these four Colts, brand new, still in their original boxes, with cleaning kits. He gave me two and kept two. I gave one to your dad, and kept the other."

"Where did Chuck get them?" I asked.

"He told me some BS about the PD passing them out to good citizens so they could protect themselves and their families. I wanted the gun, so I didn't ask a lot of questions. You know Chuck, always has something going on. Could have gotten them anywhere."

"It appears they were the property of the National Guard," Jean-Paul told him.

"I'll be damned." For some reason, George found that bit of news to be amusing. "All this time I thought Chuck lifted them from the police department."

"For heaven's sake, George," Karen offered, thoroughly nonplussed by the revelations of the afternoon. "Stolen federal property. In my house. What are you going to do about it?"

Once again George seemed not to hear her, and I began to understand how he coped.

"Maggie," he said, "I was a little surprised that your dad accepted the gun when I offered it to him. I wanted one to protect my family. You know, 1979, those were crazy times. There were still remnants of the Symbionese Liberation Army around here, robbing banks and setting off bombs. We had Black Panthers and La Raza and women burning their bras. And then Fay got shot by that guy. Jesus, I could not keep track of it all. But your dad took it all in stride. Didn't seem to worry him. We live in interesting times, he'd say."

Jean-Paul chuckled to himself; the phrase meant something to him. I didn't ask what because I wanted to keep George on topic. I gave Jean-Paul's hand a squeeze and turned my attention back to George.

"If Dad was taking things in stride, then why did he accept the gun?" I asked.

"Because of that woman," he said. "Your mother. I guess you know by now that she was stalking you. Even got into your house one night. I thought he might want protection if she tried that again."

My turn to be nonplussed. I managed to ask, "You knew about Isabelle?"

"Not the gory details," he said, smiling again. "Honey, we were right next door here when you came to live with your folks. An extra little kid shows up one day and people are bound to notice."

"What did Mom and Dad tell you about me?"

"Not much. Back then, adoptions were confidential. We didn't think there was much to say."

"I asked Betsy about you," Karen chimed in. "But clearly it was a topic she did not wish to discuss. And when Betsy doesn't want to talk about something, she absolutely won't."

True enough, I thought.

Again, George went on as if his wife hadn't spoken. "When that woman started showing up, your dad told me she was the birth mother and she had some psychological problems, and he and Betsy sure would appreciate our help keeping her away from you if we saw her sneaking around."

"Did you ever see her?" I asked.

He nodded. "A couple times. Once, I saw her hiding in the bushes by the house. We just got used to keeping an eye on you folks."

"George, our guests need their drinks freshened."

"Thank you, but no," Jean-Paul said, taking my hand and encouraging me to rise with him. "We need to check on the barbecue."

As the Lopers saw us out, Karen made conversation of her usual sort.

"I saw the locksmith van at your place yesterday. Were you having the locks changed?"

"We did, yes," I said. "There was break-in on Thursday night, so I thought it was a good idea."

"A break-in, oh my," she gasped. "No wonder you were willing to pay the locksmith Sunday prices. Anything taken?"

"No," I said. "When the police showed up whoever it was went out a window and over the back fence."

The Lopers, smiling, exchanged knowing glances. George said, "It's more likely that he went out through the gap the boys made in your fence."

"You know about that?" I asked.

"Everyone does," Karen said. "At least, everyone who had kids your age. You think we didn't keep an eye on what you kids were up to?"

Her parting comment was, "Don't forget to take one of the new keys down to Chuck Riley."

"Why would I do that?" I asked.

She shrugged. "We always have. All of us. In case of emergency, you know. He is—well, he was—the police."

I was dialing my mom on the phone before Jean-Paul and I reached our front door.

"Give Chuck Riley our house key?" Mom's reaction was a guffaw; I wish I could have seen her face when I asked her if she had. "I would not give that reprobate the time of day, much less access to our house. Whatever gave you the notion that I would, dear?"

"Karen Loper told me 'all of us' have left a key with Chuck the Cop," I said, grabbing the wine bottle off the kitchen counter as I followed Jean-Paul and his platter of raw meat out to the backyard.

"She and George may have trusted Chuck with their keys," Mom said firmly. "But the Lopers are great friends with the Rileys, and we never were. As far as old Chuck being a cop, hmm. I think that when his department suggested that he had put in his twenty years and should retire, immediately, he lost some of his cop credibility. If he ever had any."

"He was forced out?" I asked.

"That's what Ben Nussbaum told us, but I don't know the details. Probably got in trouble over one of his money-making schemes. The Rileys always seem to be in over their heads," she said. "How did the topic of keys even come up?"

"Karen saw the locksmith at the house when I had the locks changed."

"Why did you have the locks changed?" Mom asked. "Did the housing office ask you to?"

"No," I said, refilling Jean-Paul's wineglass and taking it to him. "Someone broke into the house, so I thought it was a good idea."

"Dear lord, we've never had a break-in before. Were you home?"

"I was," I said, not reminding her about Isabelle's nighttime call.

"Margot, darling." I could have kicked myself for telling her about the break-in; now she would worry. "He didn't..." She couldn't even say what she was thinking. "You weren't hurt?"

"I never saw him. He just disappeared into the night."

"Thank God for that."

I laughed. "I love you, Mom. The first question everyone else asks is what was taken?"

"As far as I'm concerned there's nothing in the house of real value, except you," she said. After a little pause she asked, "Were you thinking it could have been Chuck?"

"The thought crossed my mind," I said.

"Whatever else Chuck might be," she said, "I can't imagine he's a sneak thief. But I'm glad you changed the locks."

While Jean-Paul cooked, Mom and I talked about the last few house details to be sorted out. I told Mom we should be finished with everything by the following afternoon and be back in LA later that night.

"And then what?" she asked. I knew her question was several layers deep. Jean-Paul, the Normandy project, my situation with the network, the future for her and me once the house—our last physical link—was gone, were all wrapped in there somewhere.

"I leave for France August first," I said.

There was a long pause. I knew that my discovery of Isabelle and her family in France had opened old wounds, a fresh reminder of Dad's affair. And though she fought it, she couldn't help but feel that in some way I, too, was betraying her by getting to know Isabelle's family. She always tried to sound supportive, but I had come to expect long pauses before she could bring herself to utter words of encouragement for the film about my grandmother, Isabelle's mother, in Normandy.

I heard some false starts before she said, "Margot, is it possible that the break-in had anything to do with the questions you have been asking about Trinh Bartolini?"

"It's very possible." I hadn't told her about Larry or being shot at by Lacy, and I didn't intend to. She's not the only one in the family who can keep secrets.

"Margot, dear."

Uh-oh, I thought, this conversation was about to get very serious. Only my mom called me Margot, my legal name. And when she pronounced that name as she did then, with a ton of gravitas, I knew to be prepared.

"Margot, dear," she repeated. "On your account, I have been on the receiving end of a two-pronged browbeating delivered independently by my oldest and dearest friend, Gracie, and your Uncle Max, whom I raised from the time he was a scruffy little nose-picker until he was a licensed attorney."

"What have I done now?" I asked, making a note of the nose picking.

"Not you," she said. "It's what I didn't do. They both have the idea that by not telling you about Isabelle as soon as you were old enough to handle the information, I actually put you—your very life—in jeopardy."

"Maybe," I said. "But there's no point beating yourself up about it now."

"Except," she said in stentorian tones. "They both have decided that if I don't tell you what you want to know about Trinh, I might be putting you in jeopardy again."

"Dear God," I said. "What do you know?"

"Where to begin?" She sighed heavily. "All right, yes, there was another man, but it wasn't what you think. Trinh learned from the Red Cross that her sister Quynh was missing. Then she was contacted by someone who had proof of some sort that Quynh was being held for special punishment because she had American relatives. This person told Trinh he could get Quynh out of Vietnam, but it would be expensive. Trinh persuaded Bart to take out a second mortgage on their house to get the money. After they paid, they were told that the price had gone up. Bart, who is no man's fool, understood they were being extorted and went to the police."

"Did he go to Chuck?"

"More likely he went to the police chief," she said. "There were always issues between the Rileys and the Bartolinis. Chuck was a Vietnam vet, and he brought a whole lot of ugly opinions home with him."

"Did the police do anything?"

"I have no idea," Mom said. "Whatever they did, if anything, it didn't stop anything. Trinh had no money of her own, and the extortionist kept after her, telling her horror stories. So she asked an old friend for help, but he turned her down, too."

"Was the friend Thai Van?" I asked.

"Yes, it was. She didn't ask him for money; she was too proud for that. She wanted him to use whatever connections he had in Vietnam to find Quynh, to learn whether she was even alive. But Van said it was too dangerous to ask questions, meaning dangerous for Quynh, but I think it was too dangerous for his group as well. He and Trinh had a terrible argument about it; she was desperate."

"And Trinh told you all this?"

"She didn't have anyone else to talk to, and she was really very frightened."

"Father John is in the business of listening."

"Father John told her to pray. And so far, that hadn't worked for either her or Quynh," Mom said.

"Where does the other man come in?"

"She was told she could pay Quynh's ransom with something other than money."

"With sex?"

"I'm afraid so. I told her she would be crazy to do that. We argued about it, and she stopped talking to me."

Her voice broke and it took her a few moments to get control again. After a long breath, she said, "Maggie, I made a terrible mistake. Rather, your father and I did. When Trinh told me that she was being blackmailed for sex, your dad went straight to the FBI."

"You probably should have done that in the beginning."

"It was a mistake," she said. "Trinh was dead within the week."

Chapter 19

SOMETIME DEEP IN THE NIGHT I awakened, naked, a lovely ocean breeze blowing across my skin. Jean-Paul was sprawled on his back, snoring softly, one arm under my pillow and the other across his bare chest. I got up quietly and went to the bathroom.

The day had been warm. Our old house had no air-conditioning because it is so rarely necessary. In the evening, as is our habit in the summer, I had opened all the upstairs windows and bedroom doors to let the breeze off the Bay cool the upper floor so it would be comfortable for sleeping. But before we went to bed, I had closed them all again, or thought I had, except for the windows in our room and Max's.

On my way back to bed, more awake than before, I realized there was also a breeze coming from across the hall. I slipped into a shirt Jean-Paul had draped on a chair and went to the door to look out. We had left the door ajar to listen for Max. When he got home from his dinner with Father John we were already asleep. But he made enough noise that it registered with me that he was in and had locked both of the deadbolts on the front door.

The house was absolutely still. I could hear Max snoring in the room next to ours and Jean-Paul's steady breathing behind me, but nothing more except the wind in the trees in the yard below. The door to my old bedroom moved gently back and forth in rhythm with the wind. Out of habit, I thought, I must have left the windows open in there. The breeze was lovely and we were on the second floor, so I pushed the door further open to let the air flow through to our room. Because I was up, again out of habit, I walked on down the hall to take a look at the entry through the mirror in the stairwell. Everything appeared to be as it should be.

I went down the stairs to double-check on things. There was no need to do this. All the downstairs doors and windows had new locks that we carefully secured before we went up to bed, and I'd heard Max shoot both front door bolts. I think that, because it was to be my last night in the house where I grew up, I went down out of nostalgia more than anything, a last nighttime look at the old place, its familiar shapes and shadows.

When I got to Dad's den, I went inside and checked the window the burglar had gone out through on Thursday night—it was closed and locked—and stopped to look around. There were empty spaces where Dad's big chairs had been; his bookcases were dark hollows. But I could still feel his presence in the room, imagine that the susurrus of the wind outside was him rustling papers on his big desk. Satisfied that all was secure, I said good-bye to Dad again and turned to go back upstairs to bed, to curl into the contours of Jean-Paul's body and fall asleep again to the lullaby of his quiet breathing.

I never saw movement, never heard a sound. Strong arms grabbed me from behind and spun me off my feet. Before I could yell, a hand clamped over my mouth and pressed my head back against a broad, hard chest. The smell of scotch and sweat got stronger as I struggled to get free. I pulled at the arms confining me, bit and scratched and kicked, feeling impotent, panicked, trapped, as I was carried into the far dark end of the den. I couldn't scream, I could hardly breathe, but I could flail my bare feet, hoping to topple anything I could that might rouse Max and Jean-Paul. I sank my teeth into the fleshy palm over my mouth and felt my captor wince, but he would not loosen his grip.

We were pressed into the corner behind a door, his back against the wall, when he put his lips on my ear. I thought he was going to bite me back, but he whispered, "Shh. Maggie, stop fighting. Please. It's me, Kevin. Stay quiet, I beg you. Someone's in the house."

When I stopped struggling, slowly, gently, he set my feet on the floor, uncoiled his arms, and turned me to face him. I moved my jaw back and forth — it was sore. I was still terrified; why was Kevin in the house? He mouthed, *Sorry*, and put his finger to his lips, a plea to be quiet, and then he kissed the top of my head as apology, the way he would when we were kids and he had been an ass. I held up my palms, asking what was happening, but he only shook his head.

Under the murmuring wind, I heard a floorboard creak and knew exactly where the intruder was: on the far side of the closed dining room doors. I also knew how he had gotten into the house without a key. In the dining room floor there was an access hatch for the gravity heater under the house. A determined intruder could get into the heater area by getting into the crawl space under the house. Once he reached the heater, he could come inside through the hatch.

I grabbed Kevin and started toward the door to warn Jean-Paul and Max, upstairs sleeping. He raised a hand in front of me, an order to stop, and waited until I nodded agreement that I would stay put before he began to move on stocking feet along the edges of the room, headed for the hall. By then, the intruder had already put his weight on the creaky floorboard at the base of the stairs: he was headed up. I panicked and bolted forward. Kevin turned and pointed at me. I saw the gun in his other hand and stayed where I was.

The intruder was on the third step, where the banister makes a sound like a bird peep when anyone steps on the riser, when Kevin went out the door.

"Police," I heard him say as the hall lights blazed on. "Stay where you are. Put your hands where I can see them. Stay where you are, stay where you are. Drop the weapon."

Gunfire cleaved the night quiet. I hit the floor and started crawling toward the telephone. Kevin's bulk suddenly blocked the light streaming in from the hall, but he didn't make it into the room before he fell to the floor. Lying on his side, facing me, with a bloody hand he pushed his weapon toward me before his eyes closed. Whoever was out there was now running up the stairs. I knew Max and Jean-Paul had heard the gunshot and would probably be on their way to investigate. I held the gun at combat-ready with one hand as I punched 911 with the other. I laid the phone down and tried to pull Kevin further into the den, to get him behind closed doors. When I heard the dispatcher connect, I yelled, "Officer down, officer down. This location. Officer down. Active shooter."

"Bitch!" The shooter pounded back down the stairs headed toward us. "Shut the fuck up."

He'd reached the door, a looming blackness backlit from the hall. I was ready to fire when a gun blast spun him. I heard him swear, saw him grab his arm, saw him turn and raise his weapon before a second shot dropped him on his back.

Lying in the middle of the entry hall, Khanh Duc met my eyes and managed to say, "Bitch," before he lost consciousness.

I kicked Duc's gun into the den, well out of his reach, before I ventured to look into the hall. Jean-Paul, as naked as the day he was born, stood on the top step holding the smoking Colt.

"*Merde*," he said, coming down the stairs. "I didn't have an opportunity to zero in the sight. The gun pulls right. First shot only winged him. You okay, *chérie?*"

"Yes." I turned on the den lights and knelt beside Kevin. There was a bloody mess on the right side of his chest and he was having trouble breathing. I ripped open his shirt and put pressure on the bleeding wound. He began to cough blood.

Still holding the Colt, Jean-Paul knelt beside Duc, felt for a pulse. After a moment he looked up at me and shook his head. "*Fini.*"

Max called out from somewhere upstairs, "All clear?"

"Come," Jean-Paul said, kneeling beside me. "Bring towels and a blanket. A lot of towels."

Max came down at a rush carrying an armload of towels from the hall bathroom and dragging the duvet from his bed. When he saw that Jean-Paul was naked, he took off his bathrobe and threw it over Jean-Paul's shoulders.

To help Kevin breathe, Jean-Paul elevated his shoulders so that Max could place the rolled duvet under him. Kevin's eyes fluttered open, saw us, managed a wan smile, before they closed again.

The sound track to this entire enterprise was the 911 dispatcher trying to get someone's attention. Max picked up the phone and demanded to know where the hell the paramedics and police were.

"I don't give a great goddamn about a barricaded shooter in the Marina. I have an officer down here. Detective Kevin Halloran of the

Berkeley PD has a sucking chest wound so you damn well better get someone here now. Do you hear me? Now?"

Again, Kevin managed a little smile. Max kept the connection open, but he set the phone on the floor beside him.

As we kept pressure on Kevin's wound, the bleeding seemed to be under control, at least externally. With his shoulders raised he breathed a little more easily, but he needed more help than we could give him and he needed it very soon. The three of us stayed on the floor beside him, taking turns applying pressure. Watching the clock, hoping for sirens.

Duc's black sweats were covered with dirt from under the house. It made sense that he knew where the outside access to the crawl space was because he had spent a lot of time in the backyard with Dad, and probably would have used the faucet that was right next to one of the grated openings. Kevin's clothes were a bit rumpled, but they were clean.

"Max, I heard you bolt the front door when you came home," I said. "How did Kevin get in here?"

"I brought him home with me," Max said.

"Home from where?" I asked. "I thought you were having dinner with Father John."

"Father John invited Kevin along."

"Why? I thought you were having scotch and confession."

"Yeah, that was the agenda," Max said.

The towel under my hands was saturated with blood. When Jean-Paul took over from me, he put a fresh towel on top of the other and pressed. I wiped my bloody hands on my shirt and turned to my uncle. "So?"

"Father John is dying, Maggie," Max said. "He has some unfinished business he wants to take care of before it's too late, but he's stuck behind the seal of the confessional so there isn't much he can do by himself. When you think of all the people who have unburdened themselves to John, the secrets that he carries around—how he can look some of his parishioners in the eye knowing what he knows about them is a mystery to me. The thing is, he's heard the confessions of your parents, the Bartolinis, Kevin's folks, the Rileys, Quynh, Larry Nordquist, and I don't know who all. He's a smart man, our

Father John. He couldn't help but put some of it together. Other than advising his parishioners to do the right thing, his hands were tied."

"Did he unburden himself to you and Kevin?" I asked.

"He couldn't, could he?" Max checked the clock on the wall; where were the paramedics? "When I showed up at the rectory, Kevin was already there. It didn't take long to figure out what was up. John used an old lawyer's ploy; I do it all the time when I'm at trial. If I can't get evidence in one way, I'll get it in another. And that's what John was doing. He got Kevin and me together, directed the conversation onto Trinh's murder, and except for some occasional nudging, he left the rest to us. We had dinner, and then Kevin and I went over to the PD to go through the murder book and the paltry evidence that exists. We put together what he knew, what I knew, and the information you came up with, and made a couple of phone calls."

"Did you get anywhere?" I asked. Kevin's eyelids fluttered; I put my hand along his cheek and he grew still.

Max glanced over at Duc's corpse. "Looks like someone thinks we did."

I picked up the phone; the dispatcher was breathing on the other end of the line. "Where the hell are you people? It's been ten minutes."

"Responders are on the way," she said.

"How long?"

"They are on the way."

We did not hear sirens. Max said, "Maybe we should put him in the car and take him to Emergency."

"Moving him could be dangerous," Jean-Paul said. "It's a tough call."

Max puffed out a long breath, glanced at the clock again; the hands had hardly moved. To be useful, I got up and unbolted the front door. On my way back, I spotted Duc's gun where I had kicked it. I grabbed a tissue from the box on the desk and used it to pick up the gun. It was a Colt Commander, identical to Dad's.

"Jean-Paul," I said, taking the gun to show him.

"What's the serial number?" he asked, gesturing for Uncle Max to take over with Kevin. I turned the gun over and found the engraved numbers. As I read them off, Jean-Paul compared them to the numbers on Dad's Colt. When I finished, he held out his hand for the gun. "Both came from the same shipment by the manufacturer to the Armory."

"How did Duc get that gun?" I asked, thinking aloud, not expecting an answer. Mr. Loper told us that Chuck Riley showed him four new Colts, still in their boxes. How many did he actually have? And who all had he given them to?

Sirens and flashing lights, at last, raced toward us, coming from both ends of the street.

Chapter 20

PARAMEDICS SWEPT IN WITH THEIR GEAR and went straight to work on Kevin. One of them pulled me aside, looked deep into my eyes and asked, "Are you injured?"

"No." I was covered with blood, as were Max and Jean-Paul. Pointing to Duc, I said, "I think that one is beyond your help, but the rest of us are fine."

He bent over Duc, put a stethoscope to his chest, felt his wrist for a pulse and shone a light into his eyes. The sergeant in charge checked on Kevin first before he asked about Duc.

"Goner," the paramedic said, draping his stethoscope around his neck as he got to his feet. "Call the coroner, have him send the meat wagon."

Within a surprisingly short time, Kevin was on a gurney with an IV in his arm, a blood pressure cuff and a heart monitor attached, and a wide pressure bandage around his chest. Everyone inside the house stopped what they were doing and made way for the paramedics to wheel Kevin out. Jean-Paul and I followed them as far as the front door.

"Is that Kevin?" Chuck Riley, out on the lawn with a clutch of other neighbors, rushed toward the gurney but was pushed back by an officer wearing riot gear. "Is that Kevin? How can that be Kevin?" He appealed to the cop to let him through. "Hey man, that's my boy. Let me—please let me—"

The cop didn't seem moved by Chuck's plight. But Chuck kept at it until the ambulance doors slammed behind Kevin's gurney and lights and sirens started up again. As the ambulance drove off into the night, Chuck seemed near collapse.

The sergeant let out an ear-splitting whistle to get the crowd's attention.

"There's nothing to see here, folks," he yelled out. "Please go back to your homes and let us do our work."

The neighbors, roused from their beds, some still in pajamas and slippers, drifted off home. Chuck stubbornly stayed behind. He took a step toward the front porch, saw me in the bloody shirt, froze for a moment, and then screamed out, "What did you do to Kevin?"

The sergeant stopped him cold, got in his face and ordered him to go home or he'd be arrested for interfering with an official investigation. I was curious to see what Chuck would do next, but after hearing murmurs riffle through the crowd: *"Maggie's covered in blood"*, *"I heard Kevin's practically living here now"*, *"Is Lacy out of rehab?"* I took Jean-Paul's arm and stepped back inside.

Most of the policemen took off when the ambulance pulled out. Two stayed to watch the front of the house, and four more, counting the sergeant, were inside protecting the crime scene. After all the chaos of the last half hour, the house settled into an eerie silence. There was nothing to be done until the scientific teams and the detectives showed up, except wait. Staying at a distance, I looked around at the rubble the paramedics left behind: the clothes they cut off Kevin, a heap of bloody bath towels and used dressings, and the disposable wrappings torn from various medical paraphernalia. Amid the mess, I saw the butt of a gun, one of the Colts. I leaned close to Jean-Paul, nodded toward the gun, and asked, "Is that Duc's or Dad's?"

"Duc's," he said.

I went up to the sergeant and asked, "You're in charge here?"

"Yes, ma'am," he said. "You're the resident, right? We'll get to you when we can."

"I thought you'd like to know that the shooter's gun is there on the floor." I pointed at it.

"Thank you, ma'am."

"And I would like to know, what the hell kept you? For nearly fifteen minutes you had an officer down and bleeding. Where the hell were you?"

He blushed a furious red. "We got swatted."

Jean-Paul came up behind me and put his hands on my shoulders. "What is 'swatted'?"

"It's been going around and I guess it was our turn," the sergeant said. "We got a couple of calls that there was an active shooter at the Marina, hostages taken. There was a big party down there earlier tonight, the Chamber of Commerce, so all the bigwigs in town were there. We called up SWAT, paramedics, fire, put the hospitals on alert, and…" He didn't finish the list. "It was all a prank. Probably some fraternity guys having a kegger."

I nodded toward the still uncovered corpse of Khanh Duc. "You might want to check that man's phone records."

"You think he made those calls?"

"All I know is, in the middle of the night, a man dressed in black and carrying a gun crawled under my house to get inside. And you guys were busy somewhere else when he did it."

"Do you know him?"

"I met him once," I said. "His name is Khanh Duc. He grows roses."

"Sir, if you please." Jean-Paul opened his arms wide to show his blood-saturated front. "May we clean up a bit?"

Max, listening in, scowled but didn't say anything.

The sergeant looked at the three of us and at the bloody bath towels and the rolled up duvet. "You get all that on you taking care of Halloran?"

"For fifteen minutes," Max said crossly.

I leaned closer to the sergeant and said, "There are a lot of men here. I'd like to put more clothes on."

He shrugged. "Go ahead. We're setting up the crime scene now so it would be better for you to be somewhere else. The detectives will be here soon to talk to you, so don't be too long. And don't wash the clothes, okay?"

"Fine," I said, taking Jean-Paul by the hand. "Thank you."

We wasted no time getting upstairs. Uncle Max followed us into our room.

"You know the sarge is going to take a hit for letting us wash," he said. "He should have waited until we'd been checked for gunshot residue first."

"*Oui*," Jean-Paul said, slipping his arm around my waist. "But I prefer not to start a diplomatic firestorm. Maggie, will you join me in the shower?"

I smiled at him and said, "*Oui*."

"See you downstairs," Max said, retreating.

"Max?" I called after him. He stopped in the doorway and turned to me. "You never said why Kevin was here?"

"I'll tell you later," he said. "We need to get cleaned up before the detectives get here and stop us."

Max was already downstairs when Jean-Paul and I went back down. The big man himself, the police chief, had arrived, and he didn't look at all happy. I heard Max tell him, "Don't be too hard on the sergeant for letting us clean up. I didn't fire a gun, neither did my niece. And the boyfriend has diplomatic immunity so you can't talk to him unless there are representatives from our State Department and his government present."

Jean-Paul squeezed my hand. I leaned close to him and whispered, "Is that true?"

"Not exactly, but it sounds good, doesn't it?"

The three of us were taken into separate rooms, Max and I for questioning and Jean-Paul to be out of earshot so that what we told the detectives about the events of the evening wouldn't taint his own account, if the legalities of that ever happening could be sorted out. Jean-Paul volunteered to be sequestered in the kitchen so that he could start a pot of coffee; the chief thought that was just a dandy idea.

The chief, Tony Wasick, a good-looking man in his fifties, conducted my interview himself, in the dining room with the big doors closed.

"Miss MacGowen, what the hell has been going on here?" he asked, clearly piqued. "The body count from this address alone over the last two days has doubled my murder rate for the year so far. Throw in the burglary call overnight Thursday, and that makes your house the scene of the biggest crime wave we've had in Berkeley since I became chief five years ago. I know who you are and I know what you do. Have you pissed off some mobster with one of your TV shows and he's come gunning for you? Are you up here hiding out, making life tough for me and my guys?"

"I'm sorry, but no," I said. "My mom moved into a smaller place, and I'm only here to clear out the family house for her. Whatever is behind all the mayhem belongs entirely to you."

"To me?" Like the rest of us, Wasick had been dragged out of bed in the middle of the night, and he looked like it. The first whiff of fresh coffee coming from the kitchen distracted him for a moment. He turned his attention back to me. "You want to explain that?"

"I can only speculate," I said. "There seems to be something in this house that someone wants very badly. And I believe it has something to do with the murder of Trinh Bartolini over thirty years ago."

"The Bartolini case. Jesus." He let out an exasperated breath, paced off a tight half circle. "When I heard Kevin was shot at your house, and that his father-in-law was out front getting froggy, hell, I figured it was a personal thing. Never occurred to me that it could have anything to do with the Bartolini case. Talk about lost causes."

"Kevin?"

"No, the Bartolini case," he said. "There's just not enough evidence left from the original investigation to work with. But Kevin won't let it go."

"Kevin has new evidence," I said. "Your crime lab found DNA from three people on Mrs. B's shirt," I said. "That's major evidence."

"Sure." Wasick did not sound convinced. Or maybe he was just tired. "And thirty years later, what are the odds we'll find those three people?"

"The odds aren't bad," I said. "The victim's son will give you a sample so you can segregate her DNA. For the other two, you might begin with the man who broke into my house tonight."

He thought that over before he wrote something in his notebook. "The coroner will get a sample from the guy."

"Chief Wasick?"

He cocked his head, looked up.

"What do you know about Chuck Riley?"

"That knucklehead?" He lifted a shoulder. "Not a lot. I know he was on the force for a while, but that was before my time. Now he works security at a bank in town."

"You know he was the original detective on the Bartolini case," I said. "If the Bartolini case is, as you said, a lost cause, is it because Chuck Riley botched the investigation?"

He smiled. "Who's asking the questions here?"

A uniformed officer came through the kitchen door carrying two mugs of coffee. Grateful, Wasick wrapped his hands around a mug and blew on it until it was cool enough to drink. Revived a bit, he spent the next hour having me tell him, and retell him, about the shooting and the break-in and anything I knew about Larry Nordquist and Khanh Duc.

"Are you making a film about the Bartolini case?" he asked.

"No, absolutely not."

"But you've been going around town asking questions about her," he said. "If you're not making a film, why would you do that?"

"Because that's who I am," I said. "And that's what I do."

"Too bad about the film." He managed a little smile as he closed his notebook. "That was my only shot at being a movie star. And now you tell me it's *pfft*. Gone."

"You never know, Chief," I said. "Are we finished?"

"For now." He picked up his empty cup and headed toward the kitchen for a refill. With one hand on the door, he paused. "There will be more questions later. In the meantime, I'd appreciate it if you let us handle the media swarm gathering on your front lawn. We've had enough excitement for a while; let's not invite a circus."

"Suits me," I said.

He saluted me with his cup as he pushed through the swing door and went into the kitchen.

I opened the dining room's big double doors and looked out. Duc's body still lay in the hall outside the door to Dad's den, but someone had covered him with a yellow plastic sheet; his feet in black sneakers stuck out of the end. While I was with Chief Wasick, the crime scene technicians had arrived and gone right to work. I looked at their handi-work with dismay. Wherever bullets had lodged in the old lath-and-plaster walls, there were now foot-square gaps. Two big pools of blood, taped off, were soaking into the bare oak floor, the one under Duc still slowly oozing outward. Forget the simple house cleaning scheduled for later that morning. Now I needed to find bio-cleanup specialists to take care of the blood and a handyman to repair the walls. More time, more money, I thought, feeling guilty for even considering the practicalities of the aftermath created by that horrific night. I was sorry about Duc, though what happened to him was his own damn fault. I was deeply sorry for Kevin's pain, but I'd had a message that he was out of surgery and was listed as stable so I could crawl safely away from the edge of panic and give in to the inevitable letdown.

A young woman technician swept past me, headed for the heater access hatch in the far corner of the dining room. She knelt on the floor and began dusting the hatch and the area around it for fingerprints. Duc wore gloves when he came in. But had the intruder Thursday night? Was Duc the intruder?

The tech caught me watching her. "You shouldn't be here," she said.

She was right, I was in the way. It would have been nice to be able to go upstairs and take a nap, but the stairway was blocked off by crime scene tape because Jean-Paul had fired down at Duc from the top step. So I collected my computer from the kitchen counter where I had left it charging the night before and went out to the front porch and curled up in one of the big wicker rockers. There were four uniformed officers in the yard, so I felt safe.

When Chief Wasick asked me the inevitable question about making a film about Mrs. B's murder, I'd almost said, "My dad already made all the film that needs to be made on that subject." But it would have been a flip comment from an exhausted interviewee, so I kept the thought to myself.

Eight months ago, when I found out about Isabelle, I said that I would never make a film about discovering the truth about my parentage. Too close, too personal, potentially too hurtful to people I love. But, in two weeks I was leaving for France to make a film about Isabelle's family and their farm estate in Normandy. It won't be a film about discovering Isabelle, but she, and my dear dad's infidelity with her, cannot be ignored. Given time, I might find an angle to the Bartolini case that would make a good film subject. I wasn't taking bets on that film ever happening, but I began to think about the little collection of Super 8 movies I found locked in Dad's desk just the same.

There were twelve film reels hidden in Dad's desk. Because they were locked in a strongbox, out of curiosity on the afternoon I found them, I went straight to the local network affiliate's studio and spent a few hours converting the Super 8 reels to digital format. I'd wanted to know why these few, out of the hundreds of reels Dad shot over the years, were hidden away. More secret mischief, Dad? I wondered when I began screening them. The first time I spotted Isabelle, I knew Dad was recording Isabelle's violations of the restraining order against her.

I had been shown photographs of Isabelle and had met her once, briefly, but I was fascinated when I first saw her on film and was able to see the way she walked and gestured and canted her head to one side coquettishly whenever she caught sight of Dad. After that first glimpse of her, I had fast-forwarded through all the other parts of all the films looking only for her. But when I came across the fight between our little neighborhood gang and Larry Nordquist and his toughs, I stopped scanning for Isabelle and bore down on that scene, that day. The fight was a like a crease in the map of time, a demarcation between life before, and life after, Beto's mother died. I pushed Isabelle aside and studied that reel frame by frame. For the last few days, I'd intended to go back through the other reels to see what I might have missed, but there had been so little time and so few private hours.

Up at the top of the street, above Grizzly Peak, the sky was beginning to brighten. Full of expectation, cocooned in my corner of the porch, I opened the computer and began watching the old home movies, one at a time. The dates on the reel headers were the dates the films originally were processed, not the dates they were shot. Estimating time frame by my hair, clothes, and body development, I didn't bother watching films that were dated more than a year before or a year after Mrs. B died. That left me with four reels. Of the four, the third reel was the closest to the day Mrs. Bartolini died.

I'm standing on the sidewalk with Sunny Loper. Dad is obviously inside the house, shooting through the window on the front door. The two girls who live up the hill come into the frame, and we join them. I'm wearing the same red high-tops I wore in the fight reel, but they are not yet as scuffed as they were on that day. How long do a kid's canvas shoes last? Considering all the walking we did and the way we played, they probably wouldn't last more than a few months.

Dad scans potential hiding places for Isabelle before he catches up to us again. When he does, there are seven of us. The Bay Laundry and Dry Cleaners van stops in front of the Miller house, so it's probably Thursday, the regular delivery day for our neighborhood. A white-haired driver hops out carrying a blue-paper-wrapped bundle and hangers with plastic-sheathed dress shirts. He knocks on the front door, hands off his cleaning, and is back in his van headed up the street in the time it takes Evie Miller to come down her front steps, cross the street and join us. Around the curve, Mrs. B waits in front of her house with Beto. She's wearing a pink pullover and a gray pleated skirt. Mr. Loper drives past in his green Volvo and waves. Lacy and Dorrie Riley come out their front door, turn and speak to someone inside, the door closes. They cross the street, greet Beto and his mom, and wait for us.

Dad steps into someone's yard and films us through a gap in some kind of foliage. Mrs. B clings to Beto a bit longer than usual before she kisses him and releases him when the rest of us arrive. She stands on her driveway, watching us walk away. The camera jerks to the right, catches Larry Nordquist following us at a distance. Larry passes Mrs. B without greeting her; she is intent on our retreating backs.

The image becomes a slurry of blurred colors as Dad runs while the camera continues filming. When the focus is steady again, Dad has crossed the street. When he walks past the Bartolinis' driveway, Mrs. B is gone. Isabelle, back toward the camera, emerges from behind a hedge and sets off in our direction. Suddenly she stops, turns, pauses for only a moment, and then she begins to run away. Dad follows her until she turns up a side street, no longer following us. The camera is still running when Dad takes it down from his eye. The neighborhood is now upside down as Mrs. B walks up a neighbor's front steps. The door opens and she goes inside.

"Bastard," I said. I reversed the film to the frame just before the door opens and flipped it right side up. I enlarged the image of the door as much as I could without losing the integrity of the image, and ran the sequence forward in slow motion. The door opens, someone can be seen standing there. I froze the image of the figure in the door, brightened it, enlarged it one more click, captured it and sent it to Guido with a request to enhance the image as much as he could and send it back.

I looked up when I heard the Lopers' back door open, the soft clang of a trashcan lid, and the door close again.

"I think, from the look on your face, *chérie*, that something is up." Jean-Paul was perched on the porch rail, watching me. "Should I worry?"

"Possibly." I gestured for him to come closer. "Look at this."

I ran the film sequence again. When he saw Mrs. B go into the house, he nodded.

"I see," he said. "You think she is not going in for a visit and coffee, yes?"

"Yes." I turned off the computer. "Do you think it's too early to call on the neighbors?"

"In what time zone are these neighbors?"

I pointed to the Loper house next door. He smiled his upside-down smile and held out his hand to help me up. Before we went next door, we went inside to tell Chief Wasick why I wanted to go see the Lopers. I started at the beginning, with Dad's film, and told him about Larry's history of spying on the neighbors and his recent mission to make amends, the extortion of Trinh Bartolini for both money and sex and that Larry saw her with another man. He winced when I brought up Lacy Riley Halloran shooting at us on the freeway Saturday.

"You think all of that—any of that—has some bearing on what happened here last night?"

"I do. Let me show you something." I opened my computer to the sequence I had shown Jean-Paul. As Mrs. B walks across the street, I froze the image and asked him, "Do you know who that is?"

He took a close look and shook his head. "Should I?"

"That's Trinh Bartolini."

"I only know the case in broad outlines," he said. "Kevin's been working on it, but I'm not up to speed on the details. That's her, huh?"

"Yes." I restarted the sequence. When the neighbor's front door opens, I froze and enlarged the frame. "Now, do you recognize *him*?"

His interest perked. "You said she was being extorted for sex, and that Nordquist saw her with someone. You saying it's that knuckle-head?"

I closed the computer. "We may know more when Kevin gets the report on the DNA found on Mrs. Bartolini's shirt. But until then, a good place to start is next door."

Maybe he was just tired, or maybe he wanted to get us out from underfoot, but with some caveats he agreed that we could go.

"Hello, neighbor." George Loper, clearly surprised to find us knocking on his back door at the crack of dawn, pushed open the screen and welcomed us into his kitchen. He wore shorty pajama bot-toms and a T-shirt, his sparse white hair standing up in random spikes. There were dark circles under his eyes; he, too, had been robbed of peaceful slumber. "Come in, come in. Glad you've come over, Mag-gie, Jean-Paul. Gladder yet to see you're okay. Karen and I were just real worried when the paramedics showed up last night; no one would tell us a damn thing about what happened. We headed over to check on you, honey, but the cops told us to go home in no uncertain terms. We're getting pretty used to the police being over there regularly, but seeing the paramedics, well… Just glad you're okay. Karen was so up-set she had to take a sleeping pill. Sit down, coffee's fresh. Whatever happened?"

"Another break-in," I said, pulling out a kitchen chair.

He paused, holding mugs in both hands. "For cryin' out loud, what is this neighborhood coming to? Who got hurt?"

"The intruder," Jean-Paul told him, which was true enough for the moment.

Before George could launch into the inevitable barrage of follow-up questions, I asked him, "Those guns you said you got from Chuck, did he give them to you?"

"Give, as in give for free?" He chuckled at that as he poured coffee. "You know Chuck, always working a deal. No, we paid for the guns. Less than sticker, but we paid for them. Why do you ask?"

"You told me he showed you four guns," I said. "But I was wonder-ing how many he had to sell."

"You'd have to ask Chuck." After he said that, a sudden thought seemed to jolt him wider awake. "What happened over there last night have something to do with those damn guns?"

"Perhaps." Jean-Paul took the mugs from George's shaking hands before he could spill coffee all over. "The man who broke into the house last night had a Colt from the same armory shipment as Maggie's father's, and perhaps your own."

"I'll be damned." George had to sit down. "I'll be goddamned."

"When was the last time you saw your gun?" I asked him.

The question seemed to baffle him, but after a moment he pointed toward the ceiling. "I keep it where I can put my hands on it quick if I need to. I checked it when I heard the sirens, just in case, you know. It's where it's supposed to be. You weren't thinking my gun—"

"Just making sure," I said.

"Is that what Chuck was yelling about out there earlier, someone ask him about his gun?" He didn't wait for an answer. "I could've gone out and shot him myself when he started in. I'd just got Karen calmed down—you know how Karen likes to keep up on her neighborhood and she was not one bit happy that the cops sent her home—but as soon as we heard him, she wanted to go out there and get into the middle of things, probably make a nuisance of herself. I know my dear wife rubs some people the wrong way, Maggie, and a lot of folks think she's just plain nosy. But Chuck, he tells her what's going on and lets her talk his ear off. The comings and goings at your house the last couple of days have kept their jaws pretty busy."

"I can only imagine," I said.

"You gotta give Chuck credit though. He's been keeping an eye on your place all summer. Says he's worried about squatters. Vacant house, you know, can be a magnet for mischief. And he wasn't wrong. That Nordquist character was hanging around, and no one wanted that, least of all Chuck. You know, because of the boy's criminal background."

"Did Chuck ever confront Larry?"

"Funny thing," George said, shaking his head about something he obviously did not find funny. "But it happened the other way 'round. They had a pretty good shouting match out here one day, but it was Nordquist who confronted Chuck. Chuck told Karen the guy was just venting an old grievance about an arrest Chuck made years ago when Nordquist was still in high school. Happens to cops all the time; some people just can't seem to let go of bad feelings, you know."

Under the table, Jean-Paul squeezed my knee. Larry had apologized to me, but he also wanted me to make amends for pain I caused
him. Did he ask Chuck for an apology? Or did our Peeping Tom have
something else on his mind to discuss with Chuck? I covered Jean-
Paul's hand with mine and smiled at George; Karen wasn't the only
Loper who could talk your ear off. I did not interrupt his flow.

George reached around for the coffeepot and topped off our mugs.
"Chuck told me that the other day when he was on duty at the bank
he spotted Nordquist hanging around Bartolini's deli. He said he
went over and told Nordquist to scat, but Beto came out and said it
was okay, said the guy was waiting for you. Well, that made Chuck
nervous, thinking about what the con would want with you. So when
you showed up he caught Nordquist's eye and made like he was going for his gun and the guy took off running. Chuck got a kick out
of that."

"I wondered why Larry ran away," I said, remembering Larry lurking along Shattuck behind me; he was dodging Chuck, not me. I had
a hunch Chuck was more worried about what Larry might say to me
than he was concerned for my safety.

"Did Chuck ask you to keep Larry away from me?" I ask.

"Well, sure, honey. We look after our neighbors, you know. There
was no reason for you to be bothered by that overgrown delinquent.
I can't tell you how many times I had to shoo him off the property."

It was so easy to get information out of George that I almost felt
guilty—almost—when I fed him another question.

"Your roses are beautiful this summer," I said. "Did you ever meet
Dad's friend Khanh Duc?"

He furrowed his brow, shook his head, and then the light dawned.
"Duc? The guy with the big wholesale nursery?"

"Yes, Duc."

"Sure." He nodded with some enthusiasm. "Whenever I want anything for the garden, Chuck takes me down to Duc's nursery, gets me
a good price. Have you seen his place, south of San Jose? It's huge,
covers lots of prime real estate. That Duc's a real enterprising guy,
gotta give him credit for putting together something like that. The
specialty there is roses, but he carries just about everything you can
imagine. If you need some plants to fix the mess all those people

trampling in the yard made of your Dad's flower borders, you go ask Chuck to hook you up with Duc."

"Chuck and Duc are good friends?"

"I wouldn't say they're good friends exactly," George said. "Not backyard-barbecue good friends, anyway. Chuck told me he was an early investor in Duc's business and he didn't mind letting Duc show his gratitude from time to time. But friends? No."

"Interesting," I said, squeezing Jean-Paul's hand. "Very interesting."

From somewhere above us, Karen called out, "George?"

"You'll have to excuse me, folks," George said, pushing himself back from the table. "I better go see what the wife wants. When she takes a sleeping pill she wakes up a little disoriented. Don't want her to fall again."

We thanked him for the coffee, apologized for dropping by unannounced at such an early hour, and saw ourselves out the back door.

"So?" Jean-Paul asked when we were outside, headed home.

"Now we know where Duc got that gun," I said. "We keep tripping over Chuck Riley, don't we?"

"He seems a bit of a bungler, but I think he is an adept manipulator of people," Jean-Paul said. "Perhaps dangerously so, yes?"

"Yes." I held my phone on my open palm; the connection to Chief Wasick's phone was still open, still on speaker, as it had been during the entire conversation with George. "Chief, you there?"

"I am."

"Did you get it?"

"The whole confab," he said. "Interesting."

"Where is Chuck Riley?" I asked.

"I heard enough to send a squad to pick him up."

Happy to hear that Chuck wouldn't be out loose for a while, I closed the connection and slipped the phone into my pocket. Our front door opened just as we reached the porch and crime scene technicians, apparently finished, filed out past us carrying their gear and bagged evidence. With no fanfare, Duc's body, zipped into a green plastic body bag, was wheeled out among them and deposited into the coroner's unmarked white van. Almost as reflex, Jean-Paul and I both turned to see if anyone was watching from the Loper house, but saw no one.

The last man out handed me a certificate releasing the scene and a card with the numbers of local crime scene cleaners. I dialed the first number on the card and arranged with the dispatcher for a crew to come as soon as possible. For a small additional payment, I was told, a crew could be at the house in an hour. I said, fine, whatever, peachy, just come. Now would be good.

Chief Wasick, standing in the open front door, eavesdropped on the transaction.

"Any word on Kevin?" I asked as we walked up the steps.

"Doc says he should be okay." Wasick crossed his arms over his chest and sagged against the doorjamb, weary, ashen-faced, as he watched the coroner's van pull away from the curb. "Until we bring in Riley, I've posted men at the ICU."

"*Until* you bring Chuck in?" I said, thinking that Chuck should be in custody by now. "He lives just down the street."

"Yeah, but he seems to have stepped out. The wife said she doesn't know where he went. The logical place for him to go is the hospital to check on Kevin, but he hasn't turned up there, yet."

"When you find him," I said, "might be wise not to tell him right away that Duc is dead. Let him worry that Duc is talking."

He smiled grimly, "Hey, who's the cop here, you or me?"

"You sound like Kevin," I said.

"I'll take that as a compliment; Kevin is our best investigator." His voice cracked when he said Kevin's name. "I should have paid more attention when he told me he was reopening the Bartolini murder. A favor for a friend, he said. There was so little to go on—a thirty-year-old case—that I never thought he'd get anywhere with it. Poke around, make his friend happy. But now, Jesus." He canted his head toward the bloody mess visible through the open door; I dreaded going back inside. "What did he set in motion?"

I said, "Ask the original investigator."

"Yeah, Riley." Wasick went over and sat on the porch rail, gazed out across the long shadows of early morning stretching across the lawn. "For all of his problems, Riley had a good record as an investigator. But he sure did a piss-poor job on that one. I thought maybe he was off his game because he was too close to the case, lived across the street from the victim. But now…"

He shifted his focus to me. "Was Riley covering his own butt? Did he shoot that woman?"

"I don't know if he pulled the trigger," I said. "But I'm very sure he had a hand in it. Trinh Bartolini was being extorted for sex and Larry Nordquist, the neighborhood Peeping Tom, knew who the guy was. Riley didn't want Larry to talk to me. And now Larry's dead."

"What was Riley's hold on her?"

"Fear for her sister's safety," I said. "Wouldn't you expect that if a woman were murdered not long after she and her husband went to the police to report that they were being extorted by the local agent for the people holding their relative for ransom in Vietnam, the homicide detective assigned to her case would pursue that lead?"

"Sure."

"There's not one word in Trinh Bartolini's murder book about the ransom demands or a police inquiry about it."

He scowled. "Kevin told you that?"

"I saw it for myself," I said.

"I'll have a word later with Kevin about showing you the murder book, but it is interesting. You think Riley was in league with the extortionist's local agent?"

"Maybe not in the beginning, but from the time the police were brought in, yes. Old Chuck Riley, always on the lookout for a little spare cash, extorted the extortionist who, unless I am mistaken, is now zipped inside a green body bag on his way to the morgue."

"So far, that's a lot of speculation," Wasick said. "Have any solid evidence?"

"That's your department," I said. "It's your case. I have faith you'll turn up something. Duc came out of Vietnam with nothing, but managed to turn that nothing into a very substantial business. It's worth looking into."

Jean-Paul, who had been quietly listening in, said, "If you don't mind, Chief, I will make a call or two. Records of Duc's land purchases will not be difficult for you to find, but international bank transactions, especially very old ones, will require help of a certain sort. Maggie, shall I inquire whether the FBI has records of your parents' report and any follow-up investigation?"

"Can you do that?" I asked. A little Gallic shrug was the response.

Jean-Paul was already punching numbers into his phone when he turned to go into the house; the man was full of surprises.

Wasick seemed puzzled. "He said what?"

"Jean-Paul has resources," I said.

"Who are you people?"

I tried to imitate Jean-Paul's shrug. "When Kevin gets the DNA report from Mrs. B's shirt, with luck you'll have your solid evidence."

"The DNA report came in from the lab yesterday," Wasick said. "Whatever Kevin saw in it upset him enough that he ran out to talk to his priest."

"He ran out to get drunk with my uncle," I said, turning to go inside. "Please excuse me."

The blood on the entry hall floor was congealing and beginning to smell. Taking shallow breaths, giving the mess a wide berth and keeping my eyes averted, I went looking for my uncle. I found him in the living room, asleep on a sofa.

"Uncle Max." When I shook his foot he opened one eye. "Kevin got the DNA profile from Trinh Bartolini's shirt?"

"He wanted to talk to you about it. That's why he came home with me last night. That, and he didn't have enough for cab fare; we put away a tidy bit of scotch after dinner."

"How did you get home?" I asked. I hadn't seen the rented Caddy out front.

"In a cab." He yawned. "I offered to lend Kevin some money, but he said something about wanting a farewell tour on a leather sofa. He wasn't making a whole lot of sense by then."

"What did he say about the DNA?"

Max propped himself up on his elbows and yawned again. "He said he was an idiot and that you were right."

"About?"

"Hell if I know. Maybe *in vino veritas*, but in scotch there's just a lot of slurred words after a while."

Chief Wasick had followed me in.

"Chief," I said, "we need to see the DNA report. Where is it?"

He addressed Max. "She's kind of bossy, isn't she?"

"She can be," Max said, smiling at me fondly. "And she can be a

force of nature when she is on to something. I believe it would be wise
if you produced that report."

"The report is at the station." The chief bowed from the waist as he
swept an arm toward the exit. "Shall we?"

"As soon as the house cleaners come," I said, turning Max's wrist to
see his watch. "About half an hour."

"Maggie?" Max managed to pull himself upright. "Lana called.
The network funded your account at start of business this morning,
New York time."

"So, that's done," I said. We were staying with the network for the
Normandy project, and I didn't know how I felt about that. There
was relief that the project would go forward, of course, but also some
disappointment that we were still entangled with the old network—a
problem child—instead of making a fresh start with a new backer.

"To tell you the truth," Max said, "I was surprised that the network
came through. Apparently the push happened when someone on the
New York goon squad picked your name off the morning news feed.
He immediately sent in the order to fund."

"Saw my name?" I said, puzzled.

"Actually, this." He took out his phone and flipped through his files
until he found what he wanted, a photograph. He handed the phone
to me. "Lana says it's gone viral. I hope Jean-Paul doesn't take any
flak because of it."

"Holy crap," was all I could think to say when I saw the image.
There we were, Jean-Paul and I, standing shoulder to shoulder at
the open front door, barely dressed and covered in blood watching
paramedics wheel Kevin to an ambulance.

Jean-Paul heard me and came in from the dining room to look over
my shoulder. He muttered, *"Merde,"* and went back to his call.

Chapter 21

IT WAS STILL EARLY WHEN we got to the police station, though we'd been up so long it felt like midday. The Civic Center was just coming to life, city workers beginning to straggle in, paper cups of coffee clutched in their hands as they dodged the cadre of young skateboarders who use the public sidewalks, ramps and stairs as their private skate park. And, of course, there was a fair cross section of street people drinking out of paper bags or sleeping off the night before on shaded benches. Max, Jean-Paul and I managed to negotiate our way through wheeled youth and panhandlers and get through the front door of the police station without incident.

The rookie cop on front-desk duty expected us. He led us out of the police lobby and through a maze of cubicles in back. We passed Chief Wasick's office door and went instead into the detectives' bull-pen. Tony Wasick was at Kevin's desk studying the contents of the manila file folder open in front of him. He glanced up when we came in.

"It's interesting," he said as the three of us peered over his shoulders. "Very interesting."

When Kevin sent Trinh Bartolini's shirt to the lab for testing, he had also sent along a sweat-stained T-shirt belonging to Chuck Riley, the baseball bat belonging to George Loper, a plastic fork Bart Bartolini had used, and a chewed-on pencil he lifted from the pencil cup on Dad's desk. Beto gave him a bamboo flute that he remembered his mother playing, from which her DNA sample was extracted. Of the five samples, only two matched the DNA on swatches cut from the bloody white shirt she wore when she was found. They were hers and Chuck Riley's.

When I saw that Chuck Riley's semen as well as some of his blood were found on the shirt, I felt like crying and laughing and maybe doing a rain dance at the same time; fatigue, let-down after a very bad night, both or neither, I didn't know what all, made me feel just a bit giddy.

I reached around Wasick and put my finger on a line in the lab report: a small amount of Chuck Riley's blood was found on the back of her shirt. I said, "Riley was behind her when she was shot."

"Looks like it," Wasick said. "She took a frontal hit, middle of the chest. The bullet passed through her and may have grazed him. So, the question is, if he was behind her, who pulled the trigger?"

"Ask Riley," I said.

"When we find him, we will."

Max chimed in, "You certainly have enough to get a search warrant for Riley's house, Chief."

"Thirty years after the fact, what am I looking for and where am I looking for it?"

"Riley's bedroom or whatever dungeon he took that dear woman into. Take up the carpets, check the walls, look for blood, a gun, a bullet hole. A souvenir he kept of her, maybe."

"*More* than thirty years, counselor." Wasick rubbed tired eyes.

"It's a long shot," I said. "But it is a shot. If Chuck Riley won't talk, we may never know exactly what happened to Trinh Bartolini. Larry Nordquist is another matter. After all that I have seen and heard, I am just awfully damn certain that Chuck whacked Larry to keep him from talking. I have faith in you, Chief. You'll find what you need to convict Chuck on that one."

"We'll see," Wasick said, closing the file. "We'll see."

We had learned what we came to learn, and now it was time to go. I offered Wasick my hand. "Thank you, Chief."

He took my hand in both of his and looked directly, pointedly, into my eyes. "Like the murder book, you never saw this report. Got it?"

"Of course."

He rose from his chair. "Now, if you folks will excuse me, I have a nap to take. I'm too old for all-nighters."

Jean-Paul, Max and I walked up to the Bartolini deli for breakfast. Beto's wife, Zaida, was busy with customers, but she took the time to tell us that Beto was at the hospital with his dad and that Bart was having a pretty good day, all things considered. Beto had run into Kevin's son at the hospital, so he knew in broad outlines what had happened the night before. And because Beto knew half the staff at the hospital from either school or the deli, he was able to get regular updates on Kevin's condition. Zaida told us that Duc's bullet had pierced Kevin's lung and shattered a rib on the way out. He had lost a lot of blood, but no other vital organs were damaged. He was still in the ICU, still asleep, and his condition was stable. Good news all around.

After we ate, though a nap sounded like a very fine idea, no one was in a hurry to get home until the crime scene cleaners had time to finish removing the gore. Jean-Paul and I decided to walk, to get some fresh air, while Max, playing the martyr, volunteered to go home to check on progress. He said he would call Lyle, to get a referral for someone to patch the walls and to paint; Lyle had contacts.

After we saw him off, Jean-Paul and I headed up Shattuck to take the shortcut across the Cal campus. I wanted to show him where I had spent a great part of my growing-up years, and where I had earned my degree.

The day was already warm, uncomfortably so. But the campus under its canopy of redwood trees was sweet-smelling and cool, a lovely break from the ugliness of the night before. Instead of cutting straight across, we wandered arm-in-arm along Strawberry Creek, through the Phoebe Apperson Hearst Grove, and then over to the physics building where my dad's office had been for so many years. I was feeling a bit wistful, wondering if I would ever take that particular walk again. Saying another good-bye to Dad.

Jean-Paul interrupted my reverie. "Tell me, my friend in television, if you were to film a dramatization of the murder of Trinh Bartolini, how would it unfold?"

I rested my head against his shoulder and thought for a moment. "I can think of various scenarios, but the one that makes the most sense to me after seeing the lab reports would begin with Mrs. B in bed with Chuck, his house, drapes closed to keep the room dark so she wouldn't have to see him, gritting her teeth, praying he'll finish and roll off her. They hear someone in the house. He pushes her or she falls off the bed, bruising her bottom and her shoulder when she lands on the floor. She grabs the first thing she finds to cover herself—his shirt. Chuck ends up standing behind her. Was he trying to hide, or to use her as a shield?

"Someone opens the door. Maybe he, or she, has heard a man's voice inside. In the darkened room he sees a man's white shirt, assumes it's Chuck, aims for center mass and shoots."

Jean-Paul thought that over before he nodded. "I can see that, yes. But who opened the door?"

"If this is my story to tell, it would be someone who intended to take out Chuck and made a terrible mistake when he shot her. I don't know anyone who would want to hurt Mrs. B, but I can't say that about him."

"Khanh Duc?"

"He's certainly on the top of my list," I said. "The Bartolinis paid Quynh's ransom through him, and then somehow Chuck infused himself into the situation. Did Chuck, always looking for a deal, offer Duc protection from a police investigation in exchange for a cut of the proceeds? If that's the case, then when my parents brought the FBI aboard there wouldn't be much Chuck could do to shield either of them, and was probably a liability. He would certainly hand over Duc to save his own scrawny butt. Maybe he asked for too much and Duc wanted him gone."

"If that is what happened, then I would expect Duc to try again when he missed killing Riley the first time," Jean-Paul said. "We learned last night what Duc is capable of."

"Unless Chuck told Duc that everything would be exposed if anything happened to him. Duc certainly thought there was something in our house that he needed to get to. Was Dad supposed to have evidence of some sort squirreled away?"

"He did, if you recall. Isn't that how you became involved?"

"True. Nothing that I found in Dad's desk would incriminate Duc, but we don't know what Riley might have told Duc."

"What about the husband?" Jean-Paul said. "Is it possible that your snooping Larry tells Bartolini, Senior, that his wife is making visits of a certain variety to Riley? In a rage, Bartolini grabs a gun and goes across the street after Riley. He shoots, but it is his beloved wife he hits by mistake. *Catastrophe.* He is distraught now, of course. Riley foils the murder investigation to save his own—what do you say?—sweet ass, because it is highly problematic to explain why there is a naked dead woman in his bedroom without getting into some grave difficulty. Instead, he dumps the woman's body and destroys the evidence he can. And there you have it, impasse for thirty years."

"Chuck's wife would have the same motivation as Bart," I said.

"In that case, which one was she gunning for?"

"They were both hit."

"It is a fine puzzle, *chérie.*"

The rest of the way, we talked about anything except the people in my neighborhood.

When we got home, the cleaning crew was still at work inside. We found Max out front helping Toshio Sato unload the plants he had brought to repair the ruined flower borders. The two men were arguing affably about what should go where.

Jean-Paul went up onto the porch, a quiet place to return calls, while I went over to greet Mr. Sato.

To the plant discussion, I contributed, "Think tidy, hardy and low maintenance."

"Not good enough," Max said, waving off what I'd said. "We should at the very least try for some approximation of my brother's planting scheme. Red, orange, yellow, and so on."

"Max, Max, Max." Mr. Sato took off his hat and wiped the sweatband with his big white handkerchief. "Yesterday I asked Duc to give me some good plants for Al's borders, and this is what he gave me. I got pink begonia, I got yellow lamium, I got white shrub roses, and I got some rosemary makes a nice blue flower in the spring. You want something else, you go get it. But don't fool around 'cuz I got grandkids to pick up from lacrosse camp this afternoon."

At the mention of Duc's name, Max and I looked at each other. He shook his head; now was not the time to announce Duc's death to Mr. Sato. So far, the coroner's office had released no information about Duc.

"So, Tosh," Max said, "are you and Duc good friends?"

"Nah, the guy's a pain in the ass, but he knows flowers," he said, putting his hat back on. "As long as we talk flowers, we get along okay. If you're thinking of driving all the way down there, don't bother unless you want to pay retail because Duc didn't come in today. Now, you gonna give me a hand here or do you want to stand around talking?"

"Mr. Sato," I said as he sank the end of a shovel into the soil of the flower border. "I was wondering, if Duc worked with you, why don't I remember meeting him before the other day? Every Monday I would say hello to you and your helper. I never knew them very well, but I'd like to think I would remember them."

He pulled off his hat again and wiped the sweatband with his big handkerchief. "That's because Duc never worked for me on Mondays when I did your yard. Guy worked two or three jobs. Mondays and Fridays, he drove a delivery truck, I think."

"Did he?" I caught Uncle Max's eye but he just shrugged. "Could he have worked for Bay Laundry and Dry Cleaners?"

"The laundry?" Mr. Sato thought that over as he settled his hat back on his head. "Yeah, I think it was the laundry. I remember he used to pick up dirty tablecloths after big weekend parties. He'd salvage all the wilted centerpieces, recycle the vases and florist foam and junk, save it for when he opened his nursery."

"Mystery solved," I said, thinking Duc had just hit the Trifecta: motive, means, and opportunity. "I'll go see what's happening inside and get out of your way."

I was allowed into the living room, but everything from five feet beyond the front door was sealed off behind plastic sheeting. Jean-Paul and I had decided to pack our things and go to a hotel until we could hand the house keys over to the university. Max was leaving, too. He had a late afternoon meeting in LA with Lana and would be leaving for the airport in a few hours. But because of the wall of plastic sheeting, we couldn't get up the stairs until the crew left.

They wouldn't need much longer, I was told, because as crime scenes go, this one was relatively small. The man I spoke with launched into a lurid account of a mass shooting at a crack house down in Fremont, but was summoned back to work before he got very far into his tale. I was not unhappy to see him slip back behind the plastic.

Just for information, I called Lyle and asked him how long he thought it would take for workers to finish the house cleanup and repairs. He went through the list I gave him: the blood was being dealt with, a plasterer was scheduled to patch the holes in the walls made by the lab people, then some new paint, and finally a thorough general house cleaning before we handed the keys to University Housing.

"Four days, maybe more if some flooring needs to be replaced," he said. "Guido told me you guys are headed for France in a couple of weeks. Is this going to put you in a jam?"

"It is, but it has to be done," I said.

"Maybe we can do each other a favor," he said. "We have a friend, broke up with his partner, needed a sofa to sleep on, so we took him in. He's a good guy, a very good guy, and we've enjoyed having him. But Roy's parents are coming out for a visit day after tomorrow and I think it would be better for all if we don't have an extra person around while they're here. What if I send him over to you? He doesn't have any disgusting habits I'm aware of. He works from home so we can put him in charge of overseeing your workers, make sure everything is done right."

"If he's willing, it would be a godsend," I said, feeling a mountain lift from my shoulders.

"No, honey, it would be a Lylesend. Let me go get him so you can work out the details."

"You're my guru."

After a brief conversation, arrangements with the friend were made. He would leave the City before freeway rush hour that afternoon and arrive at our door as soon as traffic allowed. After we said good-bye, I called Evie Miller at the housing office to tell her that there was a delay for some repair work. We put off her inspection for a week — it didn't seem to be a problem for her. By then, my truck should be finished and I could take care of both tasks in one quick trip.

It was early evening in France. I called my French grandmother and told her when Guido and I planned to arrive. She was delighted, especially so because the government had recalled Jean-Paul from his consular post and he would be returning to France at about the same time. "Such a nice young man," she said. I suppose that to a woman in her nineties, a man of fifty could be considered young.

Out in the hall, there was a great rustle of plastic and hardware as the cleaning crew got ready to decamp. I was handed a bill that made my eyes water. Thank God, Mom had good home owner's insurance.

"There was a nice coat of wax on the hardwood floor," I was told by the man who handed me the bill. "You're lucky. There won't be much of a stain at all."

I followed them out and found Jean-Paul dozing on the porch in the wicker rocker with his feet up on the porch rail. Max and Mr. Sato seemed to have settled their issues. The plants, still in cans, were arranged in the borders as they would be planted. Mr. Sato was working on the roses I had managed to salvage so even if the colors in the flower borders would no longer follow the order of the color spectrum, at least some of Dad's beloved Chrysler roses would be among them.

Peace, at last, I thought, looking out across the lawn, enjoying the fresh breeze off the Bay, the slight salt tang in the air mixed with jasmine growing on a trellis in the Lopers' side yard. There had been a time when I knew every person on the street. During the short time I had been back, I came to understand that the big secret my family kept, namely my origins, was petty stuff compared to the secrets some of our neighbors held tight. What a terrible burden, I thought, a secret could be.

I said a silent farewell to them all, and went inside to pack.

Sometimes, when something is entirely out of place it takes a moment to realize what you're actually seeing. The red leather jewel box was lying in the middle of the upstairs hall, open and upside down. I felt a moment of panic until I saw the dragonfly brooch a few feet away and apparently intact. It was only when I stooped to pick up the brooch that all the implications of it being where it was flooded in, and real panic ensued. I pushed open the door to the room I had been sharing with Jean-Paul and saw a jumble of clothes and books and overturned drawers in the middle of the floor. All of the furniture had been pulled away from the walls and left in higgledy-piggledy disarray.

My first thought was that one of the cleaners had come upstairs looking for loot, but that made no sense. A little pilfering, sure, but not this, not a thorough tossing; a member of the crew would be sure he'd be caught. That's when I saw that a window in my former bedroom was broken. I went over and looked down, saw the ladder against the side of the house. During the cleaners' hubbub downstairs behind the plastic wall, someone had broken in upstairs. My next thought was to get the hell out. Now.

I ran down the hall, clutching the brooch in one hand while I tried to pry my phone out of my pocket with the other. He was no more than a blur, a flying tackle launched from the side out of Max's bedroom door. He dropped me on my belly and slapped the phone out of my hand as he pulled my arm behind me, bending it up toward my shoulder until I thought it would pop out of the socket. With his other hand, he pressed the tip of a knife against my throat.

I cried out, "What do you want?"

"You know damn well." He stank of old sweat and hot fear. "Where is the letter?"

"What letter?"

"Her letter. She hid it in this house."

"I don't know anything about a letter."

"You do," he said. "You showed it to my son-in-law."

I heard what sounded like "whuff," and suddenly his weight was off me; his knife hit the wall beside my head and skittered down the hall. I came up off the floor running.

"Maggie?"

I turned at the sound of Jean-Paul's voice. He had Chuck Riley face down, hog-tying him with the cord from Uncle Max's bathrobe.

"Did he hurt you, *chérie?*"

I shook out my arm; it hurt. "Where did you come from?"

His chin flicked toward the end of the hall. "I came up to find you."

"But—"

"Please telephone," he said as he bounced Chuck's head on the floor and ordered him to quit squirming.

I retrieved both my phone and the knife. Why bother with 911? I called the chief of police. "We have your man," I told him. "Please send someone before he gets too squirrelly." And then I called Uncle Max, who was still in the front yard, and suggested he should get upstairs, pronto.

"Chuck," I said, keeping my distance in case Jean-Paul lost control of him. "Tell me about the letter."

"Fuck you," he said.

"Okay, then. Who pulled the trigger that day? You were standing behind Trinh Bartolini when she was shot. Who pulled the trigger?"

He strained to look up at me, seemed confused by the question. "How could you know that?"

"Who shot Trinh Bartolini?"

He suddenly lost his starch, stopped struggling and turned his face to the wall. Through choking sobs he said, "God, she was so beautiful."

"Was it Duc?"

"That damn gook, he didn't have to do that."

"He was aiming at you."

"He was only supposed to scare her," he said. "To make her back off. The feebs were asking questions. We needed her to stop before she fucked up everything."

"You gave him the gun," I said.

"So what?"

"You blackmailed him after he shot her, didn't you?"

"I couldn't let him get off scot-free, could I?"

"For killing her? Or for failing to kill you?"

"Both, I guess. But it doesn't matter anymore."

"What have you been looking for?"

"A letter." He raised his head as sirens approached. "She said she wrote a letter, and that if anything happened to her or to your family, the letter would come to light."

"You think it's in this house?"

He dropped his face to the floor, defeated. "I know it is."

"You broke in to look for it."

"Old George Loper was afraid someone would find Al's gun," he said with a smirk. "Fuck the gun. That letter is a bomb. A nuclear bomb with my ass in its sights."

Chapter 22

"Jean-Paul." I snuggled against him in the backseat of the San Francisco consul general's Town Car, happy that Rafael was driving us to the airport. "What is it that you really do? I mean, what did you do before you accepted the consular appointment? I know what you've told me, but you're always just a bit vague about it."

That shrug again. "I'm a businessman. A quite boring businessman."

"That's what you always say, but I don't believe it anymore."

"No?" He smiled, a funny little smile that was full of secrets.

"No. Exactly what kind of business are you in that you can make a call and someone tells you that Thai Van, an obscure man, died in a jungle shootout thirty years ago? You traced a very old shipment of guns, with serial numbers, from the manufacturer to the U.S. Army by placing a call. Another call and someone faxes equally old records of Khanh Duc's international bank transfers from a bank in Berkeley to an account in the Cayman Islands, and from there to Bangkok, as well as regular payments to his 'employee' Chuck Riley. Quite boring businessmen don't have that variety of contacts no matter where they went to school."

"But, my dear, it was a very good school."

"But a school of a very certain sort," I said. "They also teach whatever form of martial arts you used to take down Riley?"

"When a man sees the woman he loves held captive with a knife to her throat, who knows what he is capable of doing to free her?"

"You never quite answer the question, do you?" I said. "Monsieur Bernard, when you go back to France and pick up where you left off, exactly what will you be doing?"

"I won't pick up where I left off at all," he said, smooching my cheek. "I will be with you, a fresh start."

"Okay," I said, pulling a slender book out of my carry-on bag. "Let's trade information. I will give you this book if you give me a straight answer."

He looked at the title and laughed: *Opticks: Or, a Treatise of the Reflexions, Refractions, Inflexions, and Colours of Light*, by Isaac Newton. "This is what you have to bargain with?"

"All things are not what they seem," I said. "Pure sunlight seems to have no hue, no color at all. But in fact, it has all the colors that exist. You wear the mantle of a quite boring businessman, but we both know you are anything but; you are, my friend, very colorful. The same can be said for this book."

"You find this book fascinating?"

"No, quite boring," I said. "Difficult to read, especially for a child. After my father read it with me when he was teaching me about optics, he could be very confident that I would never open that book again. But, like you, it holds a very interesting secret."

He pressed the book between his hands, felt the cover, and then he smiled. *"Bien sûr.* May I open it?"

"Will you answer my question?"

"Of course, my dear. If we're to share a life, you will need to know everything."

"Then go ahead."

He opened Newton's treatise and thumbed through the pages before he flipped to the inside of the back cover, ran his fingers around the edges, found the tiny slit Dad had made near the spine, and slipped out an envelope.

The day before she died, Trinh Bartolini mailed a letter to my parents. She apologized for getting angry when Mom advised her to report the extortion to the authorities. She wrote,

Where I come from, officials are not to be trusted. I had hoped that in this country that would not be true. But I have found that it can be. It is an official who asks of me a price I would rather die than pay. But, for the safety of my husband and my son, I will continue to do what I know I must. I beg you not to turn against them because of what I have been forced to become. And I beg you to tell no one, especially the police.

Help me protect my dear husband from ever learning my shameful secret. I am afraid for what he might do. A man from the FBI came to my house today and I had to tell him that you were mistaken. Please help me and do the same. If they investigate further Bart will find out and others might become dangerous.

Whatever happens to me, please look after my Beto. Tell him his mother will always watch over him.

Jean-Paul read through the letter twice before he slipped it back into its envelope. "She was afraid."

"She had reason to be," I said.

"Is this what Riley and Duc were looking for?"

"It isn't what they thought it was, is it?" I took the letter from him and slipped it back into its hiding place.

Jean-Paul watched the San Francisco skyline slide past his window. After a moment or two, he turned to me. "How did you know where to look?"

"I took one last walk-through before we put the house into the hands of Lyle's friend. I was thinking about Dad and what he would have said about the flower borders now—pretty enough, but what's the point of the pattern?—when I saw Newton's *Opticks* on the shelf. I couldn't bring myself to put it in the library's book sale, and it isn't special enough for the university, so I left it for the tenants. But in the end, I couldn't abandon it. One day I might be a grandmother and I might want to teach my grandchildren about the nature of light."

He smiled his upside-down smile. "Nothing gets past you, does it?"

"I might be slow on the uptake, but I usually get what I'm after," I said. "So, I showed you mine. Now it's your turn. Jean-Paul, what is it that you actually do?"

He wrapped me in his arms and pulled me against him. "Well, to begin…"

About the Author

Edgar Award–winner Wendy Hornsby is the author of ten previous mysteries, eight of them featuring Maggie MacGowen. She is a retired professor of history at Long Beach City College. She welcomes visitors and e-mail at www.wendyhornsby.com

More Traditional Mysteries from Perseverance Press
For the New Golden Age

Albert A. Bell, Jr.
PLINY THE YOUNGER SERIES
Death in the Ashes
ISBN 978-1-56474-532-3

The Eyes of Aurora (forthcoming)
ISBN 978-1-56474-549-1

Jon L. Breen
Eye of God
ISBN 978-1-880284-89-6

Taffy Cannon
ROXANNE PRESCOTT SERIES
Guns and Roses
Agatha and Macavity awards nominee, Best Novel
ISBN 978-1-880284-34-6

Blood Matters
ISBN 978-1-880284-86-5

Open Season on Lawyers
ISBN 978-1-880284-51-3

Paradise Lost
ISBN 978-1-880284-80-3

Laura Crum
GAIL MCCARTHY SERIES
Moonblind
ISBN 978-1-880284-90-2

Chasing Cans
ISBN 978-1-880284-94-0

Going, Gone
ISBN 978-1-880284-98-8

Barnstorming
ISBN 978-1-56474-508-8

Jeanne M. Dams
HILDA JOHANSSON SERIES
Crimson Snow
ISBN 978-1-880284-79-7

Indigo Christmas
ISBN 978-1-880284-95-7

Murder in Burnt Orange
ISBN 978-1-56474-503-3

Janet Dawson
JERI HOWARD SERIES
Bit Player
Golden Nugget Award nominee
ISBN 978-1-56474-494-4

Cold Trail (forthcoming)
ISBN 978-1-56474-555-2

What You Wish For
ISBN 978-1-56474-518-7

Death Rides the Zephyr
ISBN 978-1-56474-530-9

Kathy Lynn Emerson
LADY APPLETON SERIES
Face Down Below the Banqueting House
ISBN 978-1-880284-71-1

Face Down Beside St. Anne's Well
ISBN 978-1-880284-82-7

Face Down O'er the Border
ISBN 978-1-880284-91-9

Elaine Flinn
MOLLY DOYLE SERIES
Deadly Vintage
ISBN 978-1-880284-87-2

Sara Hoskinson Frommer
JOAN SPENCER SERIES
Her Brother's Keeper
ISBN 978-1-56474-525-5

Hal Glatzer
KATY GREEN SERIES
Too Dead To Swing
ISBN 978-1-880284-53-7

A Fugue in Hell's Kitchen
ISBN 978-1-880284-70-4

The Last Full Measure
ISBN 978-1-880284-84-1

Margaret Grace
MINIATURE SERIES
Mix-up in Miniature
ISBN 978-1-56474-510-1

Madness in Miniature
ISBN 978-1-56474-543-9

Wendy Hornsby
MAGGIE MACGOWEN SERIES
In the Guise of Mercy
ISBN 978-1-56474-482-1

The Paramour's Daughter
ISBN 978-1-56474-496-8

The Hanging
ISBN 978-1-56474-526-2

The Color of Light
ISBN 978-1-56474-542-2

Diana Killian
POETIC DEATH SERIES
Docketful of Poesy
ISBN 978-1-880284-97-1

Janet LaPierre
PORT SILVA SERIES
Baby Mine
ISBN 978-1-880284-32-2

Keepers
Shamus Award nominee, Best Paperback Original
ISBN 978-1-880284-44-5

Death Duties
ISBN 978-1-880284-74-2

Family Business
ISBN 978-1-880284-85-8

Run a Crooked Mile
ISBN 978-1-880284-88-9

Hailey Lind
ART LOVER'S SERIES
Arsenic and Old Paint
ISBN 978-1-56474-490-6

Lev Raphael
NICK HOFFMAN SERIES
Tropic of Murder
ISBN 978-1-880284-68-1

Hot Rocks
ISBN 978-1-880284-83-4

Lora Roberts
BRIDGET MONTROSE SERIES
Another Fine Mess
ISBN 978-1-880284-54-4

SHERLOCK HOLMES SERIES
The Affair of the Incognito Tenant
ISBN 978-1-880284-67-4

Rebecca Rothenberg
BOTANICAL SERIES
The Tumbleweed Murders
(completed by Taffy Cannon)
ISBN 978-1-880284-43-8

Sheila Simonson
LATOUCHE COUNTY SERIES
Buffalo Bill's Defunct
WILLA Award, Best Softcover Fiction
ISBN 978-1-880284-96-4

An Old Chaos
ISBN 978-1-880284-99-5

Beyond Confusion
ISBN 978-1-56474-519-4

Shelley Singer
JAKE SAMSON & ROSIE VICENTE SERIES
Royal Flush
ISBN 978-1-880284-33-9

Lea Wait
SHADOWS ANTIQUES SERIES
Shadows of a Down East Summer
ISBN 978-1-56474-497-5

Shadows on a Cape Cod Wedding
ISBN 1-978-56474-531-6

Shadows on a Maine Christmas
(forthcoming)
ISBN 978-1-56474-531-6

Eric Wright
JOE BARLEY SERIES
The Kidnapping of Rosie Dawn
Barry Award, Best Paperback Original. Edgar,
Ellis, and Anthony awards nominee
ISBN 978-1-880284-40-7

Nancy Means Wright
MARY WOLLSTONECRAFT SERIES
Midnight Fires
ISBN 978-1-56474-488-3

The Nightmare
ISBN 978-1-56474-509-5

REFERENCE/MYSTERY WRITING

Kathy Lynn Emerson
How To Write Killer Historical Mysteries:
The Art and Adventure of Sleuthing
Through the Past
Agatha Award, Best Nonfiction. Anthony and
Macavity awards nominee
ISBN 978-1-880284-92-6

Carolyn Wheat
How To Write Killer Fiction:
The Funhouse of Mystery & the Roller
Coaster of Suspense
ISBN 978-1-880284-62-9

Available from your local booksto
or from Perseverance Press/John Daniel & Compa
(800) 662–8351 or www.danielpublishing.com/perseveran